Joe Carol—
with appreciation.
Enjoy the flight!

Joe Fry

ALSO BY LAURIE FOX

My Sister from the Black Lagoon
Sexy Hieroglyphics

THE LOST GIRLS

A NOVEL

LAURIE FOX

SIMON & SCHUSTER

New York   London   Toronto   Sydney

SIMON & SCHUSTER
Rockefeller Center
1230 Avenue of the Americas
New York, NY 10020

SIMON & SCHUSTER and colophon are registered trademarks
of Simon & Schuster, Inc.

For information about special discounts for bulk purchases,
please contact Simon & Schuster Special Sales:
1-800-456-6798 or business@simonandschuster.com

Book design by Ellen R. Sasahara

Manufactured in the United States of America

1   3   5   7   9   10   8   6   4   2

Library of Congress Cataloging-in-Publication Data

Fox, Laurie Anne.
The lost girls / Laurie Fox.
p. cm.
1. Middle aged women—Fiction. 2. San Francisco (Calif.)—Fiction.
3. Peter Pan (Fictitious character)—Fiction. I. Title.
PS3556.O936L67 2004
813'.54—dc22   2003 059168

0-7432-1790-X

For Sue Bender, who believes

The intensity of the longing is what does all the work.

—Rumi, translation by Robert Bly

Had I been a man I might have explored the Poles or climbed Mount Everest, but as it was my spirit found outlet in the air. . . .

—Amy Johnson, British aviatrix, *Myself When Young*

Since You Asked

 WAS warned against it, lectured, teased—even threatened. But it was bound to happen: *I grew up.*

I grew up with purpose, I grew up with alacrity, with an excess of insolence and a daring lack of contrition. In so doing, I made a small dent in the heart of a young man, a boy really, whom I left behind in my drive towards self-knowledge and sophistication. For all I know, to this day he remains disappointed in me—and defiantly, stubbornly young.

I paid dearly for my act. I married well; I bore and raised a ravishing daughter. Then I lost both husband and daughter to inner worlds that I am not equipped to enter. Which is why most nights I sit alone at my window, the fabled storyteller with a dearth of stories to tell the children she meets. For the only tale left is too hideous to confess—full of adult heartbreak, adult wistfulness.

You could say mine is a story with a hook. A hook to a boy who hardly exists anymore, except in glimpses of my husband, in piss-poor dreams of flying around rooms like a damn fairy, in the stranglehold the past has on the imagination.

When I was thirteen, I seriously believed that if I conjured up "happy thoughts," I could float above the world. This belief had a poetic logic that wasn't lost on me. Nowadays, the rare happy thought occurs to me as I look out at the San Francisco Bay. I meditate on lifting off, then touching down—on losing and finding myself in one fell swoop. And then I recall a boy who wanted too much from life; a grown man who wanted too little from me; the pressing needs of a dozen young boys. Such unhappy thoughts send my spirits crashing. A shame because, when I was thirteen,

I was chock-full of possibility. I was magic incarnate! They called me the Wendybird, a creature admired by one and all, and flying was as natural to me then as sitting is now.

Like all fairy stories, mine begins in the shadows—with one particular shadow called Pan. For I am fourth-generation Darling, the daughter of the daughter of the daughter of Wendy Darling, the original guide to the Other World. We Darlings all refused to surrender our family name, giving up instead a host of other essentials: our dewy youth, our equilibrium, a clear-cut sense of what is real. We donated our young bodies in Springtime and worked those bodies to the bone—scrubbing, laundering, sweeping—our ropes of strawberry hair tied up or back. We became consummate caregivers at an age when most children are looked after by responsible adults and given the opportunity to succeed or fail under loving eyes. Not unlike that of maids and nuns, our character has been shaped by service, by devotion. And, like nuns, we formed somewhat uneasy alliances with men. We all fell deeply in love at too tender an age and learned of loss before the sun set on our teenage years. We discovered that what young men offer is fleeting and slippery, and quite possibly the most glamorous adventure of all. Our hunger has been great and a certain kind of boy was food to us. Of course, boys don't want to be eaten alive—they want to be mothered. Too bad, then, that not all of us are good at this, not properly motivated.

Whenever we've confessed our common histories—to fathers and teachers and clergy and doctors—we've been met with silence, or worse, hospitalization. The four of us, plus my own daughter, Berry, have been misdiagnosed as "delusional," our awfully big adventures reduced to psychotic episodes. Thankfully, in the nineties—the 1990s—my own melancholy bears a more charitable name: *Seasonal Affective Disorder*. It's a serious affliction—have you heard of it?—but one that can be treated successfully with pills and light therapy.

Still, one cannot easily dismiss our talent for self-delusion. We Darling girls take pride in our ability to craft whole worlds out of nothing but velvet curtains and blue patches of sky. And we never apologize for our visions—we've earned them. In my own case, I eschewed all pills the day I sprang myself from the psych ward. I'm tired of pretending my past is suspect, fabricated, faulty. It is what it is. And I can't tell this story if I'm fuzzy at the edges.

Like most of the women in my family, I have been excused from intimate friendship—from decent, normal life. I have been touched by magic and hurt by magic. But to live *without* magic would have been a tragic waste of a life—don't you think so? I have to believe this. I must believe that my dream was real and that reality can be an adequate, even satisfying, dream. In the same way my great-grandmother once sewed Peter's shadow to Peter himself, I must sew the two halves of my life together. To make the cloth whole.

 **PART**

ONE

What is an adult? A child blown up by age.

—Simone de Beauvoir, *La Femme Rompue*

I

HE DAY Mother took me by the hand to visit Great-Nana Wendy in the hospital, we promised each other that when the past came up, we would change the subject as casually as changing the sheets. We would not validate Great-Nana's stories, no matter how tempting or true. In this way, we would speed her recovery. At the time I didn't understand why she had been locked up like a thief, for one's memories can't be stolen—they belong to you for life. However, Dr. Smithson patiently explained in the dreary hallway of Guy's Hospital that Great-Nana had, in fact, stolen whole scenes and conversations from storybooks and made them her own, put her own psychic copyright on them. He went on to say that the voracious reading she had done in her youth had harmed her irreparably, that she couldn't distinguish fairy stories from real life, and this made her a "dangerous woman."

Mother suppressed a giggle, then guffawed openly: "Christ almighty, what rubbish!"

Dr. Smithson grimaced. "Mrs. Braverman, I'm not joking. If you recall, we picked up your grandmother after the neighbors spotted her straddling the sill of her second-story window, dangling her legs and talking to the Moon. She was babbling about comets, about *steering clear* of comets. I can assure you, after four days of extensive psychological evaluation, the results are conclusive: your grandmother is delusional. What you refer to as *whims* could make it very risky for her to negotiate the simplest activities: crossing the street, shopping for groceries. Consider what would happen if she spotted a 'buccaneer' at the supermarket—would she draw a 'sword' from her handbag and go on the offensive? You must think of her welfare, not your own interests."

Mother took a preparatory breath. She fluttered her lashes and placed her tiny hands on her hips, drawing attention to her thrilling hourglass figure. "Buccaneer? What in the world? I'm sorry, doctor, I don't quite follow." She winked at me broadly, like Shirley Temple in *Little Miss Marker*.

Dr. Smithson patted his forehead with an ornate monogrammed handkerchief. "Mrs. Braverman, surely you've heard the stories?"

"Stories?" Mother said. "Why, I'm not sure."

"Yes, yes, the tall tales. Mermaids, pirates, Indians. Don't tell me your grandmother doesn't regale you with this poppycock?"

I could see that Mother's calm was eroding. She shook her head sharply and her coiled plait came loose, falling open suggestively between herself and the doctor. "Nana's faculties are unassailable," she said.

"I beg to differ, Mrs. Braverman. For one thing, the flying. Your grandmother doesn't talk of flying around the parlor?"

Mother smiled a bit too widely, showing off her glossy niblet teeth. She looked as if she was about to devour the man. "Hmm, let's see . . . does Nana talk about flying? Well, only on *Wednesdays*, does that count?" She let go with a snort.

Dr. Smithson reddened and bowed his head.

"Well," Mother continued, "if that counts, then, yes, she speaks about flying. But what's the harm in that? Everybody talks about flying, women do these days. Really, if you don't discuss heightened states of consciousness, you're considered provincial. And Nana is nothing if not cosmopolitan. Her friends are legends, I tell you. Cocteau, Isadora Duncan, Huxley. Have you never read *The Doors of Perception*? No? Well, you're in for a wild ride!" Mother patted the physician's back. "You see, my grandmother isn't mad, she's *progressive*."

"Mrs. Braverman."

"Call me Margaret," Mother encouraged. "No, call me Maggie."

"Mrs. *Braverman.* Your grandmother is seriously ill. This is not a matter of how artistic or liberal she is. She honestly believes that she flew off to some sort of funfair when she was a girl. And that she will return to this counterfeit world when she dies."

"How perfectly cyclical," Mother said.

Dr. Smithson heaved a laborious sigh and, changing direction, bent over to address me. "You *do* want your great-grandmother to get well?" he asked simply.

"Mummy says she's not ill," I answered reflexively, chewing on my curls. "Mummy says, if Great-Nana is ill, then we're *all* ill." I smiled up at him; he was a handsome man after all.

"Right. Well, let's go see her then. I'm recommending a live-in nurse, but you can judge for yourselves."

EVERY Sunday morning until I turned five, I'd spent a few enchanted hours in Great-Nana's presence. Splayed out on the Persian rug in her sitting room, I played amid the clutter—sheet music and watercolors, stuffed owls and marble busts of young, muscle-bound men. Born in 1953 and living in the shadow of the A-bomb, I was an anxious child who tended to cringe when emotions ran high between Mummy and Daddy, who both felt some time spent with Nana was time well-spent, indeed. Of course, Mummy didn't always approve of Great-Nana's methods.

"To be young was very heaven," Nana liked to sing as she bounced me on her knee. While Wordsworth had written this about the dawn of the French Revolution, for my own time period he couldn't have been more on the mark. "To be young was very heaven, Wends," Nana would repeat, eyes fogged with mist—or memories.

"*You're* very heaven," I'd coo in return, and she'd blush down to her garter belt and silk stockings. Then she'd slip me—a slip of a girl—off her knee, inviting me to bang my bum on her threadbare rug. This was her way of illustrating that falling from heaven, when young, can land you on the nursery floor.

"I'd much prefer hell as the entrée to life," she mused one afternoon after dumping me on the floor. "The *main* entrée, with heaven for dessert! You see, a main course of heaven just makes you hunger for more. Yes, give me hell as the entrée, and heaven much later on—when a person can fully appreciate it."

"My bum hurts," I complained. "Do I have to fall *every* time I visit?"

"If you learn how to fall properly now," she advised, "it won't hurt so much later. When life is painful early on, the pain of growing up won't come as such a shock."

On hearing this homily, Mother, who had been curled up on the settee with *The Second Sex*, hauled me off to the kitchen, telling her own grandmother to stifle herself. "You are a piece of work, Nana. You really have no business turning *my* daughter into a neurotic. When it comes to nutters, you take the grand prize!"

"And your daughter, the little peanut, is first runner-up!" Nana said, eyes blazing.

I nodded studiously, twisting a strawberry-blonde curl with my forefinger until a few hairs broke off. At the time I wasn't clear on what a *nutter* was, but I was quite sure I didn't want to be one.

EVEN though I am now forty-two—an *old* forty-two—I recall the very moment I set eyes on Great-Nana that cheerless afternoon in the hospital. She was in her cups, as Mummy liked to say. Most amazingly, the nurses hadn't gotten wind of this, allowing her to sip her "parfait" through a straw; by the time we arrived, she'd been working her way through a thermos for hours. The schnapps had been smuggled in by Daddy, a connoisseur himself, and the only one of us who could spring for private quarters. Apparently, the two of them had spent the morning sipping, watching the news, and gossiping about Princess Margaret's sex life. Upon hearing us approach, Daddy had fled in a mild panic, a phantom whose only traces were the Player's cigarette fumes he'd left behind. He hated running into Mummy—"the grand divorcée," he called her.

Daddy and Mummy's path as a couple had taken a permanent detour by the time I was five. I hardly remember him from those early, stormy days. By my teens, however, every fact about him had been colored in and criminalized by Mummy. In her eyes, Daddy was a cretin, Daddy was a dildo, Daddy was a dumbfuck. In the fifties, went her mantra, Daddy had left the two of us to go fly his little airplanes and build his big airplanes. And, in the sixties, to start a hip company called Brave Hearts Airlines that played pop rock in the terminal and served weak French roast in the air. But as much as Mother demonized Daddy, my heart never blackened at the thought of him. Fathers are not exchangeable at Harrods or Nordstrom; you're stuck for life with the one you've got.

Obviously, Mother didn't share my opinion; she got rid of Daddy the night he went paragliding on the cliffs near Dover. Well before there were kits for such things, he rigged up the glider himself, then downed a few pints, stripped to his smalls, took flight abruptly, and mooned the world. In a second coup de grâce he crashed in a patch of ripe tomatoes. Why Mummy didn't laugh at this is a mystery, but I believe it had something to do with me. Now that he was the parent of an impressionable girl, she scolded, he should put an end to all the stunts—the silly hot-air ballooning, the sophomoric scuba diving, and God knows, the rock climbing, the pub-crawling. It was time to come home and stay put. Unfortunately, Daddy's appetite for life had to be fed on an hourly basis, and he fed it.

My parents' divorce was swift; there was money enough for everybody, enough for Mummy and me to leave the country for good. Hastily uprooting us from the suburbs of London, Margaret Darling Braverman planted us in the fragrant hills of Berkeley, California, where her "psycho-spiritual ideas could take root." On the west coast of America, she could do her hatha yoga openly, worship her goddesses, and begin her career as an author of books on self-improvement.

Upon arriving in the East Bay, I recall that the Queen Anne Victorians seemed pleasantly familiar; but the birds of paradise, the gladioli were alien to my eyes, almost wanton. On clear afternoons, you could see both bridges—the Bay Bridge and the Golden

Gate—from our backyard deck while hamburgers smoked and sizzled on our brand-new barbecue. On foggy, marine-layer mornings, you could scan this same vista and see nothing. Goodness, I was homesick for England and yet confused by my good fortune. Courtesy of Daddy's bank account, I'd been given a new life as an American girl, but at quite a steep price: I had to content myself with stolen glimpses of my father on advertisements for Brave Hearts Airlines.

"Look at Dummy!" Mother would shriek, slapping the telly whenever Daddy's face lit the screen.

"That's *Dudley*," I'd correct her, "your *ex*."

X is one of the last letters in the alphabet, Mummy routinely pointed out; she liked to play up Daddy's failed status as often as she could. Dudley Braverman, CEO of Brave Hearts Airlines, had been reduced to one letter in our house in the hills, and I grew up longing to know the mysterious Mr. X. There had to be more to him than a handsome daredevil businessman who occasionally donned an eye patch.

In the private regions of my mind, I referred to Daddy as "Your Ex-cellency" and, by the mid-sixties, dreamed of flying off to London on one of his jazzy Brave Hearts jets, where the stewardesses strutted the aisles in white patent-leather boots and tartan minikilts. In these reveries, I was seated between Michael Caine and Dusty Springfield, and we'd chatter nonstop about the dark side of show business. After exchanging phone numbers with my new friends on the plane's final approach, I'd sashay down the ramp and plunge into Daddy's outstretched arms on the tarmac below. On his shoulders he'd carry me through customs and, when asked to declare what items he'd brought into the country, he'd confess: "One fabulous daughter whose value is . . . invaluable!"

Save for an inaugural spin on the runway, I never did fly on Brave Hearts Airlines. Mummy made sure we gave all our business to BOAC and Freddie Laker, and later on, to Virgin Atlantic—Daddy's biggest rival. In this way, we lived as if Daddy were already dead, a burden of grief that weighed me down as a child and endowed me with a grave disposition. My only solace was our annual visits with Great-Nana Wendy—the stories she spun about Daddy!—for through the years she and Dudley remained as thick as thieves. Nana's memories, though, often proved faulty; her narratives tended to confuse Daddy with Pan. This was forgivable, I suppose. Both were boys of some charm who refused to play by the rules. Both loved flying more than the world itself (and forgot about the world from time to time). Both Daddy and Peter made you feel extraordinary in their presence. But that was the catch: you had to be in their presence.

As I said, Great-Nana Wendy was in her cups the day Mummy and I ventured into her hospital room. After flushing Daddy's smoke out the tall windows, we settled in for the afternoon. I had never visited a real live crazy person and didn't know what to expect.

Nana wasted no time. She waved me over to the bed with a pudgy, liver-spotted hand; her fingers were dressed with so many gaudy costume rings I had to shade my eyes. "I like to entertain the senses," she explained. "The more bijoux the better." When she noticed me staring at the little ruby number on her pinkie, she slipped it off and said, "It's yours, buttercup."

A bit awed, I approached her bed. "Closer, my little bird," she sang in a flutey voice. "Come sit with me, darling. Alight *on* me, for God's sake!"

I inched nearer, until she reached out with two fleshy arms and forced me onto the bed, pressing me into her generous bosom. "There now. You've exhausted me, child. Give me your ring finger."

I was confused—*every* finger of Nana's was a ring finger—so I stuck my entire right hand in her face. She chuckled and slid the glittery red-stoned bauble onto my longest digit, then bent over to kiss it as if I were a princess.

"All right. Enough of that." She waved my hand away. "Jewels can blind you, fool you into thinking that *this* world's the best place in which to bide your time. Now, child, close your eyes. Go on. Good. Now please try to imagine the worst possible thing."

"Nana!" Mummy cried from her chair in the corner.

"Hush. Don't interfere. I want Wendy to hold a monstrous thought in her mind's eye. Got one?"

I nodded enthusiastically; I was good at conjuring up really bad stuff. I thought of Tootles, my dear puss, flattened by a lorry, his guts spilling onto the pavement. Tears pooled in my eyes and dampened my cheeks. I sniffled and chewed on my bottom lip.

"That's the spirit!" Great-Nana applauded.

"Can I open my eyes?" I whimpered.

"No, dear. You've just begun to make use of your powers."

"But Nana, I see millions of dots. How very strange!"

"Well, we Darlings tend towards the strange. We *veer* towards it."

"How about veering towards a nap?" Mother interrupted. "Really, you're scaring the girl."

"I'm scaring her for her own good. Now, buttercup, imagine that you could escape this world of death, old-age pensioners, and frightfully bad weather."

Through squinting eyes, I caught Great-Nana winking at my mother. Mummy was right: I hadn't a clue to what Nana was getting at. Plus, I could smell the schnapps on her breath, her signature lavender toilet water mingling with stale bath powder.

I opened my eyes without permission. "You're not scaring me, Nana. I just can't see."

"That's it!" She smacked the mattress with flattened palms, then propped herself up and cast off her blankets. "You can't *see*. You haven't experienced such a world, a place where animals and humans and rocks and vegetables live in harmony—and with such esprit de corps. But it exists, it exists. . . ." Gazing out the window, she smiled appreciatively at nothing.

Even in the hospital's bad light, my great-grandmother looked beautiful; she glowed from within. In spite of the spirits and her medication, Nana's heavy-lidded eyes danced with life, and her aquiline nose—the nose all Darling women quietly endured—appeared queenly, compassionate. When it began to twitch something awful, I stuck a tissue under it and caught a sneeze.

"Whew!" Great-Nana sighed. "My conviction makes me wild with passion. And passion always makes me sneeze."

"Okay, Grandma." Mother clapped her hands like a headmistress. "It's time to sleep it off." Rising from her chair with authority, she crossed over to the bed, managed to coax Great-Nana beneath the covers. Then, when Mummy had for all intents and purposes returned to her chair, Nana flung back the bedclothes. "I'm just getting started!" she roared.

"Christ," Mother sighed, and held her hands towards heaven.

"Mummy, we're *Jewish*. Are we not Jewish?" I mimicked her pleading gesture.

"God, that's a tough question. You see, Wends, I'm a Wiccan-slash-Buddhist, a Wicca-Bu, if you will. It's your father who's Jewish. As for your great-grandmother, well, she's a *fabulist*."

"Very funny," Nana said. "You're awfully droll, ducky. But," she continued, "you are absentminded when it comes to history. You've forgotten everything crucial. For instance, crocodiles. And all the key personalities."

"Like fairies and mermaids and pirates?"

Great-Nana smiled slyly.

"Oh, Nana, really."

"Don't oh-Nana me. It's time to talk to the girl. How old is she?"

"Six."

"Heavens, we're almost too late."

Mother rolled her eyes in my direction, as if to signal that Nana was potty.

"But he comes earlier and earlier each time. We've got to be prepared!"

"Who comes? Who?" I was wild with curiosity. "I'm prepared for anything, Nana. I'm a Brownie," I assured her.

Great-Nana shook her head and clicked her tongue, as if I, her sole great-granddaughter, had been prepared for all the *wrong* things. "Margaret," she told Mummy, "please be a good girl and let us be. We've got business."

Mummy opened her mouth to protest, but left the room in

defeat. After a minute, though, she stuck her head in the door and gaily announced, "I'll be in the hallway, if anyone might possibly need a mother."

Ignoring her, Great-Nana directed me to pull up a chair. She offered me some lemon drops from a beveled-glass dish on her night table and, with a trembling hand, I took a sweet. "Take your time with it," she instructed, "melt, don't crunch." I sucked away with deliberation. "Now, open the curtains," she told me. "Super. Now, the windows. Excellent. Now, poppet, back to the chair." I followed her instructions to a T. "And this is the hard part, dear, for you really have got to open your mind. It's time. It's past time, really."

A sharp breeze rippled through the cramped room, raising goose pimples on my arms. My teeth chattered like castanets. But Great-Nana's attention was fixed on the sky. Perhaps her eyes tracked clouds or birds or airplanes; I couldn't make out what she found so fascinating.

Finally, she pierced me with a look of vexation, blinking in slow motion. A single freckle showed through her thick alabaster foundation. "You must pay attention, Wendy, because I only have the energy to say this once." I searched her gray eyes expectantly. "They—the physicians—have decided that I need constant observation because I happen to be having too much fun. And this fun threatens their boring little ex-*is*-tence!"

"Eggs and stains?"

"Sssh, child. I am here to warn you."

"Warn me?"

"About eternal youth. About Neverland. About boys and men and death. But not in that order. Men come last. Remember, they always come last."

I nodded as if I understood the lot of it, the ways of the world. Nana appeared newly refreshed; her liquid eyes brimmed with an excitement tinged with fear. She raised her right hand, surely about to spank me, then smacked her own forehead instead.

"Nana!" I objected.

"Listen to me, poppet. When you turn eleven or ten or—God forbid—eight, you will meet a boy."

"Yes," I said agreeably. After all, this sounded like a *good* thing. "But when exactly, Nana? I meet boys all the time."

"You do, do you?" I nodded like a horse in a circus act. "Oh, well. I hadn't thought of that. But this boy, he's not ordinary."

"Daddy says no one is ordinary. Daddy says we are all *extra*-ordinary!"

"He does, does he?" Again I nodded. "Well, your father is awfully optimistic."

"Daddy likes people."

"*Daddy* has a frightfully high opinion of the human race." Great-Nana stretched her arms over her head and yawned extravagantly. "But what he failed to mention is that some of us are extraordinary in extraordinary ways."

This sounded tantalizing, like a riddle. "Is the boy nice? Is he handsome?" I asked.

"Wendy, the point is, he's *too* nice, he's *too* handsome. You shall fall for him uncontrollably, head over heels and against all logic. Against all common sense."

From her toiletry bag on the bedside table, she scavenged for a lipstick, then took great pains to apply a deep shade of plum to her lips. Even at six, I wondered if she'd fallen for this boy herself.

"I don't understand. What's the bad part, Nana?"

Looking less wan now, Great-Nana lifted herself high in the bed and gave me a peck on the forehead. "The bad part? Oh, the underbelly." She scratched her nape and wound a stray wisp of tangerine-colored hair round her pinkie. "This boy, he will take you for a ride. He will open you up to miraculous things—caves the size of department stores, coves the color of daiquiris. Stars that are luminous, numerous, and numinous!" Here she cackled like a madwoman. "He will make you his queen and then his mother and then the mother of all the boys in his neighborhood."

"Sounds funny," I said. "Like a dream."

"Yes, darling, you are absolutely right. It *is* a dream. . . ." She stared off into the ether. After an absurdly long pause, she added: "His name is Peter. He will come for you and you will have no choice but to follow. Your mother will insist on it. Just like I insisted that my daughter, Jane, go with him and Jane insisted that Margaret do the same."

"But where *is* Grandma Jane?" I asked.

"Jane, where are you, my sweetheart?" she called out. Then, she closed her eyes and hummed. Just as abruptly, she put a finger to her lips. "Don't interrupt. When you grow up, Wendy, you will encourage your own daughter to follow this boy."

"But where will he take me? Does it hurt?"

"Hurt? God, yes. But only later when you can't be with him anymore. The beginning, however, is unimaginable."

"Then how can I imagine it, Nana?"

She arched her heavily penciled eyebrows. "It's *magical*. I can hardly put magic into words!" Then she softened and patted my head. "Wendy Darling, you *deserve* magic. You *deserve* the unimaginable. You just have to open your mind to . . . the Story. Shall we take it from the top?"

"Yes!" I cried with a certainty that I found startling.

"Jolly good show," she said, both of her cold hands clasped in mine.

"You will wake one starry night to discover a lad squatting on the floor, bawling his head off. It's always the same thing: 'boo-hoo-hoo.' The boy is crying his eyes out because he's either lost his shadow or lost his fairy, or forgotten the end to a fairy tale. You know, the usual alibi, the usual ruse."

Were the doctors right? Was Nana bonkers? I stifled a giggle and she pressed on: "I repeat, you will wake mid-dream, frightfully confused by footsteps and blubbering. Upon encountering such theatrics, you will say, 'Boy, why are you crying?' Not the best opening line, I grant you, but it will do. My beloved Jane knew from the outset that the pathetic, whimpering creature was Pan, but she kept tradition alive by dutifully repeating: 'Boy, why are you crying?' Of course, your own mother, Margaret—never one to miss an opportunity to be clever—dispensed with tradition and blurted out, 'Hey, gorgeous!' Then she waltzed circles round Peter, showing off her see-through nightie, and watched his eyes pop out of his head like a cartoon cat. But I am digressing." Nana squeezed my hand so tight I let out a little cry.

"During your first meeting with Peter, he will tell you how invaluable you are, that he cannot survive without you. He will claim that he needs you like no one has ever needed you. And you will find this most seductive—"

"What's *see-duc-tive*, Nana?"

"Good lord! Seductive is anything that makes you excited and pretty at the same time." I gave her a puzzled look. "Peter will complain that he's been without a mother for far too long. He'll swear to be your devoted slave if you'll do a bit of spring cleaning for him and his friends. Not to mention a little button-sewing, a little cooking, and a great deal of baking. At the time, this will seem reasonable, doable."

"I can do those things!"

"See, you're already taken in."

Was it true, did I believe her? Did I *want* to?

"And, most dramatically, dear, he will teach you how to . . . hover."

"You mean *fly*?"

"Well, yes, if you wish to split hairs."

"I'll be Amelia Earhart!" I bounded onto the bed and extended my arms, pretend-soaring above her tatty satin duvet. "Daddy will be so proud of me. He's always wanted me to be a pilot, you know."

"Yes, but he expected you would be using a *plane*, darling."

Giggling, I looked down to discover a still-handsome woman fallen back on an enormous feather pillow. "What is it, Nana? You said the story was magic. See-duc-tive. Are there monsters? Do people *die*?"

"Later, Wendy. Let's concentrate on the Story. So off you will go with Peter to meet his friends—strangely enough, they're all boys—and become a part of his epic adventure. Doesn't that sound smashing?"

A nurse stuck her face in the doorway. "Time for your pills, luv." A wraithlike young woman trotted in, her mannish shoes clomping, and handed Nana three yellow pills and a paper cup of water. Both women winked at me; apparently this was some sort of game.

When the nurse had retreated down the hall, Nana spat out the pills that she'd tucked, one by one, in her cheeks, and crushed them to dust in her meaty, white palms. Then she howled maniacally. Again I filled with doubt; maybe listening so faithfully to Great-Nana's stories only damaged her further—like pressing too hard on a bruise.

"Lie down with me, dear," Nana now purred. She stroked the duvet with her heavily ringed fingers.

I climbed onto the narrow metal bed and arranged my limbs around Nana's ample torso. When I was settled in, shabby duvet pulled up to my chin, Nana reprised her deranged laugh. "Isn't this divine?" she said. "We're two peas in a pod. Two Wendys in a bed. Two lost, lost girls." This sounded terrible to me, like a family curse, and I began to shiver.

"Wendy, listen carefully." This time she studied the ceiling instead of the sky. "My intention is not to scare you. Your mother does a good enough job of that. In fact, your mother is the one who has turned against males. Who is obsessed with personal justice and the settling of scores. Men! If you must know, I still love them all. When I said that they come *last,* I meant that you must always make certain you remember yourself *first.* But don't grow angry like Margaret. Or disappear like Jane." She dabbed at her nose with a tissue. "When the men betray you—and they *will* betray you—use this as an opportunity to forgive, as a heightened experience from which you can make music, write poetry, paint paintings.

"Believe me, you will be privy to a world that's more vivid than your crayons—more colorful than those snapshots your father is so fond of. A place where your creativity is queen. So plunge in, say *yes,* fall recklessly in love. Feel more deeply than your friends do. Hit the heights, descend into the depths. Kiss the lads smack on the lips and move on—like I did. I survived love and you will too. When you want to kill yourself—and you *will* want to kill yourself—remember that your Great-Nana loves you *and* your feelings. That your imagination is more powerful than your anger. And don't ever doubt me, Wendy. For your Nana is not only a flaming romantic, but a visionary who sees many things you cannot."

"What do you see now, Nana?"

"Now? I'm rather spent, dear." She faced the blank wall.

"Please tell me something. Just one itty thing."

"Well," she sighed, and pressed her palms together. "I see your future and it's . . . red-hot . . . your future burns bright as the sun!" Then she slipped her entire body, including her head, under the covers. But her queer musings continued, now muffled by the blankets: "The sun . . . its magnificent flames scorching everything in their path. Licking, hurling, annihilating. The sun, which gives us life, also burns a hole in our heart. And I'm not talking metaphorically, dear, I'm on fire. . . ."

Then she was asleep.

It was a simple question: should I cling to Nana or run?

Stepping out from her bedclothes, I tiptoed at high speed out of the room. No doubt, I had contracted my great-grandmother's illness—if I wasn't already bonkers, I'd soon be mad as a hatter. And that is how I became a burn victim of Great-Nana's imagination, for she branded her own dreams into me that afternoon, and I caught a fever that would not subside over fourteen thousand days. That day in the hospital, I said good-bye to common sense, to rationality. But what was I saying hello to?

II

OTHING that happens after the age of twelve matters very much." So said Sir James Matthew Barrie, most certainly about my great-grandmother and her "mythological" clique. But I say, *What a terrible prognosis,* our destinies fixed. I'm perhaps foolishly hoping Sir James was wrong, that those things that happen to us after the age of twelve matter very much indeed. You could say I'm betting the house on it.

Like it is for most preteens, my twelfth year was a time of arousal and unease: vexing allergies, inflating boobies, over-the-top expectations about school, about life. There were the requisite pimples and perspiration and new dance steps to learn. There was a rash of new "likes" (Pop-Tarts! nylons! Herman's Hermits!) as well as what I called the "horribles" (anchovies, beer, jocks, skateboarders). While my secretiveness and dreamy nature, accentuated by the floaty dresses I wore, tended to scare away classmates (they assumed I was silly or fey—"off" in some unfortunate way), I did have one close friend. Melanie Lawrence, a black émigré from South Africa, harbored a similar creative streak. A promising writer of mysteries, Melanie featured in her stories an African-American teenage sleuth who bore her own name. Mel and I liked to act out the plots to her stories on my backyard deck. Alas, our flights of fancy were routinely interrupted by Mummy: "Can you do something with my hair, girls?" "Would you girls mind listening to this bitch of a chapter I'm writing?"

While Melanie was entranced by Mummy—Mother's wine-colored locks were romantically long compared to the blunt, modern-looking cuts of my schoolmates' mothers—I was outraged. None of the other mothers in the neighborhood swore, and it was hard enough to build friendships when one was perceived as a weirdo.

"Your mother's so beautiful," Melanie gushed one afternoon. "I'm even thinking of changing my protagonist's name to Detective Margaret Darling."

"How about Detective Margaret Doo-Doo?" I offered and bit away at my nails.

At the time I hadn't begun to write fiction; it was poetry that piqued my interest—all that messy emotion corralled into tight little phrases. e.e. cummings was my current favorite, although Mother had recently forced Anne Sexton on me. "She'll open your eyes with a pitchfork," Mummy had said a tad gruesomely.

I'll admit that Sexton shocked me:

> Let me go down on your carpet
> your straw mattress—whatever's at hand
> because the child in me is dying, dying

I had never been in the presence of writing that revealed such stripped-down truths. Although I couldn't begin to fathom their adult mysteries, Sexton's poems made me shiver with feeling and I promised myself that I would always tell the truth as a writer. I wasn't aware that, soon enough, I'd be cloaking my own confessions in fables that starred barnyard beasts and forest critters—that obfuscations were essential for survival.

Being twelve was a mixed bag. Like other girls my age, I both dreaded and looked forward to beginning junior high in the fall: the social pressure from the boys, the social pressure from the girls, the dating, the nondating. In regard to one special boy, Great-Nana Wendy was wrong. Peter arrived sensationally late—far later than he had for her or for Jane or even for Mummy, who'd met Peter mere hours after her twelfth birthday and well before she'd been formally tipped off. Peter turned up in my bedroom on my *thirteenth* birthday, when I was, if anything, overprepared and had been waiting what felt like a lifetime. Every year, whether on the phone or in person, Great-Nana and I had had the same conversation, until I was convinced she was telling the truth. But after years of expecting Peter to make the scene, I'd aged considerably, not unlike those early American plainswomen who went mad studying the horizon while waiting for their husbands to return. The strain was even evident in my speech, for I took to stuttering words that began with P, and could hardly cry "For Pete's sake!" without slapping my cheeks with brute force.

By the time I was twelve and a half, I'd completely given up on meeting Peter in the flesh. First disappointed, then numbed by his absence—something I could hardly quantify—I added another layer of resentment to my feelings about my truant father. Worse, I was forced to conclude that my mother and her female elders were out of their barmy minds. For as much as Mother tried to convince her open-minded daughter that "Mummy is on the level," she could not produce one shred of proof about The Neverland. She couldn't even produce her own mother, Jane. And so I had to connect the dots myself: make-believe and reality are two different universes. The truth is, they have never even heard of each other.

During this restive time, I was successful in adding several inches to my height. An angular girl with a talent for performing improvised ballets and mutant strains of the Twist, at five feet, five inches, I resembled the elongated Alice in Wonderland, the Alice who outgrew her little house. Though long ago I'd made peace with my gaunt appearance—Mummy called it a "look"—the years of waiting for a boy to literally sweep me off my feet eventually took their toll, and I began to eat my way through the evenings. I rarely went to bed without consuming at least three Fig Newtons and downing a full glass of chocolate milk. For a chaser, I'd swallow a handful of Sweet Tarts—sleeping pills in my book—and nibble on cheddar cheese. Food couldn't hurt me, I reasoned. Not like boys who don't show up on schedule.

The evening of my thirteenth birthday, I happened to turn in early. Already disappointed by my teenage hormones—I was a tall, bony thing with no boyfriend, after all—I took to bed when it was still light out. Mummy had showered me with distracting gifts— Jean Naté body splash, Yardley English Lavender talc, Mary Quant eyeliner, and other teenage sundries—to make up for my lack of a love life, but I'd left them half unwrapped on my nightstand. By now, I'd given up on the whole Pan business and chalked it up to family myth, a fish story. I was more determined than ever to navigate a different path from that of my familial Darlings: I would become a professional truth-teller, a highly principled journalist. Fantasies be damned, I'd traffic in facts and all things verifiable! If something wasn't three-dimensional and rock-solid, it would have no place in my life.

After putting away a pound of birthday sweets, I found myself in a deep sleep, uncomfortably stuck in a dream about Daddy and his latest girlfriend, Amanda Cohen-Smythe. They were flying off to Fiji without me—how typical. Daddy was escorting, well, *shoving,* me off the plane, shouting, "This is Daddy's trip, not yours! Find your own trip." Screaming back at him, I lost my voice and could only hear it drumming in my head: *But* you *are my trip. You're my father!*

Then, curiously, he kneeled down on the tarmac as if to propose and lightly kissed the tip of my nose. "Bon voyage, Wendy," he whispered, once in each ear.

"But you're the one who's going away," I pointed out. "You're the one who's actually going somewhere."

"Don't be so sure, ladybird," he replied with an exaggerated wink. Then Daddy's long, lean frame towered over me; I watched him promenade up the ramp to his private plane. When a noxious puff of blue smoke issued from the engine, I knew it was time to head home. I waved good-bye to Daddy, who was already air-bound and no doubt happy; at the very least, he was en route to a place where he could manufacture the emotion.

I awoke with a start and the nagging sensation of having been left irreversibly behind. And there he was: the figment, the scalawag, the dreamboat.

I am not fond of crying boys. It's not that I'm stoic; other people's tears undo me. But I had been promised the sight of a crying boy dressed in some sort of vegetable-green getup for so long that when I finally set eyes on Peter, I saw a cartoon version of what I'd been expecting. His hair was a shambles; a forerunner of Ziggy Stardust or Bob Marley, it boasted both spikes and braids. His arms were caked with cobwebs and dirt, and old crumbs of chocolate framed his downturned mouth. His tears, mixed up with the dirt and crumbs, were grimy, too, and his outfit—distressed button-fly Levi's of unknown vintage and a Fruit of the Loom tee—was undeniably modern. The tee bore the faces of Manny, Moe, and Jack—the Pep Boys—and made me laugh out loud. Nothing on his person was green.

I'd rehearsed the occasion too many times; Great-Nana Wendy had insisted on it. How many nights had I practiced her signature line, "Boy, why are you crying?" But a moment like this was ripe for farce and, under the circumstances, I could only grin cruelly. "You're a mess," I said.

"Wha-at?" the boy stammered.

Soberly, then, I delivered my line: "Boy, why are you crying?"

"I've come for you, Wendy." His eyes studied me like a doleful puppy.

"Come for me?" I repeated, and let out an unfortunate chuckle.

"Hey, what's so funny? You find me funny, do you?"

Peter rose to his feet and rested his hands on his hips. We were at eye level now and I could see beneath the grime. Peter was astonishing-looking, deeply cute—even cuter than Jay North in *Dennis the Menace*. A faint scent of mint, or was it clove, permeated the room. And then I spotted a crude, hand-rolled herbal cigarette burning casually on the windowsill, its violet plume undulating in the half-light. Great-Nana had not prepared me for a smoker.

"I don't find you funny at all," I said, drawing a shaky breath. "I just don't believe it's you. You must be another bad dream I'm having."

"Blast, I hate bad dreams. They're worse than hurricanes. We Lost Boys can't weather 'em without a mother around. Get it? *Blast. Hurricanes. Weather.*" Now it was his turn to chuckle. He bent over to get a better look at me and I blushed, despite my superior knowledge that I was fast asleep.

"Lost Boys?" I repeated, and considered the possibility. "Oh, you're good. I just don't believe in any of this. Sorry."

For a moment he looked dejected, an abject failure of a storybook character. He took a drag off the cigarette, then snuffed it out in the potted African violet on my nightstand. Brightening, he said, "I'm so real I'll prove it to you!" Without warning the fellow blew in my ear.

"Jeez!" I hissed. I tried to swat away his hand but it was too late: the boy had taken flight. Well, he hovered a few inches from the ceiling, if *that* counts.

In spite of the tickle in my ear, I told myself to get a grip: I slapped both cheeks until they stung. But the boy bobbed resolutely overhead. So I asked him once again, though with a twist: "Boy, why are you *flying*?"

To this, he swiftly touched down, landing a little closer to my face than is proper. "The question is, luv, why aren't *you* flying?" He asked this with a smile as goofy as Terry Thomas's and an endearing cock of the head. Really!

"Because," I said, stalling. "Because I have yet to be indoctrinated. Plus, it's just a metaphor. Flying is a metaphor." I sounded totally grown-up to my mind. "In this family, we speak of flying as often as we speak of shopping."

"You're a queer girl," he said.

"Why, thank you," I answered with a curtsy.

"But you are as wrong as I am right!"

"Says who?" I challenged, sacrificing any pretense at sophistication.

"Says *me*," he said. "You are dead wrong. All wrong. Girl-wrong!"

"Girl-wrong? That's not even a word," I said disdainfully. A pinched smile leaked out against my will. "Please do get the words right. Civilization depends on it."

"That's precisely why we need you," Peter said with an earnestness I hadn't detected before. "We need to speak gooder."

Either this was a calculated attempt to extract my sympathy or he was one dumb bunny. "It's speak *better*. You need to learn how to speak better."

"See how much you can help us?"

"Us? Now I don't suppose you're referring to . . . fairies?"

"Crikey! Fairies don't need any help when it comes to conversing, they speak the Queen's English. I was talking about me mates."

Because I was mired in a dream, albeit a most convincing one, I blatantly rolled my eyes, making no effort to conceal my lack of faith in this exchange. I mean, I had heard them a hundred times—those quixotic tales of Peter and the Lost Boys—so often I could repeat them in my sleep. I *was* repeating them in my sleep! So I played along, privately hoping I would wake up before anything serious happened. Like falling out of bed. Or falling in love.

"God help me," I said under my breath.

"You know my name!" the boy cried and clapped his hands. Freshly inspired, he scrambled over to the rocking chair in the corner and began to rock violently.

"You mean, *God*? Oh, you are too much." I crossed my arms to convey exasperation, but like a cowboy riddled with fake bullets, he twitched and giggled in response.

"I *am* too much!" the boy squealed, and stood on the teetering chair. Then a look of gravity took possession of his face, if only fleetingly. "You *do* know my name, Wendy. Margaret promised me she would tell you everything."

"Oh, yes. I know more than a person should know."

His eyes sparkled like a lunatic's. "All right! Margaret was a real dolly bird, the prettiest mum of all." On hearing this, my face caved in. "But she was a stubborn girl, impossible to tame. And a tragically useless cook. Surely you can do better?"

I stood at the French windows, frozen in the pale-rose light of dawn; my room appeared to be drenched in fog—or perhaps it was my mind? Peter sprang out of the rocking chair and tiptoed nimbly, if broadly, over to the windows where I happened to be gripping the velvet curtains like a lifeline. Then, bending over balletically, he whispered in my ear: "Wendy, what exactly *did* Margaret tell you?"

I gazed into the face of the dream-boy and measuredly told the truth. "My mother and my Great-Nana Wendy—they said a young man would come, a dubious person named Peter. That I would be taken in by everything he said. And that he would spirit me away to a place where life is never, ever boring. They promised me I'd have more adventures than you can stuff into a lifetime, which hardly makes sense, and that I—why are you grinning? Excuse me, but would you please stop grinning?"

Peter sprinted onto my bed and began hopping up and down, trampoline-style. "You know my name! Isn't it the most brilliant name ever?"

"What? Oh, right. I forgot about your manners—they're reputed to be poor."

He belly flopped onto the mattress. "My manners have massively improved over the years, I'll have you know."

"Says who?"

"Says Wendy and Margaret."

"Shoot!" I blurted. *Those meddlesome Darlings.* "Well, I'm sure they're right," I said, lightly patting his head. His body jerked away from my touch. "Listen, Peter," I said, undeterred. "I'm not too great at cooking or cleaning. I'm a modern girl: I eat convenience foods and do the least amount of cleaning possible in order to free up my time to pursue other stuff."

"What kind of stuff?" he asked from a safe distance.

"Oh, you know."

"Nope. Haven't a clue." Now sprawled impishly across my bedspread, he gazed up at me and, not quite against my will, something akin to warmth flushed my cheeks.

"Well, I have my activities," I said. "Nothing as exciting as *smoking*. Stuff like watching TV, playing records, writing poems."

"Po-ems?" he asked, wrinkling his nose. His head rested in the basin of my pillow—like he owned it.

"God, what *did* those women teach you?" I plopped myself down, with great emphasis, at the far end of the bed, and fixed my attention on what little I could see out the windows: nary a star in the sky, but the high beam of a helicopter cast the whole firmament in a harsh light. "Well, you could say that a poem is an odd sort of wish. A bunch of sensations and feelings and images all blended together to make the juiciest sounds. But it's written down on paper, too."

He knocked on his head. "You lost me. Is it anything like *Jack and the Beanstalk*? *Treasure Island*?"

"Not exactly. Oh, a poem *can* tell a story if it wants to. But it doesn't have to. It's more like a child's nursery rhyme." He looked crestfallen. "Gosh, I forgot. Peter Pan doesn't like to be reminded of his early years."

"Why don't you just shoot me? Any baby who fell out of his pram, who got locked in a motorcar or abandoned in the park by his parents does not care to stroll down memory lane, thank you."

"I'm really sorry." I crawled up next to Peter on the bed, and he positioned a pillow for my head. Was *this* seduction? Was I being *seduced*? "Listen," I said, "would you like me to recite one of my poems, so you can hear for yourself?" He nodded indifferently.

With a small surge in confidence I cleared my throat. " 'Bliss,' by Wendy Darling Braverman," I said.

> *The world is a place for no one with a heart.*
> *It loves nothing. It feels nothing.*
> *Boys come and go and kiss and wave.*
> *They know nothing*
> *Of my heart.*
> *And nothing lives there anyway*
> *But a world of perfectly forgotten happiness.*

Peter spent an entire minute glued in place; for once his legs and arms stayed put. Just when I was about to pop, he said, "So that's a poem, ay?" More silence followed, then: "Are you sure?"

"Of course, I'm sure."

"But it doesn't rhyme."

"No one said it had to."

He scratched his chin like an old philosopher. "Well, your poem's bloody sad. And it's mean, that's what it is."

"*Mean*? What's that supposed to mean?"

"Of course, I don't know nothing about poems—"

"Of course you don't."

"But this one is very tough on us lads. It hardly gives us a chance."

"That's not fair. I didn't mean to say that."

"But you did."

"Well, you're wrong. And I'm the expert here," I said.

"Hey, you can't control how I respond to your codswallop. That's for *me* to decide." He leapt up on the mattress and flapped his arms like a proud rooster. A dreadful quacking assaulted my ears.

So this was *crowing*. Mummy had warned me about crowing, a horrid fusion of bragging and strutting, and she was right: it was both intolerable and undeniably cute.

"Why, you arrogant, stuck-up jerk! You can't go around deciding things." I bounded onto the mattress to accost him, which made him gloat even more.

"Oh yes, I can. I can decide that, as girls go, you are a most pleasing representative. A real peach."

"No, I'm not," I insisted. I recalled Daddy's similar appraisal, tendered so long ago that it hurt.

"And I can offer proof." Peter pulled a tiny, perfumed peach from the pocket of his baggy jeans, and held it up to my white-pink cheek. "An excellent match," he said with godlike certainty.

It was then I knew I could fall for this boy, for he had vast, hidden reserves of charm. And, as I said before, movie-star looks. I took the fruit, rubbed its furry flesh in my palm, and was about to sink my teeth in when he announced: "Come on, Wendy, it's time. Let's make like a leaf and blow!" He lifted off the bed, just a tad, and indicated that I should do the same.

By now, any remaining suspicion that this was a dream had taken a backseat, and I forgot to *try* to wake up. I honestly wanted to fly off with Peter. Who cared what kind of reality this was—it was far more compelling than the one on the ground with its sad birthday parties and no prospects for a boyfriend.

And thus I channeled all my desire into flying. I secured the peach under my pillow, then hunched my shoulders and squinted my eyes; I even got up on my toes and hopped. But it was not to be: I remained disappointingly, unequivocally earthbound.

"Haven't we forgotten something?" I cried out to Peter, who was now swinging on the light fixture like Errol Flynn. "I mean, don't I require some fairy dust?"

Peter, the little show-off, flew a couple of perfect circles around me. "You don't need dust, Wendy. That's your parents' generation. All you need are happy thoughts. So don't expect your *poems* to do the trick!" He cracked himself up with this, so much so, his snickers returned him to Earth and we were face to face on the bed again.

"All right, mister, watch out," I said, shaking a finger. This time, instead of wrinkling my brow and pumping my fists up and down, I remained perfectly still. I searched the dingy corners of my mind for something that was transporting, that would translate into genuine liftoff. . . .

I HAVE one memory of being noticed by Daddy. I was four, he was tinkering in his workshop, experimenting with different thicknesses of rubber bands for the rudders of his model planes. I happened to poke my nose through the garage door at a pivotal moment, and he waved me in.

"Step into my laboratory," he said in the rich baritone of a mad scientist. "Daddy has something to show you."

I approached cautiously; usually I was banned from entering this realm of nuts and bolts and male paraphernalia. Before I could take another step, Daddy snatched me like a hungry wolf and dropped me onto his lap. He had no idea of how robust he could be. Then he bounced me up and down till I got dizzy, directing me to withstand the terrible G forces, whatever those were, and to master my sense of equilibrium. After this exercise in nausea, he set me back on the ground and unveiled his most forward-thinking invention yet: a miniature aircraft, about four-feet long, that wasn't constructed from the usual balsa wood parts. This one was metal through and through.

"Where does the rubber band go?" I asked in earnest.

Daddy flashed a wolfish smile and whipped out what he called a "remote-control operating device," a gadget the size of a sausage roll. "No more rubber bands for us!" he cried, blonde fringe flopping in his eyes. Then he entrusted me with cradling the boxlike device while he got everything "ready for takeoff."

All systems go, Daddy tugged me by the arm, his other arm curled around the mystical metal craft; like criminals we hustled out the garage and down the block. As we passed the school yard, three older girls fell in behind us, their whispers loud and insinuating. Finally, the tallest girl, whose thick plait ran all the way to her bum, caught up with Daddy and me. "Well, if it isn't one of them *Darling* girls. I hear they're all barking mad," she said, turning to her friends. The three girls laughed shrilly, their shoulders jiggling. Then the tallest fluttered her arms like a demented bat. "Twinkle, twinkle!" she said, flapping madly, before she stepped back in line with her friends. The three girls crossed the street in a dark cloud of gossip.

"What's twinkle, twinkle?" I asked Daddy as we turned the corner.

"It's nothing, nothing at all," he answered evenly. I gnawed on my hair, not really believing him. "Sweetie, they just think . . . they think you believe in fairies."

"Silly Daddy," I said. "Fairies aren't real."

He refused to elaborate further and we arrived at a plot of land that was overrun with clover. Daddy instructed me to hand over the box and flashed his toothsome grin. Then, with mysterious purpose, he paced a wide circle on the field. Next, he cautioned me to stand back about eight meters while he placed his shiny new craft at the circle's center, and then stepped back eight meters himself. Crouching low to the ground, he mumbled something enigmatic and began flipping switches on the box. An impressive whirring sound was followed by an even more impressive silence.

"Bugger, bugger!" he swore, and wiped his forehead with his rolled-up shirtsleeve. Once more he furiously flipped switches, after which he regarded the sky with a near-religious look of desire. This time the whirring begat movement and the metal craft hovered admirably over the field with inches to spare. Pleased, Daddy flipped the largest toggle switch and his contraption took flight, buzzing above our heads in breathtaking, imperfect circles.

"It's bloody working!" he roared. "It's a bloody-fucking miracle!" Seeming to forget me in the wake of his success, Daddy followed the craft around the field, working his switches.

When the plane crashed in our neighbor's garden, he giggled girlishly, then flung himself onto a bed of dandelions. By the time I caught up with him, a couple of tears fogged his eyes. "Daddy," I called out, "are you all right?"

"All right? Daddy's *brilliant!*" He pulled me down onto his chest and squeezed me so tight I began to cough. "We did it, Wends! We did it!" Then he looked me in the eye and saw me, I think, for the first time. "What a lovely girl you are. A real peach." I blushed and soaked up all his praise like a sea sponge.

With a cheer Daddy sprang to his feet and lifted my skinny bones high above his head. The height was too much. My palms sweated, my heart banged around in my chest like a trapped animal. Daddy began to spin us—first slowly, then at high speed. "Wendy, extend your arms," he instructed. "Don't hold back. That's it, ladybird. Feel the air rush over your wings. Inhale the clouds. By George, girl, you're *flying!*"

I remember the sky that day: it was swimming-pool blue and boasted both white, puffy clouds and ominous gray ones, as if it couldn't make up its mind. Of course, *I* couldn't either: spending time with Daddy was a precarious activity. As long as he was entertained, life was good, even grand.

Daddy retrieved his toy plane, making pretty apologies to our neighbor Mrs. Slightly, and we walked home hand in hand. We entered the garage winded, the blush of victory on our cheeks. But Daddy's eyes were still rimmed with pink. I admired his sandy curls, his roguish mustache—"The man's a blonde Clark Gable," Mummy liked to say.

He wrapped the plane in newsprint and stowed it in a crate. Then, with extreme caution, he withdrew a framed photograph from his workbench drawer and dusted its glass with a flannel cloth. In the photo, a pretty woman with cropped hair and a funny helmet stared back at us. My stomach knotted up. *Was Daddy in love with someone other than Mummy and me?*

"Who's that?" I peeped, and rubbed my runny nose.

"Good God, Wendy! You don't recognize her?"

I shook my head, wondering if the lady was a member of the royal family or some movie star I had overlooked.

"It's Amelia," he said flatly.

I registered no sign of recognition.

"Amelia Earhart."

I shook my head dumbly.

"You're her namesake," he said, a trifle irritated. "She's the person you were named after."

It was true: I was named Wendy Amelia Darling Braverman.

"Amelia was an amazing pilot, Wends. The best. In fact she flew better than most men. She had the skill and grace and pluck and beauty. But no luck, no luck . . ." His beatific gaze at the photograph darkened.

"Why's that?" I asked.

He ignored the question and tucked the portrait away in the drawer. But I had seen the expression of love on his face, the one he withheld from Mummy and me. "Just be careful," he said. "Don't go bumping into things." I nodded and we left the garage in silence. . . .

⌒ "Wendy, on the face of things, your face doesn't look very happy. D'ya get it? Your *face*? *Face* of things?" Peter was shouting in my ear, jostling me out of my reverie.

"Did I fly? Did I soar?" I asked.

"Are you having a laugh? You look like your goldfish died." He started for the windows.

"Please," I begged. "Give me another chance. I may not have a knack for this, but I'm a fast learner." I batted my eyelashes just like Mummy always did.

"What's wrong with your eyes, mate?"

"Nothing's wrong. Just trying to get rid of . . . memories. Blinking is the best way to do that, didn't you know?" He shook his head. "Well, it's true. You can push them out your eyeballs."

"Disgusting," he said, drawing closer. "Aw, all right. One more try and then I've gotta fly. At least *my* poem rhymes, hee-hee! I'm a bloody rhyming genius!"

I threw myself into the task as if my future depended on it—and it *did,* according to Mummy and Nana, who both felt there's nothing more character-building than a tour of duty in The Neverland. I sat down decisively in my rocking chair and concentrated on the notion of something unquestionably lovely—a thing so grand and merry and elevated that it would eventually elevate me. *A new party dress? M&M's? Paul McCartney?* My toes remained pinned to terra firma. *Peppermint stick ice cream? Baby kittens? Mummy, when she's kind?* My heels dug into the floorboards; my bottom remained fused to the chair.

Stop this foolishness, I scolded myself. *Hang up your wings and go home.* But I *was* home; Peter was the one who was AWOL. Besides I was a resourceful girl; I could fly in other ways. Were my poems not tickets to other worlds? Surely they could take me to places no one had even thought of. I didn't need to redo what my relatives had done in spades.

And then I noticed a subtle breeze blowing beneath my toes. *Beneath!* I looked down to find myself a few inches above the rocking chair, my bum levitating in the air and my arms outstretched like

Supergirl's. So it was poetry that had done the trick—my morbid little poems! Peter was wrong: my poems might be sad things but thinking about writing them had made me wildly happy. "Look at me," I giggled. "I'm up, I'm up!"

I felt gauzy, like a whisper, a tiny ripple in the heated air. I was gazing *down* upon my Lesley Gore records, my cache of lip gloss tubes, my still-childish bedspread with its parade of ducks and swans. My stomach wobbled, my breath roared in my throat. I was both scared and inspired, and altogether convinced I would pee—it was only a matter of seconds.

"Nice going, Wendy!" Peter applauded. He gave me a standing, then flying, ovation.

"YES, darling. Good going!" Mummy was standing in the doorway, wearing a skimpy tube top and cutoffs. "Now don't fuck it up— keep thinking lovely thoughts. Up, up, up!"

It's no coincidence the word *mother* rhymes with *smother*. The moment I heard Mummy's voice, I came crashing down and even hurt one knee so badly it required cortisone. But Mummy had triumphed: her daughter was now initiated into a cult, albeit with one of its members missing in action—Grandma Jane had been mysteriously absent for over twenty years now and no one seemed the slightest bit worried.

I had triumphed too. I was off and running—well, off and flying—and Mummy was pleased with me, and maybe jealous. As for whether or not I'd been dreaming, I didn't give a fig. I'd experienced weightlessness—me, a tall, gangly teenager—and didn't care to come down before I had to.

REAT-NANA always said I had stars in my eyes, but surely that's a by-product of too much night-traveling. These days pollution has ruined all that, iced the stars with soot. But when I was a child, Orion clearly pointed the way, the constellations performing a silent ballet, and I arrived on the island drunk with light, my irises dazzled, my heart exploding with excitement.

The Neverland casts a glamour on every soul who washes up on its shores: for a tadpole like me, the place dripped with risk, with *experience*. Its surreal vistas (deserts abutting jungles! leaves that dart from tree to tree!) shook up the senses, challenged what I knew to be true.

You see, The Neverland means something dramatically different to each person who alights there. No two travelers' reports correspond. For some, the landmass is vast and overpowering, on the magnitude of Alaska; for others, it's a dot of earth no bigger than a football field. Some visitors remark on the island's vegetation, all knotted and flowerless; others swoon over the variety of flowers or rave about the forest, dense yet illuminated from above by a cluster of moons. Natives go on and on about the size of the fruit—corpulent cherries, bite-sized watermelons!—while visitors single out the taste of the vegetables: *how spicy, how tangy,* they coo. Passersby remark on the lack of good housing while those who stay put tout the architecture of the tree houses, the durability of the caves. Everyone seems to agree that the springwater is tops, practically ambrosial. But no one can agree on the color of the sky—cobalt, duck-gray, beach-glass, chamomile? Longtime residents say it's what you bring *with* you, your preconceptions, that make the place what it is. That you have to be careful lest you invest it with too much beauty or wonder. It's important not to go overboard.

In any travel brochure, it's almost too easy to play up the picturesque and avoid the problems. Think of Cuba, Tahiti, Atlantis— lovely islands all. But physical beauty dodges the big questions. You have to be vigilant where beauty runs amok. It so happened that the *psychological* tenor of The Neverland eventually got to me—it got to all girls who set foot there. For peril lurked hand in hand with wonder—it always does.

Mythological places are notable for their opportunities as well as their dangers, and The Neverland was no exception. On its stage great triumphs, pitched battles, and profound naps took place. Rites of passage were so common you could hardly take a walk without encountering an alter ego, an adversary, or a guardian fairy who lit the way. Heroes were plentiful, too—the fraternity of wayward boys, but also a loose collection of Indians: Pacific Islanders, Inuits, and Native Americans, men and women who sought balance there. By the time I arrived, though, all but two of the tribes had moved on to Hawaii, a roomier and less melancholy Pacific island.

It wasn't all simpatico in The Neverland. There was a cadre of villains who cast their lot with the Boys and the few remaining Indians. Every year, you see, a few lads failed at the Grand Experiment— to remain carefree, silly, *young*. I hate to say it, but they managed to grow up badly. It was these failed boys who turned to banditry, who referred to themselves as *blaggers, rapscallions, pirates*. In Spring, the island was lousy with these losers. Most of them went off to sea; others went literally underground, building an extensive series of tunnels for the advantage of surprise. But when the pirates were outsmarted, again and again, by the Indians, terrorizing the Boys became their primary goal. As was expected, the Boys counted the pirates as one of the island's many charms: for here was a gang of skanky older dudes with whom to engage in sport! And wasn't war the number one game of boys everywhere?

Not surprisingly, in the men's heart of hearts, they were playing for goddamn real. Lots of showy swordplay, pillaging, and plundering—the Boys couldn't have been more stimulated! But a lark for the Boys proved to be an emotional sinkhole for the girls. Known to be of a sex too smart to fall out of their strollers (and thus unlikely to end up on the island), the few girls who made their way there were regarded as prey by the men. Perhaps I don't have to tell you, but these men practiced rapine—the art of carrying away things by force. Perhaps I don't have to tell you that those *things* included girls.

It was this dark mischief, coupled with the fickle companionship of the Boys, that set the stage for my confusion in life, and precipitated a disorientation worse than the effects of any hallucinogen. So while the Boys toyed with their foes, shelling their ships with cantaloupes and tossing cow pies in their tunnels, we girls took great pains to avoid getting snatched. Which explains how, after landing on this lovely isle, my outsized fear tarnished my native delight—a ferment of emotions that even now cripples me. How I wish I could tell you what I can't remember!

There are shadows the size of grown men that cover up what we can't see, what we refuse to see. On the island such shadows grow monstrous and bullying, and worse than that, they *smell*. Like sulfur, some say, or rotten meat. I recall one particular shadow with a nasal drawl and skeletal limbs that beckoned to me like a bad mime. I tried to outrun it, tried to outsmart it. But it poured over me like a slick of motor oil. Blacked out, I couldn't see myself—but I could smell the beast.

It would be too easy to say that I was ravished. *Rape* is too strong a word, *devalued* not strong enough. For I believe the shadow had its way with me. I know it had some sort of horrid meat hook for an arm. They say it even named itself after its appendage. That this shadow was human.

Even now in my forties, I pull the chain on my night-light before I slip into bed. I shudder the moment the sun goes down and can't be held at my waist without becoming queasy—without feeling that something is terribly wrong. If I were a crime scene, I swear you'd find fingerprints on every inch of my skin—that's all I can tell you. For The Neverland is one big projection, and I had very little to project at the time.

★ ★

THE day I stripped the bandage off my freshly healed knee—my first attempt at flying had netted me a long, wiggly scar and yet a delicious new confidence about what my own limbs could *do*— Peter paid me a second visit. This time he demonstrated even less patience with me, allowing that we were already terribly late. *Late?* He grabbed a sheaf of my poems, not bothering to read a single page, and waved it in my face. "Wendy, time is a-wasting. Take a gander at your poems, do your deep thinking, and let's boogie!"

This time I didn't need the poems; the mere thought of flying by my own hand did the trick. I was out the window and, within the hour, rocketing through the blue skies over the coast at Santa Barbara. But by the time Peter and I found ourselves gliding through a yellow, poisonous film that clung to the Los Angeles basin like suntan oil, my stomach was in an uproar. It wasn't the smog that disturbed me—it was the idea of *landing*. It turns out that Darling girls, no matter how ungainly, excel at flying, but landing can be a hazardous business. To steady my nerves, then, I took a little detour and flew dangerously close to MGM Studios hoping to touch down on some old stage set from *The Wizard of Oz* and make myself at home. At this point in the journey, Oz made for a better prospect than The Neverland, for the Oz story has a happy ending while my own was still up for grabs.

But where I saw the locus of movie magic, Peter only saw rows of bland gray buildings and demanded that we press on. With haste, then, we flew off toward the stars, leaving behind the known world and the good sense that accompanies it. When Peter remarked that I looked radiant, I felt like a star myself!

⬯ I landed in The Neverland with the softest of thuds—a meadow of spongy pink flowers cushioning my fall—and then bounced in place like a big rubber ball. The flowers smelled sweetly of pink bubble gum, the kind that comes with little wax-paper comics, and each time my body banged against the leaves, I thought I heard a *boing*.

In spite of the heavenly scent and the springy flowers, my stomach was beset with butterflies. Surely, my travels to London to visit Great-Nana had always been interesting. But never eye-popping, never *intoxicating*. What's more, this trip had been notably longer than the storybooks suggested—and hence I was intoxicated and *cold*. No book has remarked on the dramatic changes of climate one must endure, or discussed the failure of one's nightgown as travel wear.

Eventually, all the excitement took its toll and my thoughts turned to safety, to self-preservation. I sat up, supported by the dense bed of flowers, and on the chance there were onlookers, tugged the flannel gown over my exposed legs. But I was all alone. I struggled to get a firm footing, only to regret it: the boy landed on my bad knee and knocked me down all over again.

"How clumsy is *that*?" I said to Peter's face.

"Dreadfully clumsy," he replied. Then he smiled with such un-alloyed pleasure that I knew I would be all right. The smile aimed an undeniable heat on my chilled skin and banged knee; I watched the goose bumps on my forearms fade, felt my stomach ease up. The boy gave me his hand and pulled me upright. Now I could see that the flowers were waist-high, their floppy leaves as long as dog ears, and that they were supported by an undergrowth of thorns. As I took in the brilliance of the meadow—the pink was so concentrated it tinted the surrounding hills and the boy's dirty cheeks; even the horizon looked rosy—Peter encouraged me to follow him to an enormous oak tree at the edge of the field. I was bone tired and yet he egged me on—with *real* eggs, mind you. Where the eggs came from and how they got hard-boiled, I hadn't a clue, but since I was famished I did what the boy said.

The great oak was distinguished by a trunk as thick as a one-hour photo booth and a silver plaque that read THE HANGING TREE: "Are people really hung here?" I asked nervously.

The boy had a laugh at that. "Not *hung*," he said. "We lads *hang* from the branches whenever we want—which is most of the time." He shook his head as if every bit of information I'd brought along with me was worthless here. Then, for a visual aid, he hung by his toes from one of the tree's stockier branches and dangled precariously. After a showy dismount, wherein he executed a double flip, the boy touched down on the ground next to me.

"Very impressive," I told him, but already his attention was directed elsewhere. He was studying me the way guys back home check out girls, and I shuffled my feet in the dirt.

"Listen, I've got to ask you a sticky question," he said finally, and I prepared myself to say *yes* to life and to love, exactly as Great-Nana had instructed. This was my first date and I wasn't going to blow it.

"Will you promise me something, Wendy?" he said with the slightest hint of pressure.

"I can promise you anything," I said rather boldly. After all, I'd just arrived and felt capable of winning a gold medal at the Olympics.

"Right." He cleared his throat dramatically. "You must promise me that you will never grow up. Do you understand?" he asked, eyes wild with hope.

I nodded gravely, but tried to look cheerful, too; our relationship was still young and open to interpretation.

"It will kill me. It will just kill me if you grow up like the others."

The others? He was referring to my own relatives, of course, and I wondered where I got the backbone to attempt something as radical as this. But isn't that the nature of new friendships—you feel that you can achieve practically anything?

I wriggled around inside my voluminous nightgown, stretched my arms and legs out in front of me, and felt my body come alive. My body was a growing thing, and yet I was about to tell him that I would put a stop to that! "Yes, I promise," I said with a clarity that came up like a burp. "I promise you I won't grow up."

He sighed like the weight of the world had left his own body and taken off into the wind; then he stood up abruptly and made his good-byes. "Cheers, Wendy, we'll see you later then," was all he said, but it was enough for me to take heed. Daddy was in the habit of saying the same thing, and I hadn't seen *him* for nine months.

Just like that, I was alone in a new dimension, without compass or flashlight or savvy tour guide. This didn't look promising. I took a wary whiff of the sweet-smelling air, then stepped onto a dusty path that offered to take me someplace special. I'm not clairvoyant—there was a hand-painted sign of a fairy pointing in the same direction. The sign said SOMEPLACE SPECIAL and who was I to argue?

That same afternoon, I met the ragtag guys about whom Great-Nana had spoken so fondly. Though they turned out to be a more recent crop of homeless, soapless youth, they were just as blindly devoted to Peter as the original gang. Funny how Peter always ended up as Lord Master, Head Poo-Bah, or His Excellency. I could never persuade the others that there should be a revolving leadership on the island—or a council that included them all. The Boys were happy to defer to Peter; they actually enjoyed being governed by someone a notch older and wiser. Someone akin to a father, but still a fool.

The path I'd chosen with such confidence ended at the banks of a creek so clear it reflected back all my imperfections. *But I didn't care!* I promptly went about washing off all the muck I'd acquired in my travels, as well as many of my misconceptions. For while I was not crazy about being left alone on the island, I now felt a surge of self-reliance—a rare optimism that had come apparently from nowhere. I dipped my wind-knotted hair in the mild springwater, and watched the strands float lazily on the mirrored surface. I half considered donating my entire body to the current and floating downstream. But when I lifted my head from the water, I was face to face with a profoundly tanned, surfer-looking fellow who sported baggy Hawaiian-print trunks and ivory dreadlocks. Though coated with a fine layer of dirt, he showed no interest in the cleansing properties of the water; instead he fished with his bare hands for guppies, tossing the slippery devils into his mouth like popcorn. I was—charmed.

"Name's Bert," he said, mouth dripping.

"I'm Wendy." I waved. "Otherwise known as the Wendybird."

"No. You're having me on," he said. With the back of his hand he wiped the last of the fish guts from the corners of his mouth. "The real O.W.?"

"Sorry?" I said.

"Blimey, the Original Wendy?"

"Well, *I'm* Wendy and I'm myself."

He eyed me suspiciously.

"Okay, I suppose you're talking about my great-grandmother. Wendy the First?" I smiled broadly at the boy, turning on the ancestral charm.

"So you know her?" he asked, agog.

"Of course. She's family."

"I don't know 'bout family," he said bleakly. "I hear stories, though. It all sounds pretty dodgy."

"Well, sure," I told him. "But not always. Sometimes a family makes you stronger, connects you to a powerful force—to history and to the future!" Now the boy looked deeply bored. "You knew her, my great-grandmother?"

"Me? Nah. But, bloody hell, she's a legend around here. The O.W. made quite an impression on us lads."

So Great-Nana's influence had continued to shape these young men. I got a little tingle. "And Margaret, what about Margaret? Did you . . . *do* you know her?"

"*Princess* Margaret? Yeah, some of the blokes had mad pashes on her. Me, I don't know the bird. But I hear good things. I hear she's tasty."

Mother would be pleased to hear it. I grabbed a couple of shallow breaths before asking the inevitable: "And Jane? Have you ever heard of Jane?"

"As in, me Tarzan, you Jane?" His lampoon was followed by a laugh that seemed hysterical under the circumstances. "Nope," he said with a flip of white-gold plaits. "Never heard of her. Is she a looker too?"

"I don't know," I answered solemnly. "I never met her."

"Are you sure ya don't mean a bloke named *Jason*? 'Cause there was a Jason hanging 'round these parts, an evil sort who lost his hand in a card game."

"You mean he played a bad hand?" I asked, amused.

"I mean he bet his own hand and lost it," Bert said. "You best steer clear of 'im, miss."

"Oh dear," I said. "But I was speaking about Jane. My Grandma Jane."

"You must mean *John*, then," Bert continued, unfazed. "There was a bloke named John 'round these parts."

"No," I corrected. "John is my great-grandmother's brother. He was a little boy when he visited the island."

"You sure 'bout that? 'Cause this John's a tall, strange-looking geezer who'll have nothing to do with the lot of us."

"Well, John's a very common name. I'm sure your John is not my Great-Great Uncle John."

"Great? What's so bloody fabulous about 'im?"

"*Great-great* is a figure of speech," I told him. "Anyway, John returned to the Mainland. He's a doctor, well, he *was* before he died."

"Died? Aw, cripes." The boy slumped against me on the sun-warmed banks; together, we dipped our toes in the fizzy, Perrierlike water.

"Hey, it's okay." I hugged the boy to my chest as if he were a toddler. He seemed to respond to my touch. "Great-Great Uncle John grew up and had this really amazing life. He went off to war, you know. World War One? He was a medic and saved the lives of hundreds of blown-up men. Later, he worked in a clinic as a baby doctor.

An ob-ste-tri-cian. So he could be present at the *beginnings* of lives. Imagine delivering thousands of babies! When he was really old, like maybe forty, John told his sister that his life was the epitome of balance. He died a happy man."

The boy looked up at me with hooded, pale-green eyes. "Did the babies have parents? Did the parents keep their babies?"

"What?" I asked, shooing a large, three-winged insect off my cheek.

"Were the babies he delivered, you know, loved? By their mums and dads?"

"Well, I didn't know the babies. But statistics show—"

"No!" he shrieked, and clung tight to my chest again. "No statistics. Give me the bloody *truth.*"

I hadn't a clue what to tell the boy, for I was a child of little certainty myself. The truth? Well, yes, all babies are loved. How could they *not* be? The whole world loves babies. What had Great-Nana said? That all of us are bathed in a cosmic love as we make our entrance into the world. Whether this love flows from each and every parent, too, I couldn't remember. And whether love will be a constant, whether it will follow us around like a faithful dog for the sum of our days—who knows?

What I *could* tell the boy was, the moment we are born appears to be the very same moment we forget we are loved. Now isn't that awkward? Shouldn't the two things dovetail, love and memory? Shouldn't a feeling that powerful be carved on a tree so no one can ignore its message? To come so far to be in this world only to forget something all-important—what kind of a journey is that? I'll bet that 90 percent of the love that surrounds us is dismissed or discounted—the cup of tea a friend makes, the letter from a faraway auntie. The fact that no one feels loved *enough* merely proves my point.

I would have preferred to die with my half-baked theory than to live with no theory at all. Or with a theory that presumes an emotional void at the heart of the universe. Believe me, I was no Pollyanna—but neither was I cut out for realism. Throughout the Spring, The Neverland would make sure of that.

So, what to tell the boy? I couldn't prove the existence of love, but I could assure him that someone must *remember* being loved or we wouldn't have the idea to begin with. Besides, his parents—those "monsters" who'd rejected him—had been babies once too, were loved once too. Or maybe not. Already I was bent on rehabilitating the boy, hoping to convince him that he was not abandoned.

It turned out that my good intentions fell by the wayside, for the boy and I were joined presently by a band of the officially unloved. Six other boys of unknown pedigrees sat down beside us on the bank, and began arguing over whose neck was thickest. I couldn't glean the purpose of such a contest or the glory of such an honor, but the whole scene was pleasantly diverting. When I proposed that *my* neck was the thickest, I was heckled mercilessly; two boys with grubby fingers even jabbed at my swanlike stem. But when I coiled one of the Boys' mildewed sweaters around my neck like a muffler, the group unanimously agreed that I'd won. I didn't get it. The boys could have cheated in a similar manner. I guess, to them, the illusion I'd created wasn't illusory. It was the new, improved reality—and was the very height of silliness.

Now being understood *and* accepted is a peak experience for any teen; which is how a girl who'd largely known disappointment now found herself on cloud nine. Of course, the entire island was one whopping cloud nine, but being accepted had cinched it. I slipped off the sweater, ready to be stripped of my winner's status. Already, it seemed, the boys had moved on to the next contest: "Which one of us 'as the biggest bone-crunching thighs?" Now this was one competition that I begged off from entering. In any dimension, it appears that boys will be boys and that large body parts play a large role.

After many more pointless contests, including "Who burps loudest?" and "Who pees longest?" I yearned to take a nap. It was only then, as I started off towards a cave that Peter had arranged for my stay, that Bert formally introduced the Lost Boys. He did so with surprising fanfare considering that I'd spent the better half of the afternoon with the guys.

"Oi, listen up, lads!" Bert hollered. "This 'ere's Wendy the Second, great-granddaughter of the O.W."

"You don't say," said a slack-jawed youth.

"Well, bugger me," said a freckled beanpole.

"Oi," scolded a now-red-faced Bert, " 'ave I got to remind you to mind your language around a lady?"

"What *kind* of language do you propose?" asked the slack-jawed boy.

"*Pretty* language," Bert said.

"None of us is pretty," argued another, this one six feet tall and counting.

"Right," said an exasperated Bert. "Just be good to 'er or I'll tie you to a tree and give you a knuckle sandwich."

I waved a friendly finger in the air. "Excuse me, but . . . isn't that playing a little rough?"

"Yeah," Bert agreed after a two-second deliberation. "Like the lady said, I'll put you through the wringer. You got me?"

"Yes sir!" the Boys chimed.

"Now let's get acquainted and call it a day."

"It's a day!" cried the Boys in unison.

"State your name and purpose," Bert instructed, nodding in my direction.

"Um, hi everybody. I'm Wendy Darling." An ominous rumbling, like thunder, erupted from the group. "Of the Berkeley Darlings," I joked. "By way of the London Darlings." The discord grew, now punctuated with rude animal sounds. "But I'm totally American, completely myself. I'm not anything like the first Wendy." A round of boos. "Sorry about that. And I'm nothing like Margaret, either. I mean, who could out-Margaret Margaret?" A couple of the guys hooted but still I forged ahead. "I'm just so tickled to be here, I can't tell you. Guess I *am* telling you. I've waited my whole life to come here and tell you!"

"Then why do ya sound so bird-brained?" asked a little guy with a skyscraper Afro and a voice that could grate carrots.

"What?" I said, startled. Neither Great-Nana nor Mother had

warned me about being disparaged in The Neverland. I could always feel like a nobody back home.

"You know, why d'ya sound like a dingleberry?" the little fellow said. The Boys glowered at me.

"Just because," I said at last. There, I'd stood my ground.

"Because why?" he pressed.

"Because . . . happiness does that. Because when you realize your greatest dream and it realizes you, you are reduced to speechlessness, to groveling, to tears."

"Oi, watch out," Bert warned. "She's gonna turn on the waterworks!"

The troupe regarded me with openmouthed stares; I gazed back at them with dreamy equanimity. After a long pause perforated with adolescent snickers, Bert assumed a military bearing. "Blimey, lads, she's not 'alf the crybaby her mother was. Time to sound off now!"

And so it was that the Lost Boys, circa 1966, presented themselves to me. Deficient in manners yet educated in the art of hijinks, each boy made an effort to bow, a motion that devolved, naturally, into a pratfall.

"Beasley!" the freckle-faced youth blurted out, bowing so low he managed a somersault into the spring.

"Toenail!" cried the slack-jawed boy with an adenoidal twang. On leathery heels, he tried to bend into a backward arch, but fell flat.

"Junior-Junior!" barked a husky, moon-faced boy in oversized boots trimmed with bright blue feathers. He saluted stiffly, then marched headlong into a tree trunk, faking a knockout blow.

"Elvis!" said the small boy with the big Afro and a surplus of moxie. After performing a ceremonial bow, he froze in place and appeared to stop breathing. None of the others seemed bothered by this in the least, so I directed my attention to the next boy in line.

"Theo," an angel-faced Japanese boy whispered, extending his sleek hand to me. I held it affectionately until, in one well-rehearsed motion, he flung me over his shoulder and pinned me down on the grassy bank. *Theo,* I repeated to myself, making a mental note.

Once I was on my feet again, the final boy, a hairy behemoth who'd won the big-thigh contest, paced circles around me, sniffing. I was not surprised to learn his name was Bowser; neither was I thrilled to be sniffed, but, in my family, one accepts attention where one finds it.

"So that's the lot of us," Bert said, ever economical in his speech. He bowed formally and without incident, but I detected a speck of shame sullying his pride.

At this, Elvis retired his bizarre "statue" pose and began moving to a powerful downbeat; strange, syncopated music blared from a hole in the tree trunk to our right. Bert and the others followed Elvis's lead, gyrating to the music in an impromptu ring that eventually snaked around—me! I watched the lads shimmy-shake and pirouette, make gravity-defying leaps. The whole performance was less *American Bandstand* than *West Side Story.* When at last the dancing fizzled, leaving an awkward silence in its wake, the Boys got down on their knees and bowed reverently, without a hint of devilry. I was so moved that I covered my face with my hands on the chance that my "waterworks" might start up. Then Bert made a daring suggestion: "I got an idear, mates."

"He's got an idear," the throng chanted.

"Let's ordain Wendy as an honorary Boy. We need her more than we could know."

"Then how do we know it?" asked Beasley.

"To *know* Wendy is to need her," Bert said mysteriously, and it was all I could do to suppress swooning. "So, 'ow about it?" Bert enthused.

"Honorary Boy!" the throng cried.

The unanimous cheering caught me off guard. A bubble of nausea made its way up my throat and I succumbed to a hiccup. For there it was, a small voice inside me wondering, *If I was being accepted for who I was, why did I have to become a* boy *in the process?*

Theo tore off into a nearby hedge of bottlebrush, only to return moments later with a necklace made of Wrigley's Spearmint gum wrappers and *real* spearmint leaves. He hung the thing around my pole of a neck, and I attempted a curtsy. "Wow," I managed to squeak out.

"'Ere ye, 'ere ye," Bowser proclaimed. "Wendy is 'ereby declared a boner-fide, gen-u-wine Lost Boy!"

The Boys whistled, stomped, and whooped, after which Elvis recited a poem entitled "Wendy's Escape from the Land of Mothers":

> *It is written that anyone*
> *Who trucks with*
> *The Motherland*
> *Is a mothertrucker!*

Bowser then hoisted me onto his shoulders and paraded me around like I was a war hero. The others fell in line behind us, singing summer-camp songs without a trace of irony. Our entourage headed off to find Peter; we were a small but powerful force to be reckoned with.

Three months later, Peter said good-bye to me for good. It's not that I wasn't homesick, just a little, for Mummy and the movies and some grown-up conversation—I'd been open about harboring such longings. But it's easier to say good-bye when someone *promises* that he will come back for you, when someone gives you his *word*.

On the day of my departure—which should go down in infamy— I hadn't planned on going anywhere on the island, let alone all the way back to Berkeley. For an entire week, I'd been shot down by the flu—sore throat, fever, runny nose, bad cough—and within hours of my first sneeze, the Boys' routine was paralyzed. They couldn't manage to feed themselves, clothe themselves, or patch up fights without me. But there was no way I was going to get out of bed and take charge.

Leave it to Peter, then, to introduce a new face on the island—the face of another girl. In the spirit of full disclosure, I should add that her *body* was likewise introduced to me, but it was too Amazonian, too perfect, to describe—and so I won't. Let's just say I would refuse to take part in a beauty contest of any kind, and my fever spiked within minutes of her arrival.

"Wendybird, I'd like to introduce a *new* bird," Peter had announced with stupendous naïveté. "She's come all the way from Minneapolis and knows a story or two. Staggeringly good ones, too."

"Shut up!" I cried. But that was all. With no energy left to fan the flames of jealousy, I sank back under the bedclothes.

Once the girl was hustled safely out of the house, Peter had the nerve to speak to me again. "Listen, pet," he said more gently this time. "You're out of commission and we Boys need to run a tight ship."

"We're on *land,* blockhead," I said, and blew into a hanky made from the flannel nightgown I'd arrived in. By now I'd ripped the gown so much and so often, it had become a minidress by default.

"That's it," he said decisively. "You're going back."

"No!" I cried hoarsely, knowing full well that I'd never recuperate on the island with certain domestic duties forced upon me. And then, as Peter drew nearer, I gripped his wrist and refused to let go. "Just because a girl gets sick doesn't mean she's done for. Really! You have to have a little patience."

Twisting free from my grasp, he rubbed his hand as if *I'd* actually caused *him* pain. "But you've been ill practically forever, Wendy, and I refuse to wait. I just won't do it!"

And so he didn't. He had Bert remove me from the strata of blankets and knitted afghans, and bundle me into three of the Boys' humongous sweaters; then he insisted that I think lovely thoughts. Given my status as a diseased person with off-the-charts head pressure, the only happy thought I could muster was of the rosemary shampoo scent of Mummy's hair. When I skimmed the ground, just a tad, we were both surprised. Peter shouted "Yes!" and it was a fait accompli: I was aloft in spite of myself.

Midair, Peter latched on to the collar of my topmost sweater—a *cardie,* he called it—and endearingly pulled me up above the haze that veiled the island. Then, with a serious face, he made some prepared remarks for which I was unprepared: "Wendy, I know you think I'm thick and a bit wonky, and you don't care for me gallivanting about the way I do, but . . . I don't want to botch this. I just want to tell you that you're a right sweet girl who—"

"—who will never see you again, right?"

"Not true," he said, looking away.

"How can I believe you?" I asked. "*Why* would I believe you?"

"You have my word," he said quite convincingly. "I guarantee . . . no, *I vow on my own mum's life* that I will come back for you next Spring. You'll see. It won't feel longer than a fortnight, I promise you. And *you* have to remember your promise."

There are certain things one cannot promise no matter how great the desire. I searched for the truth in his oak-brown eyes, which was not easy to do in the filmy dark cloud we were passing through and, with my red, rheumy eyes, said my piece: "Peter, I *want* to believe you. It's just this—the story goes that you're not so good at returning. That you shine at arrivals and first appearances. For those, you get the highest marks. But reappearances? Not so good."

I glanced over my shoulder at my feet, clad in ragg wool socks, kicking in the strong wind. And then I knew the answer: already my feet were growing. "Promise me again," I whispered.

"Just have some bloody faith," he grumbled, and flew on above the cloud cover. The west coast of America beckoned in the distance, but it looked like just another ghostly outline in a world of dreams.

BY the time I turned sixteen, all of my Springs had become extended vigils—months blackened by starless nights at my bedroom window as I waited for Peter to return, my body moored to the bentwood chair, rocking so hard I wore grooves in the floor.

I became a fixture of grief. I lived in my blue chenille bathrobe with its appliquéd moons and planets, took meals in bed, and only spoke up when Mummy pulled the plug on the telly. She liked to wrap the cord around her neck in a display of sympathy, which produced hardly a smile from me—more like a stifled sneeze.

When the thought of waiting another minute for Peter had become intolerable, I went for the instant gratification of dying. I plundered Mummy's medicine cabinet and, finding a cache of pills in rainbow shades, made my way through the color spectrum. The result was a stomach pumping in the emergency room that emptied me out and hollowed my spirit, too. Back home again, my agitated rocking hardened into immobilizing sadness. And thus every Spring since spelled danger for me.

At the time, Mother had arranged an alternative armamentarium: Jungian visualization, Bach Flower Remedies, Chinese herbs, and white witchcraft. By the time I was nineteen I'd been subjected to a smorgasbord of bodywork. Against her better judgment, she even took me to see Freudians and behaviorists. But my melancholy was as stubborn as Peter's youth. Even the most broad-minded therapists encouraged me to admit that my departures to The Neverland had been the stuff of inspiration—or dream—while at the same time congratulating me on my "gift." One object relations therapist even fessed up to being envious of my fabrications, "that sturdy inner life wherein you take shelter."

After I had exhausted all the analysts in the greater Bay Area, Mother thought a trip to London might be just the tonic. We could hang around the quiet, repressed neighborhood where she first grew up, from which she'd navigated her own departure to the island. She wondered if I might feel more validated at the locus where the Story took hold. (Like Nana, Mummy called her past the Story—all Darlings were fond of such euphemisms.)

I made the trip to London via cattle class and without much hope. Planes make me cringe and sweat—all that confined space and stale air. Mother, on the other hand, was uncommonly frisky on the flight over, chatting up the stewardesses and swilling Dubonnet. For the trip she'd wrapped herself in a frenzy of Peter Max scarves—it was impossible to make out *what* lurked underneath— and sported a pink-felt beret from which sprang a velvet pansy. Her feet bore her trademark hiking boots. In all kindness, she looked like a cross between Minnie Pearl and Minnie Mouse. When our stewardess inquired if we were enjoying the flight, I said it was not such a big deal, that I flew all the time—or used to. Mother poked me in the rib cage.

"I'm sorry," I whispered. "Of course, I don't remember *how.*" With this admission, I drew my nails across the tiny, moist window.

"It's just a temporary glitch," Mother assured me. But I knew that she had forgotten how to fly, too.

IV

N forty-odd years, I have allowed only two males into my inner circle. The first was a washout, the second my husband. Whether *he* is a washout too, I cannot say. The jury is still out and is not coming back any time soon.

Freeman, my sometimes estranged spouse, works for Skywalker Sound, designing bleeps and chirrups to vivify little rubber aliens and big rubber aliens and an entire galaxy of latex and celluloid stars. His sound endows them with personality and makes Freeman feel like God. I am more convinced than ever that he prefers the company of plastic models over human beings. Yet I also take pride in his work, which is admired by millions of impressionable children worldwide, not to mention adults who swoon when they discover he had something to do with both *Terminator 2* and *Toy Story.* Our own special song, in the first years of our alliance, comprised the five signature notes hummed by the mothership in *Close Encounters of the Third Kind.* Talk about romantic! Freeman's lips vibrated these same "erotic" tones whenever I pressed into them, which was often and with considerable greed. Even now, when *Close Encounters* comes on the tube, I can hardly watch the finale without blushing.

Freeman is consumed by his work—you can't separate the man from the job and still have a living, breathing person on your hands. It's widely known that the Noise Boys at Skywalker Ranch are perpetually on fire with extravagant ideas—I can almost smell the conflagration from my perch in the North Berkeley hills. Freeman's studio across the bay is a paradise for him, a place of daily and nocturnal revelation. Unhappily I have been locked out of paradise for many years now; I simply cannot get through to my husband, as much as I admire his commitment to mythic characters. Lest he forget, I am a mythic character too—something he discovered only *after* he fell in love with me.

WE met well before I admitted myself to the hospital, but not before I had formed the opinion that men are only boys in disguise—boys determined to race through life in cars and boats and hang gliders, leaving their girls behind in a convenient cloud of dust. We even met in the dust. I was out hiking in the Marin Headlands with my mother, Margaret, who was hauling enough food to feed the thrashers.

The Headlands begin in the mist and end in the mist, a jut of land that is frequently draped in fog but has its finer moments when one can make out the shoreline, the grasslands, the occasional wood. With the Golden Gate Bridge looming in the distance as a touchstone, the Headlands is a great place to get lost, especially with a good lunch.

Mummy was dressed that day in a rather twee outfit—billowing skirt, sheer blouse with a clot of ruffles at the neck, topcoat, and lace-up boots—the kind of impractical getup featured tirelessly these days in the pages of J. Peterman. Absorbed in the ferns and wildflowers, she couldn't have cared less about actually *getting* somewhere. With her buttoned-up look, Mummy gave off the perfume of orthodoxy, and yet she was wonderfully coarse in the way she clomped around in her boots and cursed. When she stooped to examine the shocking-pink bloom of a wild rose, she pricked her finger and muttered, "Fuck it!" On this trek, like so many others, she'd been lecturing me on the necessity of finding a man along my own garden path—someone who would prove to be the opposite of Peter or, for that matter, Daddy. It seems she no longer took either seriously; her divorce had gutted her regard for her own history and she preferred to trivialize her string of liaisons.

"Wends, do pay attention." Mummy sucked on her bleeding pinkie. "Boys are everywhere you look. You mustn't be so blinkered. Bugger it! There's still a thorn in me."

"Should I wake up and smell the roses, Mummy? *Really*. I am completely awake. I am not the dreamy girl you think I am. Look at me. At *me*, not the damn flower. I can hardly compete with a jolly thing like that." I forced Mother's jaw in my direction. "See? I am a twenty-four-year-old *woman*." I stuck out my chest and sucked in my gut. "There's at least five years of woman you're looking at. Not that that's a *good* thing. All this estrogen must have scared Peter off."

With a sigh, Mother lowered herself onto a stump—things like stumps seemed to materialize just for her. "Darling. That's not using the power of positive thinking. Please don't go there."

"Go where, Mummy? The past? I'm not afraid of it like you. Bruno Bettelheim says that tales with fairies in them are *healthy*." I sat down beside her in the dirt and toyed with a California poppy.

"Dr. Bettelheim is a fine example of a man," Mother said, desirously. "Look at what use he made of his life after the camps. God, I'd love to know his most private fantasies, how he made it through. He's one of us, Wends. A *survivor*."

Mother stretched her shapely, freckled legs out in front of her, tucking the yards of her prairie skirt between her knees. I couldn't believe she was equating the Other World with concentration camps. That was a particularly rotten comparison. And, once again, we were light years away from the real subject at hand: my body and its insistence on changing—the source of much misery.

"You *do* recall the final blow?" I asked her.

"Oh yes, your tat-tats. Most certainly the moment they announced themselves."

"That's right." I nodded.

"Goodness gracious, we've arrived here again. It's one of those *special* chats."

"Yes, Mummy. It's one of *those*."

Mother winced behind her blue-tinted sunglasses. Then she

tore off the glasses, sprang up on her tree stump, and assumed a boxer's stance. "Right-o, my pet, let 'er rip!" She cuffed me on the ear.

How I loved the riddle of Mother, her cheerful anger. She was equally passionate deconstructing the weather or sexual politics. And when it came to matters of the heart, she was consistently outraged. Mother was a vulgarian, and I wouldn't have changed that for the world.

I leapt to my feet and batted away her hands. "I'm still waiting, Mummy. But he's forgotten all about me. Eleven years ago he promised to return for me. It's been *eleven fucking years*! I mean, what could have possibly come up that was so important, so completely demanding of his time every minute of every day?"

For eleven years, I told myself, some battle or siege, fire or flood, must have displaced Peter's memory of me. For I was his greatest love—not counting Mummy and Grandmother Jane and Great-Nana Wendy. At the very least, I was third runner-up.

Mother flung her arms around my neck like a lover. I picked up her sweat, its dizzying top note of rose oil. "Sweetie, Peter's affections for you were real. *Are* real. But so is his bloody narcissism. Really, I thought we'd been through this countless times. At least forty, eighty times."

"No, that was *you* and *your* mother, Mummy."

"Not true," she said with a heavy heart. "I don't have a mother. I was sprung from the loins of creativity itself!"

"That's baloney and you know it. Anyway, stop trying to make things right. They're not hunky *or* dory. Not even close."

"All right, love. Let's workshop this issue." I raised an ironic eyebrow and she pulled on my bangs. "Have you picked up the von Franz yet? You know, the textbook I borrowed from the library?"

"You mean stole?"

"Well, it's a seminal work and we can't afford seminal works. Not since Dummy, I mean *Daddy,* stopped paying alimony."

"You mean, not since you dropped off the best-seller list." I stuck out my tongue.

"You brat. I'll have you know that *The Problem of the Puer Aeternus* is Marie-Louise von Franz's masterpiece. It explains why Daddy and Peter and your dead grandfather are all so—screwed up."

I stared at her blankly.

"Perhaps you haven't ventured beyond the book's cover?"

"Oh Mummy, that stings."

"Well, the photograph on the jacket—of the Bronze Statue of Youth—is clearly arousing. I know that looking at him does *me* a world of good—"

"Mother, the point?"

"The point is spelled out by the book's subtitle: *A Psychological Study of the Adult Struggle with the Paradise of Childhood.* In other words, Peter is a big baby. The poor dear can't *evolve.*"

"Oh, that's deep, that's really helpful." I tore free of her arms.

"Sweetie, Peter's no different from those surfers who monopolize the beach in Santa Cruz—charismatic, yet startlingly empty inside. You can never possess him. He belongs to nature."

"I don't wish to possess *anybody.* I just hate being forgotten. *How dare he.*" I kicked at a rock and watched it break into bits. "Look!" I twirled around. "I'm stunted too, just like Peter. Except I'm stuck in hell, not paradise."

"Now aren't we being a touch melodramatic?"

"I have a *degree* in melodrama, Mummy. Don't you remember? Perhaps you've forgotten me too."

"Oh, poor nobby no-mates! You slay me." Then she pretend-fainted, throwing herself down on the dusty trail—she always could outperform me. Yet Margaret was the only known Darling who hadn't succumbed to madness: her medley of lovers, pre- and post-Dudley, had made certain she got attention around the clock. Of all the Darling women, Mummy alone had the confidence of the Truly Loved—or Madly Worshiped.

"Sweetheart," she said, "do keep your heart open, won't you?"

I lay down on the trail next to her, caring nothing about the dirt in my hair, on my clothes, up my nose. We must have looked like two women felled by a deer hunter.

"My heart is closed for the summer, Mummy. I just don't believe they're out there, those boys who *allegedly* grow up. Despite my limited experience, it's clear to me that men are eternal babes in the wood. . . ."

∞ . . . outstretched on the earth's floor, I sensed the planet spinning ever-so-slightly, inching along in its trip around the sun. I must have dozed off. But there was something strange about my sleep: a raven-haired boy loomed over me. At least his shadow did. When I cried out, he had the nerve to plunk down next to me, setting his muscular limbs alongside my scrawny ones. Oddly enough, I was thirteen again, not yet fully developed.

Squinting up at the sun, my eyes took in a world of unparalleled beauty: the sky was a most serene periwinkle, dotted with fluffy cotton clouds that appeared to spell out my name. (Perhaps my own narcissism had gotten the best of me.) And yet it was snowing too! Crystals the size of snow cones fell on the ground to my right. I shivered, then was warmed by a current of temperate air. Encircled by desert *and* jungle, forest *and* lagoon, I had to laugh: this place was as familiar as the ring on my finger. I had forgotten so much!

The boy and I giggled conspiratorially.

"Why it's my biggest fan!" I teased, and reached over to tickle him on the belly.

"No it isn't," he said, pulling away. "I'm my *own* biggest fan. See?" He waved his hands overhead, creating a luscious breeze; it carried the hint of mint and lemon.

"What a grand fan you make," I said.

The boy brayed, then bounded up and began dancing a free-form jig, one that today would appear more punk than folkloric. "I'm grand, I'm so grand," he sang, so many times I was persuaded to pull an ugly face. Before I could comment on the boy's revolting love affair with himself, he stuck a banana in my mouth—one freshly plucked off the tree to our left. He fed it to me slowly, and it was delicious.

"Thriz izz so grood," I said.

"Sorry, can't understand you. You really shouldn't speak with food in your mouth."

"Oh yeah?" I countered after a final swallow.

"Yeah, yeah, yeah. Blimey, I'm a Beatle!"

"Hardly." I scowled.

The youth scrambled up the banana tree and swung athletically from its lowest branch. I bolted up from the ground, and was about to tickle the boy's bare feet when he recoiled. "Naff off," he said.

"Where*ever* did you pick up such language?" I scolded.

"From your mum, who else?" With his lips he blew a raspberry—how sophomoric—and then began crooning "She loves you, yeah, yeah, yeah" until I planted a palm over his lips.

"And just *who* exactly is this person—the *she* who loves you?" I taunted. The love of his life was standing right in front of his nose, yet the boy was bloody oblivious.

"The she who loves me?" he repeated, voice muffled. "Couldn't tell you." He shrugged. Then he bit into the flesh of my palm.

"Ow!" I cried, withdrawing my hand.

"But *you* can tell me something," he said.

"Yes?" I said, anticipating another bite or perhaps some vain request. Against my better judgment I drew closer.

"You could tell me that blinding good story again—the one about the Beatles coming to America? Plee-eze," he pleaded, kneeling for emphasis.

"Oh, all right," I groaned.

We sat on a log cushioned with daisies—a very odd log. And though I assured the boy that all mothers read to their children in an intimate fashion, he refused to lay his head on my lap. Of course, I hated him for that.

"Once upon a time," I began, with all the energy I could marshal in the face of romantic disappointment, "there were four talented lads from Liverpool who could make music like the gods. They flew to America on Pan Am and on February 7th, 1964, they landed at John Fitzgerald Kennedy International Airport, where a gaggle of screaming mimis awaited them on the tarmac."

"Stop." The boy extended his hand like a crossing guard.

"What, you're bored already?"

"No, it's a corker of a story. It's just, I need to remind you about tickling me. And putting your hand on my mouth."

"Yes?"

"Don't."

"What?" I asked.

"I said, don't ever touch me again. I am not to be touched."

I WENT to swat his hand, but there was no boy sitting beside me or hovering overhead, only the midday sun in a cerulean sky, warming my cheeks and highlighting my shock. I brushed the sleep from my eyes—*I'd been sleeping?*—and turned my chin to face Mother. She was arranged fetchingly on the ground, skirt fanned out as if she were Scarlett O'Hara. "You were saying, dear?" she prodded.

"What, Mummy?" I rummaged through my thoughts. "Oh, right. I was saying that I've decided to find true happiness in being alone. I no longer expect to be pleasantly surprised by men. And I can't carry a torch for a man who doesn't exist. It isn't fair!"

"*Wherever* do you get these ideas?" she said, sitting upright.

"From you, Mummy. From you."

Her cheeks were smudged with soil now and her topknot was in a tumult. To tell the truth, she looked sexy.

I remained draped on the path, vowing never to rise again. Of course, I made vows like this the way other daughters promise to brush their teeth and go to bed early. Crossing my arms defensively, I closed my eyes to the world and tried to imagine nothing, something I wasn't good at.

"Coming through!" called a sweet, high-pitched voice, interrupting my little stab at serenity. Dust streamed from a pair of navy-blue Converse sneakers that were attached to the longest legs I'd ever laid eyes on. The legs were planted like a bean stalk a few inches from my waist. "I said, hello down there. Guys?"

I looked up to meet the haunted eyes of a young man with a bird's nest of ice-blonde curls. A so-called grown-up. He appeared to be carrying some sort of portable reel-to-reel, and his ears were encased in geeky, oversized headphones. Yet another male tuned in to a fantasy world. But, then again, he was gaunt like me!

"Hey, are you guys okay?" he asked.

Mother sprang up from the ground. "Clearly, we are not *guys*. But, yes, we're quite well. In fact, we are tip-top! And you, are *you* tip-top?"

"What?" he said, shading his eyes. I stretched my Patti Smith tee-shirt down over my stomach, and slowly got to my feet. "What?" he repeated.

"Well, if you'd remove the bloody headgear and look in my direction, you could hear the bloody question, couldn't you?" Mother said.

The young man shook off the headphones in an aw-shucks sort of way; he set his Nagra tape deck on the ground.

Mother moistened her lips, repositioned her braid, and patted down her gathered skirt. Little puffs of dust issued from its folds. "I said, isn't it a smashing day? We've decided it's perfect."

"That's cool. A committee of two decides that today, July 20th, is the best day the Earth has ever witnessed. And two Brits."

"We're Americans!" I blurted out, not quite clear on Mummy's status.

"Hi, I'm Freeman," he said casually, and pointed to himself as he said it. He then bent down to examine the spot where I'd recently been horizontal. "Okay, okay, okay. I just don't get it," he said. "What's so special about the ground?"

"My *daughter* is what's so special." Mother rested a dainty hand on each of his broad shoulders.

"Mummy, don't. We were just looking at things in the dirt. Bugs."

"I agree with your mother," the young man said, rising to his full height. All three of us blushed in unison.

"It's the bugs," I repeated to no one in particular. It was then that I realized my cheeks must be streaked with dirt, my hair a jumble.

"Listen," he said. "Would you mind if I recorded you saying 'It's the bugs'? I like the sound of it."

"Oh, I don't know," I demurred.

"It'd make me really happy," he said with a dopey grin.

"Well, *your* happiness takes precedence," Mummy broke in. "Say it, darling!"

Over the course of ten minutes, I managed to say "It's the bugs" twenty times into Freeman's microphone—and this before I knew how far "the bugs" would take me. We were playing a game, were we not? Mother had assured me that all meetings with men were games—that I must participate fully if I wanted to go home a winner.

I HAVE to admit, Freeman's passion for documenting every sound along the path that day really turned me on. I was knocked out by a man who had every inch of the imagination of Peter, but who lived on terra firma. Who was tethered to *this* plane. Of course I missed the obvious: Freeman was tethered by a cord to his tape deck, a connection that rerouted his attention from me to a world of crackles and squeaks and discordant bleeps.

Mummy has always insisted that my encounter with Freeman was kismet. In fact, she stepped aside that day and let the two of us improvise, retrieving *The Female Eunuch* from her backpack and parking her petite derriere in the shade of a eucalyptus.

Picking up on Mother's cue, Freeman pointed down the trail. "Did you know," he asked, "there's something completely awesome down by the beach?"

"Really?" I said, amused. "Because I've had my fair share of awe."

It was then that I risked looking into his angular face and, I swear, saw my own. His was a Scandinavian version of my Anglo/Russian-Jewish countenance—paler, blonder, unfreckled. Sweet and uncomplicated. If you don't count the monomaniacal eyes and the cunning smile.

Mother waved us off with a melodic *ta-ta*, her motives as transparent as her blouse. With unchecked glee, Freeman led me in the direction of a little-known beach. As we made our way over the coastal cliffs, negotiating the ice plant and the occasional poppy, I couldn't stop smiling. Freeman declared his allegiance to Monty Python and even performed their complete catalogue of silly walks. *Goofy is good,* I told myself, and thanked God for this reprieve from my usual black thoughts. As we chatted, we brushed against each other like old friends, inches away from holding hands. All the while, Freeman took refuge in talking about music composition, explaining why certain sounds are too subtle to record faithfully. I let him carry on for minutes about things I couldn't fathom; concepts like *feedback loop, flanging,* and *stochastic resonance* hardly resonated with me, but I relished hearing about a cult as mysterious as my own sect of aerodynamic girls.

As we stepped out at last onto a deserted, pebble-tossed beach, Freeman made a preposterous claim: "If you listen real hard, you can hear the world turning on its axis."

I could only respond with a wise-guy grin, for I had experienced this axis-turning only an hour before and didn't recall any particular sound. Nevertheless, I cupped my hand to my ear and said "aah." I was making an effort.

"What?" Freeman asked, excited. "You actually hear something?"

I nodded bravely.

"So tell me what you hear. Describe it!"

"Sorry."

"What?"

"I don't have the words," I confessed.

"Because you can't hear it. Right?"

Once more I nodded, mildly ashamed.

"You can't hear it because it takes training. *Years* of training." He stooped down and fingered a pink stone, then cast it in the direction of the water. It missed the tide by a wide margin. "You have to learn to screen out the ambient sound, the foreground noise," he said.

"Oh, I see," I said neutrally, then tugged on his jeans jacket.

"Excuse me, but isn't that a little arrogant? I mean, doesn't it somehow suit your purpose that *you* can hear something I can't?"

"And what purpose would that be?" he challenged.

"To make me feel inferior, of course."

Freeman shrugged. "I just wanted to share something beautiful. It was a present."

By now, we had reached the point where the stony beach meets the green-gray water. Freeman turned his back to me, perhaps in disgust, or maybe he was listening to other sounds I couldn't hear; he had marched into the ocean with his Converse sneakers on. Slipping off my high-top tennis shoes and crew socks, I darted into the water and sloshed my way over to him. From behind, I grabbed at his waist. I have no idea what possessed me to do this; a waist is a very private province. Freeman recoiled at my cold hands, then turned to face me.

"Thanks for my present," I said. "I will use it wisely." Then I delivered a kick to my own right shin for sounding like a princess.

With bemused powder-blue eyes, Freeman now looked through me, no doubt preoccupied with the sound of crashing waves, the dulcet hiss of foam. When I tapped him on the nose to bring him back, he blinked; then he took my wet hand in his and solemnly led me back to the beach. Hardly on solid ground, we bent our knees in unison and sat on the damp sand salted with pebbles. I didn't care if my jeans were soaked to the calves or that my butt would flaunt two round wet spots; it was worth it to be close to this young man with the big ideas.

"Good," was all that Freeman said before he held a palm to my cheek and kissed my sea-moist skin. "Good," he repeated before he left a soft, dry kiss on my chapped lips. Then he took my strawberry-blonde hair in his hands and played with it—for minutes. I was so excited by this strange contact that I wanted to bite him *and* thank him. And when he coiled my hair into loose Princess Leia buns (*Star Wars* had opened in May and was still the rage), I did the latter—I thanked him for *everything*. My gratitude seemed out of proportion; we had known each other for barely two hours.

But I was aroused by a boy who was capable of growing whiskers and turning gray at the temples.

Freeman held a stray lock of my hair up to the sky, which was rapidly clouding over. Exposing my chilled right ear, he blew warm air on it and whispered "Thank you" in return.

"I haven't done a thing," I said.

"You *listened*," he said. "And you *believed*. In fact, you have the look of a believer."

"You don't know the half of it." I chuckled.

He let go of my hair and we kissed gingerly, brushing off any grains of sand that interfered with our purpose.

★ ★

FREEMAN was as charming with Mummy as he was with me. But while she found him the ideal suitor, I found him painfully sunny. He was endlessly upbeat, possessed of a happy-go-lucky nature that appeared to be the antithesis of my own. It's no secret that, by my mid-twenties, the gloom that had set in during my late teens now pervaded all my days, sunny or not. Besides, I didn't trust blondes. They looked blithe even when harboring the worst moods. And Freeman's bad moods would never hold an Elavil to mine. Nevertheless, I was intrigued.

The morning after we collided into each other on the hiking trail, Freeman joined Mummy and me for breakfast at Le Bateau Ivre, a Viennese-style coffeehouse on Telegraph Avenue that reeked of dark-roasted beans and Old World romance. Immediately we went into "couple" mode, nodding and teasing and elbowing each other. Lacking common knowledge about music or literature, we boldly completed each other's sentences and applauded each other's jokes. Freeman even fiddled with my hand under the table, tenderly counting my fingers and toying with Great-Nana's boulder-sized ring.

The entire time, Mother sat woodenly in her high-back chair, drinking her *Mokka mit schlag* in short, brittle sips—how she hated being on the periphery. In a transparent bid to grab the spotlight, she offered Freeman a generous dollop of her whipped cream and he promptly went to work, painting his face with the stuff. The foamy goatee and eyebrows he gave himself charmed my pants off, and I returned the favor by sucking my empty water glass so hard I sealed it to my lips.

"Very attractive, Wends," Mother observed. "I've always considered sucking the perfect strategy to snag a man."

"Mother!" I chided.

"It totally works for me," Freeman offered. He picked up his own glass and followed suit.

Mother rolled her eyes as if to suggest she was dining out with children; but she blew me a kiss when Freeman wasn't looking. Even though Mummy wasn't the center of this specific universe, I saw that she took some pleasure in her daughter's success, and I winked back.

FROM the very beginning Freeman and I set opposing agendas. He required of me a certain cheerfulness—a quality I lacked but could feign (Daddy had required the same of me)—and I asked that he indulge me in my pain: put up with my frequent crying jags, my phobias about hugging, about fishing. My fear of being held at the waist was not uncommon, doctors assured me, but my fear of fish and meat hooks was as weird as they came. I did not want my new boyfriend to demand that I "just get over it." Our agreement to tolerate each other's quirks was understood; there was really no need to discuss the particulars.

As I said, Freeman turned out to be deliciously silly (which made cheerfulness much simpler to fake). After we finished breakfast at Le Bateau Ivre, he invited Mummy and me over to a local recording studio, where he asked me to repeat "It's the bugs" another twenty times into a microphone ("Sound like you worship bugs, Wendy"). Then he asked the same of Mummy. Her rendering of this phrase turned out to be earthy, verging on carnal. From that day on, Freeman took to calling Mother *Mae West* (he liked to puff out his chest like a bodybuilder in her presence), and the two enjoyed an intimacy that was, at the outset, lost on me.

Despite his chumminess with Mummy, Freeman never failed to paint a smile on my sorry face. Plus, he incorporated me into his art. The "bugs" tape quickly became the centerpiece of a composition that would become his master's thesis at Berkeley. A joyful melange of voices, it celebrated our meeting—and distorted it. The music was tender, it was pretentious, it was elegant, it was button-pushing. And in a postmodern gesture, he incorporated bars of the *Love Boat* theme song, a fact that endeared him to his classmates if not to his professors. For the piece's debut at Zellerbach Hall, I was prominently onstage for everyone to see—well, to *hear*—and thus felt unusually present in my new boyfriend's life. Freeman was showing the world I existed, not that anyone could trace the voice in the piece to me. On tape I sounded like a banshee on steroids (and Mummy like an alien hooker), but I was proud to be a part of the composition and, in the front row, beamed conspicuously at my talented new beau.

After the concert Freeman made the social rounds in the lobby, introducing Mother and me as his "gals." Unfortunately, as the evening progressed, the camaraderie between Mummy and Freeman grew loose and liquored, and I ended up ditching them both for the privacy of a nearby ladies' room.

And this is where our agreement kicked in, the silent bargain we'd made about pleasure and pain. After a half hour of sitting in a bathroom stall, memorizing the graffiti and inventing a few lines of my own, I showed my waterlogged face in the hallway. Freeman was both baffled and worried, while Mummy was merely angry. Now that I *finally* had a lover, she felt I shouldn't fuck things up, and she said so right in front of Freeman. He took me aside in a small rehearsal room and let me know I hadn't screwed up—an act of kindness for which I shall be eternally in his debt. In turn, he allowed me to bitch about Mummy's intrusive nature; I even blurted out that *she* was the one who'd pushed Daddy away, once upon a time. (I hadn't yet considered the glaring similarity between Freeman and

Daddy: they were both members of the Puer Aeternus Club for Men, and as such, would push off for distant, more compelling shores with little provocation.)

Freeman listened to me with a childish impatience and yet heard me out, rubbing my hands and head as if I were a puppy. I liked this a lot. Alas, to deal with his discomfort with anything that smacked of conflict, he resorted to invention. In minutes, he conjured up a dozen nicknames for me: *Wendolyn, Window, Wenston Churchill, Wenderella.* This was a gift of no small proportion. Then he called me *Wendybird.*

"W-why did you say that?" I asked, instantly suspicious.

"Say what?"

"Why did you call me Wendybird? I mean, where the hell did *that* come from?"

Freeman dropped my hand, which he'd been stroking lightly, and appeared mortally wounded. "I don't know. Just the British sixties thing. You know, women are *birds,* men are *blokes.*"

"Oh," was all I could manage. And then, "I'm sorry, okay? I ruin everything. Well, not *everything,* just the good things."

He smiled tautly and shook his head. "Okay, okay, okay. Let's get back to those good things, hey?" I nodded and he escorted me back to the reception, where we found Mummy encircled by music students—all male. She was leading them in an animated chorus of "There Is Nothin' Like a Dame," though only a few knew the words. As a result of her gyrations, her tight black sweater had crept up her tummy, revealing her belly button.

"Oh, Mother!" I whined, propping my hands on my hips.

"Oh, Wendy," she echoed. "When did you become such a grown-up? What a disappointment you must have been on the island. What a wet blanket."

I can't tell you how much this hurt me; Mummy could be so unconscious. Though Freeman hadn't a clue at this point to what she was talking about, he'd seen and heard enough. "Mae West," he whispered, "let's make like a leaf and blow!"

At this, Mummy tittered like a teenybopper and bade farewell to her admirers: "Cheerio, boys, this town's not big enough for the ten of us!"

The three of us waltzed out the door in dramatically different moods, Freeman clinging to the idea that everything was all right, me clinging to the idea that it wasn't, and Mummy still glowing from all the male attention, her cropped sweater showing off her bare midriff like Barbara Eden in *I Dream of Jeannie*.

V

N a flight back from Boston last week after visiting my publisher, I spent the better part of five hours sifting through the wreckage of my marriage to Freeman, its pieces too small to add up to divorce or separation, but sharp nonetheless. Freeman, now my husband of seventeen years, was still the boyish guy I nicknamed *Man* from the get-go. I've always fancied the sweet literalness of *Man,* its Neanderthal sensibility. Besides, *Free* was too painful a reminder of what he wanted most from life, and I could never give him that. Giving a person his or her freedom was beyond my power.

Through the years I'd felt entirely free *within* the institution of marriage; fastened to something bigger than myself, I could drop my anchor in Freeman's reality. Unfastened, I would surely have spun out of orbit and landed in a tomato patch just like Daddy had. It's clear that I needed the safety and predictability of a partner who, over time, permitted me to speak about the unspeakable. Marriage to Freeman also provided the illusion of structure, enough to experiment with my writing, my childhood poetry having given way to absurdly tall tales that brought me a decent living as a children's book author. My lifestyle was modest, on par with my talent, and I tried to keep a lid on the depression. Plus, Freeman would be there when the going got tough—at least that was always my theory.

Back in 1976, though, marriage to Freeman wasn't in the immediate cards. Living together not only made good sense politically but was the vogue. And I was really in no rush to jog down the aisle. In The Neverland my domestic skills had been tested exhaustively and, to tell the truth, I'd failed: I hadn't had a clue about baking bread or sewing buttons, a budding feminism having gotten in the way of learning such practical matters. However, it so happens, I could sweep like a demon.

At the impressionable age of thirteen, I took to the broom faster than you can say *Cinderella*. Sweeping afforded me solace, suffused me with purpose. With broom in hand, I could process all the strange goings-on in a world that made sense only half of the time. And so I swept Peter's mucky cave, his mates' messy grottoes, the stables where they sheltered a hodgepodge of beasts. And when I returned to the Mainland, I swept the floorboards of our house like a girl possessed.

After ten years of dedicated sweeping, I showed such a belief in its therapeutic power that Mummy persuaded me to write a book on the subject. She had just climbed the charts with her own self-help rant, *The Pan Pathology: Refusing to Grow Up and Other Ungenerous Traits*, and wanted me to follow her on the pop psychology path. With little conviction, I took pen in hand and stared down the page—but nothing occurred to me. I could hardly rally the women of my generation to take up the broom; we had just gotten accustomed to wearing bras again, and housework was still thought an impediment to higher consciousness.

★ ★

FOUR impetuous weeks after our meeting in Marin, Freeman helped me move in to the many-gabled Victorian in the flatlands of Berkeley, where he rented a studio (his own living space was a mere half gable). At the time this seemed like a good idea, but when I finally gazed out the window of his apartment, instead of taking in bridges and skyscrapers and a sky full of stars, I saw nothing. And nothing is what I felt inside when I gazed in his eyes; I was so stunned that a man could like me *and* live in a house (as opposed to a tree or a cave) that my heart froze over like an ice cap. Sometimes getting what you want is too much to feel. And so you don't.

In my numbness, I did find Freeman's apartment pleasantly disheveled: the vaulted ceiling gave an impression of roominess, and the clutter—mike cables and power panels and something called a fuzz box—faintly echoed Daddy's garage workshop. A coffee-stained futon on the floor in the corner was topped off with a musty patchwork quilt, and the single bay window was sheathed in torn lace, the lone feminine touch. Posters of Brian Eno and John Cage were thumbtacked to the wall above an altar of avant-garde LPs stacked halfway to the ceiling. The whole place was marvelously seedy, a set director's idea of *la vie bohème*. Best of all I saw a grand opportunity here for sweeping.

After I stumbled over one of three guitars propped against a wall, Freeman pointed to the bed and said "sit," as if I were a trained tiger. I sat as directed, happy just to be away from Mummy's meta-physics. Her curious ideas about relationships and destiny had ruled the roost for over two decades now and, frankly, I wasn't all that clear on the difference between her and me. Just because we shared an unreliable childhood secret, we were not the same woman, I reminded myself. While Mummy had waded in a pool of lovers—more like a whirlpool of jerks—and dipped her big toe in the puddle of love more times than I can count, I had had one "simple" encounter with an asexual, flying boy. And for all the affection Mummy routinely received, her heart had become indifferent to men (no doubt a product of Daddy's indifference), whereas my feelings for men were merely frozen, but ready to thaw at the warmth of a kiss.

And kiss we did, that first day in the apartment. With all the agility he demonstrated as a guitarist, Freeman peeled off my near-Victorian layers of clothing: a root beer–brown pullover, pilly and soiled with ink at the cuffs, a chambray blue work shirt with a W embroidered on the breast pocket, and a fifties western-themed cir-cle skirt, under which waffle-weave long johns shielded my chilled limbs. On my own I slipped out of my bra and panties. I kicked off my boots and, with each foot, scraped off knee-high argyle socks.

"Sheesh, Wends, are you sure that's everything?" Freeman said as I lay naked and shivering on his quilt. "Are you sure you haven't forgotten a barrette or something?"

I slapped him on the bum, which was milk-white and goose-pimpled. The radiator clicked away, trying to keep up with the sinking temperature; the bay window had clouded over with condensation. Throwing my arms around Freeman's neck, I drew him fast to my chest: "Be my blanket or I'll freeze to death."

Freeman lowered himself to the bed. While my height had thankfully topped out at five foot ten, his was such that, even when we lay side by side, my head barely rested on his shoulder. "Better?" he asked.

I nodded and inhaled his smell, a mix of Dr. Bronner's soap and herbal shampoo. The bouquet carried me off for a second; when I returned he was pulling on a nipple with his teeth, so subtly I imagined a spider crawling across my flesh. But when he placed his hands around my waist, I pulled back and involuntarily slapped his wrist. "Stop," I said.

"What?" he asked, looking up with flushed cheeks.

"I need to see you, Man."

"I'm right down here, woman." He waved merrily.

"Really," I added with a serious face.

"Hey, I'm just getting started on a brilliant piece of music." He puckered his lips and I curled over to meet them halfway.

"I need to tell you what Dick said."

"Dick?" He sat up rigidly, casting a puff of air across my legs. "Dick Clark? Dick Tracy?"

"Philip K. Dick, the *Blade Runner* guy. You know, *Do Androids Dream of Electric Sheep?*"

"Do androids dream of electric sheep?" he repeated. "Ya got me."

"No," I objected, "that's not the question."

"Then what *is* the question," he said, wiping his forehead clear of curls. "I'm not in the mood for games. *I'm in zee mood for luff.*" He broke into song, his crooning on par with Bugs Bunny's.

I crinkled my nose as if something smelled bad. "Man, listen to me." I pulled at the indomitable tufts at his crown. "Dick said, 'Reality is that which, when you *stop* believing in it, doesn't go away.' I repeat: when you stop believing in it, doesn't go away. Isn't that something? The *stability* of everything! This is what I've been looking for. I don't need to prove myself to anybody."

Freeman drew his long, hairless legs up to his hips and rocked his body to keep warm. He looked vulnerable, like a freshly shaved poodle. "You don't need to prove yourself, period," he said quietly.

A warm spring of water leaked from my heart. Then, too quickly, the sensation was gone. "Don't you see, Man?" I said. "Everything can go on without me! All those other dimensions don't need *me* to keep them going. They're freestanding." In a dramatic enactment, I stood up on the futon and rotated my arms like a windmill. "Just because I'm here with you doesn't mean there aren't other dimensions *out there*."

Freeman offered a close-lipped smile, more pained than winning. Then he stood up on the hard-cotton batting and folded my hands into his, fanning our arms out on each side. Flush against each other's chest, we remained pinned to the wall, suspended in a very old dance. Somehow Freeman managed to slip his hands behind me: he cupped my buttocks and let out a whoop. This eased the tension of the moment and I collapsed into the cave of his armpit. He licked my neck, his tongue rough like a cat's, then he gathered my hair and twisted it up and off my nape. Now his thin, cracked lips pressed against my mouth, his legs folding around me. I lost my balance and slipped down onto our tangle of bedclothes. Freeman followed me down and we began to slither and twist, pulling on each other's skin with hands and teeth, whatever was available. He entered me with an endearing gentleness, lightly strumming my lower back as if I were one of his beloved guitars.

Now he silently worked his rhythms—bobbing, swaying, pausing for the briefest of meditations. When we did speak, it was in an exchange of sighs and pleased whimpers, though at one point he inquired if I was okay. I answered that I was fine on several planes.

We remained glued lip to lip for hours that afternoon. When we finally unhinged ourselves, I coasted over to the mirror to check out the damage: my mouth was swollen and distorted like a circus clown's. But I was weirdly content: I hadn't the slightest desire to sweep! When Freeman slipped away to take a shower, I deliberately ignored the cobwebs of his life—the crumpled balls of Post-its, the wires and white-gold wisps of hair. No longer numb, I allowed myself a brief happy thought and floated above the ground for a sensational three seconds.

FREEMAN emerged from the shower and dressed his skinny self in head-to-toe denim. When he looked up, he found me standing motionless in the middle of the studio, both hands gripping my suitcase. "Wendy, is that a suitcase in your hands or are you just happy to see me?"

"Oops," I said, wondering if perhaps the Spring air had fooled me into thinking we were right for each other. I set down the luggage on the studio's worn planks.

"You look like a person who's seen *multiple* ghosts. Come 'ere," he called, head cocked towards the bed. I ran into his arms and we rocked on the futon all over again. "Maybe we should talk about this moving-in thing?"

"Oh, absolutely," I agreed. "Let's discuss it."

"Okay, for starters, where will *you* sleep?"

I was just about to slither away when I caught the joke and slammed him with his pillow. "You're a horrible, cruel person! And what's more, you're not very nice."

"Sorry, Wends. Couldn't resist."

I broke down anyway; I could never keep tears down. Freeman apologized again, but he quickly tired of feeling bad. Like a tot, he appeared to change moods in record time: irritation slipped into glee, boredom into curiosity.

"Hey, Wendolyn, check this out!" He raced over to his turntable and begged me to listen to "The Chipmunks' Christmas Song," a cut off an old LP. After lowering the needle with awesome finesse, he closed his eyes and purred, as if nirvana could be found in a novelty song. When the piece ended, he pounded his knees: "This is the exact feeling I'm going for—distorted happiness."

"Ah," I replied, wondering if he shared the same goal for us.

"You don't get it, do you?" I shook my head. "I want my music to capture the unadulterated joy of the Chipmunks—to be a tad off-kilter. Off is good. On is boring."

"I'm off," I said boldly. "Is that why I'm here. Because I'm off?"

"Yep, afraid so. You're so off you're perfect."

No one had ever called me perfect before, not even Peter when we were close. Despite it being an obvious lie, I felt an obligation to return the compliment. "And you, you're so perfect, you're off the charts of perfection. Can't even find you on the map—"

Freeman put a hand over my mouth. "Wenderella, you'll sleep with me, in this bed, until the Pacific Ocean dries up and the foothills tumble into the sea."

Given that the old house was built atop the Hayward Fault, practically at ground zero of a Big One, I realized that geology might undermine his good intentions faster than he knew. Still, his silly promise, stolen shamelessly from song lyrics, appeared genuine, and we both postponed discussion of our couplehood for another, more somber, day.

FROM the moment I moved my desk and writing files into Freeman's studio apartment, I became increasingly dizzy-headed and had trouble breathing through my nose. I also experienced a low-level nausea that Freeman's friends assumed, with clichéd winks and nudges, was a clear sign of pregnancy. I was stumped: I had never been sick in the traditional ways, having favored hallucinations of raffish pirates and fluorescent pixies. Mummy chalked the whole business up to NWS—Neverland Withdrawal Syndrome— but I knew better. It was flat-out anger that hounded me.

No question, Freeman was an adoring and adorable man; his flair for whimsy was unparalleled on the planet. And he was smitten with me in the way young women expect and deserve. I just hadn't expected to take care of his world to the extent it needed caretaking.

It turns out, he had sprinted from an all-nurturing mother to the flimsy security of living with me—he'd been on his own for only three months before I intruded on the scene. So my presence was now more than convenient; it was paramount to getting the laundry washed, the meals cooked, the rent paid on time. Not that Freeman was lazy; he spent all-night sessions at his desk composing music with the dedication of a monk. I couldn't fault his drive or passion. He just didn't see those things that needed tending to—and sometimes those things included me.

My shock was great. How could I have forgotten that a person possessed with a teeming creativity and a daft sense of humor could be heartless on a regular basis? I had always assumed that creativity and heart go hand in hand. It wasn't that Freeman didn't enjoy my presence; in fact he insisted on it. He required a ready audience for his pratfalls, but mostly he needed another set of ears to listen to his nonstop stream of sounds. Lucky for me, I liked the music; I was inspired by all the novelty, the raw unvarnished notes. And when he surfaced from his marathon bouts of writing, he would scoop me up in his arms and "notice me" to pieces, hailing me "Wenderella, Queen of Composers!" and tossing me in the air as if I were a stuffed animal. Unfortunately, my nausea made these moments difficult.

My writing suffered too, not a surprise to women who join forces with charismatic men. Navigating by my own compass during the day—Freeman's class-load was at an all-time high during his final year of grad school—I had more than enough time on my hands for mythmaking. Each morning at the honey-colored library table we ate on, I set out the tools of my trade: Olivetti-Underwood typewriter, thesaurus, thermos of hot coffee, and, in case I lost my way, *A Woman's Dictionary of Mythology, Folklore and Symbols.* Against the wall I propped a eight-by-five-inch glossy of Margaret Darling—her book jacket photo. It was a rare glimpse of Mummy looking gentle and benign, and for some reason, it sustained me.

Unlike most frustrated writers, I did not hesitate or procrastinate; I filled sheet after sheet with words. Alas, each page bore variations of the same story: a family of deer (father, mother, and two sloe-eyed does) that, despite their obvious affection, cannot keep track of each other. Each eventually wanders off in one of four directions and spends the rest of its days trying to reconnect with the others. Transparent, yes, but like most children's stories it dealt with the big themes, the psyche's top-ten list.

I titled my collection *The Dear Deer and Their Wayward Ways*, and in spite of the raves it received from Mummy, publishers found it "confused," "groggy," "muddled in its structure and ambitions." All too soon, my promising fables of deer endowed with the gift of speech and high degrees of empathy soured, and I took to writing parables about sickly hedgehogs that harbor thoughts of gorging themselves on cheese in one final food binge. My new allegories weren't pretty. When I tried to return to the deer chronicles, I couldn't see the forest animals for the trees, and soon an oppressive lightheadedness plagued me, the dizziness begetting confusion, the confusion begetting a blanket of sadness under which I shielded an unbidden rage. I'd become groggy like my stories.

After four months of living in a fugue state, it was time for a showdown. On unsteady feet I stalked Freeman around the apartment; he had blown through the door after midnight, ablaze with musical ideas that involved charcoal briquettes and matches. Bent on discovering the best method for amplifying the sound of flames, Freeman had until 9 A.M. the next morning to puzzle this out. Pacing the tiny room in lopsided figure eights, he muttered to himself, even hopping onto chairs and the futon to hasten the flow of ideas.

I emerged from the bathroom wearing only his pajama bottoms, and waving the tops in the air. "Ahoy, matey!" I said. Freeman dropped the footlong matchstick he'd been using as a baton and shot a rare, penetrating look at my breasts. Then he resumed his high-strung pacing. So this was what I had been reduced to—a strip act?

I swaggered up to him, and tried to stop him with a kiss at the neck, then a pat on the ass; but he shoved me out of the way.

"No!" I screamed, and shoved back. At this, he froze in place and furrowed his white-blonde brow. But his mouth wore the smile of betrayal.

"What's so amusing?" I demanded. "What's so fucking funny, you can smirk while I am freaking out?"

"Sorry, Wends," he said softly, the corners of his mouth still upturned. "I'm busy and you—you make a lousy Viking, or whatever you are."

"I'm a pirate," I said, folding my arms over my chest.

"Well, you're way cute and the last thing a pirate wants to be is cute."

"You want cute?" I got up on my toes to meet his eyes. "Let me show you cute." I ran over to the utility closet, grabbed the broom, and began to swat at my own head with the bristles. When I failed to make a dent, I rotated the broom like a baton twirler and hit my head with the wooden handle. "Oh, much better," I cried. "I'm finally getting my head together!"

Freeman wasted no time. He seized the broom from my tensed fists and threw it against the wall; then he dragged me over to the futon and forced me to lie down with him. I slipped under the quilt, ashamed and flinching with pain.

"Okay, okay, okay," Freeman said, shaking me harder than he realized. "What's this about—your work?"

"No," I whimpered through the quilt. "It's about *your* work. *My* work is going brilliantly—all my furry forest creatures have grown fangs and turned into bloodsuckers. I've got a whole new series brewing: *Bambi, The Bitch from the Hell Regions.* A little derivative but it will sell."

"Well, *I've* never heard of it, if that's any comfort." Stunned by his kindness in the midst of my pain, I could hardly accuse him of ignoring me. But I did.

"I just feel left behind here, Man." I emerged from the quilt. "Your work tends to confine me to certain regions—like the Arctic."

"What? I mean, *what*?" Now he looked as stunned as I did.

"Your really superinventive work?" I continued. "It takes up all the space in this house. You *know* I support it, that I support *you*. I just don't want to be an afterthought. This is such a cliché. It's just, I am your biggest supporter. I am president and vice president of your fan club. Sergeant-at-arms, too. But I'm also your lover. And, *as such*, I don't want to be squeezed in between the hours of one and two A.M. We fan club presidents deserve more—"

"It's before one," Freeman interjected, "and we're talking now, aren't we?"

"Oh, that proves my feelings are wrong, doesn't it? You are absolutely correct. Because it's *before* one, we *have* no problems! What could I have been thinking?" I pounded my already throbbing head and rolled over on my stomach. The feather pillow swallowed my face.

"Hey you." Freeman lightly massaged my scalp. "Don't hurt the mind I love. It's my mind too."

"What?" I gasped, and flipped over to face him.

"Your mind is my mind. If we live together long enough, we'll merge—like in a Vulcan mind-meld—and you'll instantly grasp my ideas." He winked at me like a coconspirator.

"Uh-huh," I nodded. "And what about *my* ideas? Will you understand *them*? Or will they become your ideas?" I narrowed my eyes, hoping to stare a hole in his logic.

"Which ideas are those?" he questioned, with all the earnestness of a Cub Scout. When I failed to answer, he said: "Sure, your ideas can become mine, if they want to."

I shot up from the futon and screamed, "Arghh!"

Freeman covered his ears protectively, something I had never seen him do. These were the same ears that could listen to the Stones in the front row at the Oakland Coliseum, that relished being in the wake of trains and jets.

"Did I offend you?" I asked.

"Well, I need to take care of my boys," he explained, patting his earlobes. "Listen, I don't get why you're so worked up. I mean, we can share ideas, can't we?"

"Yes, we can *share*. I just don't think you have any idea of my ideas." I wasn't so sure *I* had a handle on them, or if they were worth a hill of beans. "Like, for example, do you know what I'm working on at the moment?" He appeared to be lost in the pattern of his plaid flannel shirt. "Perhaps I could offer a small clue?"

Freeman exhaled audibly, then stretched his lanky arms around my neck and pulled me solidly to his chest; I caught a whiff of his tangy deodorant, the musk of charcoal on his hands. Just when I expected him to take me up on my offer, he said, "Okay, okay, okay. What do I know?" He scratched his scalp with simian glee. "Well, I know you're writing about hedgehogs who've contracted some sort of disease and gone nuts. I know you're not happy about this. I know you want to find out why the hedgehogs are so sick and violent. That that's important to you. I know you haven't figured out how to make them well again. That the leaves in the forest where the hedgehogs live are also diseased or limp or something. I know I could express this musically, but that words . . . words are, you know, tough for me. I know I love you more than words, but the thing is, you are so taken with your theory of being left behind that you can't see I'm here with you *now*. That being with you now should count for something. I want it to count!"

I studied Freeman's milky cheeks, now flushed pink, and for once, I took him on face value—the pale-blue eyes boring into me, the thin serpentine lips pursed in frustration, the noble aquiline nose. And so it came to pass: I returned to a landscape wherein Freeman was a ghostlike presence, but a ghost who loved me like a rock. Within hours, my nausea and dizziness faded into the background, and I could breathe without resorting to a medley of nose sprays. (I collected nose sprays like other women collect perfume bottles.) I pushed my just-below-the-surface resentment deeper still, and again took up sweeping (as a tranquilizer) and dish washing (because who else would get around to it?).

Repressed anger served me well: my stories took on a shadow life that would have made the Grimm Brothers proud. Even Mummy lauded me for crafting characters of stunning ambivalence. A rabbit that hated hopping. A bear that couldn't hibernate. My rabbits and bears were neither good nor bad—they were deformed and troubled characters in a complex world. And the endings of my fables were inconclusive, just like my own story was turning out to be. I was a girl with a boyfriend who would love her till the cows came home, but who was not coming home with the cows himself.

I CONTINUED to lead the cheering for Freeman's music. After all, his life of the mind showed no signs of slowing down. Still at work on his thesis, he'd also picked up a modest commission from a fringe arts organization. By now, Freeman had left behind any vestiges of affection for the Chipmunks and for comical sounds in general. His enthusiasm for fire sounds had matured into a religious zeal for water and wind sounds, and his reputation for articulating the elements of nature was growing.

Our few hours together were spent in the wild; we took labor-intensive hikes with the sole purpose of capturing the sound of flowers, stones, and the occasional beer can bobbing in the creek. During this phase, Freeman dismissed all synthetic sound, and his compositions reflected this bias. I continued to worship the music he created and ended up attending a lineup of new-music concerts that would have tested the soul, and ears, of the most open-minded aficionado. But—hello!—I was in love with a man whom I considered a genius—shouldn't that alone have defused any problems that surfaced over the years?

My nausea returned seven months later. Along with the vertigo and stuffed-up nose. Freeman and I sat in silence on the pier at the Berkeley Marina one nippy afternoon, sipping hot chocolate and dangling our feet over the murky gray water; he was bent on recording the slap-slap of the waves hitting the posts, and I was focused on sniffing drafts of sea air, hoping to discern something salty about it.

"Honey," I said, propping up my head with my hands.

"Quiet," he replied without looking up.

"Sweet . . . heart."

"Not now. It's high tide. Stand by for greatness!"

"Oh fuck it," I said and proceeded to throw up. We both watched in awe as my vomit trickled over the pier and into the chop several yards below.

"Bad milk?" Freeman asked. His trusty gear had picked up the sound of the expulsion.

"No, no. Bad dreams. Really, hallucinations. I'm, uh, too dizzy for words. I can't even tell you."

"Tell me what?" he queried.

"Well, if you shut off that damn machine we can talk!"

Eleven months of living together and I still hadn't uttered a syllable about The Neverland. Not a day went by when I didn't weigh the danger of hiding my history from Freeman against the danger of telling him everything. Confessing all would be a big relief, but I could not risk turning into my great-grandmother, who now required a full-time attendant at home. Neither could I risk ending up like Grandma Jane—missing in action, a dim memory in *her* mother's mind.

Freeman punched the stop button on his tape deck, then grimaced as if in pain.

"Okay, I can tell you something," I said, catching my breath. He looked over my head and out to sea. "I'm dizzy and don't know why. Well, maybe I do. My dreams are full of people I used to know. Lovely and unlovely people. A man who kissed me against my will and a flying boy who refused to kiss me. Well, he gave me buttons and called them kisses. Isn't that clever? He was the cleverest boy I've ever known." Freeman arched an eyebrow. "But he was very forgetful. He didn't remember things. Like me. What was I saying?"

"Wends. You're not making sense."

"Well, making sense is highly overrated!"

"Are you trying to tell me about other men in your life? Because I don't . . . I can't follow your logic."

"Because there *is* none. That's why I'm nauseous: there's a dangerous lack of logic in my head." I held my stomach with both hands and doubled over.

Freeman watched helplessly as I vomited into the bay a second time. When it appeared that I had finished, he surrendered his denim jacket and threw it over my quivering shoulders. For minutes we said nothing, swinging our feet above the anxious waves. Finally Freeman rubbed his eyes with his fists. "Wenderella, you need to see somebody."

"I see *you*—you're a body."

"Very funny. Someone other than me. Someone who can clear up your confusion. I mean, I know your parents were difficult—are difficult—and even a little kooky, but this is beyond me. I don't know who these people *are*, the scary man and the superboy. Are they real guys? Are they characters in a fable you're working on? I'm thinking maybe you're being cryptic on purpose. That I'm not *supposed* to figure this out." He stood up and shook his curly mop. "Am I right? Are you trying *not* to tell me more than trying *to* tell me?"

"What are *you* trying to tell me?" I struggled to my feet. "That I'm fabricating my past?"

"I said nothing about your past."

"That's because you know nothing."

"Agreed. So, are you going to tell me? Is that what we're doing here?"

"No, we're here to record the finest waves the ocean has to offer. That's the agenda of the day. The agenda for all time."

"Okay, okay, okay. I get it. It's jealousy time. You're jealous of my music." He began pacing perfect circles on the pier, always resorting to geometry when things got heavy.

"No, I'm jealous of your childhood. Can I have it? I mean, could you just give it to me for Christmas?"

Freeman stopped in his tracks and squinted at the water. I detected a smile inside the squint. "You think my life was a breeze? That I'm a shoo-in for Best Childhood by a Child Prodigy?"

"Yep, I do," I said with a confidence only the clueless can afford.

Freeman knelt at my side, still refusing to look me in the eye. "Well, you pinned the tail on the donkey: my childhood was pretty darn near perfect. My mother, Eleanora Duse Ullman, was so beautiful she dazzled me into thinking I could be another Mozart if I wanted it badly enough. My sister, Babette, was already a virtuoso on the violin by age seven. My father—Dr. Max Ullman, Polymath—wholly expected his son to follow him on the polymathic path to freedom. Let's just say I was a major disappointment to my father by the age of ten. He was always out of town, being brilliant full time. Listen, if you want to be jealous, be jealous of something simple. Nobody, not even me, gets out of childhood without putting up with brain-fucking complexity."

I nodded numbly in the direction of San Francisco. It was true: Freeman was gifted with a mother who'd been mesmerized by his boyishness; a woman who'd responded to his cleverness and humor with the kind of affection reserved for babies. In turn, he'd suffered an emotionally distant father who was also geographically beyond reach (those Ullmans were nothing if not peripatetic). So with a windfall of devotion from one parent, and a dearth of discipline from the other, Freeman had no reason to do anything other than what he wanted. What he *wanted* to do was get lost in a world of sound.

I sidled up to my boyfriend and nuzzled his cheek. "You're right, Man. I just feel so alone with my own story sometimes."

"So why don't you tell it? Write about *people* instead of forest creatures."

"I'm hardly ready for that. I can't even *smell* things, let alone write about real stuff, especially the past. Those Darlings, the ones who have spilled their beans, have paid dearly for the spilling. I'm talking isolation, shock therapy."

"More cryptic allusions. Help me, Wends. Help me understand just five percent." He selected an empty Coke bottle from the rubble on the ground, and cast it out to sea. "Wow. Listen to that *plink*."

But I was too far away in my thoughts to hear a bottle skirt the waves. An aristocratic gentleman sporting a topcoat, a tweedy three-piece suit, and a ridiculous, Dali-like mustache was sizing me up, running his hand down my calf as if I were a beast of burden. "Good

God!" he cried, nodding and smiling crudely. "We've a strong girl here. A girl who could serve a higher purpose. *My purpose.*" Then he smacked his lips, drawing his tongue back and forth over a voluptuous lower lip until it glistened in the moonlight. *Moonlight?*

I drew a sharp breath. The man brushed my cheek with a cold, metal protuberance fastened to his French cuff. *No!* I tried to scream, but no sound formed in my mouth. He flashed a snaggletoothed grin and, with his palm, forced my jaw to meet his. Though the warts on his nose were massive and his acne scars unkind, he obviously fancied himself a handsome chap. With a jerk, he let go of my head and began swaying to and fro, rocking to some internal melody. I spotted a neat, oily braid tucked inside the collar of his topcoat. Cheap cologne assaulted me.

"I know you," I said quietly.

"Of course you do," he assured me. "All girls know me." He paused, as if to consider the magnitude of his claim.

"Go away," I pleaded.

"Re-al-ly?" he said with obvious pleasure.

"Yes, really."

"Oh, darlin', I can't. I really can't." The man removed a handkerchief from his coat pocket and dabbed at the saliva on his bottom lip. I noticed the cloth, initialed *J. H.,* was practically drenched. "But I *can* serenade a pretty girl. That I can do." He cleared his throat of a surfeit of mucus, then recited a vulgar sailor ditty:

> *A pirate's got to ply his trade*
> *By stealing all the things God's made.*
> *When stealing doesn't do the trick,*
> *Use a stick or gun, a knife, a prick!*

Then he forced a laugh—a maniacal, cartoon laugh as startling as his steely touch. I withdrew from the menacing hook, which was ingeniously attached to his wrist.

———

I MUST have passed out on the pier, because Freeman was shaking me awake, his voice thundering in my ear: "Wendy, come back! Follow the sound of my voice: Ahh-ohh-ahh . . ."

I looked into the bugged-out eyes of my boyfriend, the adrenaline of the moment before still pumping through me. I took a couple of deep breaths and, lo and behold, could smell all manner of things: salt, fish, the hot chocolate on his breath.

As relieved as I was to regain my sense of smell, I was nonetheless terrified to the bone: the past was quickly intruding on the present—whether or not I wrote about it. And whether or not I had the courage, I would have to confide in Freeman. I prayed he wouldn't turn my little melodrama into a comic opera, or worse, another Broadway musical. I had always preferred the anonymity of my illusions. But what's private only feels manageable. Soon I would follow my Great-Nana's lead—spill my beans and suffer the consequences.

 PART

TWO

Children do not give up their innate imagination, curiosity, dreaminess easily. You have to love them to get them to do that.

—**R. D. Laing,** *The Politics of Experience*

VI

HOSE who say the present is informed by the past are being kind, being courteous. The present is routinely blown up by the past, again and again, as if by pirates, whereas the past never shatters—it's steadfast, fixed in memory like the brightly colored pages of a beloved children's book. The words, the pictures never fail you. Unlike real life. Real life pales in comparison with the past. It's flatter, grayer, disturbingly dim. We could do without it altogether if we believed in something bigger. *If we truly believed.*

Nana always said that real imagination requires patience with a world that pushes it aside. For the world does not wait for anyone: it plunges headfirst into the reality most of us call *misery.* To counter this, she said, we must wade courageously in a different direction, towards what most people call *fantasy.* What I now prefer to call *faith.* For if you can look at frosted corn flakes and see fairy dust; if you can find beautiful pictures in a breast cancer scar; if, by glancing at it cockeyed, you can transform a hovel into a home, you begin to see how believing is really a kind of seeing. Why would we want to believe, otherwise?

★ ★

WHEN Freeman related my little incident at the pier to Mummy, he abandoned any nuanced detail in favor of the graphic and sensational. "Listen, Mae," he said on the phone, "Wendy's off the hook. She's *gone.*" I took this as a criticism, but was really too dazed to protest.

Mummy raced over to our apartment in her Ford Galaxie 500. Not bothering to knock, she blew through the door like a funnel cloud. Perhaps it was her cacophony of scarves and the flowing bell-sleeves of her djellaba that made me think of weather. Or the hot air that all worried mothers expel.

"Wendy, darling, it's your mumsters! I am here to save you from yourself!"

Frantic, Mother whirled about the futon, on which I was laid out like a casualty. Then she produced, prestidigitously, a hot-water bottle from her backpack. It was still burning to the touch as she placed it on my forehead. For what purpose, I cannot be sure; I mean, my forehead was not the problem.

"My poor, beleaguered puss." She bent over to give me the sort of insinuating kiss reserved for girls who have outgrown their mothers, and I turned my face away. "So, we're a bit green about the gills? Well, I've got some Chinese herbs that are brilliant. *Voilà.*" From a rumpled paper sack, she poured a mound of stinky roots and leaves into her palm. "Delicious," she confirmed, sniffing at the aromatic twigs.

I winced at the faint penciled writing on the sack. "Mummy," I croaked, "that stuff's for rising wind. You know, gas."

"You brought her medicine for farting?" Freeman said. "Jesus, Mae. Can't you concentrate for once on Wendy's issues? Rising wind is *your* thing, I believe."

Mother gave him the evil eye, a scolding more Snidely Whiplash than Mr. Hyde. "Freeman, dear, would you please catch up? Wendy requires the most enlightened remedies available. And anything that becalms the stomach also becalms the mind. The stomach is our way in."

"I prefer to focus on the mind," he said. "I prefer that Wendy see someone who actually has initials after her name. Not one of your witch doctors. Someone whose wisdom isn't written in Sanskrit or pictograms. You know, someone who can talk theory *and* prescribe. A little Valium wouldn't kill her."

"Valium schmallium. Wendy's not going to take something so

common. Her problems are special and so should her drugs be." She repositioned her own photograph on the library table. "This really should be framed," she said.

Noting the lack of furniture in our apartment, Mother reclined on the hardwood floor as if on a chaise lounge, and took a moment to adjust her frenzy of scarves. From a deep pocket she removed two dainty, silver bells, courtesy of Gump's department store, then closed her heavily mascaraed eyes and hummed. There she sat, my little Buddhist/Wiccan mother, droning on with the best prayer bells money can buy.

In Perry Mason–like deliberation, Freeman crossed over to Mother and kneeled beside her chanting, swaying body. He clapped his hands twice, disrupting her showy communion with the spirits. But Mother hardly blinked; apparently she'd lapsed into a deeply meditative state.

"Christ, Ullman," she eventually moaned. "Have you no respect for the weird?"

"None whatsoever," he answered, then made a grab for the bells. He proceeded to ring them offensively, like a village idiot.

All too quickly Freeman was absorbed in the bells' sweet tinkling. Inspired, he tossed a bell down Mummy's back and she howled. As her laughter fed on itself, I heard its echo of desperation, perhaps the feeling that she'd failed me.

"Earth to Mummy, Earth to Freeman! Hel-looo!" I waved. Their eyes wandered leisurely over to me on my pillowed throne, as if acknowledging someone faintly familiar. I threw up my arms: "*C'est moi*, the lunatic."

"Hush, darling. Don't talk that talk." Mother held a fertility-ringed finger to her lips, at once the kind kindergarten teacher. I may have spotted a tear making its way down her cheek, but with Mummy you could never be sure. Her moods turned on a very unstable dime.

Dashing over to me now, as if some new emergency had just availed itself, she ordered Freeman to plug in a heating pad she'd stuffed into her well-stocked backpack. Then, with genuine feeling, she fluffed my bangs and petted my brow, which mainly served to knock the water bottle off my forehead. "Who's my girl?" she sang out for the world to hear, then whispered furtively: "Have you told him yet?"

"Just now," I said weakly, "in the broadest strokes."

"Oh shit," Mummy said. "Then don't expect him to be psychic. He's a good man, but remember: he only believes in *three* dimensions."

"Yeah, Bartok, Boulez, and the Bee Gees."

"Now don't underestimate the composer. He *will* get it in time."

"Well, why don't you start the conversation?" I challenged her. "Why don't you get him up to speed?"

"You know it's not my place to say anything," she said. "I may be an interfering bitch, but I know how these scenes must be played."

"Hey, kids, I don't wish to spoil the party," Freeman said, joining us on the futon, "but we really need to find someone Wendy can talk to. I know she saw everyone in town when she was a teenybopper, but surely there's some new guru around. Someone who specializes in . . ."

"In?" I said mournfully.

"In advising beautiful young women who, uh, live with talented composers and hallucinate."

"Brilliant save," I said.

"Well," Mother smacked her lips, "there's this supposedly phenomenal Marxist psychologist, a Dr. Milton Pease, whom my rolfer recommends. Did I mention how brilliant he is? Furthermore, he's a stand-up comic! Wendy, doesn't that sound perfectly yin-yangy?"

I wheezed like a beached whale.

"So the question is, sweetie, would you consider seeing another doctor in a long line of nutters?"

"Sure," I said foggily. "The comedian angle might come in handy when I tell him some whoppers."

"Don't make fun," Mother said.

"Yeah, I'll see the guy."

"Good girl," Mummy cooed and pinched my cheek. "I'll ring

him up tomorrow. And now for some tea," she announced with false good cheer. "Freeman, would you mind brewing some of this?" She foraged in her backpack for a wax-paper packet of more stalks and leaves, and tossed it with a pained look to Freeman. He caught the packet and returned the look, which to my mind read "hopeless," like a last-ditch prayer.

I AGREED to see the Marxist-comic shrink—two times a week for six weeks—on his economical trial plan. Disappointingly, though, Dr. Pease approached my personal history with a complete lack of humor. During our first meeting he accused me of being an "ersatz Scheherazade." I blanched at this but was secretly flattered. I mean, who wouldn't want to be compared to history's greatest spin doctor!

Pease's office was offbeat, bordering on slovenly. The moldy walls were hung with a couple of amateur seascapes and a "Free Albania!" poster; the place stank of old socks and gym shoes. Displayed among the textbooks on dust-coated shelves were props that appeared to be rejects from a Gallagher act: a giant blowup banana, a meat grinder with fake sausages hanging out its mouth, jelly jars of confetti, a tired rubber chicken.

Though the setting had dramatic potential, our communication, it turned out, was a flop. During my testimony Pease often appeared restless or sleepy; he was periodically dismissive. His long beatnik face grew creases as I spoke, and his ungroomed Jewish Afro scared me.

It didn't take much time before a few of the comic props—Harpo Marx horn, shaving-cream pie, seltzer bottles for spritzing—proved more entertaining than the doctor himself, and I took to toying with these whenever Pease appeared either bored or excessively serious. Over the weeks, he turned downright morbid, his eyes watering at the wrong parts of my story and using inappropriate language: "You really put a nail in the coffin with that anecdote" and "You're depressing *me*, dear." When I finally complained to Mother about the doctor's ill-timed gravitas, she did some checking around. From her druggist, a gossip of the worst sort, Mother learned that Pease's career as a comic was presently in the toilet. It turns out that, during the wrap-up of a painfully unfunny night at the Comedy Store in Hollywood, the good doctor had punctuated a weak joke by taking out his penis. No one in the audience had been the slightest bit amused—the LAPD especially lacked a sense for the absurd—and Pease had spent the night in lockup entertaining the other fuckups.

So *this* was the person in charge of my psychic health? The finest the Bay Area had to offer? I wondered whether Mother had an opinion; she usually had three. But she just pooh-poohed the penis rumor, chalking it up to envy.

"Not penis envy?" I groaned.

"No, *professional* envy. Other shrinks do half the business Pease does. He's *that* good. Supposedly."

I committed to finishing the program; Mummy had such high hopes and it would get her off my back. Ironically, the only progress I made was of the comedic sort. As Pease slid deeper into the jaws of despair, I sharpened my storytelling chops. The forest creatures of my fables began to lighten up, find the laughter inside the tears, even throw off their legendary bitterness. With tales of their newly droll exploits I entertained the doctor as best I could, as he sank further into an unprofessional funk. Every once in a while, he manifested a tortured grimace, which I took for a smile, a vote of confidence in my work. This made me feel all warm and fuzzy, if only for a second. My private thoughts were still haunted by the image of the snaggletoothed, one-handed gentleman; his visitation was not something I could easily laugh off. Was he a figment of my past or a harbinger of my future? He had wanted me to join him. But where? How? When?

During our final weeks together, Pease managed to rally his emotions and sense of duty, and he delivered the psychological goods. In two dimly illuminating sessions, he tried heroically to teach me that "fantasy can't add up to anything solid." With very little time left on the clock, he labored like a hostage negotiator in an effort to make me understand just how flimsy and untrustworthy my illusions were, assuring me that "*il*-lusion only results in *de*-lusion." Like that's a *bad* thing. After a battery of bizarre tests ("Fill in the blank: The Vietnam War was an atrocious—" "Atrocity?" I answered), Pease arrived at an underwhelming diagnosis: "Wendy, all this Neverland talk suggests you are a profoundly gifted and enterprising woman. But—and here's the thing—you also have a distinct tendency to avoid responsibility."

He looked away from me then, as if ashamed of his own lack of faith, and I gifted him with the flicker of a smile.

At the conclusion of the trial plan, Pease telephoned Mother and Freeman. He made a big deal about their participation in my cure and demanded that we convene as a foursome. Within twenty-four hours, we congregated on a rustic bench at the Berkeley Rose Garden, a spectacular terraced amphitheater designed by the Works Progress Administration. Unfortunately, the day was such a knockout, the four of us could hardly focus on what we had come to discuss. The sky was that woozy Technicolor blue most people find irresistible, and the roses, which through most of the Spring had been shy and reticent on account of the drought, were now strutting their florid stuff.

We sat on the bench in an unfriendly row—Pease, Mother, Freeman, with me on the far end, as though I were being pushed off. Under such tight conditions, we were forced to look straight ahead instead of at each other, and I wondered if this was all part of Pease's plan.

After his ritual hemming and hawing, and exaltations about "how far-out the day is," Pease clapped his hands once and said, "Now then."

Mother cried, "Out with it!" but she sounded almost cheerful. I noticed her sizing up the lanky doctor as she fooled with her sherry-colored locks.

Pease cleared his throat for effect and without further stalling *did* come out with it, the most hackneyed bunk I'd heard in years: "All right, people, here goes. Our Wendy suffers from a massive propensity for the theatrical, the artificial, the staged. To my mind, and I

really have great insight into this sort of disorder, she could use—
no, she requires—an extra-strong dose of reality: a job in a factory, a
stint as an inner-city schoolteacher, or, dare we allow ourselves to
imagine it, a tour of duty in the military.

"Instead, she takes refuge in a tenuous children's book career,
which only promotes her 'problem' and does nothing to counter her
superstitions, her apparitions, her phantasms. On the contrary, her
writing encourages her suffering. Not a real shocker to *you* folks. If
it were up to me, if I were her boyfriend or her mother, I would urge
her to stop the notebook scribbling and put an end to the contem-
plative, self-obsessed life. I would get her out in the world, pronto!
Wendy needs to participate in real life close-up, not from the foggy
distance of her dreams. There, I said it. Any reactions? Comebacks?
Put-downs?"

Pease let go with a sad, rheumy laugh. Fixing his gaze at the
electric-blue sky, he placed a hand on Mother's shoulder to console
her. A whistle issued from his nose.

Mother was visibly outraged. In what Dr. Pease might have
called a "staged, theatrical" fit, she flailed at him with her tiny hands,
which were encased in rainbow-striped Guatemalan mittens, and
proceeded to stamp out a young rosebush with her hiking boots.
"You must be mad, Doctor. I mean, tell us something *new*. Tell us
something we can work with." She snapped off a prize-winning Lili
Marlene and jabbed the air with it.

"Put the weapon down, Margaret." Pease spoke in a steady,
unruffled manner.

"Not on your life, Doctor."

"Then on your *daughter's* life. For her sake, I'm asking you."

Mother tucked the rose behind her right ear and grinned mili-
tantly.

"That's better," Pease said. "Now, you were saying?"

"I was saying, I've paid good money to find out that my daughter has a fantasy life that scares the living daylights out of you? That,
in your expert, well-seasoned opinion she should become Rosie the

Riveter on the swing shift? I should shoot rivets into *your head,* Pease."

For the first time since I'd met the man, he let go with a belly laugh; he really appeared happy in a sloppy, carefree way.

Leaving Mother and Pease alone, Freeman took my hand and led me down the terraced steps to the lowest level of the garden. I stumbled along, feebleminded. Despite the teeming beauty, I was heading into a tailspin. I'd just spent six weeks with a shrink as depressed as I, albeit with half the creative juices, and wondered what it all added up to. I hadn't made a bit of progress in calming my mind; in that department Mummy's tea had outperformed Pease. True, I'd gathered a little literary momentum as my children's stories took on semihappy endings (a failed attempt to appease Pease). But if I had to choose between weathering preposterous problems in a suspect dimension and good old depression in this one, the answer was as clear as the Mermaids' Lagoon, where once I splashed blithely like an otter: the lunatic fringe was my motherland. It was where I belonged.

THE day at the Rose Garden wasn't a total loss. It appears that, after their initial flare-up, Mother and Pease got on like a house afire. This wasn't altogether unexpected, as Mother tended to take the Hepburn-Tracy approach to relationships: an early round of adversarial sniping followed by a lukewarm détente and the laying down of spears (in this case, thorns), and for the big finish, a plunge into the other person's arms with abandon, or what psychologists might call a lack of self-esteem. What Mother saw in Pease escaped me. But I believe the idea of a man whipping out his penis at a comedy club had sparked her initial interest and then served to maintain it over the run of several months.

No doubt they had loads in common. While Pease was a bona fide shrink, Mummy, the layperson, had achieved popular success with her self-help tomes, *The Pan Pathology* and, more recently, *Happy Harpies: Women Who Sound Off & Get Even.* In a calculated move, Pease took to poring over her books as if they were the Dead Sea Scrolls, often reciting passages out loud to make Mummy blush. Surprisingly, he enjoyed being dominated by her personality as well as her intelligence. They both loved talking about behavior more than anything in the world. And I have to believe that Pease whipped out his punch line often enough to satisfy Mother's sexual hunger, or else the whole thing would have been doomed from the start.

That afternoon in the Rose Garden, Freeman and I also got a bonus. Stopping at a footbridge so we could take in the sound of Codornices Creek—"It burbles like a baby, Wends"—Freeman made a startling admission. During the six weeks when I'd been preoccupied with the hokum from Pease's therapy sessions, it so happened that Freeman read every word of a book by Great-Nana's friend. He'd curled up with a lavish edition of *Peter Pan in Kensington Gardens*, illustrated by Arthur Rackham, that he'd found in Mummy's library, shelved among other mainstays like *A Room of One's Own* and *How to Win Friends and Influence People*. I was dumbfounded, at a rare loss for words. And I feared our future anew.

"So?" was all I could manage to say.

"So now I love you even more. Does that help?"

"Well, it's a good place to start," I conceded, rubbing moist eyes. I peered over the rail into the creek and began nervously looking for fish hooks. What else could I do under the circumstances?

"And I think it's a great story," Freeman said. "I know it's a classic and all, but it seems absolutely modern, really cutting-edge."

"Oh, it is! It is!" I said, trying to get beyond the fact he'd called it a *story*. Perhaps it was my own fault: I'd only recently revealed my early indoctrination at Great-Nana's hand; I still referred to my experiences as "really powerful hallucinations."

"I can see how this fairy tale has had such a strong influence on your family," Freeman continued. "Why you've all borrowed it as your anthem. It's very, uh, cool. And no wonder you're having this Hook guy make personal appearances in your dreams—he's a creepy bastard. I'd dream about him, too, if my family had talked about him my whole life. I mean, it's totally natural that you've fixated on this thing. It's got so many levels. It's intense, compelling stuff—I'm even inspired to write music about it."

"Oh?" I said limply.

"Yeah, I've already begun a piece called 'Pan the Refusenik.' You know, how Peter flatly *refuses* to grow up? I'm throwing a Russian melody into the mix."

"You're completely confusing things," I said. "A refusenik is a Soviet citizen who is refused permission to emigrate." He looked at me like I was the one who was confused. Growing increasingly anxious, I rapped my knuckles on the pendulous rail that ran along the footbridge.

"Hold on, Wends," Freeman said, fearing I might jump down all of four feet into three inches of water. He restrained me with his delicate musician's hands, then shook me like a snow globe. "I won't let you do it!"

"Man, you have no right to read that book," I chided him. "It's private."

"You have got to be kidding," he said. "It's in every library in America. Are you, like, into censorship now?"

"No. I'm into *respect*. Respect for the living." When he screwed up his nose, I realized how shaky that sounded. "It's just, I wish to respect the privacy of the people in the *story*. They deserve to be given a wide berth."

Freeman took my left hand and guided me away from the bridge; he didn't care for the possibilities it inspired. "Next time, we go with a therapist I choose. Someone really happy with his life. Is there such a thing as a happy doctor?"

"Oh yeah," I answered solemnly. "The kind that delivers babies. They understand miracles better than anybody."

"Are you telling me you need to see an obstetrician?" he asked.

"I'm telling you I need a miracle."

VII

N obstetrician came in handy, for I was pregnant before you could say "Prepare for landing."

Berry was not an accident: for years I had dreamed of a young child who looked like Mummy (petite, with burgundy curls) and behaved like Daddy (capricious, mad with ideas). In these dreams, the child would run circles around me until she made butter out of air, a shameless steal from *The Story of Little Black Sambo.* Then I'd swallow the butter, shoveling it in my mouth with a big wooden spoon. In seconds I'd become so huge I couldn't move my legs. The dreams always ended with me making a dent in the earth with my newly acquired mass, and wondering if I'd ever get off the ground again. The child would wander off and I'd grow weak from calling her name. Once awake, I'd feel both heavy and bereft, the weight of her absence adding to my own.

For contraception, Freeman and I practiced a method lifted from music composition—the John Cage doctrine of chance. So absorbed was Freeman in his work that, when he surfaced, we hurriedly took advantage of life's little essentials: dining, concerts, movies. Alas, sex was always fourth on the list and so rarely indulged in that we routinely forswore protection. Protection was no use; I knew I would take the familial path. I would have one child—a daughter—just like Wendy, Jane, and Margaret. There was never any doubt. And she would take off into the night without a good-bye kiss to her mother. In that light, contraception could only be seen as an obstacle to destiny, a postponement of the inevitable.

So it was that, at the indelicate age of twenty-five, when other women were putting off marriage and families until they'd soaked up every drop of free love, I put on the veil, courtesy of B. Boop's Vintage Frocks, and hobbled down the aisle with a secret growing in my tummy. No, not the child. I told everyone I knew that a baby was in the works. But I couldn't talk about the cost of being a girl in this family. I couldn't admit to myself that another Darling would pay dearly for having the nerve, the guts, the utter audacity to grow up.

★   ★

MY outdoor wedding was brisk and uneventful: I kept Mummy and Daddy in the dark and out of the picture. That's the storybook version. In truth, the whole business was operatic and notable for its multiple rounds of vomiting. For one thing, Mother officiated; in addition to taking graduate classes at the California Institute of Integral Studies (she was planning to become a *real* psychologist to give her books some heft), she'd taken a correspondence course in Astral Ministry. The ceremony took place in the same rose garden where Dr. Pease had once held court. I was incensed that Mummy had invited the shrink but as she was still sleeping with him, she felt justified.

The weather for the wedding was classic Berkeley fare—mystic coastal fog begetting midday sunshine begetting rudely chill winds in the afternoon. We had prepared for this and placed Pendleton blankets on the rental chairs for our guests. Shivering and awaiting our cues, Freeman and I cloistered ourselves in the two park bathrooms across the street, knocking on our shared wall like prisoners of love. If I had known Morse code, I might have tapped out *SOS.* Not *Save our souls,* but *Social obligations suck.* There was still time to make a run for it and marry privately in a faraway kingdom where parents aren't allowed.

As the ceremony got under way—with a tape-recorded snippet of "It's the Bugs" followed by a cheerful, well-intended "Wedding Bell Blues"—there was a marked stir among the spectators. Peeking out at my guests from behind the redwood pergola at the top of the amphitheater, I witnessed a lot of neck-craning and crying out. Had Grandma Jane showed up, twenty years off schedule, to properly send me off? How I longed to meet Mummy's mummy, to understand the forces that had always been at play.

The disturbance turned out to signal the courtly entrance of Great-Nana, who was carried into the garden by three beefy college students (members of the UC Berkeley Wrestling Team, per their jackets) and set down in the front row for all to consider. She was handed a silver flask by one of the thoughtful young men, who then covered her exposed calves with a special mohair throw.

Just hours before the wedding, Daddy, too, had whisked in—in his case on a private Gulfstream jet, having exchanged places with the pilot for much of the trip. His navigatory prowess had put him in an especially jaunty mood, which was critical, he let it be known, if he was going to be "on the same continent as the grand divorcée." That morning, I'd watched from Mother's backyard deck as he made himself two Bloody Marys in the kitchen. After swilling down the second, he began to cough violently; I thought his chest would explode and the wedding might have to be called off. Finally catching his breath, he wandered outside where he found me, stone-still, taking in the view but comprehending nothing.

"Nerves?" he asked, grinning.

"Always," I answered.

"Wendy," he said, steadying himself against a potted palm. I looked away, for he really was too handsome. "Wends," he began again, squinting at the bay. "It's obvious that, as a father, I've been too . . ."

"Otherwise engaged?" I said, chewing on a split end. I hadn't anticipated a lecture this late in the program.

"But you've never been far away in Daddy's thoughts," he continued. "The truth is, you're extremely important to me. Of colossal importance—bigger than the Concord!" he added, reaching a bit.

I nodded like a bobblehead doll; I'd heard it all before.

"I mean it," he continued. "The *idea* of you is more compelling than anything I could ever imagine. But the fact of you . . . well, I'm not good with facts."

"You mean children, Daddy. You're not good with children."

He scratched boyishly behind his ear. "My princess is getting married and I haven't a clue what to tell her!" Then he hiccuped, gulping in air.

"It's okay, Daddy." I patted his back as if he were the child. "Because, you know, I only get married once!" I winked broadly.

Regaining his balance, he clung to my shoulder and tried to cozy up. His neck smelled of ginger and cloves, and I swooned just a little.

"The truth is," he said with a catch in his throat, "the world is too blooming big. Unreachable. Unknowable. I would have urged you to explore it, to steer clear of obligations like *husbands*. But it's a bit lonely out there on the limb. So marry the chap." He gave my shoulders a squeeze. "You and Freeman are doing the right thing with the nest-building, the baby-making. God knows I'm not the best role model—just look at me. Daddy's a goddamn icon! Everybody loves me and nobody knows me. Just think of what I could have achieved if I'd had a family, too."

"You *do* have a family," I said.

"Quite," he said flatly.

"Uh, Daddy." I looked him in the eye. "Is this speech really about me, because if it is, I'm missing something."

"Just don't wish for too much," he said, checking the horizon.

"Not a problem," I told him.

Then, spotting Mother through the window, Daddy stepped back into the house to greet her, his smile looking cagey again. Mummy had packaged herself in a low-cut, sexed-up crimson gown. "Sears?" he asked sweetly, and winked at me through the glass. Apparently, Mother's ministry license from the Cosmic Life Church also gave her the license to don a peculiar hat (a yarmulke of confused ethnicity—ribbons and rickrack on madras). Later this outfit would prove successful in drawing attention away from the bride as she grappled with a nasty bout of nausea. For this alone, I'd be grateful.

CONTRARY to what you might expect, being a pregnant bride had a definite upside: for once my chronic queasiness was socially acceptable. Immediately before I made my entrance, I heaved in the park bathroom across the street; then, as if punch-drunk, I wove through the sympathetic crowd at the top of the steps.

It's important to add that I looked spectacular. My wedding dress was the same smashing number Great-Nana had gotten hitched in. Naturally it was loaded with Edwardian affectations: it had lace, it had ruffles, it had flounces. It was seeded with pearls and dripping with crocheted balls and flowers. My store-bought veil could have been put to good use by Christo—to wrap the state capitol. In short, I *was* the wedding cake.

Daddy was waiting to escort me down the aisle, several flights of terraced stone steps. He looked rakish in the extreme and I fell under his spell all over again. His moussed golden locks were freshly peppered with dark-blonde streaks, but no gray—he regularly saw to that. His silk eye patch complemented the dapper Brioni suit he'd bought for the occasion, and he wore matching black Adidas sneakers.

After giving me an almost erotic buss on the lips, he brushed the hair from my ear and whispered: "Wendy Amelia Darling Braverman."

"Yes, Daddy?" I said.

"It's time."

I wriggled my nose.

"To fly away, ladybird!" Then he flapped his arms like a tipsy pelican. My heart swelled at such extravagant, effeminate swooping; I giggled and cupped my mouth. Not wishing to abandon Daddy, I flapped my arms shyly in a single flutter. The guests applauded. I flapped a second time and could feel the blood rush to my cheeks, shame and embarrassment all mixed up with ancestral pride. Again the guests cheered. Inevitably Daddy and I winged our way down the aisle, a twin blur of black linen and cream silk.

Amid the bustle, I swear I left the ground. The wind rushed under my sandals; I could feel its tickle, hear its faint thrumming. My nausea momentarily worsened—the smallest change in altitude could go right to my head—then it gave way to a mild euphoria. Thanks to my ankle-length gown, no one noticed the irregularity, save perhaps for Great-Nana, who sniffled bravely into her hanky, then blew a real honker. Mummy was too busy endearing herself to the audience, blowing kisses to friends and strangers alike, and re-arranging her décolletage. She winked at Pease so many times one might have thought she had Tourette's.

When Freeman materialized, I was relieved to see how normal he looked. At the last minute, he must have decided against the blue-jeans-and-tuxedo-jacket combo that was so popular, and opted for a beige linen suit with tee-shirt. Black high-top tennis shoes winked at me from below sharply creased pant cuffs.

I smiled winsomely at my groom. Freeman deserved that much for marrying a problem who toted around a second problem inside her. Of course, *he* never would have regarded our union in this way. He still believed that, over time, I would calm down and that the child I bore would have a squeaky-clean slate when it came to her mental health. The crucial thing was that we were nuts for each other. The fact that I was occasionally starved for attention shouldn't have mat-tered. Neither should have Freeman's expert avoidance of gainful employment.

Though he'd started a paper route for the *San Francisco Chroni-cle,* after two weeks of tossing papers in the dark, Freeman accused his vocation of disrupting his creative flow. How dare it! Thereafter, he'd returned to life as an unemployed composer (what other kind was there?) and we'd made a go of it with a small infusion of cash from the artistic Ullmans, my tiny advance from my first book, *Fer-rets Are Free,* and by cashing in Brave Hearts Airlines stock, my sweet-sixteen gift from Daddy.

I had never felt comfortable asking my parents for money; ever since leaving home, I'd striven to demonstrate my independence on the material front if not the emotional one. Besides, Mother was spending her book royalties as quickly as the checks came in—being a voluptuary didn't come cheap. And Daddy's generous impulses were entirely fickle: an offering of cold cash might be followed by an icy admonition to "be brilliant in your field, Wendy, or give up the ghost."

That day, my wedding day, I'd rightly expected to be a ball of conflicting emotions. Jittery. Rhapsodic. Numb. Standing in front of my family now, not to mention Freeman's, not to mention a swarm of Mummy's closest male friends, I tried to concentrate on what was good about life—not *my* life specifically, but the Big Picture. For one, I had a warm albeit funky shelter. Two, I ate really clean organic food (this was Berkeley, after all). And three, there'd been a mercifully long interval between quakes of the geological sort.

But what about the Small Picture? The knowledge that Freeman was a creative ally should have been enough. I honestly *expected* him to leave someday; if he stuck around, I'd be pressed to revise my sexual politics and we couldn't have that.

So, stepping onto the outermost brink and shaking like the Cowardly Lion, I tallied what I felt to be true:

- One, I was lucky to be wanted by somebody.
- Two, I'd never have to worry about whether such a charismatic guy would hang around for the whole show. (He wouldn't.)
- And three, once *he'd* flown the coop, I'd feel devastated and unforgiving, but in no time revert to my native loneliness. As loneliness was a state with which I was ridiculously intimate, I really had nothing to fear.

True, my tally did not include a baby. While the Ullmans insisted that we marry, Freeman and I could have coasted along very nicely, thank you, without a sanction from the government. For there was never any question my baby daughter would take the name Darling; in my family this was nonnegotiable. Freeman, only too happy to record the subtle sounds of pregnancy, had yet to focus on what came after.

So, having itemized the verities and finding myself still vertical, I snuck a look at my sweet, goofy husband-to-be and saw . . . my father.

Why was I marrying a near-clone of Dudley Braverman?

I believed in happy beginnings.

Bundled in his suit—a sheepish boy in men's clothing—Freeman took my hand with great tenderness as he had on thousands of occasions, then proceeded to squeeze the life out of it. No question he was scared. In order to survive the ceremony, I tactfully withdrew my hand and pretended to adjust the train on my heavily garnished gown. When I glanced up, we both caught the remorse in each other's eyes. Freeman was sorry for being a nervous Nellie (after all, the entire tribe of Ullmans was in the audience, looking remote and intellectually underfed); and I was sorry he was saddled with the Darlings and the Bravermans—most especially, with their lone offspring.

"All right, kids." Mother cleared her throat and took a sip of wine from a crystal goblet on the makeshift podium. The wine had no religious significance; she was simply a glutton for a good Chablis.

"Let's get this r-r-r-oad on the show!" she trilled, then whooped like a rock star. No one laughed, but Mother continued as if she'd been howlingly funny: "My daughter, Wendy, a postmodern bride who doesn't really *need* to marry and become a slavish subject of the state, but rather feels that this wedding is a private affair of the heart concerning only those who love her—" Guests exchanged sidelong glances. "And her smart-arse Mozart of a groom, who doesn't really *need* to settle down with one woman, but feels obligated because his best girl got preggers—"

"Mummy!" I shrieked.

"Let's have a little fun, shall we? We are gathered here today in the memory of two individuals who have decided to give up their personhood—"

"Mae!" Freeman growled under his breath. The guests in the front row tittered.

"Don't get your knickers in a twist," she hissed. "I'm just trying to spice this up. The ceremony *you* wrote is leaden and corny."

"How dare you, Mother," I said as discreetly as I could. "This is my first and only wedding, and you are *not* going to screw it up."

Freeman took hold of Mother's twiglike wrists. "You're fired, Mae."

"But you two need me. You can't carry on without a *professional.*"

"Gee, ya think?" Freeman hoisted Mummy in the air and set her down several yards from the podium. Then, wearing a wiggly smile that spoke volumes, he returned to address the crowd: "Okay, okay, okay. We're gonna try and continue with the ceremony as written by Wendy and me. But let's take a moment to acknowledge my mother-in-law, Margaret. She was the perfect warm-up act, don't you agree?"

He encouraged a round of applause and the guests sluggishly obliged. From the corner of my eye I spotted Mummy fuming in the background, half obscured by a bush of flaming Red Devil roses.

The wedding moved forward without further interruption (though Mother's performance became the stuff of legend). Not to say that our wedding succumbed to convention: without the services of a minister, Freeman had to assume the role and improvise. This added a silly rhetorical ring to the proceedings: "Freeman, do you—do I?—take Wendy as your—as my—awfully lawful and bedded wife?" "I do." "And do you—do I?—promise to cherish her but not place her on a pedestal too often?" "I do."

To legalize the whole thing, Freeman and I got married again the following Monday in a subdued civil service at city hall, with Great-Nana serving as our witness. By this time, Daddy was safely in the air, jetting back to Brave Hearts headquarters, and Mother was holed up in her house, vowing never to speak to me again.

★   ★

HAVING a child requires little imagination as far as biology goes. Anyone can *give birth*. But believing in your child's future takes the vision of a Bucky Fuller, the faith of Joan of Arc, the lunar-mania of Jules Verne. It takes an artist to conjure up a space for your girl or boy that's boundary-free and fraught with beauty: a place to climb a bean stalk or don a riding hood.

Let's say that, as prospective parents, Freeman's and my fears were only outmatched by our speculations. Quaint notions like: our baby will know the world is a kind place if she listens to early Judy Collins. Or, Wonder Woman comics will come in handy to empower our delicate flower. Or, whole wheat ensures wholeness. Like most parents, our ignorance gave us an edge over chaos. Like all parents, we would muddle through.

During my pregnancy, I did my best to keep things upbeat around the apartment. I stayed away from movies by Godard and Bertolucci, and satisfied my cinematic jones with Woody Allen and Truffaut. I read daily from the scripture of *Mary Poppins,* and played Mummy's *The Sound of Music* LP until the grooves gave way. I avoided all Sylvia Plath in favor of e.e. cummings, and took to wearing fruity pastels, even in the dead of winter. Freeman joined my Mickey Mouse Club for Pregnant Women and took to supplying cute voices and sound effects for a phalanx of cartoon characters that he watched on Saturday morning television. He turned the volume all the way down and, with a mysterious box called a synthesizer, substituted a menagerie of electronic howls, squawks, and moos. Over the months, he became astonishingly good at this, a one-man band with infinite resources, and we both wondered where such talent would take him, if indeed there was a destination.

By the time I was four months pregnant my nausea was at its apogee. I couldn't imagine it getting any worse, as my imagination had abandoned me at the three-month mark. Even the *thought* of a cracker made me hurl. Desperate to offer some relief, Freeman created a stream of soothing sounds on his synth to distract me, and occasionally he succeeded. One evening he played tapes of two of my favorite songs—Joni Mitchell's "Blue" and Laura Nyro's

"Lonely Women"—but with a twist: onto these fabulously bleak tunes he mixed tracks of fairylike xylophone notes. He hoped the resulting hybrid would trigger some neurological switch that, given time, might suppress my nausea and, if I was open to the ironies, make me chuckle. He called his technique *Freeman-phonia*. I called it folly but the thing is, folly *worked* and I was able to regain equilibrium and move about the apartment.

A tad more sentient now, I had the niggling feeling that Freeman would rather be making tinkly sounds and animal noises than finding real work. When I questioned him about this, he met me with predictably deaf ears: "Wends, listen to this: *ping-pling p'zow-ping*! It's sheer genius!" So I'd listen to whatever and nod, wincing with faint approval.

In the eighth month of my pregnancy, we moved in to my childhood home in the Berkeley hills. It goes without saying that we needed the space, but we also wanted our child to be closer to nature. (In a truly lopsided exchange, Mummy took up residence in Freeman's student quarters to be closer to the coeds who championed her books.) My old bedroom was converted into the nursery and its hardwood floor refinished; all the damage from my manic rocking was smoothed over. I even installed a chair that didn't rock—a chaste white wicker armchair.

It was here, in this setting, that I began to worry about our family's future. It's not as though I could say to Freeman, *I'm* a grown-up and you're not. Just because my stomach was inflated to the max didn't mean I'd graduated into bona fide adulthood. No, my thoughts and ideas were still controlled by the past, if not held completely hostage. For it was not long after moving back in the house that I began to receive visits from shapes and colors and voices and weather that, I knew all too well, had nothing to do with my pregnancy and everything to do with my childhood. Trapped inside a time bomb of a body, it was almost too easy to take the plunge: I gave in to the assorted shapes and colors, voices and breezes, immersing myself in a world where one's body had little meaning.

Incorporeality was everything in The Neverland. If you asked anyone what he weighed, he would just laugh like you'd made the cleverest joke. But if you asked what flavor the sky was, you'd get a serious answer that went on for paragraphs.

The visits always began with a rousing gust; at least I don't *remember* flying. As usual, I'd be in the bathroom, undressing for my morning shower, ever astonished by the pretty curve of my expand-ing belly. I'd lightly pat my stomach, instructing my baby to "get ready for life on the outside—it will blow your tiny mind." Only here, in the privacy of the bathroom, did I feel comfortable with the idea of being a mother. I'd picture my little girl and me at the city museum, pointing and laughing at the paintings, admiring the mas-terworks and dismissing the rest. And then I'd catch my smile in the bathroom mirror and fill with such lovely thoughts of mother-hood—thoughts that were at odds with my usual dread.

It was then I would sense a brash, alien current of air pricking the tiny blonde hairs on my forearms. Soon I'd pick up the scent of lavender and anise circling round the tight space, and taste some-thing cool on my lips—a coolness akin to spearmint. I'd begin to feel lightheaded and weightless, in spite of my considerable weight. By and by, a pink fog would hover overhead, leading me inside the shower stall—to a place that would soon make sense. All too quickly, though, the fog would recede into the pink tiles and I'd question what I'd seen. Then, just when I was about to turn on the spigots, the fog would reappear, its gauzy fingers imploring, *Hurry, this way!* and I'd stop everything and wait for instructions.

First came the voices—cartoonish yet familiar, as if my oldest friends were speaking at forty-five rpm. Usually it was my name they spoke in unison, which put a smile on my chilled lips and warmed me from the inside. Then came circles, trapezoids, oc-tagons, triangles—not so much floating in the air, but rotating like a carousel in my mind. Each flaunted its bold, saturated color as if I were in elementary school and just learning about the forms objects take. At a leisurely pace the shapes would settle into a landscape that I could eventually make out as the building blocks of mountain, la-goon, and forest. Giddy with comprehension I'd jump into the air and shout: *rock! water! oak!* Each thing I called upon bowed in the only way it knew how: wobbling, rippling, bending. This never failed to strike my funny bone, and I'd giggle until the sight of a boy took my breath away. Then I'd pass out like some sort of drama queen.

Sometimes Freeman would find me in the shower stall, dry and clinging languorously to the spigots, or laid out like a drunk on the pink tiles. With barely concealed anguish, he'd lift me out and set me down on the bath mat, then feed me a glass of water from the sink. He'd chastise me for opening the bathroom window on "such an insanely cold day," and then close the window with a ferocity that puzzled me.

But there was a single morning when I traveled well and far. I touched down without incident and woke up blinking like a newborn. I'd returned to the site of the crime—the very spot where I once swore to Peter that I'd never, ever, cross-my-heart-and-hope-to-die, grow up.

∞ A week before Berry was due—by this time we'd arrived at her name, a homage to the great man of letters J. M. Barrie, Nana's first crush and the person who'd christened her *Wendy* because she called him "my Friendy" in her toothy way—I found myself sprawled on the well-worn spot under The Hanging Tree, Pan bobbing over me from on high.

In a flash—like a film with crucial frames missing—he appeared in front of me, smirking like the wicked lad he was. With impressive haste he removed the green, paisley bandana tied round his noggin, hippie-style, and fastidiously tied it to my wrist. Then, with a single obnoxious tug, he yanked me to my feet.

"Well, if it isn't the Wendybird," he said. "So, once again, I've rescued you. What d'ya have to say for yourself?"

"Ha!" I protested, noting that I was uncommonly huge in The Neverland. But Peter didn't seem to notice; he didn't appreciate that thirteen years had gone by.

"So that makes twenty-two thousand successful rescues, *that's* what. A new world record." He stuck his vulpine face in my startled one, and I turned my puffy cheeks away. I'd just seen something that made me cower.

"What's the matter, tongue got your cat?" he jested.

"It's nothing," I said with false aplomb. But my eyes hadn't deceived me: a couple of nut-brown whiskers were sprouting from Peter's chin and, I swear, his voice was lower.

Could it be that Peter had, God forfend, *aged*? Ripened like the peaches he so fancied? Perhaps he'd glued some fake whiskers to his jaw for a theatrical skit, some burlesque wherein he played a pirate or reenacted his triumph over the multiple descendants of Captain Hook?

"Then why're you staring at me like you've just seen Casper the Friendly Ghost?" he asked, mouth ajar.

"Because I *have* seen a ghost. You're ever the ghost, Peter. Don't you know that? All this"——I made an exaggerated sweeping gesture—"this is one big ghost story compared to the rock-solid story I live in. My world is sturdy and durable. It takes precedence over yours. At least that's what they tell me." Bowing to the pressure in my head, I fell to my knees.

"What's this all about, li'l lady?" Peter spoke in that wooden John Wayne voice I'd taught him so long ago. "Is it because you're a li'l fat and a lot taller? *Freakishly* tall, actually?"

I shook my head and sniffled. He stroked the air above my head the way one touches a stranger's dog. "Now then, lass," he said more compassionately. "Why don't you tell us the story of Peter Pan and Wendy. That'll be good for a few laughs."

Yanking the sleeve of my Lanz nightgown (as was customary on the island, I was packaged in a virginal, white-flannel shroud), Peter led me to a hammock woven from cast-off button-down shirts he'd pinched from the Salvation Army; he sat himself down an arm's length from me. For a few peaceful minutes, we swung under the shade of a Torrey pine. The magnificent tree reminded me of the Southern California coastline, especially the cliffs at La Jolla where Daddy went hang gliding whenever he graced America with his presence. One more beautiful vista from which he ignored me.

As Peter and I rocked more turbulently on the hammock, old, unwanted notions began to surface, not the least of which was the hurt and the shame of Peter's chronic absence during my interminable teen years. It was the very thing I'd forgotten on arrival, too easily distracted by the perfumed scenery. In rapid succession more stinging memories made themselves known: the fact that I was pregnant, that I had a "boy" back home. I was dizzy and sickened by the contradictory images of my bifurcated life, the sum of my experience as a changeling. It all added up to an unfinished piece of work—one defective young woman.

"Peter, our story is not some comedy," I told him. "It's a *tragedy*. An especially tragic one." Once again I sniffled and rubbed my nose, destroying any chance to look fetching.

"Girl, the way you talk!" Now he was mimicking the black vernacular he'd picked up from listening to a popular sitcom. So he'd visited the States recently—was he seeing other girls?

"The way I talk isn't the problem," I said. "It's the way I make decisions. Just think, I could've stayed on with you and the Boys— where the hell are they, anyway?—and had a perfectly interesting life as some sort of mother. But I don't know if I *want* to be a mother. I can hardly take care of myself! If I feel any pull at all, it's towards you, Peter, and that thing we can never speak of."

"Pull? Thing?" He vaulted off the hammock and stuffed his hands in the back pockets of his jeans.

"Don't be cute."

"Can't be helped. I *am* cute."

"I mean, girls have needs. There's a *human* need for . . . intimacy. Attachment."

Peter crouched in the dirt, resting his forehead on his knuckles à la *The Thinker*. He appeared to be deep in thought—but was that possible for a boy who defined "reflection" as his handsome mirrored visage in the Mermaids' Lagoon?

After a stagey pause, he sat down on his haunches. "Wendybird, I, uh, can't. I just can't. Not after Jane."

A shudder ran up my arm, though it was undetectable beneath my commodious nightgown. What did Jane have to do with *us*?

"Grandma Jane?" I asked, quaking.

"Dead right," he answered.

I couldn't believe I was competing with a phantom girl—a relative no less! Maybe she was still around here, hiding, biding her time. "Is she here, Peter? Is my grandmother . . . on the island?"

He took inventory of everything in the room—everything but me. "Haven't seen the bird for ages," he said.

"Oh," I said, disappointed. "What was she like, Peter? Was she anything . . . like me?"

"She's *exactly* like you, but even taller and skinnier!" His eyes widened as if reviewing some delicious memory.

"I meant her *inner* qualities, her personality."

"Oh," he said, furrowing his brow. "That's what's so strange."

"What's strange, what?" I asked.

"Well on the inside, Jane's exactly like *me*. Fearless, resourceful. The girl fancied me so. I, uh, tried to indulge *her* needs, but it was a nightmare. I mean, I found all the soppy stuff stupid."

For the first time in a thousand days, I was voiceless, struck dumb by life's cruelty. Had Peter experienced s-e-x in all its sweet and playful variations? Had he and Jane revealed themselves to each other, and then entwined their naked bodies until he recognized that he was a part of her—and she a part of him? Had he understood with any gravity that sex was flawed, that you can never truly know someone inside out?

I looked into Peter's unblemished face: despite the appearance of those few pert whiskers, he still had that *Tiger Beat* thing going for him. The guy was Davy Jones cute, Peter Noone cute. If any experience had etched itself onto his creamy features, its mark had promptly vaporized in the Neverland air. Only Peter's eyes betrayed how lost he really was, abandoned too many years ago to remember anything of substance about his ignoble beginnings. The image of the bars his mother had installed on his nursery window remained just that—a memory he could no longer be certain of—though surely his heart would recall this injustice whenever a new girl he brought to the island decided to return to her family. No, Peter didn't seem to know sex. If he did, it was one great adventure that hadn't registered a whit.

Stock-still on the hammock, I wiped my face with the hem of my nightgown. I no longer felt so completely tragic; in fact, I detected a little objectivity creeping into my feelings for Peter, the sort of distance that might even save one's life. I turned my back on him and crossed over to a rock that, fortunately for me, was shaped like an easy chair. In crude calligraphy, the letters M + P were carved into the stone, a schoolgirlish heart circling the sentiment. So Mummy had gotten here first! Her slimy snail tracks were everywhere I went on the island. Any youthful proclamation of mine, any poetic expression of my love, must have been considered so redundant by Peter as to be trite. But look what Mummy had done with her adolescent yearnings—turned them into polemic, not poetry! Poor Peter had ended up as fodder for Margaret Darling's diary, not to mention its unavoidable follow-up, a suite of self-improvement books. Surely I had a chance to do something more literary and enduring with my experience—but what?

"What's happening, baby?" Peter drawled. He must have caught Wolfman Jack's show while squatting on the windowsills of America.

"Peter, so much is happening I don't know where to begin." He raised an eyebrow. "For one thing, I'm married."

There followed the kind of silence that can only be filled by birds and insects and the movement of stars. Then, in a contained outburst, Peter kicked up dirt with his work boots and batted a thick ivy hedge with his fists; this before scrambling up a far branch of The Hanging Tree to settle in and stew.

I seated myself on the chairlike rock and remained on red alert: I didn't want to miss a thing. Even when the sun took me in its gentle arms and joined forces with a swell of aromatic breezes, I resisted napping. I was far too agitated. The very idea of *Peter* pissed off at *me*! But I must have passed out in spite of myself, for I awoke to a sky specked with constellations that were completely unfamiliar. No matter; I was at home among the unfamiliar. I shook my legs and tried to get the blood flowing. I slapped my cheeks and watched as a fine silver dust, perhaps some sort of glitter, purled off. For minutes, I devoted myself to smacking my skin, fascinated by the opalescence I was stirring up.

At last I spotted a figure moving along the horizon; Peter cast a golemlike shadow under the plump, full Moon: his head appeared swollen, his arms two snakes. As he came around in front of me, I could see that he was toting an enormous basket woven out of straw, twigs, and odd bits of cloth. I hopped off the great rock to meet him. "Hey there, handsome," I said, hoping to negotiate a truce.

"Hiya," he said softly, glancing down at his dirt-caked boots.

"Listen, there was no right way to tell you," I said. He continued to study the ground. "I mean, you never showed me the slightest interest and I—"

"Well, I'm showing you something *now*," he said, raising the basket in the air between us. He turned the whole business upside down, and out tumbled scores of buttons. Pearl buttons, tortoiseshell, abalone. Bakelite, brass, and gold. He must have been saving buttons for months, *years* even.

"I brought you all the kisses I've collected over the last couple of days," he announced matter-of-factly. The effect was so beautiful I began tearing up again, the glitter on my cheeks illuminating my surprise. "They're incredible, Peter. I've never seen so many buttons in one place!"

He turned away before I could check out the reflecting pools of his eyes. When finally I was able to find my voice to say "Oh my god, thank you," Peter was nowhere on, or above, the horizon. He had vanished in the strong light of the Moon. I screamed out his name— "Pee-ter!"—and sifted through the soil with my hands. Like fine jewels, the buttons—Peter's kisses—sparkled in the moonlight, offering palpable proof of the beauty in this world. "Peter!" I cried again, the buttons I'd just amassed spilling every which way.

"OH SHIT." I pounded my head and bit my lip and pulled on my hair. It wasn't long after this childish display that I found myself curled up on the shower tiles, Freeman shaking his head and wearing his now-habitual mask of chagrin.

"Sorry, your little friend's not here. Just me. You ended up with me." He turned on the water, made sure it was good and hot, slammed the shower door, and walked out without further comment.

By now, we were beyond arguing the fact of Peter's existence. Sometimes Freeman humored my romantic ravings; other times the mere mention of Peter's name made him tense up. But I never forced him to believe me: I sensed the potential for being deserted was at an all-time high.

I hauled my pregnant self up, peeled off my soaked clothes, and began to scrub every inch of my dazed body. No one had ever given me so many kisses.

VIII

UST seven months after Freeman and I tied the knot (as tightly as we could under the circumstances), our baby girl arrived. All too quickly it dawned on me: it would be my duty to inform her about the ways of women, to help her distinguish between kisses and buttons. It would be my mission and my burden, and, if I could remember how, it would be my pleasure.

As is expected of every Darling female, no matter how book smart, I learned about women's wiles in The Neverland. More precisely, I learned about *fairies*, who seem to have appropriated the worst qualities of my sex and made a go of it. This species lives openly on the island, though it's true the fairy population isn't what it used to be, given the great number of skeptics who prevail nowadays. As one might expect, fairies are comely creatures and whimsical to a fault. But anyone who thinks it's a party to live among fairies should beware: they are fiercely loyal and fiercely jealous, resentful, bitter beings!

God knows, I'm not a woman-hater. But these "fairies" give fairies a bad name. They hitch themselves slavishly to the human male and it's all over—you can count on their jealousy to undo any progress you've made in the relationship department. One can always try to befriend a fairy, reason with a fairy, even fly alongside a fairy (though I don't recommend the last: their baroque loop-de-loops and flamboyant figure eights will have you crashing in no time).

The sprites love to triangulate and manipulate; they thrive on one-upmanship and will expose your ineptitude at every turn. While your indignation at being outmaneuvered will make you long to squish the creatures as if they were gnats, you will be forced to shelve this idea. Before you ever get the opportunity to swat one, a nymph will limp over to your beau and complain about your bullying her. "No way!" you will cry, and she'll answer "Yes, *way!*" or something to that effect, but more literary. Remember: fairies excel at everything, especially proper English.

So, what is at the root of the fairies' taste for rivalry? Quite literally roots—white snakeroot. Fairies nibble at clusters of this brilliant white flower, which everyone knows causes tremors. Curiously it also triggers a rabid suspicion in fairies. An ethnobotanist would have a field day with the chemistry of this plant! Still, let's not discount the fairies' fabled origin as the source of their spitefulness. J. M. Barrie speculated that fairies came to life when the world's first baby's scream matured into a melodious giggle, and this single laugh broke into thousands of funny sound bites that evolved into light-emitting pixies (don't ask me how, the New Physics is quite daunting). The mites soon found themselves whizzing about The Neverland with no natural enemies—until one of the Lost Boys lured a girl from the Mainland onto the premises, and lo, the fireworks began. It is said the boy's patron fairy went ballistic as she watched the human skillfully romancing *her* guy; without a shot fired, the fairy had fallen from number one on his list to a devastating number two. Her humiliation complete and broadcast 'round the island, the fairy's bright twinkle soon dwindled to a dull, diffuse luster, not unlike that of a cheap night-light. In short order, human girls became the fairies' foes—not even the nymphs' contempt for sea dogs could match their antipathy for girls.

Now, competition for a man's attention is an old, sorry story. I know of what I speak: I'm still flitting around Daddy vying for his. And with so few girls finding true love these days, you'd think the fairies would lay off our case. I mean, couldn't we *sympathize* with each other about being dismissed so abruptly or just plain forgotten? With children turning their attention to video games—taking their noses out of books and pointing them at computer screens—the fairies' days are numbered. They need a quorum of believers to survive.

Finding myself in my forties and still adrift, I admit that I feel the same way: if I can encourage you to believe in me, perhaps you'll stick around. If I can convince *me* to believe in me, perhaps I'll finish this story.

My first brush with females of the fairy persuasion occurred on my second day in The Neverland. Just minutes after Peter had given me a tour of the island—a rather hurried, perfunctory expedition that shared much in common with the Universal Studios tour I once took with Daddy ("You got your pirates, you got your Indians, and then there's me!")—I was assaulted by a pest no larger than Great-Nana's cocktail ring. And just as gaudy. It (she?) appeared to be swathed in a silver-sequined bathing suit that was positively blinding in the glossy sunlight. Mummy always said that a little Bob Mackie goes a long way.

"Wendy, meet Cher," Peter announced with swollen pride.

The tacky bug buzzed around me like a Russian MiG. The rhythmic batting of her wings against my cheeks made my skin itch, but her sparkly aura cast a certifiable spell. I was agog in her presence. Surely, fairies come with a load of apocryphal baggage: their ability to guide lost persons is said to rival bloodhounds'; their charitable acts have been written down indelibly in the great children's books; their ethereal attire has inspired countless Halloween costumes and froufrou prom dresses. Indeed, what young girl hasn't prayed for a fairy to help her out of a jam, to lead her out of the woods and into the arms of a happier family? Despite the warning bells that Great-Nana had sounded, I still expected fairies, at their core, to be good-hearted.

I wish I could tell you that I held my own against the sprite. Instead I fell backwards and tumbled over a bottlebrush bush that had no business being there. This made the fairy twitter so hard she practically snorted, a trait unbecoming in any species.

As Nana had predicted, Peter, who happened to be at my side, sided with the *fairy* when it came to enjoying my misfortune; he hooted and whistled as if I were a circus act. The fairy and Peter were in cahoots, too, when the nymph settled on my nose for a prolonged, if agitated, nap. Peter asked me to take this as a compliment but I knew better. Plus, my nose itched. The irritation became so intense I caved in to baser desires: I flailed at the pest with a bottle-brush branch, swatting and screaming, "Off, you little creep!"

In response, she bit me hard on my right nostril and took a fair-sized chomp out of my right earlobe, all the while issuing dainty bell sounds that might have been considered "pretty" under other circumstances.

Ever so helpful, Peter was quick to translate: "Cher says she's sorry—"

"Oh, well. I guess I can accept that," I said, rubbing my nose with my free hand.

"Let me finish," Peter continued, winking at the fairy; she'd taken refuge under a biggish grape leaf.

"Cher says she's sorry, but your nose was simply too tempting— it's constructed so generously and all." My jaw dropped. "She adds: 'I'll wager you could land a B-52 on that thing.' "

"Well," I said, massaging a tender earlobe, "you tell the *bug* that at least I have *character*. I mean, I can't even *see* her nose. How much character could her face possibly have? You can't even make out its features."

The fairy tinkle-screeched, if there is such a sound—like arpeggios of the highest notes on the piano, but worse.

As before, Peter translated: "Cher says, 'Ha!' "

"Ha?"

"She finds your fixation with character priceless," he explained. "She says that character can't hold a candle to beauty. That character never lasts."

"What?!" I shrieked.

"That character never—"

"I *heard* it. I just can't believe it. Where did she grow up? In a cave?"

By now the tinkling was so high-pitched I expected every mutt on the island to come running.

"Yes. The answer is yes," Peter interpreted. "Fairies protect themselves from inclement weather by making their homes in caves, you know."

"Oh, I give up," I huffed, still brandishing the bottlebrush. But there was no use in poking the fairy in the eye when I couldn't *find* an eye. "Peter," I sniveled, "why does she hate me so much?"

"She says you smell of devotion. That, in the vernacular, you *stink*. Remember, Wendybird, she's protective of me and the Boys."

"Well, isn't devotion a *virtue*?"

More insane tinkling; even Peter covered his ears.

"Give it to me straight," I begged as the racket subsided.

"Uh, you're not going to like this. Cher called you a busybody, a meddler, the worst kind of wench. A tall, skinny girl whose fat heart gets in the way of her wings."

"I don't *have* wings," I protested.

"'Precisely,' she says."

Peter took my militant swing at the fairy as a strong exit cue. With impressive foot- and wing-work, the two retreated to another part of the forest, leaving me alone with a sore nose and a confusion about women that, I'm loath to admit, hasn't cleared up to this day.

★ ★

As if fairies weren't role models enough, I also learned about women from mermaids, those alleged sirens of the deep. They're deep, yes, but not *profound* in the way one would hope. They don't read and they're not that self-aware or emotionally complex. It's intuition that keeps them afloat.

Through the years, mermaids have acquired a bad reputation, but they're really not so awful. True, they have a gift for seduction—

but should they have to apologize for their beauty? They *could* try to be a little more conscious of the effect they have. Mermaids—as a rule—give such little thought to their actions, claiming to be instinctive creatures and not responsible for men's myopia. That may well be so, but it doesn't set the stage for healthy relationships. (The sailors don't usually *drown*, you know; they're just too humiliated to report back to their captains. After being lured from their boats and reported dead or AWOL, it's simply too embarrassing for them to show up on deck with those lovesick looks and telltale love bites.)

At the age of thirteen, I was wholly taken with the *idea* of mermaids and even gave some thought to joining their ranks. A pipe dream, yes, but as the whole island was one massive pipe dream, why not?

⬮ I met my first siren while hiking on the coastal cliffs one gray, draggy afternoon. (The islanders' mood was regularly projected onto the canvas of the sky.) The sea creature had the dreamy look of a young Elizabeth Taylor—snow-white complexion, plump lips set in a closed smile, ropes of sable-colored hair pasted to her bosom, eyes like chocolate kisses. Needless to say, she set my heart aflutter. Coiled around a missile-shaped rock that broke rather violently through the waves and ended in a single spire, she spotted me, arched one brow, and simply uttered "Oi." I couldn't tell if this was a mermaidian gurgle, a Cockney hello, or a Yiddish lament. "Oy!" I shouted in return. To this she let out a shriek, slapped her muscular tail so hard it created a wave of its own, and sank back into the indigo water.

I sat down on the cliff and waited for what felt like an hour before the water parted again. Just when I questioned the integrity of my vision, up shot the raven-tressed girl. She was in the company of two other sea creatures: a flat-chested waif with blond, Twiggy-short hair and a voluptuous, brown-skinned siren whose spiral locks were woven into what we now call cornrows, dozens of them, tied at the ends with wisps of seaweed. I stared openly at her breasts. My eyes then traveled nervously from one mermaid to another—studying, gawking, ogling. I was so taken with the sirens that I forgot to compare myself unfavorably to them! So transfixed was I, the impulse to lower myself into the water became all-powerful and, after negotiating the steep path, I slipped into the opaque liquid to join them.

Dog-paddling over to the fish-women, my unsexy nightgown stuck to my skin like an unwanted shadow and my ponytail shook loose until the sopping strands plastered themselves to the little buds that were my breasts, not unlike the tresses on the dusky-haired beauty! I was swimming among the mermaids now, splashing and blowing bubbles and feeling somewhat overheated, despite the gelid water. I wasn't certain whether I'd been accepted into their sorority or if they were merely tolerating me, but as far as initiations go, I couldn't imagine one more sensuous—or troubling. For immediately after the mermaids convinced me of their friendship, they deserted me to toy with a sailor. He'd drifted into the lagoon in a sad, leaky boat, sloshed in more ways than one and unaware that his actions would lead to an erotic dead-end. No sooner had he jumped from the boat than the women surrounded him and began cooing *ooka-ooka, ooka-ooka*. In concert they nipped at his flushed cheeks and pawed at his wind-cracked mouth. I couldn't see what was transpiring underwater, though his sighs suggested a few epiphanies were in progress. Each time I descended into the murk, I could make out only a tangle of shadows.

Now ribbons of torn clothing floated desultorily to the surface. Two knee-high boots bobbed aimlessly on my left. Finally, it seems, the fellow had had enough, for his lusty laughter dissipated into grunts of exhaustion and only the smallest hint of pleasure remained on his lips. Frankly, his despair was palpable.

I decided against intervening—at the time I had little experience in the ways of men and women, let alone men and *mermaids*. Instead I offered a meek hello. Assuming I was another sea creature come to sample him, the sailor swam to his boat like a man pursued by the Devil. When I turned back 'round, the three mermaids were gone, foamy swells and pearly clusters of bubbles sputtering in their wake.

So what did I learn from all this? That women are bad, or *mad*? That sensuousness hurts others? God, no. I learned that women tend to overwhelm men; men simply can't handle our presence, it is that rich. I learned that we should stand back a few feet to let men breathe. Of course we can't. It is our nature to be close, to dig in, to nestle in the arms of another. We crave and deserve nearness, contact. "Touch me and I'm yours," we say. "I give myself to you." And this is a *good* thing. It is a good thing to devote ourselves so fully, a spiritual thing if you will. Too bad it comes off as clingy. Too bad it makes monsters out of us.

It would be years before my daughter bothered her pretty head about the conduct of women and men; fourteen years, in fact, before I had the temerity to utter Peter's name in her company. One could say I was afraid of my own shadow, to lose the one thing that had roused me from my long-held dream: a person who really needed me. Berry ushered in an era of glorious selflessness, a reprieve from my preoccupation with abandonment, a chance to pay attention to worldly matters. She was better than any story I could have made up. Freeman, too, adored her, though there was a lot of white noise in his head for his daughter to compete with.

In the beginning, the Darling-Ullmans were a comic, motley crew: a father with no life experience to speak of, a mother with little experience outside her books and delusions, and a prescient child who had her whole life spread out in front of her like a magic carpet.

It took all of ten minutes to discover that Berry was unlike the other Darlings. After she wriggled out of me in record slow time—Mummy cheering me on with "You'll kill the munchkin with indecision if you don't push harder!"—Berry didn't make a peep. The whole scene at the hospital was downright eerie. Even as the doctor patted her on the behind, Berry remained mum. It was only when he tripped over his own valise and took a spill that Berry acknowledged our presence. She volunteered a gummy grin and let go with an almost depraved chuckle. "Nice kid," the doctor said before he limped off to attend to a badly skinned knee.

Berry turned out to be a regular tomboy. The least dreamy of all the Darlings, she was action personified, forever tree-climbing, roof-climbing, pinning down horrid little boys on the grass. And did I mention the *mouth* on that child? I don't know where Berry picked up the words she knew.

She was stocky with small, defined muscles and had a habit of swaggering down the street like a bantamweight boxer. Unlike the rest of us, she didn't freckle: she wasn't cursed with our chalky, quick-to-burn complexion. Neither were her locks strawberry-blonde, straw-blonde, or claret—there was not a hint of red in her hair. On the contrary, Berry came into this world with creamy olive skin and a dense, chestnut mane; she appeared somber instead of lighthearted, Gothic instead of lyrical. Her emotions flickered not on the surface, but burned deep in a well. We were surprised by her severity—surprised is not the word, we were grateful. Our daughter was a wake-up call, her tough-guy stance a breath of fresh air, her moodiness just the tonic for our fantasy-centered lives.

Berry wasted no time in establishing her turf. By the time she'd turned one, she was in the throes of the "terrible twos," scratching and biting like a feral cat, and yet conversant in the alphabet and the names of animals. At two, she could write her own name, to which she added teeth and whiskers. She "mellowed" at the age of three, at once dropping the fierce feline act and adopting the persona of a skittish mouse. We let her play this out until she tired of eating cheese and scurrying through holes in the cardboard wall we erected for her.

In late Fall of that year, Berry began crossing the street to Tilden Park, where she quickly learned about snakes and newts and salamanders. She also learned that acting human could be interesting, even lucrative. We showered her with stuffed animals and gave her a tour of the Oakland Zoo, where she could see firsthand how animals were treated by humans. When Berry was four, we finagled our way into a private showing of Walt Disney's *Sleeping Beauty* and exposed her to those "benevolent" fairies Flora, Fauna, and Merryweather (though I was a bit anxious about perpetuating certain falsehoods about "imaginary creatures"). We even took her on her first airplane ride—in a Learjet with Daddy at the helm—to give her a sense of the Big Picture.

By the age of five, Berry had logged a lifetime's worth of sensory experience: she loved rolling in the earth, covering every brown inch of her skin in soil. A born guttersnipe, she pocketed stones and shiny trash that she found curbside, displaying her finds triumphantly each evening at the dinner table. She ate flowers. She perked up at the sound of horns and sirens (no doubt a product of her father's aural fixation), and was elated on the most miserable, wet days when the hills were socked in with gloom. She considered moths and aphids her "pets" and had an inexplicable fondness for bees, which she stuffed live in her overall pockets and then forgot for a spell. Later in the day, she would fumble in her pockets for a tissue and end up getting stung. But she never complained: the pain was her reward for forgetting, she said.

Yes, Berry was an odd girl. But oddness was practically encouraged in mid-eighties Berkeley, and my daughter soon fell in with a formidable clique of oddball children. Many of the kids were older than she and wilder. Many of them had tried pot or had been subjected to therapy before they could read. Some of them wore dreadlocks; others swore like pirates. A few were pesky thieves and none seemed happy; at least I rarely saw them smile. But Berry found their darkness comforting and I couldn't blame her: by the time she started school, her father's music had gone "loony tunes" (à la Spike Jones), and her mother's fairy stories had become treacly, frivolous affairs. Berry turned out to be the rare child who eschewed sugar on her bran flakes and wrinkled her nose at chocolate bars. In her opinion, sucking on lemons was "rilly cool" and pickles were the finest dish on the menu. She even rooted for the villains in cartoons. (A Cruella DeVille poster became a staple on her bedroom wall, which was painted a beastly shade of green.) As much as I had wanted a normal life for my daughter, I had to admit that Berry would never make prom queen or even first runner-up. She was destined for graver things.

LOOKING back on our early years as a family, it was Berry, not me, who abetted Freeman in his quest to come up with sounds. Freeman and his young collaborator used Saturday mornings as a kind of mad-scientist laboratory, setting up shop in front of the television with a collection of high-end electronic gear. Together they embarked on a weekly ritual of making a ridiculous amount of noise. First, Berry would spin the TV dial until she landed on a cartoon series that the six-year-old didn't find "dumb." Then she'd cry, "U-ree-ka, I found it!" To this, Freeman would perform a "hallelujah" jig in front of the TV screen until Berry called "Places," an announcement to which Freeman would respond by racing to his equipment and Berry to the remote control, where she'd lower the volume until you could barely make out the cartoon voices and background music. Then the two would settle in for hours, creating sound effects for a rich assortment of humans, aliens, and beasts; animate and inanimate objects; actions, gestures, movements; meteorological and geological events; explosions and implosions. I was impressed. Freeman had a real gift for coming up with the appropriate clangs and plops and gassy projectile sounds, which Berry would embroider with her kiddie hiccups, raspberries, and ooga-oogas. The sound he conceived to accompany the Roadrunner as he raced off cliffs (only to flatten into a pancake on the hard earth) was unparalleled to my ears.

Devoted to pushing the envelope until it could hardly bear more pressure, Freeman began to spend more time refining his cartoon sounds than writing "serious" music. (After seven years of living with me he'd given up completely on looking for work, claiming that his skills were "too specialized for the market." Besides, the Ullmans wouldn't let their son starve—though they weren't as sanguine about Berry and me, whom, they felt, siphoned off energy from his genius.)

Like most geniuses, Freeman insisted on one hundred percent innovation, generating sounds that were "profoundly new." With his Mellotron and Moog synthesizer and a medley of effects pedals, he was able to produce the coolest space-alien bleeps and the most stirring elephant stampedes. Over the months, he began to record his sound effects for what he christened the Ullman Library of Din, and the tapes quickly became fodder for musician gatherings around Berkeley. At one particularly lifeless party where the guests listened sleepily to Esquivel records, Freeman produced a tape he'd made to accompany an old *Rocky and Bullwinkle* cartoon. Not only did it energize the party, it motivated a shaggy, bearded guy from Fantasy Studios to approach him on the couch to talk shop. When Freeman left the party, circa 2 A.M., he was drunk on praise and a couple of beers, and the lightheaded recipient of an honest-to-god job as a sound engineer.

WHILE her father was in the studio he had created in the garage, wrestling with his first assignment (he had only the weekend to come up with credible sounds for a robot spider on a children's record), Berry sat at her usual post in front of the TV watching the parade of Saturday morning cartoons. I disapproved, but I was *working*.

Berry ran into the kitchen, where I was agonizing over a story about two weasels who attend charm school. "Mu-Mu," she cried, "listen!" She opened her mauve O of a mouth and out came a torrent of madcap characters: a haughty British queen, a big-hearted Brooklyn gangster, an adenoidal astronaut.

"My," I said, utterly floored.

Once again she ran through a repertoire of voices. Her lisping bunnies and smart-ass parrots were spookily on target, her archvillains downright scary.

"Go show Daddy," I urged. But Berry remained willfully in place, fingering her swarm of curls. "Honey," I assured her with a pat on the head, "your father *needs* to hear this."

She gave me a hangdog look, so I scooted her, both hands nudging that diminutive tush, into the garage. We found Freeman at his mixing board enmeshed in a snarl of patch cables, tapping his bare feet and whistling a grating rendition of "The Love Boat."

"Go on," I coaxed her.

Berry took two steps forward, swinging her ropy arms at her sides. "D-Daddy," she stammered. But her father barely lifted his head, which was encased in top-of-the-line Sennheiser headphones. After five minutes of quiet observation, Berry mounted a Bose speaker, then scaled her way up Freeman's back. She pried off the headphones and hollered "Boo!" into his right ear.

Now she tried out her best stuff on him: a husky-voiced femme fatale; a pip-squeak weight lifter. Anything to get a rise. Freeman listened to his daughter with glassy, faraway eyes. At one point he smiled and nodded before being consumed by what could only be his own inner music. This served to increase Berry's volume—the more she was ignored the more proficient she became, trotting out chatty cows, caustic crows, wily wolves. And for her pièce de résistance, she aped the president, Ronald Reagan.

After this showstopping performance, Freeman pried Berry off his back as if to say "your time's up." Then, without warning, he scooped her up in his arms and gave her a whirl. "That's my girl!" he sang before setting her down on an amplifier as though she were a cup of coffee, and returning to his mixer. "Now tell me," he instructed, "what do ya think of this cool spider sound."

"S-spiders don't make s-sounds," Berry replied. Hopping off the amp, she sprinted through the garage and back into the house, a rattlesnake hiss sputtering from her lips. Freeman glanced up at me, standing erect at the door.

"Spiders don't make sounds," I said, echoing my daughter, and returned to work on my weasels.

★ ★

UNLIKE a lot of girls her age, Berry got her rebellious rocks off. She had come into this world with a surplus of aggression that didn't sit well with society's notion of sweet young things. I was certain that this negativity hadn't come from *me* and wondered if Mummy's unresolved feelings for Daddy—or her own mother—had skipped a generation. Fortunately, my daughter's uncanny ability to moo and howl and squawk and bleat, all in the name of creating a character, allowed her to let out a great deal of hostility without hurting anyone, including herself. Thus, she ended up being the first Darling to enter adolescence without leaving a host of mental health professionals in her wake.

Throughout the run of her childhood Berry was never demonstrably happy, but she didn't seem to be looking for good times. Freeman and I took her grimness as a reflection of our leftist politics and wore her creativity as a badge for our postmodern parenting. We were especially fond of Berry's need to personally break the sound barrier.

The night she turned eleven, the neighbors reported Berry to the police—she was hollering "Killers!" at the top of her lungs, straddling the side fence and laying into it with her cowboy boots. She seemed to be screaming at no one—I hoped it wasn't us.

I ran outside to check on her; the howling had become cadenced and strangely musical. Her concentration thrown off, Berry stopped mid-scream and blinked at me. "Howdy," she said hoarsely.

"Berry, what's wrong?" I asked.

"Name's not Berry," she said.

"All right," I allowed.

"The name's Shiva, Destroyer of Worlds."

"Okay, Miss Destroyer. What's this all about?"

"We saw a movie in school today," Berry reported. "About that nuclear bomb guy."

"Bomb guy? You mean, J. Robert Oppenheimer?"

"Exactomundo!" she cried, getting worked up again. "Oppenheimer the Terminator. You see, when they tested his bomb and he realized all this shit was gonna rain down on innocent people—he said, *actually* said, *Now I am become Shiva.* See, he *knew* he was a murderer."

"Uh-huh." I nodded thoughtfully, as if I understood anything about the mind-set of preteen girls. "And how did that make you feel?" I asked therapeutically.

"What?" she barked.

"And that made you feel all what?" I repeated softly.

"Mu-Mu." She paused dramatically. "Sometimes you have too much energy."

"Me? You mean me?"

"I mean people. People explode. People have explosives inside them. Like dynamite and plutonium. So much of this stuff, they need to kill something. But they don't. But they still feel guilty about wanting to. They feel ashamed, like murderers." She tucked her head into the crook of her elbow and let her forearm hang loosely.

"Berry. I mean, Shiva." She smiled. "Do *you* feel like killing stuff? Is that what this is about?" I climbed up on the fence to join her, and scanned the flat, dirty sky.

She kicked the heel of her boot into the fence and we both rocked in place. "Sometimes I feel like a bomb, that's all I'm saying. You don't have to be scared or anything. Sometimes I have to go off, too."

Freeman wandered out the front door to join us, a Sony tape recorder slung over one shoulder. Perhaps he believed that documenting sound actually solved problems.

"Sorry, Dad. Show's over," Berry said, hopping off the fence. She took a bow, but her pointed little gesture was interrupted by a squad car pulling up to the curb. We all watched as a chunky police-woman got out and marched up our driveway. She was puffing heavily and looking deadly serious, her nightstick bobbing with each lumbering step.

"Hey, folks. I'm Officer America Fuentes." Freeman and I each shook her large gloved hand. "We have a report of a young woman at this address wailing awfully loud for this time of night—thought there might be trouble. Could that young woman be you, Miss?" She got down on one knee to look Berry in the eye.

"Yes it was," Berry answered, amused by all the formality. "But Officer—I wasn't wailing. I was *keening*. There's a difference."

"Keening," the policewoman scribbled in her log. Berry raised her hand like she was still in class. "Yes?" the officer said.

"So what time of night is best for such activity?" The officer cocked her head, cleared her throat. "You said I was too loud for this time of night," Berry said.

America Fuentes grinned and squinched her earth-brown eyes. She released a sigh that seemed to make her smaller, and made another entry in her logbook. "Name, please?" She tossed Berry an inscrutable look. "Name?" she repeated.

"Shiva Darling," Berry said, and ran off to the house. She keened one last time as a parting shot.

Freeman and I finished up with the officer, promising to be better parents or at least more vigilant ones. She encouraged us to do our best, then raced off to respond to an altercation at a downtown yoga studio. Back in the house we found Berry/Shiva sprawled on her bed, remote and incurious as she flipped through a stack of comic books she had received for her birthday. An hour later, I knocked on her bedroom door. There was no response. I pressed the door open to find her doodling pictures of atomic bombs; a riot of psychedelic pastels lit up her notebook pages.

I telephoned Mother. I wasn't sure if I wanted her advice, but her insights were always fanatically different from my own, and besides, she had had experience raising me—that had to count for something.

I told her about the scary wailing and kicking, the talk of murderers. "Why is Berry doing this?" I half whispered into the receiver.

"That bitter pill!" Mother said gaily. "She does sound a little wonky. Are you *sure* she's your real daughter?"

"What are you implying, Mother?"

"Well, Berry doesn't really look like any of us." More ill-timed laughter on her part.

"You're talking about your own granddaughter, Mummy."

"Wendy, this is elemental stuff. Are you even paying attention?"

"What are you getting at?" I said.

"You *know*," Mother said, "that you can only suppress the shadow for so long before it comes home to roost. You know that,

Wends. And when it returns, more fortified and all-knowing, it's going to bite you in the bum!"

"Uh, what do you mean, *for so long?*" I asked.

"For so many goddamned generations. You can't just sweep things under the rug without accumulating dust mice, dear."

"But *I've* nothing to hide, nothing I've swept under. I express *everything.*"

"I seriously doubt that. But even so, this isn't all about you. You've a very shallow idea of history."

"Do you mean this is about *you,* Mummy? Is Berry expressing some of your leftovers?"

"Darling, I may be a narcissist, but I'm afraid I can't take all the blame. Berry's behavior could just be the usual, random hostility of adolescents. Or her venting may very well be the culmination of generations of repressed anger—anger that's never been sorted out from mother to daughter. We're talking karmic predestination, cellular inheritance. We're also talking abandonment on a cosmic plane!"

"Abandonment?" I said, shaken by her words. "I'm not your darling," I told her and hung up.

I'D pretty much expected my daughter to serve as my literary muse, assumed she would inspire in me a flotilla of children's books—each one more daring than the next. Sad to say, then, that she found my fables "spastic." It wasn't my words that offended her—words were her friends—it was the cute, furry creatures that she couldn't stand. Whenever I explained that, in the overmined tradition of Aesop, these animals were stand-ins for real people, she forced the issue: "If you mean *people,* Mu-Mu, then why don't you say *people?*"

It was hard to admit that my daughter's sensibilities ran darker than my own, but there it was: my stories were l-i-t-e in her eyes. Still, I reasoned, not every child can handle real, live humans in their fables—humans who act oafish, indifferent, or cruel. So it was that

I'd regularly regret using Berry as my audience. Those times when I could screw up the courage to read a few pages to her, she would listen politely and then feign a hunger for French fries so great that it could only be quelled by a trip to McDonald's. Once inside the Golden Arches, she relished collecting those plastic glasses with pictures of *famous* animals on them. At such times I was a saint.

The afternoon before the publication party for my newest collection of fables, *Weasels Are Doing It for Themselves,* I alighted on one of two rocking chairs in the living room, and teetered on its edge as what could only be a panic attack set its teeth in me. Its timing could not have been worse. My breathing came shallow and arrhythmic, and my thoughts (*my animals are wimps, my animals are fakes,* I'm *fake)* veered recklessly into the oncoming traffic of my mind. A head-on collision, I hoped, would put me out of commission; I could cancel the reading and take to bed.

A cancellation wasn't to be. Upon discovering her mother unhinged like the Tasmanian Devil, twelve-year-old Berry walked over and stabilized the chair. "Mu-Mu!" she cried, fanning her stocky body across my lap. "Enough."

So startled was I at this intervention that I immediately ceased having crazy thoughts. Berry threw her arms around my neck and, mimicking her father, asked if I'd like my back scratched by "one of the best in the business."

"Why not," I agreed, breath still sporadic.

With stubby, soil-filled nails, Berry began to doodle all manner of shapes on my back, asking me to guess each tickling configuration. Weasel? Hedgehog? Gerbil? I wondered where she got the courage to draw the very creatures she hated reading about in my books.

"Thanks, honeydew," I said at last, motioning for her to stop. "Now I've got a zoo of beasties on my back."

"Your skin's all red and gross," she said dully, then raced towards the doors to the backyard deck.

"Wait!" I shouted.

Berry whipped around. "What now, Mu-Mu?"

"Come here," I said, gesturing with both hands. "It would be really good for your mother to talk to you before she reads in public tonight. I'd like your blessing before I show this stuff to the world, you know?"

Berry hesitated, her corkscrews rising and falling in the heated current that swept through the room. Then she turned her back on me and faced the plateglass: it was one of those remarkable days when you can see clear to Alcatraz Island: hot and dry and shimmering with gold. I was in competition with the weather, it seemed.

"Please," I asked more forcefully. Berry obliged me this time, inching her way over as if hobbled by foot pain. Her tiny pillow of a butt settled on the rocking chair next to mine.

"Dearest creature," I said and bit my lips. "If it helps any, I'm not going to read to you."

"Good," she said with a chilling conviction, " 'cause I'm never going to like it." Spellbound by the sunlight as it streamed through the glass, she regarded the sailboats rounding the bay, the eggshell-blue sky.

Why a child would boost her mother's esteem only to shatter it minutes later was a mystery I preferred to leave alone. Who knew what poison lurked in those brambles? Still, I couldn't help compounding the hurt: "Never? You mean, *really* never?"

"Yep." She joggled her chestnut curls.

"Oh, I don't know. Someday you'll be curious about my stories. I swear it." I reached over and tickled her tawny belly.

Berry squealed, and for the moment I was in the presence of a regular little girl. Then she slapped my hands and stood up. "Never," she said softly but coldly, and marched out on the deck. I watched through the glass as she ripped the leaves off a eucalyptus branch and tossed them in the air. The leaves rained down on her head as if fulfilling some biblical prophecy.

This "never" business undid me. For the next hour or so I remained glued to the chair, paralyzed with doubt. My stomach juices roiled, my head throbbed. As absolutes go, *never* was supposed to be a *good* thing. The Neverland, also known as Never-

Never Land, had always smacked of positiveness; there, positivism, a doctrine that claims sensory perception is the only way we can know the world, was the law. *Never-never* also suggested *in no way,* as in "In no way should you fear," or *unprecedented,* as in "You've never seen the likes of this!" *Never* was a comfort word: "Never shall you go wanting, be sick, grow old."

How could I have missed the obvious, that *never-never* was a double negative, that it could conceivably mean "You will never find your way home." That "You will never grow up" was a *bad* thing? To me, *never* had always been the highest rating, on par with *incomparable, ideal, perfect.* The Neverland, an ideal that lived on in my mind if no longer in practice, was a place where you were never alone, never hungry or without hope, and most certainly, never crazy.

Great-Nana's grandfather clock, newly imported from England, struck the hour of four, and I was roused from a vicious cycle of half dreaming, half obsessing. To be candid, I could hardly tell the difference. I pulled my hands through my hair: I still had three hours before the reading during which to gather my thoughts and my composure.

As I shook off the lethargy that had seized my legs, Berry strolled in, arms full of plant life, her hands dusted gray with earth. She'd snapped off the heads of dandelions and was now cradling just the stalks. There was really nothing to say.

"I'm coming tonight," she announced.

"Oh, really? I'd rather that you . . ." I stopped short and went to my bedroom. Berry followed me into the room. "Please wash your hands if you're going to grace me with your presence," I told her.

Without a word, she stuffed her crappy bouquet into a tall, waterless vase on my dresser and stomped out. The air circling in her wake was shot with static. I threw off my bathrobe and collapsed into a summery frock, its flowers belying a certain lack of blood in me. Studying the face in the dressing-table mirror, I saw a woman who looked a little too shocked by life, a woman who had no business raising a child.

———

THE night-sky was gorged with stars. By the same token Gaia Books was flush with strangers; I recognized a few friends of Mummy's in the Right Livelihood and Enneagram sections, but that was all. I steadied myself against a bookcase, thrown by the crunch of people milling about. I'd isolated myself for so long and so successfully that the only attendees I knew were those people I met on my rounds: denizens of the coffeehouses where I occasionally worked on my laptop, the postal clerks who sent off my manuscripts. As I made a mental note to nurture a few relationships *outside* the home, Mummy Dearest barreled through the doorway with Freeman and Berry swinging on either of her arms; she was wearing two shiny buttons—WOMYN TAKE BACK THE NIGHT and U.S. OUT OF MY UTERUS—on a dress woven out of hemp. It looked indestructible. Mummy brushed each of my cheeks, not really kissing them. "Oh-my-goddess!" she cried, flinging her attention on me like a shawl. I recoiled into a shelf of books on Forgiveness.

"Hi, Mummy. Hi, Freeman. Hello, Berry," I said mechanically. "Let's all sit down," I suggested, deflecting the fuss.

"Tish tosh!" Mother said. "You've been sitting all day. Now is the time to stand up for your ideas!"

"Mother," I whispered. "Please don't raise my consciousness any higher than it is." She was about to blurt out perhaps another slogan when she saw my face, corrupted by pain, and parked herself in a front-row chair. Berry trailed off to the Ecology aisle, where, one hoped, she could edify herself with a few volumes not penned by relatives. Freeman, set loose to roam, migrated to the Ambient Music bin, where he was captivated by a CD featuring the sounds of whales in labor.

After five minutes of accelerated bustle, somebody clanged a gong and a turbaned black woman spoke commandingly into the mike at the far end of the store: "All right, people, let's get down to business. It's my pleasure to introduce Wendy Darling, the author of *Ferrets Are Free, Lally and the Blue Hedgehog,* and *The World According to Chloé the Cat.* She's just published a collection of contemporary fables that is truly divine—a divination of the truth in a way we're unaccustomed to hearing it. Via *animals,* that is. Well, I guess there *are* other authors who use animals as a way in, but trust me, her work is completely original." I smiled weakly at the audience and flooded with the same fear that had immobilized me all afternoon. "Let's welcome Wendy Darling to our house, tonight," the turbaned woman said. The ringing applause gave me a jolt, and I steeled myself for the task at hand.

"Weasels," I said definitively into the microphone. Then I cleared my throat and began again: "*Weasels Are Doing It for Themselves.* A silly title, to be sure, but one that both empowers us (well, if we were *weasels*) and makes fun of empowerment. Now, why would we want to make fun of empowerment?" Here Mother raised her hand, but I shook my head no. "I'll take questions at the end, okay?" The whole room nodded in agreement. "I make fun because what kind of a world is this where we aren't *naturally* empowered, where we have to grab at power?" A woman began to cough spasmodically. "So, I asked myself, what is the essence of the weasel? Mania. Enthusiasm. Eccentricity." Freeman turned his attention to the ceiling fan, which was making a lovely whirring sound. "I wrote this book of interlaced stories to celebrate mania, enthusiasm, idiosyncrasy, if you will. If you won't, then it's just a few stories! Really, I am interested in entertaining you above all else. The politics come second or even third." Here, I glanced at Mother, who was shaking her head either in a rare instance of concurrence or else ruing the moment. And then I spotted Berry in the last row making what could only be a weaselly face. A little misty-eyed, I nodded in her direction and cracked open the binding of my crisp new book. "How the Weasel Got Its Spots," I read.

IX

T's no secret that my daughter's disappointments out-paced even my own. So it was that Berry began the seventh grade with a chip on her shoulder. She refused to wear dresses, opting for camouflage pants and tops that didn't blend in with any environment. She shaved her leg hair in distinct rows, as if cultivating crops. The only makeup she applied was a smear of kohl to her (already spooky) eyes. My baby looked like a raccoon with striped legs. Conveniently the Goths were still in fashion, which might have been a consolation, but most of *those* kids steered clear of Berry. It wasn't style that was responsible for her look: her resistance ran deep, erupting on the surface in weird little outfits.

During spring break, I decided to force Great-Nana upon Berry. Perhaps things would end up just the reverse, with Berry preying on her great-great-grandmother, whom she referred to as *Triple-Nana* or, more simply, *Triple*. Remarkably, Great-Nana was still hanging in there at the age of 95, though she'd been slowed down consider-ably. After an unexplained fall from atop her chest of drawers, whereby she'd suffered whole-body bruises, she'd been moved by Daddy to All-Saints Sanitarium just outside of London, where the potty elders of her generation held court.

A Dr. Deepak Wolfe, zealous disciple of R. D. Laing, was in charge of the premises. True to Laing's doctrine, Wolfe had no problem with the denizens of All-Saints acting out their wishes, fears, and fates within the clinic's vast grounds. In fact he appeared to encourage chaos. Alas, it happened that, after so many years of being free to "do your own thing," the patients had pretty much expelled their inner demons, and now Wolfe missed observing these impulses. The current populace, he'd complained to me over the phone, was a rather stable lot, with only a few eccentricities leaking out from time to time—quirks that Wolfe literally applauded. He had worn his hands out clapping for Great-Nana, who upheld a daily regimen of attempting to fly off the second-floor balcony. Whenever the nurses grumbled about the dangers of such whims, Dr. Wolfe pointed out the soft landing of grasses below. As if a few green blades could save a nonagenarian's life. Ever childlike, Great-Nana still had the capacity to think lovely thoughts, and I didn't understand why she never achieved liftoff. Nevertheless, I was grateful for her failures.

So, why bring Berry into a climate of old folks' fading manias? I wondered if she might find kinship here, a community wherein differences were more than tolerated—they were celebrated. I also hoped to scare the living daylights out of her, to stun her into kindness.

For our British Airways flight to London, Berry and I were bumped up to first class. While I hardly ever dropped Daddy's name in the course of daily life, I wasn't above cashing in on the Braverman name—all Bravermans were considered airline royalty. And though Brave Hearts had fallen recently on hard times— Daddy desperately needed a financial partner to keep the fleet aloft—its legend appeared secure. Most British pilots had grown up singing the snappy Brave Hearts jingle; based on "Heart" from *Damn Yankees*, the jingle stuck in the craw of even the most sentimentally challenged fliers:

> *We've got heart,*
> *Miles and miles and miles of heart.*
> *When you're flying high in the air*
> *Brave Hearts is there from the start.*
> *For us, flying's an art!*

You'd think, after all these years, that Berry and I would be immune to the jingle's charms. Not so. After we boarded the plane and settled in to our spacious seats—bottles of Evian and fresh-baked brownies at our disposal—the flight attendants gathered in the aisle and hovered over us wearing sappy grins. A male steward "just happened to have" a harmonica in the pocket of his pressed khakis, and he sounded an introductory note: *Hr-rum!* The crew ambushed us with two rounds of the jingle, in three-part harmony no less. When they arrived at the fourth line, they hastily substituted whistling for the name of their competitor. Berry and I broke out in cheers; we loved a good prank.

The remainder of the flight was uneventful: Berry buried her head in Stephen King's *Carrie*, while I busied myself with worrying, a very poor use of the imagination. Shaking off my fears, it seems, was becoming a full-time job. For the bulk of the trip, I tormented myself by fantasizing about being trapped in a fireball of jet fuel and steel, plunging headlong from the sky. I worried about Berry's rickety self-esteem; I fretted about the state of my marriage; I dreaded seeing Great-Nana in a deteriorated state. As for Mummy and Daddy, they were evergreen presences in the worry province of my mind. I was a Hall of Famer myself.

The jet touched down with an emphatic thud. The thud being prophetic at best, I grabbed my daughter's hand and wrung it with love. She shook me off, blowing me a patronizing kiss.

"To Granny's, to Granny's," I sang poorly but with a lilt. Berry pulled a sour face. She hated it when I lifted idioms from children's books. "Talk like an adult," she ordered, "or don't talk." Berry was a wounding little brat, but I couldn't help adoring her. I never blamed her for the hurt she caused; it was easier to dump my frustration on my own mother, who could take it.

We took a minicar from Heathrow directly to the sanitarium. Why we didn't freshen up at the hotel first is a mystery. Perhaps we couldn't wait to get a dose of Great-Nana's fabulousness—no doubt we were in serious need. Just in case it was Nana whose spirits needed brightening, I wore a loden-green tweed suit of forties vintage, with bright emerald tights and olive-suede desert boots, while Berry's hairy legs were partially cloaked in black fishnet stockings, her feet clad in gladiator sandals. My daughter's bantam figure was sheathed in her all-purpose uniform, the extra-large tee. This one bore the message: FREEDOM'S JUST ANOTHER WORD FOR NOTHING LEFT TO LOSE. Berry's look was completed by a white, boiled-wool coat on which she'd sprayed zebra stripes. We both wore berets encrusted with a medley of buttons. Subtle we were not.

Dr. Deepak Wolfe met us at the clinic's front gate, a wrought-iron affair that was flung open in a cavalier fashion, as if tempting the patients to escape. Like his name, Wolfe was a heady blend of East Indian dark good looks and British idiosyncrasy. In each hand he held a saucer on which a teacup of Earl Grey wobbled.

"Come," Wolfe said. Taking our teas, we followed him down a path of flagstone steps, banked on each side by a meticulously mowed lawn of inspiring dimensions.

"This is just like in the movies!" I whispered to Berry.

"This *is* the movies!" Wolfe enthused.

Berry and I were directed to sit on a rock-hard bench in the lobby, our teacups set before us on a standing tea tray with the initials A.S.S. inlaid in mother of pearl. *All-Saints Sanitarium.* Berry stifled a hiccup of a giggle, while I uttered a staccato "Ha!" Dr. Wolfe sat opposite the tray on a punishing high-back chair. "Nothing is padded here," he explained. "We wouldn't want to make our guests feel like they were problems."

"Problems?" Berry echoed.

"You know, off their trolleys."

Berry stared straight ahead, stone-faced.

"Honey," I said, "he's on our side." Then to Wolfe: "My daughter identifies with the nutcases."

"Bully for her." Wolfe clapped good-naturedly, a dot of perspiration on his brow.

"Doctor Wolfe," I began again.

"Call me Deep."

"Sorry?"

"Deep, for Deepak. Not to be confused with you-know-who."

"Oh-ho!" I stammered. He folded his linen napkin into a tiny turban which he propped on his head. "You mean you're *not* a guru?" I teased, sounding crushed.

"Not if you ask my wife. She thinks of me as one of the guests."

"Guests?" I repeated.

"Our preferred term for *patients*," Wolfe explained, removing the napkin. "Has the ring of a grand hotel to it."

I took a generous gulp of the Earl Grey and managed to dribble it down my chin and into a bra cup. Wolfe patted my chest with a linen napkin from the tray, and I flushed with a faint sexual heat. Dr. Wolfe was a smallish man, almost jockeylike, with a huge disproportionate head that sat upon hunched, narrow shoulders. His hazel eyes had the boiling intensity of Ben Kingsley's and his glasses fogged up when he got excited, which appeared to be most of the time. The mouse-brown gabardine suit he wore was dated, loose-fitting; it washed over him like a drab wave. I found Wolfe's bagginess attractive, save for his shoes. I'd never been fond of those Birkenstocks that progressive shrinks find so unassuming. And it was winter, for God's sake.

"Doc-tor Wolfe," I said, with greater definition.

"Deep," he corrected.

"May we see her now, *Deep*? May we see Berry's great-great-grandmother?" I stood up, tried to show a little backbone.

"No," Wolfe said tersely.

"No?"

"That was a *joke*. A very unfunny one," he added to himself.

During this exchange Berry had pulled a red Magic Marker from her army knapsack, and set about drawing a scary monster on her tea napkin.

"Brilliant," Wolfe whispered, now fingering the artwork. "What have we here, a princess?"

"Hardly," she upbraided him. "It's a picture of my inner brainworks."

"As opposed to your outer brainworks, I suppose? Perhaps you're right, Berry, but I highly doubt it."

"What?" she snapped, and threw him a dirty look.

"Well, I believe your psyche might look something more like this." Wolfe produced a felt-tipped pen from his roomy jacket and began marking up his own napkin. With broad strokes he sketched a cookie-cutter princess, one begowned and bejeweled with stiltlike high heels and a conical hat. Berry commented by pointing a finger at her mouth. Undeterred, Wolfe dipped the napkin in his tea; we all watched the ink bloat, the lines fatten. The end effect was wonderful, an abstract mess of a princess.

Wolfe wrung out the napkin and began stuffing the damp thing in his jacket pocket. Then he turned to Berry and said: "Sorry, would you like it?"

A budding smile parted her lips. "It's me, totally," she told him, and accepted the cloth, spreading it out on her lap to admire it.

After this exercise in bonding, Berry and I got our way. Wolfe escorted us to Great-Nana's "flat," really a room off a poorly lit, mile-long hallway in a mansion that must have been grand in its youth, even stately in its adolescence. Today it was merely substantial. As Wolfe rapped lightly on Great-Nana's door, Berry and I sucked in our breath. We were prepared for anything—anything but her demise.

"Enter at your own risk!" Great-Nana cackled, and we exhaled twin sighs of relief. The two of us stuttered into an oxygen-deprived chamber with its shades drawn, its contents littered in every direction. Great-Nana had reproduced the same anarchic look she'd achieved so long ago in her own house. As before, there was no clear surface on which to sit, just layers created by her beloved bibelots— a stuffed robin here, a kaleidoscope there, a silver heart locket with a tiny photograph of a fair-haired girl.

When my gaze settled I spotted Great-Nana in the far corner, a cloudy figure at best. In place of the robust redhead I'd known in my youth, I saw a limp gray thing confined to a wheelchair. She still had that impressive pillow of a bosom, and eyes that suggested they'd been privy to miracles—I'm hard-pressed to convey how the light moved *through* the iris rather than stopping cold. But the body had dwindled, the face wizened, and instead of encountering the embodiment of vitality, I found myself in the presence of a ruin.

"Wendy Darling! Berry Darling!" With diminished bravura, Nana extended her arms; they remained suspended in the air for us to fill.

Berry approached, unsure of herself, her heavy backpack propelling her forward. Helplessly she grabbed on to Nana, seizing her elbows. "Triple," she said in a hush.

"Goodness, child. You're damaging the merchandise."

But Berry refused to release her, her affection for Great-Nana a force to behold. Smiling, I tasted the envy rising in my throat. Eventually I forced my way in and embraced my great-grandmother.

"Of course the merchandise is already damaged," Nana said, waving us off. "But it's priceless nonetheless." She patted her bosom, enjoying the fact that she could still advertise her best feature.

"Yes, Nana," I said. "How could we forget." I turned around to address Dr. Wolfe, but he'd yielded the room to us Darlings.

Berry drew two folding chairs up to Great-Nana's wheelchair while I lifted the window shades—both windows had been padlocked, I noted.

"What's up with the windows?" I asked Nana. She gave a wink that suggested nothing in particular. "Nana!" I shouted in her face. "The windows."

"It's an experiment," she explained. "Dr. Wolfe wants to see if I can imagine flying without actually, you see, having to jump. He's that way, you know."

"What way?" I asked.

"He prefers that we use our noggins." She smiled vaguely at the ceiling.

I took the chair on the left, and Berry seated herself to the right of Great-Nana. The three of us succumbed to silence then, searching our respective kindred faces. We gave the ancestral ghosts a few minutes to emerge and take snapshots—after all, three generations were represented here.

"I'm flummoxed," Great-Nana said finally.

"That we're here together," I said.

"No!" Nana shrieked. "That Jane's missing all of this. Where *is* she, the little twit? I cherish my daughter but she insists on living so—far away. Which isn't very considerate, is it, *Berry*?"

Berry's head grew heavy, hanging down at her chest; she set her teeth in a thoughtful underbite. "No," she whispered. "I guess not."

"Stuff her. Jane's not considerate of others. Look what happened to *her* daughter." We all got a chuckle at Mummy's expense.

"Nana," I interrupted, "do you have some idea of where Jane is?"

"I have loads of ideas. But no, I was only speaking of her character, not her location. Sometimes I can't imagine how a person could do such a thing to her own mother . . . and then I can." She fell silent again, turning the wheelchair away from us. Her slippered feet tap-tapped the chair's footrest as she fooled with her dressing gown, tying and untying the satin ribbon at her neck. Her hands shook as they patted down her nest of gray hair; it still had a tangerine cast to it. Then, to make a point, Nana positioned the wheelchair to face us. "Berry," she said soberly. "You're traveling *light* these days?" She shot me a look that could skin a chicken.

I dipped my chin, indicating no, Pan had yet to enter my daughter's life.

"Oh dear. Oh dear."

"What is it, Triple?" asked Berry.

"Here we go again," said Great-Nana. "Wendy, my handbag."

"Sorry?"

"Handbag, please. We're getting out of here."

"Is that wise?" I asked. "You seem a little . . . tired." Though I was not one to collude with doctors, Great-Nana was ancient and I didn't want to wear her out.

"Don't ruin things, Mu-Mu," Berry said. "She just wants to go out on the town. Right, Triple?"

"Right-o," Great-Nana said.

We stuffed her leaf-embroidered handbag with pill bottles and outfitted her in a wool-felt kelly-green coat. To finish the job, we bundled her shoulders in a fringed shawl and affixed a pointy woolly hat to her head. So the Darling penchant for the odd chapeau had originated with Nana!

DEEPAK Wolfe entertained the peculiar British confidence in the restorative powers of the outdoors, and with his blessing the three of us made our way to the village of Cooke. He'd agreed to let us borrow his Saab hatchback as long as Great-Nana was forbidden from taking the wheel. Her taking the wheel, I'd assured Wolfe, was an impossibility: Nana would be far too busy talking to consider driving. But I hadn't counted on twisting my neck the first time I wandered into the wrong lane. "Shit!" I cried. "These English roads have got me confused."

"Move over, dearie," Great-Nana said.

"Let's sit this out a minute," I cautioned, and stopped the Saab in the dirt bordering the left lane.

"It's obviously my turn to drive," said Nana. "It's *been* my turn for the last twenty years. Don't take it away from me, from *us*."

I sat rigidly in the driver's seat, refusing to give it up; my neck told me any sort of movement might be trouble. In the passenger seat, Nana began humming those five notes "tooted" by the mothership in *Close Encounters*—how could she know what they meant to me? Berry, who was crammed into the back with the folded-up wheelchair, whistled along, amused by the generational dynamics. She seemed—patient.

"We could split the difference and let me drive," Berry volunteered when it was clear that we were going nowhere.

"Yes, let the girl drive if you're not going to permit me the honor," Great-Nana said. "So it's not the logical thing to do. Logic can be a bloody nuisance."

"Right on, Triple!" Berry cheered.

I could see the headline in the *Times*—YOUTH, WOMAN, AND

WOOLLY-HATTED DOWAGER IN TRAGIC, ILLOGICAL ACCIDENT—
and summoned the strength to get back on the road. Someone, I
reasoned, had to be the adult: I was, by default, that person.

There were no further incidents on the drive into town; my two
passengers grumbled but behaved, and a spell of calm descended
on the external world. I was taken in by what I could see head-on:
the verdant fields and hillocks, a graceful weeping willow.

The village of Cooke was one of those cultural backwaters where
the children grow up bored and go bad, and the adults prepare for
old age prematurely. To tourists like us, it was paradise. Church,
chemist, baker, butcher, stationers, tea room, grocery shop,
newsagent, video shop, pub—what else would one need on the way
to the grave?

Our glee was palpable and expressed immediately upon arriving: Great-Nana flung open the passenger door and shrieked, "Air,
glorious air!"

I searched my door panel for one of those electronic lock buttons, failing to realize that a button was unnecessary. Great-Nana
was poignantly stopped in her tracks. Without her wheelchair, she
was an invalid; no small wonder that she'd taken up flying again.

"My chariot!" Nana ordered and Berry hopped to. She unfolded the wheelchair and installed Great-Nana as masterfully as if
she'd been her longtime assistant. Berry's actions floored me. Had I
missed a rare submissive streak in her character? Could it be that
my daughter was *generous*?

The three of us stood in a line at the curb facing the high street.
Great-Nana pointed to a folksy sign that read SCONEHENGE and
the decision was made to pop in to the bakery. As we entered the
shop, Nana sat erect in her wheelchair. She winked at the man
behind the counter as if she were a regular, which gave me a certain
chill. Not to worry, I told myself, she's a winker.

"Gaston!" she called to the elderly man. His white uniform shirt,
with *Gus* embroidered in blue thread above the pocket, told a different story. "These are my pretties," Nana announced, "Wen-dy and

Ber-ry. Gaston, give us the sordid biscuits, the whole lot of them, would you?"

I smiled, remembering this venerable family pun: growing up, we all called *assorted* biscuits *sordid* biscuits—what makes sense to a child's ear. Gaston selected three of each cookie the shop offered, and piled them high on a plate. "Three coffees," I added.

Great-Nana snapped open her handbag and shuffled through a deep inventory of junk. She withdrew something shiny and pocketed it in her coat. "Wendy, pay the man, would you?"

We took our seats at a wobbly table near the window and ate covetously, like refugees, our lips dusted with confectioners' sugar. The moment Gaston's eyes were off her, Nana withdrew a silver flask from her coat pocket and spilled something from the vessel into her mug. I smiled knowingly. Nana always said that drinking in moderation took the edge off altered states.

Thoughts of Daddy came to mind. "Has Dudley been by to visit, Nana?" She squinted at me, preoccupied. "Nana, have you seen my father?" I repeated.

She took a long drag from the coffee, holding the mug in both hands like a child, then peered over its rim for what seemed an inexcusably long time. "Not for donkey's years," she said finally. "Isn't he handsome, though? Isn't he the dog's bollocks . . . ?"

After polishing off her gypsy cream and chocolate digestive, Nana insisted on getting a haircut. We marched into Betty's Beauty Mark like Dorothy & Company entering the Emerald City. The salon's habitués, mostly in their sixties and seventies, must have appeared as youngsters in Great-Nana's eyes, for she called them *girls* and quickly began to dominate the proceedings.

The ladies were mesmerized by Great-Nana's rhetoric—she spoke surreally of "those crocodiles in the House of Commons!" and called Thatcher "That scandalous buccaneer!" Notwithstanding, she addressed the denizens of the salon as *Honeybunch* or *Precious*, and managed to compliment each with something unique: "You smell precisely like plum pudding." "You have that chic Princess Margaret thing going for you." "If she hadn't met a sticky end, I would think you were Jean Seberg in the flesh."

In a matter of minutes, the ladies anointed Great-Nana "Queen of Cooke." Her batteries recharged, Nana rose from her wheelchair and took two regally faltering steps in the direction of Betty, the proprietor. It was then I realized that she could walk when she wanted to, that the body still worked once it got properly revved up. No wonder Great-Nana's flights of fancy on the balcony had threatened to result in bona fide sprints across the sky. She had a will that could bend steel, not to mention those bothersome laws of physics.

"Make me red again, Betty! Flame red, bloodred, cardinal-sin red." Nana patted her faded, frizzy tresses. "Delicious-apple red, the lacquered red of Chinese boxes. Hell, make me communist red. Just do it!"

Betty, a heavily pancaked bottle-blonde and the youngest of all the ladies, escorted Great-Nana to her station. "Get on the love train!" she sang with a Liverpudlian lilt.

Once installed in Betty's swivel chair and swathed in terry cloth towels, Nana swiftly dozed off, soft humming sounds issuing from her nose. When she stirred from her nap forty minutes later, her tresses were as red as cows' blood.

"Triple, you'd better call the fire department," Berry said, shaking Nana's shoulders. "Your head's on fire."

Great-Nana brushed the sleep from her eyes and stared at her reflection in the booth's deco mirror. "Oh Christ," she said. She inspected the back of her head in the pink plastic mirror that Betty held up behind her. "Well," she said finally, "it's a dog's dinner, but it's *my* dog's dinner!" She smiled widely, revealing a smear of magenta lipstick on her teeth.

The hen's den of ladies closed in, fondling the new do. Not only was the hair fire-engine red but it was cropped short. A tight, bright crimson cap. "Isn't it divine?" Betty crowed. "Isn't it the last word in red?"

Berry squeezed Betty's arm. "I want one, too," she said. "But black, make mine black."

"Your curls," I pleaded. "Your gorgeous curls."

"You don't have any sovereignty here," Nana chimed in.

"Okay, Ber," I conceded. "And while you're at it, I might as well do something with my rats' nest."

Which is how we spent the afternoon in Cooke: reading *Hello!* and *Woman's Own,* and having our hair snipped and dyed. While Berry and I went under the scissors, Great-Nana entertained Gaston, who had dropped by with individual slices of blackberry crumble, plastic cutlery, and paper cups of hot chocolate. What was *he* doing here, I wondered. They excused themselves to the front of the shop, Gaston pushing Nana's wheelchair like an old hand.

Berry, in the booth next to me, was in the decisive hands of Betty, who swiftly sheared her thick locks. I wanted to weep—why is the sight of cut hair always so painful? When Berry's ink-colored do was finished, it looked, well, ghoulish. Maybe it was the sculpted peaks that ran from ear to ear, like a sideways mohawk. Berry dubbed the style "the Statue of Liberty," and dared anyone in the shop to hate it. We were, to a woman, speechless.

In contrast, my new cut was on the subtle side: short but unruly—pixieish you might say—with raspberry highlights that mimicked my real color, only more fiery. I felt more exposed than usual and yet I enjoyed the current of air tickling my ears, a familiar lightheadedness. As I shrugged off my oilcloth smock, Great-Nana was set before me like a magistrate. She examined me closely, then covered her mouth. While she didn't gasp out loud, it appeared that she wanted to.

"What is it?" I questioned. "What have I done?"

"It's him," she said flatly. "You've become *him.*"

I paraded over to the full-length mirror at the front of the shop, and struck a rakish pose: hands pressed on hips, jaw thrust at ceiling. Then I saw what she saw and gasped too. With my emerald tights and olive-green boots and my hair clipped in shaggy, razor-sharp batches, I resembled Pan—the Pan who graces picture books. And here I'd been thinking "Mia Farrow in the sixties," or, more heroically, "Joan d'Arc." But Pan? I'd never had an interest in becoming his doppelgänger. If anything, I was his antithesis. This would never do.

Great-Nana sensed correctly that it was time to leave the salon and motioned us outside, Gaston in command of her wheelchair. Why Gaston was sweet on Great-Nana, I had no idea. For one thing, he was a young man of seventy while she was firmly planted in her nineties. Yet the two seemed to share an unshakable confidence in the world, the becalming idea that nothing stays the same for long. This single idea could take the sting out of a bad marriage—or a haircut, I presumed. Which explained their steady laughter over the red fright-wig that had landed on Great-Nana's head. Gaston and Great-Nana couldn't stop going on about how "daft" she looked and fracturing themselves in the process. Berry made plain her displeasure with Gaston for usurping her job of promenading Great-Nana around town, and sulked openly on the street.

We ended up at the local graveyard, where Gaston felt we could enjoy a measure of privacy. He helped Nana onto a stone bench while Berry took a seat on a small stone crypt. I rested atop an ornate headstone inscribed with three heartbreaking lines—

CYCLOPS
BELOVED PUSS
1910–1910

—and wondered how the kitty had succumbed. When next I looked up, I saw Gaston running around Nana in circles, her shawl flapping behind him like Superman's cape. Beguiled, Nana flung her woolly hat in the air and cried, "Bravo!" Just as quickly, Gaston returned the shawl to her shoulders and her hat to her head, and gave her a peck on the cheek. Now short of breath, he hobbled off in the direction of the bakery, turning around every few feet to wave at us.

With the departure of Gaston/Gus, we Darlings were thrown together again. Nana hardly had the strength to call Berry and me over to her, and resorted to fluttering her hanky like a flag. Forming a tight, tribal circle with Nana on the bench, we took a few minutes to warm our bones. Finally, Nana drew herself up, the famous bosom rising, and asked to be transferred to her wheelchair again. Berry had the honor of fixing her in place.

"Well?" I asked, greedy for details on Gaston. "It looks like you have a beau."

"You cheeky monkey," she said. "He knew Sidney, that's all." Nana rearranged her woolly hat so that her newly cropped hair stuck out in little bunches like a clutch of red posies.

Sidney Farrington had been Great-Nana's first and only husband; all the other suitors were, in her parlance, *paramours*, and a few lucky chaps, *mon amours*. Sid hadn't lasted long. Having been truant for the birth of Jane, it was little wonder that he made infrequent appearances in Nana's reminiscences. It's not that he'd expired early, though by now he was most certainly dead. Instead, he'd been as mercurial as Pan and headed off to sea around the time Great-Nana got in the family way. It wasn't the Royal Navy that seduced Sid—careerism was not his thing. Rather, the life of Gauguin had served as his inspiration and he'd left his post as trainee accountant at Rigby & Platt for painting and the South Seas. Initially, Nana had been drawn to Sid's pragmatism, which she felt would stand in high contrast to her own artistic nature. Once married, though, Sid began to show his true colors: a dabbler in oils *and* at boxing and boating, he turned out to be a daredevil who could have gone head to head with Pan. Great-Nana had been both irked and secretly delighted, for her excursion to The Neverland had suffused her with a joie de vivre that wouldn't quit. But the couple would be thwarted when it came to making a decent income if they both proceeded down creative paths. Hence, Sid had begrudgingly stuck it out for a while at Rigby & Platt—until the couple's Sunday morning lovemaking bore fruit. In fairness to Sid, Great-Nana would only say this: "He had a little talent." The heartache that resulted from Sid's desertion was more or less eased by the arrival of Jane, a "perfect baby" who quickly took up residence in her mother's vandalized heart.

And thus Great-Nana Wendy poured everything into her child: all the grief and confusion, but also the tenderness and euphoria that are the result of "befriending" men. And lest we forget, she endowed her daughter with a certain something extra—the mechanics of flight. Jane would be *equipped*. No matter whom she met or whom she loved, she'd have the know-how of happiness. The daughter would have a discipline to fall back on, though falling had been the last thing on her mother's mind.

BY late afternoon, a heavy mist enshrouded Cooke. We welcomed the change, the darkly poetic mood. Berry and I slouched on our bench in silence while Great-Nana hummed what, to our ears, was a nonmelody—a dissonant, renegade song.

"She's doing her mysterious thing again," Berry whispered.

"Your Triple works on her abstruseness like a hobby," I teased.

"I heard that, dear," Nana stage-whispered back.

Berry bowed her head, her gloomy eyes drawn to the dots of light from Nana's rings.

"And what's wrong with being a little mysterious?" Nana protested. She arched a penciled-in brow.

"It's just, I don't know, Triple," Berry said. "Mystery and fantasy take people away."

"Away?" Nana repeated.

"Like nobody's present in this family for very long. People go off. People always find something better to do." Berry snapped off the head of a wildflower and mangled it with her fingers.

I examined the gravestone of a dead baby, hoping to recede from the conversation. Great-Nana, however, remained admirably composed, ready for the ideological duel. "So when I hum something unfamiliar, that makes you, what? Anxious, dear?"

"Pul-leeze, Triple, drop the therapy. Berry pursed her lips in a classic pout. The moussed peaks shooting out from her scalp made her look especially severe.

"Perhaps you don't care for my singing," Nana observed. "But just when did your mother ever leave you? I'll wager that you can't come up with a single example. In fact, she's been present on all fronts—physical, emotional, geographical. Eternally on call. Now, if you want a good example of someone who's been left behind, look no farther than your great-great-grandmother. They say her daughter did such a rollicking good job of leaving her, no one else need ever try!"

Great-Nana, who'd been unflappable up to this point, now whipped around like a shark in her wheelchair.

"Nana." I forced myself to speak up, then discovered I had nothing material to say. Nervous, I readjusted her shawl, fussed with her off-kilter hat. Berry and I waited for someone to change the subject.

"Young lady," Nana said at last, a gnarled forefinger cutting the air. "When you think people are going away, perhaps they're simply visiting their memories. When you get older, you'll know what I mean. At thirteen, you've very few memories to visit. But I envy you. You've got a lifetime of memories to *make*."

"I'm not going anywhere, Triple. Not in a bus or a boat or a balloon."

"Somebody's feeling awfully sorry for herself."

"Oh man, you just don't get it."

"Then *help* me get it," Nana said, her gravitas emanating from a frightfully deep well. "Give it to me straight, *man*."

Berry regarded her great-great-grandmother; it took her a moment to find her voice. "It's just, people think I'm going to mess up their trip."

"Oh, I see."

"You do?" Berry asked, caught off guard.

"So tell me, old thing," Nana said. "What've you done to get yourself uninvited?"

Berry pulled at her cheeks, then shook her head back and forth, as if regretting a lifetime of blunders. "Oh that's easy. I'm, *you know*."

"No, we don't, actually. Astonish us."

"I'm not a nice person," Berry whispered.

"Hogwash!" Nana hissed. "If *you're* not good, I'm a codfish. Per-

haps that's not the best analogy, dear, for I truly *am* a codfish!"
Berry smiled in spite of herself. "And what's so great about being
nice, anyway? Tell me one blinking thing."

"I dunno," Berry answered. "You get chosen for stuff. You get
liked."

"Oh, you get *liked*," Nana iterated. "Did I ever tell you what Carl
Jung told me in confidence, before he said the same thing to all
humanity?"

Berry joggled her head, the shellacked points on her scalp
strangely immobile.

"When I was at sixes and sevens—" Berry looked puzzled.
"When my parents were upset about me having adventures that
would trump Huck Finn's, I went and— Oh, never mind, you know
about my childhood."

"Doesn't everybody?" Berry pointed out.

"Hush. As I said, when I was at a loose end, I visited Carl—we
had the money in those days. Well, Dr. Jung gave me a look that
could fill a textbook, then ever so patiently he explained how I was
split in two."

Ah, the Carl Jung story. How had I filed it away so successfully?

"Split?" Berry said.

"Yes, divided into the Good Wendy and the Genuine Wendy.
Dr. Jung convinced me to fuse the two halves."

"With a blowtorch?" Berry cracked.

Great-Nana smoothed the nap of her wool stockings with a
gloved hand. "'Wendy Darling,' Jung said, 'I would rather be whole
than good.' Now doesn't that sound like piffle?"

"Yeah, a piffle sandwich," Berry giggled.

"Well, it's not. It's probably the best wisdom Western culture can
buy. What Jung meant, of course, was that *just* being good will get
you in trouble—"

"How's that?" Berry interrupted.

Great-Nana grew tall in the wheelchair. "Because that's only half
the picture. If we suppress what Jung calls our *shadow*—tradition-

ally, the awfully nasty part of us—we end up as terribly flat creatures."

"Excuse me, Nana." I stood up then, not knowing what came next. "Don't you think Berry already excels at, you know, being difficult?"

"No doubt she does, dear. What I'm trying to tell her is that being all shadowy or all goody-goody won't work, won't get her far. But being *whole*—being kind and generous and thoughtful, *and* being an occasional pain in the arse—now that has legs!"

"Triple, I'm confused." Berry was pacing now, fully engaged. "How do I, like, handle both things at once? How do I deal with my, you know, shitty feelings, and then let out my so-called niceness? I don't even know *what* is it, let alone where the fuck it is."

"Berry!" I shouted, but it was too late: Great-Nana was sheltering my stormy little daughter in her arms.

All too quickly, though, Berry tore away from Nana's embrace. "Leave me alone. I'm not nice, so none of this amounts to a hill of beans. Unless you're talking fat, farty beans. To be whole, you gotta have all the parts, right?"

In a gesture that rivaled Mummy at her most dramatic, Berry threw herself onto Great-Nana's lap, instantly flattening the points of hair jutting from her head. After recovering from the blow, Great-Nana thumbed her nose at Berry. This seemed inappropriate, but then appropriate was another country, one rarely visited by us Darlings.

"Berry," I said, "she can't withstand your weight." Berry was and always had been a small thing—but never dainty, never light on her toes.

"That's another defect, Triple. My jumbo weight."

"Well, elephantiasis runs in the family," Nana said dryly. "I didn't want to bring it up," Nana said. "I wanted you to find out for yourself."

"That I'm a mutant?" Berry said.

"No, that your particular shadow—your true power—is not

your nastiness. Rather, your shadow is your *goodness*. You're one of those rare creatures whose shadow is the light. That's why you're having such a tough time of it. You need to integrate your, let's say, *pissy self* with something you haven't yet acknowledged—your sweetness. Sweetness can be formidable, too."

"Triple, there's no way I'm nice. No way." Berry rolled off Great-Nana's lap and stood before her, hands remodeling the raven peaks on her head.

"Sweet Jesus." Nana sighed. "What's the worst that could happen if you *were*, God forbid, a nice child?"

Berry shifted her weight from hip to hip, each hairy leg taking turns. "I dunno," she said finally.

"Embarrassed?" Great-Nana asked pointedly. *"Found out?"*

Berry bit into her cheek, nodding vaguely.

"Well, now we're getting somewhere. All you girls forget the most crucial things," Nana said softly. "When in doubt—when you perceive that no one in the world is present for you—you must learn to mother yourself. One should never expect one's *real* mother to take care of such things. We mothers are all too wracked with doubt ourselves."

For the second time in an hour, Berry leaned into the fossil-thin arms of Great-Nana. As the sun dipped below the horizon Berry clung to her great-great-grandmother, taking some of the shawl for herself. In search of a cup of coffee, I made my way back into town, leaving the eldest and youngest Darling to conspire about how to be good in the face of evil, and how to be formidable in the face of goodness. The whole business frightened me, I must confess, for I hadn't a clue to my own power, always living safely at the intersection of kindness and duty. You might say it was time for me to get run over.

X

ERRY managed to skip the whole Pan affair—or should I say Pan skipped *her*? When her period arrived at the regrettably late age of fourteen, we finally sat down together and discussed the ABCs of menstruation, sex, and death (the latter being her topic of choice). I took this opportunity to fess up to the truth about Peter: his hunger for new stories, for annual Spring cleanings, for the company of young women—precisely in that order.

"So you've read the books?" I asked casually, ambushing my daughter the same evening the first rush of blood darkened her jeans. The wind tore in from the north and beat against the sliding-glass doors to her bedroom. (We'd removed my old French windows, which blocked the sky, she said.)

"What?" she questioned sharply.

"The books. You've read them, I suppose?"

This time she answered without skipping a beat. "Yes, Mu-Mu. I've digested the Puffin classic and devoured the Penguin volume with its scholarly preface, and gobbled up the Disney Books for Young Readers edition. I've consumed the illustrated and the annotated books, seen the play and the musical, and heard the sound track. Now isn't that smart of me? I mean, *that's* preparation. Nothing can surprise me now."

Berry darted over to the sliding-glass doors and grinned as the menacing wind agitated the eucalyptus trees. "It's all a bunch of bull, you know. I mean, *come on*, Mother. We've all peeked behind the curtain and seen the gears working. There's no Neverland. It's just a *story*. You write 'em, Daddy makes sound effects for 'em, and I watch 'em on the big screen. If you've taught me anything, it's make up your own story 'cause no one else is gonna do it for you."

I regarded my daughter, her arms folded over her chest like a train crossing that allows nothing to get through. She wasn't a believer like the rest of us. In spite of her arty-farty parents and literary pedigree, she was a realist. A blasphemer in a family of believers.

"I mean, look at me, Mu-Mu." She twirled like a contestant in a Junior Miss pageant. "Even if the story *was* true, no guy—not even the cutest apparition—would want me."

"W-what?" I stuttered, dragging my fingers down hollow cheeks. "You're—what makes you say such a thing? You're amazing. You're drop-dead gorgeous!"

"Yeah, with an emphasis on *dead*. I'm just a vision of loveliness in my mother's eye. But the guys have other, let's say, funkier, ideas. Listen to me—"

"No, *you* listen to me," I said, instantly regretting the cliché. "In spite of everything your grandmother talks about—lucid dreaming and vision quests and Aboriginal Dreamtime—you think you have a handle on reality. But you don't, you don't." I curled up on her chenille bedspread, which she'd recently dyed black, and sank my face in my palms.

"That's true, Mu-Mu," Berry conceded quietly. She crept over to the bed to make sure I was still breathing. "It's just, your proof is so totally anecdotal. Hey, I'm not belittling your past or grandmummy's. But let's get serious."

"I *am* serious," I said, lifting my face so she could make out the damage. "You're denigrating us. You're making a mockery of us."

"So you're saying I have to believe in a crock of shit to be in this family. Is that what you're saying?"

"Yes," I said. "You have to believe in a crock of shit."

"Well, I don't," Berry said with quivering lips. "*Sayonara*, Mu-Mu."

The funny thing is, I believed her the moment she said it. This wasn't a feign on her part—Berry never feigned. She would be leaving us. At fourteen, at fifteen, at sixteen for keeps. On the eve of her initiation into adulthood, Berry appeared to turn her back on her birthright—the ferocious imagination that had always served her like a charm.

ALL rites of passage are paradoxical. On the one hand, there's the opportunity for personal growth, the promise of transcendence. But there is terror and disintegration, too—deep blows to the ego. No wonder that the day a mother hands off her daughter to Pan is unquestionably her worst. Of course, events of this magnitude always occur at *night*: nothing of import happens in daylight anymore. Under a shroud of vapors and shadow, when you can hardly make out your own feet, major changes take place at the molecular level. What looks solid melts in your fingers and what appears liquid bruises your knees. Matter cannot be trusted; the laws of physics are not obeyed. Pan's anarchy appeals to children and yet scares the bejesus out of adults (whose hairs stand on end, whose nails are bitten to the quick). How differently children see things. They are transported, literally. They titter when they should be screaming, swoon when they should be respectful, devout. From this moment on, they no longer look to you for comfort or protection; they no longer need your dinners, your allowances, the safe harbor of your embrace. From this moment on, they will fly on their own fuel and eat from the tree of imaginary fruit. They no longer need their mothers, all of whom have taken a bad fall and made their peace with gravity.

This is the way of the world according to Great-Nana. What a mother wants for her daughter will go unheeded, for no mother can compete with Pan. What he brings into a room is far more compelling than anything a mother can make up on the spot. And so imagination becomes the new parent: it is an irresistible force to be reckoned with, a teacher that doesn't disappoint. It keeps a child energized well after Pan leaves the scene; it keeps her warm at night and feeds her. Too bad its power fades with the years. Too bad it leaves the daughter stranded on the ground, without the ability to lift off. I know of what I speak; for I was a daughter once too.

Pan came for Berry that first night of her fifteenth year, at an hour when gale-force winds would blow him into her life without much effort on his part. He always was a lazy fellow. As it happened Berry had been sleeping lightly, waking repeatedly to check out the Joan Jett tee-shirt she wore for a nightie; she didn't want her period to ruin it. She heard the mad clattering of trees, the skeletal branches scraping the glass doors. But she nursed no fear: she was a big fan of weather, the more ruinous the better.

As Berry would relate to me later at the hospital, she'd been sitting upright in bed reading a Spider-Man comic in the fuzzy glow of the back-porch light, when the sliding-glass doors skated open to reveal the silhouette of a young man. He cut a spry countercultural figure, she said: his long rock-star hair was blown to bits, his Levi's so shrunken they clung to him like ballet tights. Despite the icy wind, he wore a holey tee with Bono's face on it, which instantly revealed he was out of sync with my daughter's taste in music.

As Peter crept towards the bed in—what else?—Doc Martens, Berry rested the comic book on her pillow and switched on the lamp at her nightstand. This cast a greenish light on the boy's countenance, which made him look fake or simulated, Halloweenish. Berry coolly sized him up, a smile barely parting her lips. While she'd just spent most of the evening denying his existence, it turns out this had been a simple act of teenage rebellion: she'd pretty much counted on Pan to spirit her away from the fantasy realm that was Berkeley. That had been Plan A. If he didn't come, and time was growing thin, she'd have to resort to Plan B, which involved leaving Berkeley on her own volition—with the help of razor blades or pills, perhaps even electricity. At the time I hadn't a clue about either plan. I assumed my daughter was coping well enough with her inheritance, a darkness that refused to give way to the light. Besides, her morbid sensibility had given birth to some notable, if controversial, theater projects. At such a tender age she was getting recognition for her pain.

We Darlings have a tradition of putting our neuroses to good use. Berry had honored that tradition with a series of performance pieces that many considered unsuitable for junior high audiences, pieces wherein Daffy Duck and Bugs Bunny were engulfed in depression and madness, or at least low self-esteem. While her cartoon voices were spot-on as always, the emotion they now tendered was deemed too raw for the children at the Waldorf school, where we most recently had moved her.

Doing her best now to control her nerves, Berry assessed the intruder who'd swept in with the storm. Not only was he *not* crying, he didn't seem to be looking for his notoriously flimsy shadow. Instead he appeared casual, self-contained. This was not the picture of desperation she'd been expecting all her life.

"Well," she hailed him, "if it isn't the boy wonder. I don't get it. Like, why aren't you crying?"

"Don't really fancy weepin' right now," he said with a sniff, raking his fingers through wet, matted hair.

"Oh yeah?" Berry challenged.

"Yeah," he confirmed.

Now the two faced off. Berry stared down the young man—he was just as amazing as the books had promised, neither too pretty nor too rugged, but a generous fusion of feminine and masculine: ski-jump nose, vulpine eyes, dancer's physique, spray of freckles, and a grin that mocked the heavens.

Bounding onto the mattress, he sent her comic book flying. "Hey, watch the merchandise," she warned, which only encouraged him to snatch the book from her hands.

"This rubbish?" he said, flipping through the pages. "So tell me, what's the deal with the spider-boy?"

"Spider-Man," she corrected.

"Yeah, what's so special about the arachnid?"

"Well, to begin with, he's one of the coolest superheroes of all time."

"I'm sorry, luv. But you've been royally hoodwinked. There *are* no superheroes, there's just me. Pan." He stuffed the comic in the waistband of his jeans, then beat on his chest like Tarzan. "I am the hero of every story!" he sang out, his voice pitched higher than what one storybook, in particular, had suggested.

"Give it back, dickhead!" Berry wrestled with Pan and the book until the latter ripped into two sheaves. "Oh great, that was a collectible," she scolded. He just smiled and withdrew from his back pocket a white leather pouch from which he extracted a yo-yo; he executed a couple of round the worlds and one walk the dog. But Berry paid the boy no mind, so absorbed was she in restoring the comic. When he couldn't stand being ignored another minute, Peter threw open every drawer of her bureau. "'Scuse me," he said, "but I've come a right long way."

Berry looked up in time to catch him pouting. "I know," she answered with unexpected grace. "I'm more ready to leave the world than you can imagine."

Resting the comic book on the lip of her nightstand, she hopped off the bed, stuck her head of newly grown-out curls underneath the bed frame, and tugged on something massive. An army-issue duffel bag, stuffed to the gills, was dragged across the floor and set before the sliding-glass doors. "There!" she said, breathing heavily. *"Andiamo."*

"Eh?" Peter grunted.

"Let's *go*," she urged, signifying the outdoors with her eyebrows.

"I don't get it," he said. "You're not the least bit afraid?"

"Fear is not an option," she stated hypnotically.

Duffel bag slung over her shoulder and clad only in her oversized tee-shirt and panties, Berry slid the door open, inviting in a blast of frigid air and slanted rain. She stepped outside to the redwood deck that jutted out ten feet from the back of the house. At the end of the deck was a fringe of eucalyptus trees that gave way to a fern-and-ice-plant-covered slope. The deck was crowded with garden furniture, and she had to negotiate her way around her father's potted plants.

Resting the duffel bag on the redwood planks, she caught her breath. "Hey," she called to the boy, "so, like, hit me with the fairy sprinkles and let's split." Her calloused feet hopped up and down, awaiting their cue.

"Right, mate, we'll be off in a sec!" Peter hollered from inside the house. "Just tell me one thing—"

"Yeah, yeah," she interrupted. *"I know stories."* She whistled boyishly into the wind. "More stories than Scheherazade. Greater tales than Grimm. More fabulous fables than Aesop." She looked him in the eye as best she could with the hard sheet of rain slicing the air between them. "Is that good enough for you, 'cause I'm getting frigging cold out here."

Peter scratched his head as boys are wont to do when thoroughly stumped. He adjusted his soaked clothing before deciding to go along with the girl, the strangest and toughest he'd encountered by far. She must have missed his leap onto the deck, for he stood before her now. "All right, sunshine. I believe you know the drill?"

"Sure do, fly boy. The happy-thoughts meditation thingy?"

"Right-o." He laughed. "But it's got to be true—you can't fool Mother Nature." He secured the sliding door with an emphatic shove.

"Mother Nature?" she said. "There's nothing *natural* about mothers. They don't have a clue. They're all helpless, every last one of them, total zeroes."

"Wendy," he said, "just a tip? It's best not to get too worked up right now."

"My name is Berry. You know, like a *berry*? And I'm not worked up. I just don't want to be reminded of the mothership." She sat down on the edge of the deck and banged on her knees with her fists.

"But you have such a dish for a mum!" he blurted out, sitting down beside her. She tossed him a withering look. "Okay, your mum's hardly a domestic goddess. She can't sew to save her life and she can't cook for beans. She can't *cook* beans! Still, the stories she tells . . . why, they're brill. Amazing, actually." Berry raised an eyebrow. "All right, you win. A couple are rather pathetic." He chuckled fondly. "Wendy's stories have the most horrid endings. She doesn't tie stuff up with a lovely bow like the other birds do—the stories end badly or just like that!" He snapped his fingers in her face and she flinched. "And they're full of ludicrous talking rodents. I don't know how she comes up with the stuff. It's soppy and depressing at the same time."

"Hey, don't go there," Berry warned, glancing up at him with smudged, raccoon eyes. "My mom makes a living with her stories. I mean, people actually *buy* them. Of course, she ran out of stories before I was ten. But we don't mention that."

"Is that why you don't dig her?"

"I can't really tell *you* that, can I? I mean, God. *You're* the problem." She sank her head between her knees.

"What the . . . ?" Peter cupped his dripping palms together and yelled in her ear: "What 'ave *I* got to do with anything?"

"Holy shit!" she cried, popping up. "Like you have everything to do with everything. You practically run this family. My dad has to keep his distance from my mom because she got screwed up by you when she was little. And guess what? This usually includes keeping his distance from me, too."

"So, what do you know? I'm the villain of a story." He took a moment to process the news. "If I'm such a bad bloke, then why're you so anxious to come off with me, eh?" He nudged her shoulder—actually *touched* her.

Berry pulled back, stretching her tee-shirt over shivering knees. "None of your beeswax," she said. Then, still hunched over, she lifted her face. "Maybe because . . . I'm a bad guy too." She had his full attention now. "You see, my mom and dad are so *good* it makes me barf. They, like, think I'm good, but I'm not. I'm completely rancid but nobody knows."

Peter's unfailing cheerfulness now gave way to a weird solemnity. "Aw, Berry. Things can't be that bad. You look good to me."

He lowered his eyes to her stocky legs, caught a glimpse of cotton panties dotted with spiral galaxies. Wanting to wipe the rain from her cheeks, he suspended his hand in the air between them. Then, feeling self-conscious, he withdrew it.

"Now the trick is," Peter continued, "you gotta concentrate on the luvvy-jubby stuff or you won't make the journey"—he eyed her bulging duffel bag—"and it looks like a journey is something you've been banking on for quite some time." She nodded in earnest. "So, listen up. Close your eyes, relax, and think of something so cool that nothing uncool can muck it up."

"Sorry, my cupboard of cool stuff is empty," she said. Standing, she shook off the excess rain like a waterlogged dog.

"I don't buy that," he said. "Surely there's something you fancy?" She looked at him blankly. "How 'bout the Queen Mum." She wrinkled her nose. "Princess Di?" She crossed her eyes. "Right, let me guess. A blinding pair of Air Jordans?"

"No," she whispered, "nothing."

"Mate, there's gotta be something that wets your whistle. Knickerbocker glories? Hot-fudge sundaes? Or some tasty bloke like, I dunno, Johnny Depp?"

"Oh please, I'm not into food or guys."

"Right. Well, how 'bout Julia Roberts? Meg Ryan?"

She smiled coyly, then covered her eyes with her hands. "There is one thing."

"Yeah?" He lit up like a pinball machine.

"You know the movie *Alien*? Like, the original? Well, it makes me feel all tingly."

"Brilliant," he said. "Well, whatever. Let's get on with it."

She watched as he scaled a nearby eucalyptus and, on what appeared to be a flimsy branch, began a warm-up session for the imminent flight: corny hamstring stretches, ankle rotations.

"Hel-looo." She waved. "The dust? I need the dust." She shot him a baleful look.

"Like I told your mum, there's really no need."

"Sorry, but I definitely gotta have the dust. Consider me old-fashioned."

"Consider me inflexible," he said, crossing his arms like a genie. "Oh, fair enough," he said when her face muscles took a break. "If you close yer eyes, pet, I'll give you Pan's full-service treatment."

He vaulted from the tree to the ground and scrambled furtively around the hillside. Then, with both hands, he scooped up some dry soil from under the deck.

While Pan dusted her head and shoulders, Berry hopped up and down on one foot, her eyes screwed shut. The "pixie dust" was redolent of the earth, she noted; it gave off the rich perfume of clay and chocolate.

"Now do yer own thing," he suggested. "Follow your bliss."

Immune to clichés, Berry remained as land-bound as a boulder. Unfazed, he encouraged her to smile: "C'mon Ber, try for a teensy bit of happiness. Show us them bicuspids."

Another no-go. Instead, Berry scowled and managed to sink an inch deeper in the earth. Conceding defeat, she opened her eyes. "I don't *know* bliss. Can you give me a little help here?"

"Piece of cake," he said. "Think beebee guns, baseball, Babe Ruth, Barney. Those always work for me. And that's only the Bs."

Again she squinted and hopped, flapping her arms like a duck. And once more she remained mired in the mud. Her head began to pound, her vision clouded over. "Can't you see I need magic? Don't just stand there, *be magical!*"

Peter let out an unfortunate burp. "Sorry, luv, but you're the one in the driver's seat. You gotta use your own petrol to get out of here." When she refused to look up, he said, "Listen, some kids just have more fuel. If you like, I'll blow on you to get you started." His cheeks swelled up like a puffer fish, and an impressive amount of air blasted the brown hairs on her arms.

Looking up now into Peter's rain-streaked face, Berry found herself warming to the idea of the boy. "My mom *said* you were a fox. You know, irresistible. But I thought that was, like, a joke."

"Your mum's right on the beam," he said. "I can't resist myself."

"And not the least bit shallow or stuck-up, either."

"Yeah, it's a puzzlement."

Berry's mouth flew open; she had not been prepared for his brand of sincerity.

"So," he asked her, "are we going to bugger off or are we going to prattle on about how ace I am?"

"Oh, fuck it," she said. "Let's give it one last try." Berry gripped the strap of her duffel bag, looking straight ahead. "And now," she announced as if in a drama competition, "I shall perform the coolest scene from *Alien*. Specifically, the moment when the acid-spewing creature explodes from John Hurt's chest and reveals itself. *Frees itself.* Of course, John Hurt dies. Who could survive a chest wound like that?"

"Not exactly your average cheery thought," Peter said, scratching his scalp. "You're not your mum's daughter, are you?" His smile was like a high beam in the light-starved night.

Without warning Berry let go of the duffel bag; her torso jerked as if electrocuted, banking sideways, then convexing. Now her sternum heaved up and down as she wrestled with some invisible monster. It was only then Berry hovered a symbolic inch in the air. "Thatta girl!" Peter cheered. But instead of rising higher, she toppled over onto the deck.

In lieu of the usual cries of ecstasy that greet Pan as he guides rookies skyward, Berry was spitting up, her tongue flying back in her throat. Peter paced beside her body, frantic and powerless. As she sputtered and moaned, her forearms coated themselves in mud. Moments later, her limbs went limp; her voice wasted away. Finally her head rested on its side, a look of generic terror forcing open her jaw. She was inert, though her eyes twitched periodically; Peter could almost make out pictures in their glassy surface.

Eventually he had to leave. It was the only thing to do under the circumstances, the only choice left for a boy who had a rough time with obligation. He took off into the storm, determined not to look back. Looking back was for sissies. But very soon he wondered if that was a myth. When he'd risen several meters above our roof, he gathered the courage—or was it merely curiosity—to hazard a downward glance. He wholly expected to see a pathetic white dot bobbing in a viscous black smear, but there was no trace of the girl. There was nothing in the violent dark but himself. And even that felt shaky.

All this I would piece together later from Berry's recollections and from what I've just now learned. At the time I was stricken with sleeplessness; the Ambiens I'd ingested couldn't compete with the severity of the storm. There was nothing to do but wait it out, wait for the world to return to its senses. For in spite of the deluge and the pills, nothing could drown out the bitter truth of the evening: Peter was afoot, I could feel it in my marrow.

The vigilance of a mother is unequaled: *we know things.* We have a capacity akin to remote viewing, a sixth sense that clues us in on the fates of our children. But it doesn't tell us how to cope with what we know or learn. It leaves our psyches undefended, overexposed. The night of Berry's fourteenth birthday, I was certain of one thing only: I couldn't protect my daughter any more than my own mother had protected me.

"F-Freeman," I stuttered, trying to rouse the body in bed next to me.

"What?" he said sleepily.

"Something's very wrong."

"Hook?" he asked bluntly.

"No, Pan." I sat up in bed.

Freeman rubbed his chin and flung the crush of heavy quilts off his chest. He thrust himself upright. "Wends, forget it." He stared out the window at the knot of trees whipping in the wind. Then he sealed his eyes again, as if praying. "Even your dad wouldn't fly in such lousy weather."

"True," I said. "But Daddy's not Pan."

"Are you sure?" Freeman baited me, then pulled the covers over his head and turned his back to me.

"Something's very wrong," I repeated.

"She's *fine,* Wends. Berry loves a good storm, the more apocalyptic the better."

"No, not like this."

"Then get up and check on her," he said, voice muffled by the bedding.

"God, that would be so maternal. I can't. I just can't." I slid back under the quilts, trying to emulate my husband. When I'd half convinced myself that things were normal, I heard an unearthly wail followed by animal-like whimpering from the direction of the yard. I jostled Freeman awake, then raced in my nightgown to Berry's room, fear setting my lungs on fire.

There was no sign of my daughter in her bed. Moreover, her duvet was turned down, the air suffused with the scent of mint. I ran outside to the deck. The sky was slowly clearing and I could detect a few stars, little balls of gas that would guide my sweetheart and Peter to their destination. She would arrive safely, I assured myself. Perhaps she would even discover the sort of happiness she never could find here in Berkeley. She would be worshiped, if only for a while—well, as long as she could stand it. Then she would learn why her mother was such a useless creature, never as much fun as her father.

I spotted a cadaverlike lump on the deck—Berry's duffel bag—and then a second lump. My daughter rested in the mud just beyond the deck. "Ber!" I called. But there she lay, like a victim of drowning, chestnut hair dissolving in black water. I pried open her mouth to see if there was some sort of obstruction, fumbled for her plum-colored tongue. It was pale pink, drained of blood. I could make out saliva at the corners of her mouth, tiny bubbles the rain hadn't erased.

"Ber," I repeated. "*Wake up.*" My legs collapsed under me.

Freeman, who'd arrived close behind me, checked her pulse, then ran back in the house to dial 911. He returned with a wool blanket to cover our daughter.

"Can't we move her?" I asked when my voice returned. I clung to his flannel robe like a child.

"See, she's breathing." Freeman held my hand under Berry's nose so I could feel the tickle of air. "An ambulance is on its way," he said.

I stroked my daughter's arm, more to calm myself than anything. Suspended in time, her coarse features and thicket of curls took on a spooky beauty. I petted her head, kissed her chilled nose, vowing to never leave her side. Of course such a promise was impractical, one more way in which I would fail her.

"It's Pan," I said finally.

"What's Pan?" Freeman asked.

"This. This *accident.*"

"We don't know *what* this is," he said, his tolerance for the Story at its limit. "This looks like a seizure. Or an overdose." He began to hum—first a Bach hymn, then something unrecognizable.

"Are you sure we shouldn't just be quiet?" I asked.

"Berry loves sound," he said. "I've got to let her know that we're here with her."

"Oh," was all I could say before my voice failed me completely. I didn't have any sound to offer my daughter.

When the paramedics arrived, Berry's eyes clicked open. I blew her a kiss, but she was too far away in her thoughts to recognize me. I held her hand, knowing she would have preferred that I didn't. The ambulance took off like Pegasus, flying through intersections with the entitlement of a god. Inside the van Berry was breathing rapidly, and shuddering. And then a staccato chanting from deep inside her throat: "Can't see anything. Don't have my passport. Don't wanna come back. Don't want nothing. Don't like you. No. Don't go. Don't go!"

As we pulled in to Alta Bates Medical Center, the sky flushed with lavender light. Berry had to be held down by two attendants as they strapped her onto a gurney. The more they suppressed her the harder she fought. At last she was hustled into the emergency room and, after a brief, bone-chilling scream, she turned down the volume. I think she simply got tired. A crew of doctors, two with five o'clock shadows, swarmed over her, putting her through an impressive drill of tests. A soft-spoken doctor, a woman who looked young enough to be Berry's schoolmate, explained to Berry that she needed to ask some delicate questions. Berry blinked as if consenting and then stuck out her tongue.

"Now don't you look pretty," the doctor said. "I'm signing you up for the Ms. Alta Bates Beauty Pageant." She handed Berry a paper cup of water, which Berry drained in one sip, then spat onto the physician's coat. "I believe we have a winner!" the girlish doctor said, raising Berry's right arm. Then she took the arm and stabbed it with a needle.

"Bitch!" Berry growled.

The doctor asked her if she was "loaded"; but Berry refused to speak and soon fell into a forced sleep. Within minutes, she looked so content that a stranger might have mistaken her for a happy child.

After an hour, she was moved a few streets over to the hospital's Herrick campus, which housed its psychiatric unit. Up on the second floor, a cobalt-haired nurse with four earrings riding up each lobe escorted us to Berry's room. The space had been painted a benign cream color and boasted a TV set mounted on the ceiling. There were no other distractions or flourishes. Freeman and I quickly settled in, pulling up two dented metal chairs to one side of Berry's bed. Our daughter looked every bit as lovely as Sleeping Beauty: composed, self-possessed, absent. I drew the covers up to her chin, at a loss for something to do.

As the hours passed with a brutal slowness, I wondered if Freeman would hang in there for the long haul or if things were getting "too serious." Thankfully, Berry's every spasm was of supreme importance to him, her sighs a secret code he longed to crack. We remained at our post into the morning, watching our daughter's belly expand and contract, assuring ourselves that she was safe. Whether or not she was sound would have to wait for later.

Around noon Berry's slurry alto woke us up. "What is it, Mu-Mu? A bird or a plane?" She stirred under the blankets and blinked at the cream-colored room she now found herself in. Her bedroom back home was that pukey dinosaur green she loved so much. "It's Spider-Man!" she rasped.

"What, honey?" I said, faking a calmness I didn't possess. "Is my honey-berry awake?" I bent over and embraced her. But she pulled back; I could feel her resisting my devotion.

"Daddy-o!" Berry whispered.

Freeman hobbled over like Charlie Chaplin on speed. She greeted him with weak applause. As he attempted to lift her, he saw that her legs were strapped to the bed; tan leather cuffs surrounded her ankles. "Hey, kid, your umbilical cord is showing."

"Silly Daddy," she said. "Everyone *knows* I was born in a test tube." He glanced over at me and I shook my head.

"From the looks of it"—his hands followed the bed restraints to their origins—"your biological mother is a *bed*!"

This time Berry clapped like a windup monkey with crashing cymbals; her laughter was hoarse and phlegmy. Freeman and I hugged each other as if we were long-lost siblings. Our daughter was alive and kicking—with an emphasis on the kicking. Despite the restraints she twitched like a little RoboCop.

I smiled colorlessly at my daughter. Her transit to The Neverland had failed spectacularly and, naturally, I blamed myself. That's what mothers *do*. We mean to protect our children from hating themselves, but in spite of our best efforts, smart kids find plenty of opportunities for raking themselves through the coals.

The following day bore improvements. Berry had a touch of breakfast—I smuggled in a sun-dried tomato bagel from Noah's—and by afternoon she'd gathered the strength to complain about her surroundings. She found her room "way banal" and, given the number of gerbera daisies that had been dispatched by the globe-trotting Ullmans, altogether too cheery. I brought in vases of weeds from our garden to even things out, which helped her mood some, and Freeman tacked her KISS posters to the stark walls. Mummy Dearest showed up in an Issey Miyake sculptural event: a black knife-pleated skirt that morphed into a single wave which swept over one shoulder to become a blouse; the other shoulder was left bare so we could consider her new tattoo, *MEN ARE MUTANTS*. From her ears hung two chandelier earrings, and her dainty feet were shod in clear-plastic platform shoes. In a matter of months Mummy had graduated from the "rich hippie" look to that of "fashion victim," a crusade to make up for lost time. It was the early nineties, after all, and only a few daring college girls wore Indian bedspread skirts and spritzed themselves with patchouli oil.

"My precious blackberry!" Mother shrieked, impelling Freeman to close the door. "Thank Buddha, you're *alive*."

"Of course she's alive, Mummy. Don't you think I would have told you if my own daughter had died?" I pulled my hair into a tense, temporary ponytail.

"No, not really, darling. You keep so much to yourself."

"I don't think that's true. I *know* it's not true." My hair fell back in my face. "How can you say such a thing?"

"Easily. With ease. Because I speak the gospel. I hope you're not asking me to censor myself because I sure as shit—"

"Grandmummy," Berry croaked, reaching tentatively for her hand.

"My sweet juicy Berry." In a beat, Mother redirected her slippery attention to her granddaughter; she hugged her bundled form. "Holy *merde*," Mother said. "You look horrible. Don't say a word. Just rest and let Grandmummy try a few of her tricks." She winked at me, suggesting that one of her "beautifying rituals" was about to commence. Mother placed her sequined bag—in the shape of a crocodile, I noted—on the hospital bed, and pulled up a chair. She fumbled in the tiny purse as if it held hundreds of items. "I only have a bit of lipstick, but we can do miracles with Chanel, no?" Berry nodded warily, too tired to object.

In minutes, Mummy had taken a shimmery stick of Purple Rain and rubbed it on the apples of Berry's green cheeks, on her sallow eyelids, her bloodless lips. She even massaged some bright color onto Berry's dark brows. The result was something ghastly, akin to Bette Davis in *Whatever Happened to Baby Jane?* My child looked like a stranger.

Incomprehensibly proud of her masterpiece, Mother held up a coin-sized mirror to Berry's face. My daughter grimaced in new pain; she inflated her cheeks as if to retch and crossed her already bloodshot eyes. Then she broke out in melodic giggles. "I love it, Grandmummy. It rocks."

"*See,*" Mother insinuated in my direction. "She's adorable."

"I never doubted it," I said, and left the two of them to their whims.

When I returned a half hour later, Berry was pawing at her cheeks, making a wreck of her clown makeup. Her eyes were twitching, her mouth ajar. "Jesus, Mummy. Call the nurse!" But Mother was on the floor in the corner, asleep or daydreaming, I couldn't tell. The pleated wave of her skirt shielded her face.

I hit the buzzer and a trio of white coats darted in, two nurses accompanied by a doctor. With astonishing precision the team administered a series of shots to the patient, and once more Berry coasted into an unnatural slumber. Her clown face collected itself; her feet stopped fidgeting. But her dark hands remained curled into fists.

"Mummy?" I said, when we were alone again. I could tell from her rocking motion that she was crying. "Look, Berry's sleeping peacefully."

Mother peeked up from the pleats and saw that Berry was subdued. "Of course pharmaceuticals are not the answer," Mummy said, rising to her feet. "Darling women don't need drugs to take them places." She picked up her purse and signaled her intention to leave. This was for the best, I knew. I needed time to find out what Peter had done to my daughter and, failing that, what he hadn't done.

I regarded Berry, snared like a tiger in a net. I could see right through the meds into her restless heart. In spite of the potions that coursed through her blood, she was putting up a brave battle. Silly doctors. It was not possible to mute my daughter's ardor. I stared at the humiliating bed restraints, now only partially concealed by the sheets. Had Berry flown and then fallen? Had she never gotten off the ground? I was determined to discover what business had transpired between Berry and Peter. I so much wanted to be of help, to mend any fissure. The only complication: I was still in love with Pan. I was still trying to determine what had transpired between *us*.

 PART

THREE

Just before our love got lost, you said,
"I am as constant as the northern star"
And I said, "Constantly in the darkness
Where's that at? . . ."

—Joni Mitchell, "A Case of You"

XI

THE doctors told me my daughter was "lost," but how could that be when I was right there beside her, her father two steps behind me? Each morning Freeman and I made our way through a labyrinth of hallways and stairwells to find Berry all over again, in the same bed rocking. She was always in the same position: knees drawn to chest, hands shielding her eyes. I suppose this was to block out the reality that is Berkeley—parents, school, and those tired laws of gravity. The incessant rocking? Repetition is a comfort, her doctor explained; it's something she can count on.

For eight days Berry had refused to speak out, to reveal one thing about *that night.* All the same her body revealed that she'd taken a bad spill: bruised from thigh to ankle on one side. She might be remote, I told myself; she might be sequestered in her thoughts. But in no way is she lost. *No way.*

I know lost. Lost is when you don't have parents, those people who adore you so much it diminishes them to see you walk out the door. Lost means that no one waits up for you to come home at night; no one brings you supper or tucks you into bed. No one would care if you forget your address and wander off; if you end up in the next town without money or clean clothes. Lost is when you can't draw a straight line from someone you love to your hungering heart. The world has abandoned you for no good reason: it has the insane notion that it is better off without you.

No, Berry wasn't lost; we were here for her whenever she was ready to show up. It was the Lost Boys who didn't have a soul waiting for them at the end of the day. And so they were the saddest creatures I've ever met. Of course they would have you believe otherwise—they would boast that they were free. But what good is being free if you are never found by love?

ON her ninth day in the hospital, I found Berry rocking in her newly minted position of knees drawn to chest; this time, however, she was talking a blue streak. No one else was in the room, so I surmised this was a one-way conversation, one that could be deemed delusional. Still, I was encouraged: even when healthy, Berry harbored too many opinions to keep them to herself—the more that leaked out the better. In the past I'd wondered if this was her way of fending off implosions, a canny survival ploy. More likely, she was following in the very large footsteps of Great-Nana and Mummy, two people never short on commentary.

"Berry," I called out, approaching her bedside.

"So he comes into my bedroom. *My bedroom.* Of course, that's the way it is with boys—they go straight to the bedroom these days. So here he is and I am so totally casual. Like I couldn't care less when I care more than anything in the world. And I let him know that I am not your typical ingenue. That I am more prepared than some dorky Girl Scout. And he looks at me with the biggest eyes, like I'm an angel or a virgin, which I'm *not.*"

"Berry," I gasped, but she continued.

"And I show him my luggage, but he doesn't *move.* I'm all packed to go and he's just staring at me 'cause I'm not like the other girls. I have my stuff ready and I'm not into small talk. He's never seen a girl so completely primed to leave home. The weather sucks, but I don't care. I don't care! That's what I'm trying to tell him: *I don't care about myself.*"

"Berry," I said again, reaching out to stroke her forehead.

"So I step outside and I'm all psyched to leave, but he hesitates—he won't give me the fucking dust! He tries to tell me the dust is, like, extinct. He tells me I can do it, I can fly by myself, which is bullshit and I know it, but without the dust I've got to try it his way. So I do the thing, the happy thoughts thing. I focus so hard it hurts. For a moment I see the dots everybody sees when they squint—those grainy, flickering things? Just when they're making me sick, I remember Little Dot, the girl in the comic book. And I laugh. Well, I *think* I'm laughing but who really knows? I laugh because, when I was a kid, I used to do Dot's voice—you know, when I read her comics out loud to Daddy?"

I nodded solemnly, patted her damp forehead with a tissue.

"Then I open my eyes and whammo! The world looks the same as when my eyes were closed. Except the darkness is now wetness and I see the twinkle-toe dots for real. *They're stars, Mother.* Stars in a wet blanket. The sky, the stars, it's all too amazing. I start crying 'cause this beauty shit makes me sad. Because I always believed there wasn't anything beautiful *enough* to make me stick around. I needed a reason and here it is, right above me, turning my whole argument upside down.

"I get so pissed about this, I wouldn't know a happy thought if it bit me in the brain. I call out for Peter—it turns out he's still there. *And he's nice.* I'm not used to nice and it hurts to feel his kindness seeping into my head. So I try again, the whole flying business. I've got his kindness in my head butting up against my stupid feelings. And now I burn in every muscle like I'm an old creature, dying off. I can't move my feet, let alone travel a thousand miles to some Coney Island.

"Somehow I manage to block out the basic hideosity of life— long enough to see the stars again. And then I'm—*hovering.* Like one inch over the deck. I get my bearings and rise like steam until I'm about twelve feet off the ground. Un-fucking-believable. But the rain. The weather's gotten extra gnarly and I'm thinking, *Jesus Christ, the timing's off.* This is when I get a picture in my head: I'm a fighter jet and I've got bombs on board. I see little explosions in people's backyards and realize they're coming from *me*—bombs are dropping from my fists. Then everything goes dark, like right before a play. I can't see a thing. No Peter, no city, no stars. The absence of stars confirms that I've lost it, I've finally lost it. I'm the first Darling in a zillion years to screw up. I mean, everyone else *made it*."

Berry was trying to sit up now, tensed like a pit bull. "Then I reach for my head—I know it's there but I can't see my body. So I fall. For miles, which is weird 'cause I was only a few feet up in the air. The math, you see, is totally off. I hit the mud. I sink. I start to become part of *everything*. And I feel what I could never feel before. I feel, well, okay. Oh God, can I say this? I feel sort of loved. I touch my mouth, it's stretching at the corners. I'm smiling. I'm a goddamn happy face. Everything's so beautiful I decide to stay this way forever.

"Then the screams wake me up, my own dumb-ass screams. I can't stop them. I grab my throat to choke them off but something forces my hand away. I'm wrapped like a mummy in something soft and dry. I still can't see a thing, but I know it's the light that's doing this, annihilating me. And so I think, what if *this* is Neverland, the final destination for girls like me?"

Berry had her back to me now. Her voice was muffled by the pillow, but I caught its note of self-dismissal, that terminal quality that comes so easily to teenagers. Then, abruptly, she twisted her head around to make sure our eyes made contact. She threw off her bedclothes and began to sob. "The End, by Shiva Darling," she said.

"No, my sweet," I whispered in her hot ear. "It's not the end."

BERRY'S absence in our house only reinforced Freeman's obsession with work. He was now pulling twelve-hour days at Skywalker, doing a lot of sound engineering for Pixar animation, and then moonlighting during the late-evening hours at Fantasy Studios in Emeryville. Having returned to his passion for composing for cartoons, he threw himself into making sounds for all kinds of cool stuff: animated dolls, toy soldiers, stuffed animals. When we *did* talk the subject was: if a Slinky could speak, what would it sound like? Do you think Barbie is a soprano or an alto? Would a yellow rubber ducky stutter or lisp? With so much on his mind he couldn't seem to remember the visiting hours at Alta Bates. Still, he pointed out, the money was good and it kept us afloat.

I didn't care about the money—I would choose attention over money any day. For me, Freeman's absence could only mean one thing: I was losing him, however slowly, but in his head he was already out the door.

Mother proved to be of no help, either. Having left town for a ten-city promotional tour on behalf of her latest polemic, *Rapunzel's Rules: Let Your Hair Down & Other Random Acts of Liberation,* she freely offered her two cents over a cell phone: "Screaming is always the best medicine, Wends. Let Berry scream her guts out. Let her do *whatever* she needs to in order to feel emancipated. Composure stinks. Having a fit is natural. Allow the animal out of its cage!"

Unfortunately, Mummy's advice didn't deviate from the sound bites she offered on her radio interviews. Her book was the only thing on which she could focus; even Milton Pease was on the sidelines until the tour was over.

As before, I tried taking refuge in my fables. When I wasn't at the hospital pacing like an expectant father, I distracted myself by making notes for a new collection. A series on serpents. A story cycle on birds. But my angst refused to be buried in allegory. I needed to attempt something new, something light and tasteless. And then it hit me—a Jacqueline Susann-ish novel would be just the thing! My first order of business, then, was to put away my animals and trot out some Beautiful People.

One morning before visiting hours at Herrick, when the fog blanketed our hillside like the great unconscious, I hunkered down at the kitchen table and, with the aplomb of a writer who hasn't a clue where she's headed, filled my yellow notepad with sentences: *He didn't want another Porsche; he wanted to strip her gears. She wouldn't get together with him tonight or any night: he smelled of old money and she preferred new. They kissed so hard a flood of juices made its way down her legs.*

Okay, this was really bad. Writing about the horrors of Hollywood wasn't much of a diversion. Berry's psychosis, it seems, had generated enough drama. Abandoning the trash novel was for the best, I knew. The only characters I had come up with in two hours' time were a diet doctor with gonorrhea and a plastic surgeon with an incurable rash. Imagine what I could accomplish in another hour! I'd failed to write one true sentence. There was no island of the mind that offered asylum; I would be forced to stay put with my grief.

Drifting across the living room like some spacey Stepford wife, I set my rocking chair before the expanse of window-glass and endeavored to get comfortable. The room felt crowded with Great-Nana's antiques, and I chose to look outward instead. Though Fall was hardly upon us, the deck was blanketed with wine-colored drifts. The gray morning mist now cleared abruptly to reveal a slate-gray sky, and the dullness of it all persuaded me to nod off.

WHEN next I looked up I saw the horrid man again—that reject from the Renaissance Fair. *How the hell had he gotten inside the house? Was he a musician friend of Freeman's?* I would have gone faint with fear if he didn't look so shabby, so warmed-over.

The man extended his right hand to my lips as if I would deign to kiss the bony thing. It was then I perceived a cologne so vulgarly floral, I might have passed out if the left hand—really, a claw—hadn't grabbed my wrist and wrung it bloodless. Now his right hand covered my mouth in case I cared to scream.

"So fah-bulous to see you again," he drawled, crouching down on Great-Nana's Persian rug. "And in such a good mood." Yawning, he exposed the clay-pink cave of his mouth: I spotted a single gold cap before his jaws clamped shut. With a pressed handkerchief he wiped a shower of spit off his lips, exactly as I'd seen him do at the pier. "Now, where did we leave off? Oh yes, the part where I shanghai you."

Again the cavernous mouth flared open, this time emitting a high-pitched titter that could have repelled fleas.

I sank back in the rocking chair. "Shanghai?"

"Oh, you modern girls like everything spelled out. Perhaps you prefer the term *abduct*? Does that have more *meaning* for you?"

Still on his knees, he crept within an inch of my left cheek. I could smell his fetid breath cutting through the stinky cologne, the bottom note of sweat wafting out from under his coat. I got up from the chair and took a step backward. Slowly he rose to his full height, towering over me like a bogeyman's shadow. As I retreated he continued to advance, making assumptions about my lack of courage. Each of my shaky steps backward resulted in a mannered vault of his own. I noticed he was wearing crocodile shoes with droopy trouser socks; furry leg hair stuck out from his ankles, wolflike.

Eventually he cornered me, his cadaverous body bearing down on my breastbone. Flush against the cut-velvet wallpaper in our dining room, I sweated like a thief. *He's the blackguard,* I reminded myself. I wasn't about to let him take something from me. Then, shutting my eyes to the world, I made an effort to listen.

There it was, Great-Nana's entreaty, roaring in my head: *Wendy, save yourself first.*

"What's that?" the man questioned. "You have nothing to say? No sparkling rejoinder? No witty quip? Gee, I'm crushed. I honestly expect more from a Darling." He didn't twirl his pomaded mustache so much as jerk on it. "Do I have to skip your generation and move on to your daughter?"

"No!" I screamed weakly, my arms batting his chest as if I were a hand puppet. What a waste I was—I could only fight back in my stories, relying on cheeky animals to make my points.

"Stay away from her," I managed to get out.

He stroked my neck with two skull-ringed fingers. "That's better," he encouraged. "Perhaps you *are* Margaret's daughter. And Jane's granddaughter."

"Jane? What do you know about Jane?"

"Don't you mean, what *don't* I know about Jane?"

"Is s-she alive?" I asked.

"That depends on your definition of alive," he said.

I stopped struggling to get free and gave his answer a moment's thought. "Where is she?" I demanded, slipping through his arms to the floor. "Give me something!"

"Here's a little something." The man stooped down and planted a brotherly kiss on my nose. "You look surprised," he said. "Perhaps you expected something more like this." This time he zeroed in on my lips, leaving a sloppy, moist imprint. I wiped my lips with my forearm, which I then dried on the pleats of my skirt.

When the awful man finished laughing—he'd sniggered so hard, a button burst off his coat—he picked me up off the floor and flattened me against the wall again. "You are mistaken if you think I'm interested in you."

"Then why all the allusions to, you know, having your way with me?"

"Oh, that. Well, it's expected of us Hooks. We have a tradition of intimidation and bullshit. Please, let's sit down." He guided me over to the white wicker love seat that faced the fireplace, and we seated ourselves as if we'd been having tea together all our lives.

"I don't get it. You're not here to . . . hurt me?"

"Well, yes, if you mean damage your self-regard. I believe I've already succeeded, no?" I didn't give him the pleasure of a nod. "Care for a lemon drop?" he asked, selecting a sweet from Great-Nana's beveled dish on the coffee table.

I coughed on the hand with the candy.

"My word, tiger's punchy." He set the lemon drop on his thick slab of a tongue and bit down on it. "Let me introduce my-thelf," he said, crunching the candy. "Jason G. Hook, grandson of James Hook, at your thur-vith." The candy gave him the slight lisp.

"Jason G. Hook," I repeated skeptically. "What's the G for?"

"Why, Grappling," he said, surprised by my interest.

"What makes you think I won't call the police?" I said, changing the subject.

"What makes you think I won't call the police?" he mimicked in a strong soprano. "Well, just maybe because I have your daughter . . . in my grip."

I steadied myself from the shock. "You're mistaken," I said.

"She's nowhere near your grip. She's a good girl, she'd never cross over to *your side*."

As soon as I said this, I knew the truth resided elsewhere. After all, Berry was a card-carrying member of the Other Side. But she would never stand for clichés like Jason Hook—would she?

"Listen," he said in a more charitable tone, "I need your voice, that's all. I'm abducting your *voice*." I stiffened my spine in the love seat. "It's patently perfect for my needs—supple, feminine. I must have it or the ship will sink!"

"You sound as hysterical as your grandfather," I told him.

"Shut up!" he screamed. "Shut the hell up."

"I thought you loved my voice," I said.

"Not another word till we get to the ship." He held a pungent rag over my nose and mouth. I was gone in thirty seconds.

WHEN my gag was removed (by a little fellow wearing the kind of pirate costume one rents for Halloween: bee-striped stockings, red satin sash, lace-up shirt that showcases chest hair), I realized that we were, indeed, aboard a ship. It was some sort of derelict freighter that was badly in need of paint. Looking up I saw a pennant flapping laggardly atop the pilot house. It read *KRAP*.

"Krap!" I shouted. "This ship is the *Krap*?"

The little guy brandished a rubber sword from his sash and pointed it at my nose. "It says *K-Rap*. We play rap music."

"This is . . . a radio station?"

"Yes, ma'am. Pirate radio." I almost fell over. The Hooks never met a pun they didn't like.

"Actually, we're changing our programming to heavy metal: 'All hair bands, all the time.' We're hoping to get new call letters this week: K-A-Z-Z. Kick ass. You like?"

"Where is he?" I demanded.

"Who, he?" the phony pirate asked.

"C'mon," I urged. "The boss."

"Bruce Springsteen? Oh, you mean our station manager, Mr. Hook."

"Did you really say 'hair bands'?" I laughed. "Yes, Jason Hook, your *capitan*."

"It's *Mister* Hook and he's waiting for you in the mess. As you is our guest, he thought you might like a square meal."

I propped my hip against the ship's railing and filled my lungs with salty air. Judging from the stench of oil, we were in the San Francisco Bay, most likely near Point Richmond—the local refinery just up the shore. I whirled around and sized up my situation. In spite of the stink, I couldn't have been held captive in more pleasant environs—picturesque cove, streaming sunlight, a stooge wearing puffy sleeves.

"Are you suggesting that Mr. Hook cooks?" I asked.

"Hook cooks?" The little man giggled, then scratched his crotch with the tip of his sword. "You gotta be kidding. As you is our guest, he got you take-out from Chez Panisse."

"Krap has quite the budget," I remarked.

"It's K-Rap, and no, we don't actually *buy* stuff."

"Oh, that's right, you're *pirates*," I said.

"It ain't called take-out for nothing," he said, and pulled at his sagging tights.

XII

OOK'S GUEST! Well I never. As much as I wanted to jump overboard, I decided to stay put. I've been a guest before and I know what's expected. But perhaps I've been too closemouthed. Perhaps you're wondering how intimately I associated with the locals on the island—if I entertained *other* guests?

Until now my covert excursion to The Neverland has always remained just that. I never felt the need to share my experience with any number of interested parties, including schoolmates and publishers. Why? Because in many respects the experience was so normal. Heightened, yet normal as far as human behavior goes. The natural beauty was quite literally out of this world, the plant life prodigious. But the humans were as perplexed and perplexing as they were back home. I recall the Lost Boys liked to poke me in the side, to finger the peach fuzz on my arms and occasionally pinch it. But so what? That's to be expected. Their lack of finesse elicited nary a squeal or scold from me. Like most girls my age, when it came to guys I tolerated a lot of bull.

It was the Boys' expectations that I found so unfair, the way they presumed certain things about my character (like bravery, strength, coordination). One could chalk this up to naïveté. Isolated from the civilized world, the Boys were clueless on so many levels. They had no information whatsoever on the subject of females, unless you count fairies and mermaids as exemplars of my sex. To the Boys I was an anomaly: I neither flitted around and whined like a fairy nor splashed about like a siren, fixated on my physical appearance. I wasn't a good swimmer and I only tolerated flying with myself at the controls.

Before me, no truly bookish girls had ever made the journey to the island, and that includes my Darling forebears, who appear to have demonstrated more aptitude than I in several aspects of island life—save for sweeping. My incompetence in all other domestic arts has been well established. Likewise I was a washout at tree climbing, cliff diving, pole shimmying, darts. The social disgrace was worse than that at Camp Nirvana, the all-denominations summer camp in Marin County, where I couldn't tie a knot to save a life.

No, in The Neverland my saving grace was my ability to make up stuff. A gift for storytelling was my lone inheritance, and I went into action whenever the Boys were exhausted by their mischief and gymnastics. In the center of a lopsided circle of logs upon which the Boys slouched and stood, I'd sit on a stump and march out my hedgehogs, my weasels, a couple of chickens, a polar bear—all residents of children's stories I'd begun telling myself as early as six years old in an effort to order the universe. True, some of these animals bore a close resemblance to the men in Mummy's books, but my characters were wholly contemporary. Hip to the Beatles and the Stones, they had political awareness, they had credit cards. And most had a conscience. All fared badly.

I admit I had trouble ending my tales, for to do so seemed cruel, too sad for words. Whenever my rambling plots tested the patience of my listeners, I'd add a gruesome touch—a swift beheading, a zombie curse. This always bought me more time with my audience. Emboldened, I'd add a drippy eye, a rabid bat. Without fail, the Boys would get overheated and begin snapping each other with river-dampened cloths—like schoolboys in a locker room. My focus, then, would falter and my audience dwindle until there was only one boy left, the one named Pan. He was the only youth who never tired of a yarn, no matter how psychologically disturbing. And so, to answer conclusively the question every therapist has posed, Peter became the only boy I entertained.

It would make scores of doctors happy if I conceded that my first love was a figment, as illusory as a teen idol on a poster. Well, he felt solid to *me*—bone-solid, flesh-solid. He even had a pulse. And so I must conclude that what I experienced was not simply make-believe. Nothing about it was simple. For one thing, the heart can't be fooled that easily. Neither can lips, cheeks, fingers. If love is a fiction, I told myself, it wouldn't hurt like hell; it couldn't be sustained like an epic tale. It would end with a bang or a whimper. But it would, without exception, end.

I say I had a "love" and yet you must remember that I was an inexperienced thirteen-year-old and any sort of touch felt like bliss on a stick. Plus the stick I'm referring to was a *real* one, with which Peter scratched my back in heavenly circles. Three times I caught him writing his name, lightly sweeping the stick over my skin, drafting letters. Far superior to getting pinned or going to the prom, I was engraved with Peter's autograph, an endorsement of affinity most girls never get. Now, to me, this *was* sex, in the sense that it was the essence of kindness. To this day kindness remains the ultimate turn-on, the swiftest route to awakening my body. I concede that this is strange.

⌒ The first time Peter and I found ourselves alone on the island, I was wrapping up "The Panda and the Chickens," a seemingly inexhaustible parable about being out of one's element. As the tale wound down—the panda finding himself in a chicken coop in the Deep South, confused and sweating profusely—I signaled for Peter to stop. I was ready to move on to something else.

"Hold your horses," he objected. "We can't leave the panda in that kind of heat."

"Of course we can. I just did."

"No," he insisted. He rolled his log over to my tree stump and sat down with a princely air of entitlement. "I need more story! You got to get the panda out of the South. How about this: And the bear clawed his way out of the chicken coop and didn't look back until he was safely home in China, his tummy full of tasty, headless chickens. The End, by Peter Pan." Peter flashed a killer smile, then melted backwards over the log, his long, freckled arms stretching to the ground.

"Peter! That's not the end at all. You know that."

"Then let's get the panda to the National Zoo, where he can have his very own iceberg."

"Wow, you know your geography," I marveled. "Listen, I'm tired. Can we, you know, *rest* somewhere? The two of us?"

At this he cocked his head, just like Lassie, in the direction of something he called the guest house—there was a *guest house*?—and gestured for me to follow him into the woods. Eschewing the beaten path, we immediately found ourselves looping backward, ending up farther from our destination with every well-intentioned step. While Peter couldn't disguise his pleasure about our lack of progress, I could barely keep my own feelings to myself—about my growing fatigue, my blurry sense of history.

"Peter, I don't get it," I announced as we rounded a familiar-looking bend. "Why am I here? Why me? Why did you choose me?"

He stopped dramatically and faced the wind. "I told you. Because of the stories. It's as simple as that."

"Nothing's that simple. There are scores of better storytellers. There's got to be something else. Something deeper."

"Believe you me, I don't know, on account of I'm not deep myself. I'm brave and nimble and legendary! For deep, you got to look elsewhere." He kicked at a stone that, embarrassingly enough for him, refused to move.

In the mounting silence, my lips fell into a pout and my eyelids grew heavy. Peter produced an herbal cigarette from a back pocket, then drew a match across the stubborn stone.

"Crikey, Wendybird," he said, by and by, blowing clove-scented smoke in my eyes. "I s'pose I fancy you because . . . well, for one, you're squidgy and you smell good. For two, I don't know. It's not something I put a lot of thought into. For three, you accept all this on face value." He motioned from east to west over the tree-swollen horizon. "You don't torture yourself about whether it's all rock-solid or just a friggin' sham. Neverland's a slam dunk with you."

"Yeah, I suppose," I said, measuring my words. I tore a wild plum off a tree, and I could swear the plum squealed.

"So why can't you be happy with that?" he asked. "Why does stuff have to mean more than it does?"

"*Everything* means more than it does!" I cried, and tossed the plum into a ditch.

"Prove it," he said.

On tiptoe I kissed him on the nape, making certain to leave a mark with my ice-pink lip gloss. "There. What does that mean?"

"Disaster," he said, rubbing the spot dry. "Absolute doom and defeat." He tightened the rounded-off Peter Pan (!) collar of his heavy corduroy jacket; it looked like he'd taken a scissors to it. "I suppose I chose you because . . . well, you don't think I'm the mutt's nuts—not like me other mates. Because you aren't quite convinced of my greatness."

"And that appeals to you?" I said, incredulous.

"It's a challenge," he said with a shrug.

"So it's *me* who's not the slam dunk."

"You could put it that way," he answered slyly, stamping out the butt of his cigarette. "What you can't say is why you chose *me*."

"But I didn't," I protested.

"Are you dead sure, luv?" Here, he blocked the path in front of me, allowing his height to make a point.

"What are you getting at?" I said, squinting up at him as if he were the sun.

"You're the one who made the trip. It's your thoughts that brung you here."

"*Brought* me here," I corrected.

"Yeah, luv, whatever you say." He bounded a few yards down the path; boredom would be setting in any second, I knew.

"Are you saying that *I* chose this place?" I asked, catching up to him. "That you had no hand in it?"

Peter spun around to face me. "Well, you took the getaway car, you found the escape hatch, you fell down the rabbit hole. I didn't put a gun to your back. You fancy me something rotten. That's right: you chose me."

Like an arrogant genie, he crossed his arms and stamped the dirt with his cowboy boots, the leather so scuffed it had been rubbed clear white. Then, to mark his territory, he drew a line in the soil with the heel of one boot, a line that circled clear around an oak tree. Peter rested his back against the tree's great trunk, taking care that his feet did not cross the line. From his deep right jacket pocket, he pulled a Superman comic and dove into its pages.

I was stunned. Wasn't Peter notorious for being the one who started this business of "choosing" girls? The one who was ultimately responsible? The few books I'd read on the subject had made it clear that the Darlings were pawns, our fates sewn to us like shadows.

What I could never tell him, what I could barely tell myself was why it mattered so much—why *he* mattered so much. There were clever boys back home, boys with sex appeal and smarts. Guys who were even capable of *feeling* if given half the chance. So what was the big deal? Why was this one guy capable of doing so much damage over so many years?

He recognized our wildness.

Peter saw that we were capable of doing damage, too. Somehow, he understood that creativity is reckless and untidy and that we could never get enough of it. All the domestic chores were bearable *because* we were allowed our "maleness," our freedom to cut up. Liberation coupled with maternal authority—does it get any better than that? The Neverland fulfilled a real dream for us Darlings: the attentions of a charming boy in a place where we held great power. Here, we were an unqualified success.

Too, The Neverland afforded me a laboratory wherein I could experiment and no one got hurt. On balmy afternoons when the heavens displayed a keen sense of humor, the cottony clouds gathering into balloon-animal shapes, I'd take long solo walks in a velvety field shot through with petunias and pansies and poppies, and spin my stories out loud. But these weren't the gritty yarns I told the Boys or the morality tales I'd publish later in life. These were troubled romances, starring me, and they fed off a steady stream of my sadness. In each I had no kin—I was a family of one—and lived behind the locked gates of Buckingham Palace in a moldering room that was all but forgotten. I made up scores of allegories on this same trope, and never even *tried* to step back and self-diagnose. Understanding would have ruined the tales for sure and weakened their power over me. The irony of inventing stories while living out a whopper in The Neverland was never far from my thoughts. The truth is, I wasn't so much greedy for adventure as unceasingly inspired here. Daddy had told me that astronauts don't stop dreaming while orbiting the Earth; likewise, the Lost Boys and the occasional Lost Girl churned out adventures at an alarming rate. It's the very least we could do.

Once Peter had digested the Superman comic (did he favor sexy Lana Lang over cerebral Lois Lane? I asked myself), we set off again for the elusive guest house. After an afternoon spent traveling in circles we arrived in a matter of minutes. Theo, the angel-faced Boy, slumped against the door, which for some reason shimmered. As we approached within a few feet, he abandoned his post altogether. Now I could see it was a silk nightgown that fell like a drape over the opening. Was the gown Mummy's—or did it belong to some nameless girl?

Drawing the garment aside, I discovered a room decked out with the best the island offered: a seaweed-woven hammock, orange daisies stuck in the walls like lollipops, even a wooden stool flown in from the Darling sitting room, circa 1909. With a spring in my step, I crossed through the portal. Where my own quarters had been dank and lackluster, I now found myself in a dry, fragrant space lit by long yellow tapers, the walls hung with cheerful Indian bedspreads.

"Would you like to come in?" I asked, word for word, as my antecedents had.

"Would I," Peter replied, but failed to stir.

"Is there a problem?" I asked. "I mean, did I forget something crucial? A password, a rhyme."

"Nope," he said, businesslike. For the first time he looked anxious, his confidence failing him. "Just got to watch it, you know."

"Watch it?"

"Well, there's history. I've got history to consider. There's Jane, don't forget."

"Jane?" I peeped, barely audible above the hammering of my heart. "Jane?" I repeated, tearing away at a thumbnail. "Do you . . . know something?"

"I know loads of things!" he exploded. "It's just, I'm supposed to think about the coincidences. I promised Margaret I would." Peter dipped his forehead, in a rare display of introspection.

"You mean *consequences*. Mother warned you about the consequences."

"Yeah," he conceded. "That's it."

"You're coming in," I said. I seized his calloused hands and yanked him through the opening, careful lest he bring down the ivory-silk gown with lace trimming. With a trembling hand I directed him to sit on the stool. How many times, I wondered, had he settled on this same spot, making goo-goo eyes at my beautiful mother? I hated her at that moment; Mummy knew how to play any scene, how to entertain a man. At this point I could do nothing that was sufficiently original, that could make a mark of its own.

The two of us sat facing each other, heavy and silent as dumb-bells. I refused to say a word for fear of sounding common, or worse, dull. His attention span at its limit, Peter cleared his throat: "Blimey, this cave's done up nicely."

"I guess it's full of memories," I said tentatively.

"Memories that would make you blubber."

"Why would you say that?" I asked him. "I mean, how could I have *your* memories? If you'd put on your thinking cap, you'd figure that out."

Peter looked away. "Me thinking cap is on, luv. I'm not famous

for having memories. I'm famous for *not* remembering things—
remember?"

I nodded, thinking *yes, it's your forgetting that's generated nothing
but problems.* Then my mind went dim. A bucket of memories—
strangely not my own—seemed to have dropped on my head. With
the clarity of an oracle, I beheld the little house the Boys had built
around my great-grandmother as she slowly regained consciousness—her fall from the sky had been the most violent of all the Darlings. I watched as the Boys uprooted a crude arrow from her chest;
she'd been a fatality on the island, if only for two minutes. I watched
as she plucked from her nightgown the flat ivory button that had
saved her life. Many years later, she would fashion it into a pin so I
might attach it to the neckline of posh frocks. The brooch was waiting for me back home in the top dresser drawer; Nana, the poor
dear, hadn't anticipated the advent of tee-shirts.

When the fog of history lifted, Peter lorded over me, looking for
all the world like a wolf in boys' clothing. If you must know, the wolf
and I engaged in heavy petting. For me he broke the rules! First,
Peter took a bite out of my neck, the way vampires in movies seduce
pretty girls. Perhaps it was more of a nibble than a bite. I only recall
the sound I made—a sound that corresponds to greed or hunger.
"Ooh," I swooned, protesting with my arms. My inner thighs
throbbed, my lips ached. I confess that I wanted to be nipped. And
to nip back. I slipped a hand under the waistband of his Levi's and
found comfort in the taut, damp skin there. As I did this, Peter took
my entire ear in his mouth and sucked on it like a lemon drop. I
would have fallen on the floor if I wasn't already sprawled there.
Instead, I groped my way to the stool and clumsily mounted it. From
this vantage point, I could look down at the boy who famously
refused to grow up. How evolved he seemed now! How mature
beyond his years!

When a couple of forehead curls flopped into his eyes, I took his
face in my hands and practically swallowed it. Well, I tried. In
response, Peter brushed his hands over the thin flannel masking my

breasts, and again my blood rattled about. "So good," I said, against my better judgment.

"You can never be too careful," he said apropos of nothing, and smacked his lips. When these same lips received mine, there was no looking down or back, only kissing and more kissing. We were not careful in the least.

To be truthful, the whole business went nowhere. By that I mean I made this part up. I only kissed him twice on the nose—that was it. I did not try to extract meaning from the pleasure. For one suspended moment, Pan repressed his revulsion at being touched and I was deaf to my mother's warning bells. Great-Nana would be proud, for I did not try to force something permanent from this entanglement. On the precipice of everything to lose, I sacrificed nothing but two kisses for a very dear boy.

I let Peter go, of course, cleaving to a wisdom that had arrived in the nick of time. We'd been nothing but pure and thus purity became our souvenir. For the first time in my life I let go of an ideal, and allowed the mere *taste* of love to take its place. It would be many more years before I'd get a whole meal.

★　★

JASON HOOK, general manager of KRAP, admired me as if contemplating a plate of dessert. In one hand he held a demitasse of espresso, in the other a bowl of raw sugar cubes. Hook waved the cup beneath my nostrils so I might take a whiff of the rich Italian roast. For once he smiled with his mouth closed; then he set the coffee before me like an invitation.

I'd accepted his offer of lunch in the ship's mess because one never refuses a meal from Chez Panisse. "Food's good," I said cautiously. "I'm just not crazy about the company." I stabbed the last triangle of *quattro formaggio* pizza with my fork. "In fact, what am I *doing* here?"

"I see your point," he said impassively.

"You do?" I said, and popped the paper-thin crust in my mouth.

"Indeed, I do. You feel that you have no truck with men like me. That men like me are scum, or worse, undesirable."

I had to laugh. Espresso dribbled down one corner of my mouth.

"I can't take you anywhere," Hook observed, wiping my cheek with a paper napkin.

"Not true," I said. "You've taken me aboard this ship." Out a porthole on my right I saw a gardenlike isle looming in the distance. But it was not The Neverland—it was the Rock, Alcatraz, that legendary lockup for lifers, birdmen, and other miscreants. "We *are* in the San Francisco Bay?" I asked.

"Right you are again," Hook said. "And I don't see you resisting me." He lowered his stringy body into the chair across from me.

"Well, that's because I'm drugged. No way would I just *come* with you."

"Where there's a way, there's a will," he sang.

"Bite me!" I said.

"How much you sound like Berry. Like mother like daughter, like *daughter* like daughter," he said. "Actually, I've no interest in biting you. I'm a gentleman, not a vampire. Your head must be stuck in some other story."

Hook was right: I *was* stuck. Neither transported to Neverland nor caught in a dream, I was an adult who'd gone missing in her own backyard—with some ridiculous villain I had manifested.

Pleased with himself, Hook set a mouthwatering flan before me on the table. How I longed to pound it with my fists, to watch the stiff custard fly.

"See, I'm not such a baddy," he said. "I'm a fun guy. A regular Joe."

"Hardly." I scowled.

"Have we forgotten everything?" he said, raising his voice. "There is always a bit of Pan in Hook, and a bit of Hook in Pan—or hadn't you noticed?"

My heart stopped for a moment, but I didn't want to give this particular Hook the pleasure. Instead I yawned openly.

"Perhaps it's time for tiger's nap?" he said lustfully. "I'm a touch weary myself. Or maybe I'm just jaded." Then he laughed at his joke as if he'd been his own audience for too many years.

"Berry," I said dully, and collapsed on the table amid the ruins of lunch.

BERRY'S medical chart revealed that she could be found in her bed at the hospital during her mother's abduction. There was no record, however, of her mother's absence from the house, and I awoke on my wicker love seat in a moist heap, dazed but curiously full. I ran to the bathroom and promptly threw up. A great deal of crust came up, mixed with black water.

Feeling somewhat relieved, I phoned Freeman at Skywalker. "Hi," I said weakly. "I'm having a bad day."

Freeman reported that work was going "bodaciously" on his sound design for animated nuts and bolts—*All Screwed Up* was the feature's working title—and he planned to work through the night. "That's good," I said. "Really," I added.

"Then why don't I believe you?" he said.

"I'm in trouble," I told him. "You know, the bad day I just referred to?"

I heard a massive sigh through the receiver. "Wends, I can't deal with this now."

"Oh," I said brightly. "Please tell me the right time, so I can be there."

"Snideness is not the proper response," Freeman said.

"Then what is!" I hollered into the phone.

"I'm just trying to keep this family together. Not doing the greatest job, but trying. What are *you* trying to do?"

"I'm trying too."

"Well, try a little harder not to make up your mind about what's happening."

"What *is* happening, Man? Hey, that sounds cool, doesn't it? Like, man, what's happening!"

"Wendy," Freeman said mildly. "Berry and I need you to be strong now."

"Well, sorry to disappoint," I said, the old nausea rising in my stomach. "Sorry that—" The words got lost in my throat.

"Stop this, Wendolyn. Time to get real."

"Ha, that's a good one, coming from you. That's all I've ever wanted to do—get real. But it appears that's not in the cards. It *appears* that I'm stuck in some portal between what's real and what's clearly insane. That neither world wants me. Whaddya know, I'm a reject in two dimensions!"

"Wends," Freeman said again, this time so softly I might have imagined it. "That's not funny."

"I'm not trying to humor you, dear."

"Wendy!" he said, more harshly now. "I just can't stand it anymore. I can't stand the anger, the ghosts, the craziness."

"And so you won't have to."

I slammed the receiver on the kitchen table, then ripped out the cord from the wall. Flinging open the refrigerator door, I removed a half-gallon of springwater from the top shelf and took a long drink directly from the jug. With the jug in one hand and a Terminator mug in the other, I retreated to the bedroom. I was very thirsty, I recall.

After swallowing a handful of ibuprofen and five or eight Valium, I can't remember exactly, I took to bed with my clothes on and the covers drawn over my head. It was clear I had a choice to make: whether to succumb to the fever dreams of Hook or the fever dreams of Berry. Why not bow to both, I told myself, and take a little vacation? My bags were packed with really bad ideas, and I was off and running. I was prepared to sleep for a very long time.

XIII

CCUPYING a hospital room down the hall from Berry wasn't as convenient as it sounds. There's little privacy to be found on a psych ward, and God knows it's tough to focus on healing with a family member in residence. But there was nowhere else to put me on such short notice.

It only took me twenty-four hours to lose my appetite for the two realities I'd come to know and love. A new, third way now presented itself, one in which I was neither mother nor wife, nor child of Mummy Dearest. I was a mean, flighty thing—a fairy, if you will. With no discretion whatsoever, I began to tell everyone who entered my room to "shut up," and with a frequency that would have frightened me if I wasn't already institutionalized. This strategy beat the pants off depression, I should add, for it requires energy to be cranky—it's proactive. In time I became adept at silencing my visitors before they could manage to peep hello. The resulting silence was complicated: I ended up with whole days during which I was alone and pissed off. If Freeman deigned to show up, I could always be counted on for a few choice epithets—"Hey, cartoon-brains!" or "Hiya, sound hound!"—and to toss chunky *Vogue* magazines at the wall. This would easily buy more time with my newly emerging self.

While the target of my bitterness was "the whole fucking world, i.e. my mother, my daughter, my husband, my Peter," its source remained a mystery to the doctors. They had their *theories,* of course, and liked to take the metaphorical road to diagnosis. To start, they chalked up any talk of Jason Hook to some "mild" form of child molestation I'd suffered at the hands of an unnamed adult. The Neverland, they said, represented a kind of idealized, controlled environment that provided a convenient escape from my trauma. This was a hoot because one never assumes *what's* going to happen next on the island—it's the epitome of spontaneity and improvisation! Alas, the experts' theory about Peter cut closer to the bone: an instant replay of Daddy, they said, but pint-sized and flawless. If that were so, I said, then why would my idealized guy go AWOL? *What ideal does abandonment serve?*

At first Berry wasn't certain what to make of my swan dive, whether to be furious or embarrassed. For some reason, though, my incarceration proved just the thing to inspire her reentry to society. It turns out that while I was preoccupied with my descent, Berry began to emerge from her confusion: she watched *Oprah* and *Ricki Lake* with a daily, near-religious allegiance; she filled entire sketchbooks with monsters that bore smiley faces; and, after weeks of refusing to speak, she became the leading voice of her group therapy sessions. The other patients came to depend on her for her humane snap judgments: "You're pure evil, Joyce, so get over it." "Word up, Doug: it's not gonna get better, so learn to love your face. *We* have."

To speed up the therapeutic process for both of us, the doctors decided to introduce Berry into my regimen of pills and talk therapy. They felt it would be healing for mother and daughter to interact for one hour every Monday, and encouraged us to share our "colorful stories," as though they were baseball trading cards. Little did they know that I had nothing to say to Berry. My days in bed had afforded me a single, if dreadful, epiphany: as a teenager who liked to "act out"—entire Greek tragedies, it seemed—Berry had punished me more than she knew. Her lack of interest in me, her withholding of love, had fairly destroyed me—I was certain of it. But I would not let her have it, refused to carve my rage into her like a perverse graffito. Words may have been my ultimate defense against my daughter, but she didn't deserve them. I'd burn up my own psyche before I would touch hers. Besides, Berry had whacked away at her own mind for as long as she was conscious, meaning her whole life.

The knock on the door was akin to a bludgeon and it swung open before I had the poise to say "Get lost." Berry entered my close hospital quarters, a microclimate of thick air sweetened by the vanilla-scented candles I favored and very likely heated by the steam from my new temperament. "Come in," I said belatedly. Without asking she sat down on the bed, keeping her distance. So the doctors had tipped her off about my promising new viciousness.

With my face hidden behind a months-old *Entertainment Weekly*, I twisted tufts of my uncombed hair. Every so often I would peek out at my "difficult" daughter: sitting before me was a young woman who, in place of her usual stony self, exuded an air of tea and sympathy. Berry's face especially had been drawn by a more compassionate artist. The once-hard eyes shone with a velvety, Bambilike softness; the full lips, normally downturned and pursed, were relaxed in a half-smile. Her outfit, though, betrayed no trace of transformation: ripped plaid tights clung to her legs while an oversized black cable-stitch sweater hung from her torso—leaving no clue as to her physique. My best guess was that underneath the shroud lived a delicious, unwanted shapeliness.

"Mu-Mu." Berry spoke musically, without her trademark sarcasm.

I looked away from my daughter, possibly for the first time ever. I couldn't bear to hear her bass note of concern, which had arrived a few minutes late in my regard. Besides, if she were really, truly caring, I'd have no right to my anger and we couldn't have that. I'd waited too long to find a safe place wherein I could rail against the unfairness of practically everything. Now, if there were to be a sea change, a new spirit of fairness, where would that put me? I'd be forced to be my good-hearted self—which would totally suck, as Berry might say. No, this was my lone chance to be vile and no one would take it away from me.

"Ber," I said weakly. "How's it hanging?"

"It's hung," she said amiably. "I mean, yeah, it's going all right.

It's gonna *be* all right. It better." So the medicine was doing its work. She studied me with her Bambi eyes and the sensation was unbearable.

"So, it's going well," I said flatly. "How very, very good for you." I reviewed the ceiling as intently as Great-Nana once had done in my presence.

"Mu-Mu." Berry reached out to touch me, the flesh of her fingers hidden behind at least a dozen rings. I saw skulls and gladiator spikes.

Spurning her gesture, I instead grabbed her right hand and dug my nails into its fleshy pad. "So everybody's getting better. How perfectly wonderful."

Berry squeezed back, and my hand lost feeling. "Mother, you can't fool me. You're not the crazy one." She winked to underscore her words, which was genuinely funny because she'd always rejected my own burlesque winking.

I smiled in spite of everything, and despite the fact that I couldn't believe I was doing so, said, "Yes, darling. You have a right to your madness. I wouldn't want to take anything so precious away from you."

Berry burst out in hot, salty tears. "Mu-Mu, how could you be so—"

"Un-*feeling*? Un-*affected*? God, am I affected," I said. "I am so affected that I've traveled the whole spectrum—from bighearted to heart*less*. It's the new, impassive me. You like?"

Berry jabbed me in the forearm, then ran out of the room. "That's my girl!" I said, cheering her on. But she was gone and I was left with my hideousness, something only the nurse's meds could appreciate.

My days on the psych ward crept by, burdened with vintage resentments and clouded by still-smoking wounds. And here I'd envied Berry for "getting away from it all." My envy, I'm loath to admit, turned out to be just one more grievance in a sorry litany. I received my daughter on Monday afternoons with the faintest aura of interest, quietly observing the fact that she was getting better while I was getting worse. Berry's interest in me was only temporary, I knew. And I could not allow anyone's concern for me to take root.

On our fourth Monday meeting, we took a stroll of the hospital grounds, stopping in a narrow, shrub-choked alley optimistically called the Sculpture Garden. In fact there was only one sculpture: a pseudo–Henry Moore statue of unknown origin and sex. Without breasts or cock it was impossible to know what to make of the thing.

Berry relaxed up against the statue, snuggling her face in its cold, abstract groin. "Mu-Mu," she crowed, "get a load of me! I'm being born all over again."

"Very cool," I said mechanically, looking away.

"Muth-er," Berry protested. "It's no good if you don't watch."

"You mean it won't kill me as completely if I don't watch."

"Whatever." She shrugged.

"What-evah," I mimicked with a curled lip. "You mean," I soldiered on, "that your actions won't count if I don't get all freaked-out like a *real* mother." I sat down at the statue's feet and picked at its thick marble toes. Berry slid down from the corpulent thighs to sit opposite me.

"Well, you never get all freaked-out, you never go ballistic," she said. "You're just *so* lenient and *so* liberal, it makes me wanna puke! It makes me actually puke."

"It does?" I said, alarmed, recalling my own mysterious bouts with nausea. "That's because you want attention," I said, hardening. "You want attention?" I repeated, a little more amped.

"Yep," Berry conceded.

"Okay. Very well. Because you've got my attention now!" I wrung the bulky material at her waist but found no flesh there. "Does it feel good? Is it everything you always hoped it would be?"

Berry shrunk back, cowering between the statue's legs. At that moment I hated myself and yet I forged ahead. "Does my attention confirm everything you've always believed—that you're really, really bad? I don't know 'cause I've lost track of your intentions,

Berry. I wonder, does my recognition hurt like hell or does it feel like God is watching over you, after all? Or does it just prove how separate you are—that something that began life *inside* me has gotten along *without* me for a long, long time. Perhaps you are so thoroughly free of me, you can remind me of this any goddamn time you want to?"

I flung my body in her direction, the skirt of my fifties shirtwaist dress ballooning in the air. When I tried to speak again, I gagged on my thoughts, my rush of ideas. Like Berry had, I sought refuge in the figure's groin and clung to its abstractions.

Berry now stood over me, her cheeks glistening with tears and drool. She pulled the hair back from my face like a curtain. "Mu-Mu, you're a really bad actress, did you know that?"

"Excrementally bad," I agreed.

"And," Berry continued without taking in air, "I know it's a family tradition to go all fetal at the first sign of trouble, but *really.* You take the cake. You take the whole freaking bakery!" She moved in closer. "And here's a news bulletin for you: I'm not free, not like you said. Because I happen to, sort of, *like* you. And you can't be free if you feel *that.* But why—when I need you the most—why do you go and put yourself in a nuthouse with me? Is that what you call attention? Because there's a word for mothers who put themselves in nuthouses. I believe they call it negligence." Berry grabbed the statue's thumb and set her mouth around it; her dark eyes drilled me like lasers.

I slapped my forehead with my palm. "God, honey. I'm, you know, *trying.* I'm sorry to have *inconvenienced* you."

"Inconvenienced? That sounds like you had to go to the bank or something."

"What, then? What is it you want from me? A damage report? I've been here for you for like a thousand years. So I screwed up just once. Just one small miserable time." My hands covered my face so she couldn't get to it.

"Yeah, you've been here. You and Daddy were always somewhere in the house. But I swear you cared more about your stories than . . . me. My whole life, I've had to compete with Daddy's noise and your stupid, poopy forest animals. Pink bears and paisley pigs."

"My bears are not *pink*. And, what you said? It's not fair."

"I don't care about fair." She held hands with the statue. "I just don't want to be a part of the Darling show. I tried to be a part of it, and it's not a good look for me. The cute native boys? The silly jokes? The sewing? If you haven't noticed, Mother, I'm into sex. Into hard, rough sex."

I dropped my hands from my face and looked straight at her. "I can't do this anymore, this mother-daughter dialogue."

"Maybe you could have written something better for us, Mu-Mu? Something publishable?"

"Yes, that's it. I *could* have written a better story. For Freeman, Mummy, you. You could say this story sucks big-time." Berry flashed a nervous grin. "I just need some rest, Ber. I need to go to sleep and wake up somewhere else. Preferably not on an island."

"I thought you were a Neverland junkie, Mommy. I thought you were due back on the island, like any minute now?" Berry mimicked a finicky person checking a wristwatch, then wiped her face clean with the cuff of her sweater.

"I'm not due anywhere," I said tautly. "And Neverland's not a life. It's a diversion, a card trick. Haven't you heard? No one *believes* anymore. Especially not in fairies—they're out of favor. Way out. And faith? Well, it's almost sacrilege to have faith. Look at *me*. Once upon a time, I had all the faith in the world. I had faith in spades. But faith is messy, there's just no telling where it leads you. Not to mention how *embarrassing* it is. Yes, compared to its alternative—uncertainty—faith is practically insane! Which may explain why I'm here—in a hospital."

Our session was cut short by Dr. Candace Song. In a matter of weeks Candy Song had made measurable progress with Berry. At first Berry had been a tough nut to crack—refusing help of any sort, she'd tried her best to alienate the doctor with snarky observations about hospital life, and then blatant attacks on Song's weight and fussy mannerisms. But Song was unflappable. Hour after hour, she held her ground, if quietly, and soon she commanded Berry's respect with her intolerance for bullshit; she earned Berry's trust with stories of her own grinding youth in a Beijing orphanage. The tools of Song's trade? Confucian sayings, pickles, and surprise visits that resulted in hugs.

Walking in now on this mother-daughter scene, Song recognized that pickles had no place in the exchange to follow. She cut to the chase with medical precision: "I've an urgent fax for Wendy and Berry Darling."

Song handed the page to me, the wiser, elder Darling. I studied the near-empty piece of paper. "It's Daddy," I gasped.

Berry and I sat down on a courtyard bench; she held the page as I read aloud:

> Wendy, your great-grandmother is dead. The same goes for
> your great-great-grandmother, Berry. Great is *le mot juste*:
> no question that our Nana was a great dame. To that end, I
> expect your presence at her memorial service this coming
> Friday. Please, for both your sakes, get it together. I've plane
> reservations waiting for you as well as for Margaret, unless
> she's promoting some new screed, and for Freeman, if he's
> not on deadline for some cartoon. Ring my office. See you
> shortly.
>
> Cheers,
>
> Daddy/Granddad

"Ch-cheers?" I sputtered.

"Triple is gone," Berry whispered.

"He could have called," I said.

"Triple is gone," Berry repeated, looking at me as if I had missed something crucial.

★ ★

GREAT-NANA'S memorial service was shockingly high-tech for a person who was, famously, a dreamy Edwardian girl. Daddy had his publicity department at Brave Hearts Airlines cook up one of those video biographies that combine still photographs, film footage, tinkly music, and voice snippets from people who knew and loved the deceased into a morbid quilt of remembrance. In a matter of days they'd assembled something remarkably polished, as if Great-Nana were a beloved brand of detergent, or better yet, an airline unto herself.

Lined up as if before a firing squad, our family sat on a wooden pew in the Poet's Corner of Westminster Abbey, where the likes of Jane Austen, Emily Brontë, and William Blake had their memorial services. Spines straight and eyes wide, we watched as Great-Nana's life unfolded before us on a silver projection screen. There we were, the Bravermans cavorting with Nana at Brighton Beach— Mummy and I waving gaily in our candy-colored bathing suits, Great-Nana concealed inside an enormous jeweled caftan; Daddy and Nana striding across our London rooftop, Nana feigning flight; Mummy and Nana at a costume ball, dressed as floozy fairies; Nana and I doing the Charleston in her drawing room, winking at the camera like showgirls.

The scratchy old footage ended with a burst of light and segued to crisp video of a host of distinguished authors and playwrights, their grave faces betrayed by the occasional eye twinkle. Each spoke deliriously about Nana as his muse, as the mother of all whimsy, as a goddess on this earth. Berry took to coughing conspicuously whenever one of the testimonies got out of hand, its platitudes so vaunted and myriad that somebody might get hurt. One novelist referred to Nana as "my sole reason for living," which was curious in light of his misogynistic tomes, but who was to argue? Another old codger, a poet of some renown, tagged Nana as his personal assistant, and this I took as a veiled confession of his lapsed status as her lover. The two had dated in the forties, I knew, during which time his poetry became infected with her harmless surrealism. Soon thereafter, he'd published a bizarre, illustrated bestiary that included a woodcut of a bird that bore a woman's mocking face. Identified as the "Darling Harpy," the creature clearly resembled Great-Nana and had caused a minor scandal. There was no doubt that the poet had loved and lost her, the end product of their relationship the inevitable, bitter poem.

Other faces appeared on the screen—Sir Edmund Hillary, Sir Stephen Spender, Sir Peter Ustinov—virtually all the Sirs. Lord Richard Attenborough spoke of the necessity for humans to go in search of otherness, to seek out other worlds and new species, a cause well championed by Great-Nana over the course of her life. At this Berry failed to suppress a titter. She associated Attenborough solely with *Jurassic Park,* that mythic home to rebellious dinosaurs that refuse to die off. A distant cousin of J. M. Barrie gave tribute to Great-Nana's needlework, of all things, and a great-aunt of Daddy's recited a poem, too many windy verses to count about Nana's "unique specialness." I was hoping the gathering of friends wouldn't gag on the treacle; Nana would have put an end to that. Not to worry: after the video ended—with a pan of the stars in the night-sky accompanied by the genuinely lovely "When You Wish Upon a Star"—Mummy rose from her pew and approached the podium. There was an audible gasp; only later did I recognize that it had come from me.

Dressed for the occasion in a screaming red sheath, tomato-red tights, and a brick-red shawl, Mother herself looked chalky, grief-stricken. Her hanky, a shell-pink tissue that was well used by this point in the service, hung limply from her right hand while her left hand gestured slackly. Her pale, damp face, lined with creases, told the same sad story.

"Well," Mother said to the assembled mourners, "what can you say about a twenty-five-year-old girl who died? That she was beautiful. And brilliant. That she loved Mozart and Bach."

"The opening lines of *Love Story*!" I bristled, and seized Berry's hand.

"Now that I have your attention," Mother continued, "I want to tell you about the grandmother I knew. Not the little girl who was close to Sir James, but Wendy the woman, Wendy the warrior!" Everyone in the pews looked at everyone else, as if their neighbor held the answer to the riddle of Mummy's logic.

"Like a sunflower, Wendy Darling outgrew her little garden. She outgrew society's ideas about bright young things, that they should be seen but not heard. The girl knew a lot of places, she had a lot to say. And, against the wishes of the literary establishment, she became an adult—an adult who would never easily mesh with mainstream culture, who was hard-pressed to blend in, whose ideas about the world were often applauded, then taken with a grain of salt. If anything, Wendy was the first woman to publicly stand up to modern, immature man—to say *sod off* to his desperate need to stay young, beautiful, and purposeless. Indeed, Wendy sent out a powerful message to males of every stripe: *Be responsible—and suffer the consequences!*"

Here I sneaked a sideways glance at Freeman, who seemed to be relishing Mother's words, though not permitting their meaning to penetrate his skull. Daddy, on the other hand, looked wildly entertained; he had moved on emotionally years ago and no longer let Mummy get to him. Berry looked bored but I knew better: she had lost an important ally and couldn't understand why everyone seemed so jolly when she was devastated.

"Now, I don't want to get all weepy on you"—Mother dabbed at her eyes with her tissue—"but it begs to be said that Wendy Darling was screwed by the mental health professionals of her day, she was screwed by the mental health professionals of *my* day, and she continued to be misunderstood by the National Health Service in her twilight years. Characterized as 'a danger to herself,' she spent these last years incarcerated at All-Saints Sanitarium"—here, Mother scanned the audience as if policing the joint—"but in fact she was only a danger to *society*. For if we choose to ignore the other dimensions—those places that can't be seen with the lights on—we are in serious danger, my friends."

Daddy squeezed my hand with a steady cadence, and I must say it felt good.

"I am here to tell you," Mother roared, "that Wendy Darling wasn't crackers. She wasn't even close." To drive home her point, Mother pounded the podium a tad roughly for your traditional memorial service. "You see, as far as Wendy's health was concerned, her vision was 20/20, her mind sharp as a pin, her attitude tip-top! And her heart, well, her heart was—" Mother's voice broke up. "Her heart was bigger than her body." She rested her shoulders on the podium and bobbed silently.

Daddy scrambled out of his seat and, with unexpected tenderness, escorted his ex off the stage. A draft whistled through the church, scattering the programs and blowing out several white tapers. When the air was still, we were left with our thoughts and the unmistakable scent of mint and clove. The emptiness seemed fitting, for no one could translate Great-Nana's essence into words. Nevertheless I gave it a try.

Filling the awkward gap created by Mother's departure, I watched my legs make their way to the stage. Shortly I found myself behind the podium, looking out at a sea of befogged, expectant faces and a few rectangles of cobalt sky. Daddy gave a nod that served to stabilize me, and I opened my mouth to speak before any thoughts presented themselves. Pervaded by a general shakiness, I combed my fingers through my graying ginger locks, a childhood habit that has never deserted me. Then, seemingly doomed to repeat myself, I gathered and regathered my hair in a loose ponytail, letting it drop and pool at my shoulders.

"My name is Wendy Darling," I said at last into the microphone. "Wendy Darling, Junior." Nothing else came to mind and I feared that that would be the sum of my remarks. "For I am every bit her junior," I said, recovering. "As Mother noted, my great-grandmother's heart and mind were vast, open to entertaining more worlds than one. She was fond of the wildest notions: synesthesia, sentiment. It was Great-Nana, after all, who taught me that sentiment has gotten a very bad reputation. If you think about it, sentiment packs the combined power of mentality—the intellect—and sensation, the senses. What could be more potent than that? In the stories she told, Great-Nana was keen to mix the two in equal parts. This balance, she said, ensured that stories grabbed at your psyche *and* your throat. Great-Nana's tales were fearless—feeling, romantic, wise, and *true*. Sadly, she never wrote them down—she preferred the role of transmitter. Now it's up to us to piece them together in the wake of her 'retirement.' I don't think we'll suffer from a lack of volunteers. Surely those children who choose to believe—in nonsense, in illusion, in poppycock—will contribute to our cause.

"Finally, I have got to share something personal." I lifted my eyes to take in the soaring South Rose Window—so the cobalt sky was *stained glass,* not the real sky at all. "None of us Darlings are sure of what we've seen or what we've experienced. None of us can swear on the Bible or swear to God about any of it. We're all shady customers in that respect. But we wouldn't change places with any of you—being certain exacts too high a price. What I'm trying to say is, don't worry about us. So what if we're unstable. Great-Nana told me: Never be jealous of the stable ones, they're all lying anyway."

This was coming out wrong. I just wanted to tell everyone that I'd fallen for Nana the first time I spotted her picture in a storybook: a brave little girl winging her way over the rooftops of London. Love at first flight, we'd always joked. I blew my nose with a fresh tissue. "I really have nothing else to say. I'd ask you all to clap, as long and hard as you can, to bring back our Wendy. But that's just, you know, wishful thinking. I will ask that, in place of flowers or cards, donations be made to the Great Ormond Street Hospital Children's Charity—the address is written on the back of your program—"

I couldn't hear my own voice. The walls were . . . throbbing, the air displaced by a crisp low pounding that could only be understood as the clapping of true believers. I bit my thumbnail and held very still, for I was not accustomed to affirmation. The clapping continued, its amplitude rising in waves. If we hadn't woken the dead, at least we were disturbing their sleep.

Freeman took this lush, ambient sound as his personal cue. At some point in the syncopated clapping, he'd mounted the stage and strapped on his acoustic guitar. In place of his trademark *barrage* of sound, we were treated to a monastically simple version of "Somewhere Over the Rainbow," which segued into the lullaby "Tender Shepherd," which flowed seamlessly into "Golden Slumbers." The effect was transcendent.

The congregation filed out in tempo with Freeman's humble guitar-picking. Mummy and Daddy and Berry and I made our way out the doors of the Abbey, leading the other mourners in a snaking line that eventually wound its way over to the Black Cat, a local pub. Looking back over my shoulder, I searched the subdued, misty faces that I found so comforting—could that old fogey be Gaston, the baker from Cooke? Was that *eminence gris* Sidney Farrington, Nana's once-upon-a-time husband? That tall gaunt lady, the fugitive Jane? And what was this—this *posse* of homeboys? They vaguely resembled other boys I had known, but this lot looked like hip-hop artists: baggy trousers, gold chains, unlaced running shoes. What in the world were *they* doing here?

That was precisely the point, wasn't it? They didn't belong here, in this world. One of the little fellows winked at me, and I got a psychic chill. Surely he meant no harm; he was paying his respects like all the others. It was the feather in his Nikes that troubled me, the still-damp clod of moss hanging on to the laces.

 PART

FOUR

All men dream: but not equally. Those who dream by night
in the dusty recesses of their minds wake in the day to
find that it was vanity: but the dreamers of the day
are dangerous men, for they may act their dream
with open eyes, to make it possible.

—T. E. Lawrence, *Seven Pillars of Wisdom*

Wendy, let me in, I wanna be your friend
I want to guard your dreams and visions

—Bruce Springsteen, "Born to Run"

XIV

REAT-NANA'S death was Berry's and my ticket out of the loony bin. Berry was handed an "honorable discharge," and while the verdict was still out on me, the doctors felt that Berry would benefit from having her mother at home. If anyone were to inquire, I'd say I wasn't exactly *cured,* but rather paroled.

Nevertheless, a new feeling of hope prevailed in the hills of North Berkeley, as Freeman, too, arranged his schedule to spend more time with us. Family life turned eerily normal: movie and theater outings, music concerts, bookstore readings. We ate together at least four times a week and remembered to say kind things to each other on these occasions. Other times were awkward and self-consciously weird. Freeman and Berry walked on eggshells around me, but I can't say that I didn't enjoy this. My shell, you could say, remained shocked, and I still required a wide berth.

For all my family's fondness for metaphysics, I'd always shown little interest in death, in what might be called its downside. Hence, Great-Nana's passing had come as a surprise. No question that I'd had my fill of loss; at times I'd even gorged on it. Girl waits for boy. Girl sort of gets boy. Girl sort of forgets world. Boy truly forgets girl. Longing and exile and amnesia—need I say more? For in spite of The Neverland's fabled love affair with life, the place was infected with loss. Just to make the scene, a boy had to forfeit a little thing called parents. Now, just who was *officially* absent—the boy or the parents—I cannot say for sure. But I *can* say that absence was the source of The Neverland's power, its dark underbelly and very

foundation. While absence isn't death, in practice it's far more insid-
ious. The lack of closure trumps your garden-variety fatalities—
your stabbings, your shootings, your overdoses, your car wrecks.

In Neverland the Laws of Absence are utterly clear, albeit cruel
and unusual: if a boy is wanted by his parents—profoundly, strenu-
ously wanted by both or even one of the people who first imagined
him—he won't find himself among banana-nut trees and mermaid-
infested waters. On the contrary, he will be content with the scarred
oaks and polluted ponds back home, the sharp fact of his significance cutting a swath through all obstacles in his path. However, if a
boy is discarded, ignored, or stupidly left behind, forgotten at the
market or at the mall; if he is violated or misused, probed and
thrown away, then nature takes its course and The Neverland inter-
venes. It's the damaged ones who are picked up by the wind.

And we can do without those blissful flying metaphors of which
writers are enamored. The left-behind child either lifts off by con-
ceiving of something finer—a life more decent—or hits the ground
with a thud and has to deal with the shit on this plane. Those few
who do both, who straddle the ground *and* the air, are torn-apart
creatures. We live in the hospitals in every community. We get to go
home when we're good and ready to shed our beliefs, the formal
proof of our absence.

OUR family continued to be rocked by Great-Nana's demise. While
she had expired, prosaically, in her sleep and not from the calami-
tous fall we'd always anticipated, we found little comfort in the
details of her death. Her will, it turned out, was a certifiable mess,
unfit for our eyes and even less suited for those of the lawyers. It
happened that her wealth resided solely in her assortment of curios
(shells, globes, marbles) and in her collection of Victorian children's
books—barely-glued-together tomes that were signed, first editions
that dealers could hardly wait to get their gloves on. Great-Nana
had had the volumes crated and put into storage when she checked
into All-Saints Sanitarium, and no one had gazed upon the books in
years. Strangely enough, her will made no mention of the collection,

not one syllable about Berry or me inheriting a volume. Perhaps Nana felt that persons who *make up* stories have no need to actually own them.

Finally, after much shuffling through boxes, Mother succeeded in locating a letter composed in Nana's endearing chicken scrawl; it maintained that her many objects of desire were to be divided among the residents of A.S.S. This should have put a lid on further discussion or rude outbursts, but we were Darlings, after all, and not easily dissuaded.

"Don't I deserve, at minimum, one little book?" I argued one morning at the kitchen table, stabbing the soft wood with my fork. "And doesn't Berry deserve more than a handful of dust? Yes, we all know that she *loves* dirt, but really. Berry's been left empty-handed!"

"Berry can't fit any more stuff in her room," Freeman said, "and you have one of the best children's book libraries in the country. Don't you think it's funny how one's objectivity flies out the window when it comes to one's inheritance?" He took the fork from my hand and returned it to my plate.

"No, *one* does not find it *funny*. I don't know, Man. I expected to be totally fine with this. But our expectations expect so much of us! I thought I could share Nana with the world, but I can't. It's not the books I want, anyway, it's her. I have nothing left of her." I hunched over my plate of scrambled eggs and onions, and appeared to get stuck there.

"Now that is just not true." Freeman pierced a ring of onion with his fork, and fed it to me.

I searched my husband's cloudless face; in the presence of tragedy, he liked to point out several silver linings, when most people freely admitted there were none. "Come on, Wends," he went on. "You'll always have those bizarro adventures you shared with your nana—her dubious remarks, her lunatic gestures. *That's* your inheritance." With revolting self-satisfaction, he poured himself a cup of coffee from our spongeware pot. "And what about that lurid thing on your finger?"

It was true: after all this time I still wore Nana's cocktail ring. Its dime-store tackiness charmed me like nothing else. Peering at the ring anew, I studied its facets, probing for fresh epiphanies. But there was no picture of the future or the past waiting for me, only my face fractured into Cubist bits. When my lower lip trembled, the picture blurred—the ring refused to reveal anything but its surface beauty.

With a thump, Berry lurched into the kitchen. She was dressed in safari togs from head to toe, a departure from her usual black-on-black couture. Freeman and I tried not to make anything of this, though as parents, we were genuinely startled. Our daughter looked as if all the evil had been drained from her and replaced with the marrow of an Eagle Scout.

"Hey," said Freeman.

"Hey," I said casually, after him. "Stalking the wild breakfast?"

Berry sank into her designated chair, a puppet too heavy for its strings. With the same debt to gravity, she poured herself a cup of coffee and slurped it without glancing up. The medication Dr. Song had prescribed seemed to be helping more than anything that I could do for her.

"Yessiree, get a load of me," Berry said finally, glancing only at her father. "I don't know what to make of it. I don't know what to make of *me*." She posed like a supermodel, then plowed into her scrambled eggs.

"Honey?" I said cautiously. "Are you, like, rehearsing a new performance piece?"

"Wends, it's just Berry," Freeman said. "No need for an explanation."

"What? Can't I be an interested party? Do I have to *feign* disinterest?"

"You have to give her room to tell us stuff," Freeman said gently. "You've got to be patient with the mysteries."

"Hel-looo." Berry waved. "Earth to alien parents. The person you're discussing just happens to be here, *in person*. Or she was just a minute ago." She shoveled some eggs in her mouth, which kept her busy for a time. Freeman and I exchanged generic looks of shame. I picked at my own meal, forgetting to taste it.

Breakfast conversation at a standstill, Berry decided to speak up. "Guys, let me give you some teenage intel: the duds mean nothing. Really. I'm just, like, *hunting* for a new personality. See? It's a visual pun." She jammed more eggs in her mouth, then downed them with coffee.

"And we support that, Berry pie," said Freeman. "You know that."

She raised her eyebrows and continued chewing.

"I suppose that you are tired of our support," I observed wearily. It had only been two months since we'd left the hospital, and Berry and I were still a little awkward with each other. "I mean, I've read that *some* parents overdo it in the support department. We're supposed to give you room to revolt, room to challenge our assumptions—to provide you with a roadblock you can run through at a hundred miles an hour. I just can't think of anything to get all hot under the collar about. Can you help us out?" I asked politely.

Berry wrinkled her nose and curled her hands into claws, unaware of how seriously cute she looked. "Grrr!" she said.

"We mean it, sweetheart, do you have any ideas we could run with?"

"You guys want *me* to help you be bad-ass parents? God help us." She shot up from the table and, carrying her plate and fork, padded through the kitchen, out the sliding-glass doors of the living room, and past the deck to the secluded hillside that had always been her sanctuary. Her safari clothes would serve her well, I thought.

"I'm a terrible mother," I said to Freeman, more to keep him at the table than anything.

"Naw, you're just a mother," he said. "You're going to get it coming or going. It comes with the job."

"But not with *your* job? Are fathers exempt?"

"Fathers are, you know, recreational. We're darn good entertainment." He juggled the salt and pepper shakers. "But mothers? Nooo. Daughters think mothers are the source of everything that's wrong with the world. Don't get me wrong, mothers are appreciated later on in life. But most of all, mothers remind daughters that the world is made out of pain, out of icky intimacy and regret. In a word, Wends, they ain't fun." He missed the salt shaker on its way down— it hit the floor and broke. Grinning, he rose from his chair and set his plate in the sink, after which he stood over it, pecking at leftovers.

"So I'm not fun," I said, standing.

"Hey, *I* think you're a barrelful of monkeys. Or is it a bowlful of jelly?" He approached me from behind, and held me loosely at the waist.

My breath came shallow and I spun around inside his arms. "You want fun? I got fun right here, pal." I pointed to my brain.

"What about right here?" he asked, planting a fragile kiss on my lips. "And here." His mouth pulled on my right ear, then traveled to the taut skin at my neck. Redolent of eggs and coffee, he proceeded to cover my neck with a fresh crop of kisses, each one deeper, more serious. I surrendered just a little, hoping to renounce the ugly bits of malice towards everyone that I'd cultivated over the months.

Giving in to Freeman was a welcome change. Surely he deserved a wife who didn't find him a fool, and Berry a mother who wasn't deeply contemptuous of her. What *I* deserved, I did not know, for kisses have a way of disarming the mind. All too quickly I became enamored of the idea that things would be all right—if not immediately then sometime down the road. It's not that I believed in happy endings; in fact I believed in endings most complicated and undermined, *if* I believed in endings at all. It was faith that kept me going. There was something else, too, something at the perimeter.

As Freeman kissed me up and down and sideways, a serene, equitable voice sounded in the hollows of my head: *None of this is real, you know.* Flustered and weak-kneed, I broke free of his embrace. It's just an *inner* voice, I told myself—there's nothing to be concerned about. I was taking daily walks, wasn't I, and using my sunlamps regularly to ward off the blues. Perhaps I needed a full, twenty-four-hour program of sunlight? Despite my experience with phantasms, I wasn't a fan of voices without bodies. I can't imagine who would be.

Visibly concerned, Freeman asked me what was wrong, and like my daughter, I ran off to the backyard deck. I trained my eyes on the seagulls as they hurried east; a storm was coming in fast. Closing my eyes now, I positioned myself against the wind—all that pressure felt good. But the voice spoke again, this time of *illusion* and *reality*, of how I'd gotten it *all wrong* from the very beginning. *Illusions are not what they seem*, it said.

Jesus, I thought, that's awfully helpful. And then I whispered into the fierce air: "Mummy, I'm scared." I didn't want to entertain voices. I wanted to be like other women: confident, clearheaded.

The next morning, as Freeman showered me with more sweet kisses, the voice was tougher, more insistent: *Your feelings of doubt are illusions.* Shock waves rolled through me. I wasn't aware of any *illusions* I had about my feelings. My feelings were my feelings, not really open to interpretation. Yes, they were ephemeral, but their authenticity could not be challenged. My feelings, no matter how upsetting or uncooperative, belonged to me alone. I wanted the voice to go away.

The voice defied analysis—insinuating and precise, I could not identify it. As it was neither male nor female, I couldn't implicate Jason Hook or ascribe it to some advice-giving ghost of Great-Nana. This left me nowhere. After a lifetime of considering and then fending off the idea that I was bonkers, I had to concede that hearing voices capped it. A common symptom of schizophrenia, auditory hallucinations were not to be taken lightly. Thankfully, no smell or taste accompanied the voice. But I became agitated even as it told me: *You are not under attack. You are not under attack.*

I reported these episodes to no one. Daddy had spent a small fortune treating the spurious ills of the Darlings, and for the first time in years we were endeavoring to cope without the services of specialists or gurus. Mummy had canceled an exorbitant round of something called feminology therapy, opting instead for a monthly freebie from Dr. Pease, really a date with therapeutic pretensions. The two of them spent their one night out a month at the Punch Line comedy club in the city, after which they'd hit the bars.

As outpatients of Herrick, Berry and I were still obligated to see Dr. Song on a biweekly basis. When I'd explained that Daddy was no longer splurging on our psyches, Song had offered us a two-for-one deal in "the true spirit of family pathology." We should have been grateful, I knew, but Berry and I were beginning to tire of our own stories.

During my private sessions with Song, I opened up only as much as I deemed prudent. I couldn't bring myself to talk about "the voice" for fear of being interned in the hospital again. Song knew that I hadn't fully recovered from my breakdown—who ever does?—but she was giving me the benefit of a very substantial doubt, and I didn't want to disappoint.

The voice persisted. It's not that it grew louder over the weeks; rather it started to make a kind of sense. Or perhaps I began to allow its logic to take hold. By now you know that I'd spent my childhood imprisoned in a tower of extremely fluffy ideas; and by ideas I don't mean the *island* or the *boy,* but the notion that I'd been deserted, that my life was postponed until a certain somebody dropped by (or my father decided he wanted me). This notion had not served me well, but I'd clung to it like a raft and it had rewarded me with a great deal of uncertainty, not to mention an overblown sense of entitlement. Like most children, I told myself I was special. Never mind that this flew in the face of the facts: an AWOL father, a preoccupied mother, a mirage for a boyfriend. But specialness, the very concept, functions like food; it keeps boys and girls going long after they've been stranded. Plus, it's an adjunct to the second most popular notion: that children are left alone because they're *not* special. These two feelings—specialness and worthlessness—can feed a whole life. I know because I've had my fill of both.

The voice worked overtime to get my attention. I was genuinely stumped: if one's feelings are only illusions, what *does* a person hold on to? My feelings had always been my compass, my one sure way to determine direction. Now if that compass was on the fritz, this left only objectivity (and everybody knows how dangerous that is). I couldn't steer a course with objectivity. Could I?

My thoughts turned to Mother. I'd never understood why she'd turned against men when it was her mother, not her father, who had deserted her. Instead she'd spent a lifetime protecting the very idea of females—in her estimation they were sacred. Margaret had placed her own mother, Jane, in a golden circle of immunity to ward off any attack Mummy might mount on her own. And while Mother railed against men in her self-help books, reducing them to amoebas or bricks, she dated them serially.

It was then I realized that I'd been so obsessed with Mummy's behavior, I'd never stopped to consider the hurt that drove it. All my life, I had struggled to separate my antipathy for Margaret Darling from my admiration for her. Surely her success in the absence of a mother was impressive: she'd transformed her hurt into something bigger than pain, something that inspired thousands of women. It wasn't her fault that she'd failed to inspire *me*.

It's the oldest story, a lonely child churning in the wake of a parent's narcissism—a child in the wrong place at all times. But I wasn't a mistake: Dr. Song had told me that daughters are meant to live out the drama of their mothers' subconscious, to implement their dreams. Whether we can wriggle free of this *responsibility*—that's what I'm asking. Somewhere in the cracks of Margaret Darling's ego—between the books and the men—I do believe she loved me. I also believe I terrified her.

One late evening Mummy telephoned in a snit; she'd meditated for hours, she reported, but couldn't purge her mind of "what had gone down" earlier that day. I was not in the mood for this: I'd just limped through the door after attending a marathon Berkeley City Council session. After five hours they'd issued a proclamation making our little community a "Nuclear-Free Zone." Appointed to the Nomenclature Committee, I'd proposed the phrase "nuclear-clear," but no one had noticed the redundancy or found it remotely funny.

I'd had my own snit about "why they engage a writer's services if they don't want wit, if they don't want elegance?"

Making light of my fatigue with a directive to "drink some Red Zinger, dear," Mother explained that she'd spoken at noon to the Commonwealth Club in San Francisco—the chosen topic, cherishment. The panel discussion had been taped by C-SPAN, and transcripts were available by mail order. Sharing the panel with Mother had been another self-anointed savant in the self-help field, as well as a truly world-class psychologist—it was the latter who'd brought up a study of Japanese children, the results of which showed they harbor an unusually high expectation to be adored. The psychologist maintained that this expectation was the right of all children. "Bollocks!" Mother had exploded on the dais, then failed to explain why. All worked up and fanning her papers, she added: "If anything, children expect to be ignored."

"I notice your own daughter is absent today," the esteemed psychologist said, smiling at the audience.

"My daughter is an adult," Mummy shot back. "She has her own life."

"Of course she does," he assured her.

"So, is it true?" Mummy asked me now. I could hear the click of her stiletto-heeled boots as she paced in her studio apartment. "Is that why you didn't come to hear me?"

"Well," I said, rationing my words, "it's true I have my own life."

"I knew it!" Mother cried out.

"But it's also true I didn't have the slightest inkling you were speaking today."

"It was in the papers, dearest," Mother said. "You had only to look."

"And the purpose of this call is?" I asked mock-sweetly.

"If you don't come, Wends, they'll think we have problems."

"We *do* have problems, Mummy." I poured myself a glass of water.

"I mean, they'll think I'm a sad excuse for a mother. They never even wonder if the *daughters* are sad excuses!"

"What are you saying, Mother? Because I really have to go. I have my own delusions to attend to." I was pacing now with the water glass, sloshing water on the blue floor tiles.

"Your own delusions. Very funny, Wends. Do you hear me laughing?" She paused to take in air. "I'm *saying* that daughters have a responsibility to cherish their mothers, too."

"But I do," I said, suppressing a shiver. "Believe me, Mummy, I do."

"Well, I didn't," she snapped. "And look what happened to me."

In the silence following this bombshell, I took a seat at the kitchen table. *Did Mummy have something to do with her mother Jane's disappearance?* The thought had never occurred to me. Removing the barrette that held back my hair, I used it to scratch my full name—Wendy Amelia Darling Braverman Ullman—in the soft, worn wood of the table. I could hear Mother scratching too, perhaps taking notes on a pad of paper. Desperate to move on to a new subject, I began debating with her the merits of *ER* versus *Chicago Hope*. Mother reluctantly went along with this distraction. After five minutes of mildly heated rhetoric, we established that she preferred *ER* with its main squeeze George Clooney and I preferred *Chicago Hope* with its manic-in-residence Mandy Patinkin. She thanked me for the phone call and suggested that its contents would show up in a future chapter of a future book.

"Oh, really?" I said. "What's the title?"

"Well, it's my most elementary title yet. I don't want to alienate readers."

"You? Never," I said. "So, spill it. What's the title?"

"Well, if you must force it out of me, it's *Mothers, Daughters*."

"Oh. Oh, shit, Mummy. Carolyn See already used that title and *her* book is a classic. Why don't you just reverse the order? You know, *Daughters, Mothers*?"

"God, no. That wouldn't be right. *Mothers* must come first."

"Of course," I said, and bade her good night. With the edge of my barrette I nicked at the word *Darling* until it was unrecognizable.

As Freeman began to take more time out from his duties at Sky-walker and Fantasy to spend with the family, I'm afraid I met him less than halfway. Privately I blamed my aloofness on the voice, whose catchphrases continued to consume me and undermine my every thought: *You are not under attack. Your feelings of dread are illusions.* I could hardly focus on a husband. When he swooped down upon me like an amiable Count Dracula, I waved him away with a dish towel; when he climbed into bed at night for small talk or a snuggle, I stuttered appreciatively, then turned out the light. You could call this lack of interest a spiritual crisis, or, more economically, a depression, but I preferred to see it as a calling, for something was surely calling me away.

Berry took Freeman's presence in the house for what it was—charity—and she exploited the attention in the way adolescents often do, holing up in her room or hanging with a small group of friends. Even in my fog, I saw that these friends held more fascination for her than parents ever could. First, they were flaming weirdos. And second, they were into the latest music and books and clothes and drugs.

Ever since Berry had taken her fall and then muffled the effects with medication, she'd been hell-bent on discovering an altered state that was good to her. For this I couldn't fault her; I was even a tad jealous. So when she began showing up at the dinner table glassy-eyed and leaden, though I should have blown the whistle, I held back. Yes, I was concerned, perhaps even anguished, but I was tired of playing the heavy. And I was desperate to get back into her good graces. Besides, Berry had never been so relaxed. Didn't she deserve a vacation from her four-alarm self?

They say that pleasant drugs lead to unpleasant ones. But I didn't feel qualified to demand that Berry "just say no"—not as long as I entertained voices. That didn't seem fair. Instead I watched my daughter from a remove. She seemed happier than she'd been in years, if a little fuzzy around the edges. I'm sure it was just pot; I wanted to be sure.

Freeman, on the other hand, was furious. Given that his range of emotions ran from genial to ecstatic, I wasn't accustomed to fury and wondered now if he might implode or, more practically, compose a frenzied piece on the electric guitar. Instead he took to sulking, staring holes in Berry's forehead, and, presumedly, her resolve. At times I fooled myself into believing that steam rose from his ears and mouth, and imagined his jaw getting stuck as it jutted out like a shelf. When his sulking failed to get a rise out of Berry, Freeman began to lecture her, talking mostly to himself. The more he pressed her to "lose faith in other people's drugs and believe in your own creativity"—as though creativity could save her like some old-time religion—the more she set her own course of action. She began to stay out late at clubs on the flatlands of Berkeley, returning home only after we'd gone to bed. She'd always had the outlaw clothes and attitude, but now she had the joints to go with them, and a couple of friends who had driver's licenses.

One friend in particular, a girl named Cody, proved particularly galling. She'd been in and out of the hospital much like Berry, but with far less imagination; in fact, she fully expected to make return visits as a badge of her coolness. The soup of drugs that Cody had legally acquired, she used to cement friendships, and so it was that Berry became a recipient of Cody's "kindness." Berry liked Cody well enough, though they had little in common besides mental illness (which Berry preferred to downplay). The thing was, Berry rightly picked up on Cody's need to be sicker than the others in their group, and let her do her thing. The two hung out together on a very slender premise: that the hurt they felt so keenly inside pretty much defined *everything* about life. Nothing more need be said.

Cody was a shaggy thing. Her haircut was a relic, a real seventies shag, and the centerpiece of her wardrobe was a sixties suede jacket a.k.a. "a mangy mass of fringe I inherited from my mother." What she considered hip appeared to my eyes as sad, almost desperate. Even so, Cody was a girl of obvious intelligence who'd decided to dress herself in bitterness and conceit—to the extent that not even my Berry could keep up with her.

It wasn't entirely Cody's fault. Her mother, a Greenpeace activist, had graced the headlines repeatedly with her virtuous piracy on the open seas. Cody's father, a professor of biology at Stanford, was even more notorious: a distinguished AIDS researcher with a theory so creative and unpopular that his department had shuttled him off to Paris. While both parents' work was admirable, even Nobel Prize–worthy, their actions took them far away from their daughter. In response, Cody, who must have recognized that she was Stanford material herself, took to the streets of Berkeley, where, like so many young people, she could get support for her worldview. She called this view "dystopian" but I recognized it right away as supremely pissed off. Hers was as universal a conviction as there ever was.

Berry's other main accomplice was Drew, a gentle "Goth" who wore a black velvet cape, enjoyed Broadway show tunes, and collected neglected teddy bears. Unlike most Goths, who tend towards the skeletal, Drew was a portly boy—"You don't have to be a waif to have a dark soul," he told me. Surprisingly free of irony, Drew smiled easily, his lips outlined in ice-blue lipstick. But he boiled over at the slightest provocation. Aware of his short temper, Berry and Cody pressed every button they could find, and even invented some new ones. I confess that I didn't understand this infighting—why *create* problems, I asked. The girls just snickered and said they were "unshackling Drew from society's expectations of jolly heavy people." A euphemism for being mean, I thought, but kept my mouth shut.

In an effort to keep Berry home one night in August, we invited Cody and Drew over for al fresco dining on the backyard deck. Though Berry called the ploy "obvious and lame," she participated in a big way, even coming up with the menu. On hand were tofu burgers, which she'd shaped earlier in the day into the initials of her friends and one massive patty that took the form of a well-endowed woman. This wasn't sexist, she pointed out, as long as a *girl* had created it. I raised one eyebrow and Freeman raised two, but when it came time to eat, we both wrangled for the zaftig burger. On the menu, too, were a mesclun salad poignantly dressed with yellow wildflowers and a pineapple Jell-O mold with floating candy corn. Apparently "mellow yellow" was the evening's theme, a fact that didn't register until dessert, when Berry brought out banana splits for everyone. Each banana was accompanied by two scoops of mango sherbet, not on top, but placed strategically on each side in a phallic arrangement that drew helpless titters from Cody and Drew. I would have laughed too, if Berry's scream hadn't cut into the gaiety like a scythe.

She stood fixed at the edge of the deck, staring up at the black helmet of a sky that was punctured by a sole, winking star.

"What is it?" I said. "What now?" The "now" was involuntary and thus regrettable.

Berry turned around to face the picnic table, then ran at me full bore, her hands reaching out to strangle something. Freeman had to act fast to draw her off me, but she continued howling and clawing at the air.

At this Cody issued tinny, birdlike screeches and Drew clutched himself like a pillow. "You're not helping," I told them. But it was obvious that an alarm had sounded in their heads and I didn't have the means to turn it off. My body shook badly. I know I had hurt my own mother and now, it seemed, my daughter wanted to hurt me; a couple of her nails had even scored my neck and it was bleeding.

Freeman continued to restrain Berry, whispering assurances in her ear. Once her breathing stabilized, she tried opening her mouth, but nothing came out.

"Ber, please," I said, maintaining my distance. "What did you see? What did you hear?"

"That's just it," she said finally, addressing only her friends. "I don't see anything. I don't hear anything. My parents are so fucking creative that they've sucked up every image and idea there is. There's nothing left." She pointed to the unilluminated sky. "See? Null and void."

Cody, whose screeches had been in competition with Berry's, now ran to her friend and grabbed her arm. "It's cool, B. Let's go home."

"She *is* home," Freeman said, and pushed Cody away. Drew remained silent, holding his belly and rocking in place.

"Time to say good night, Cody," I said, hand still protecting my neck.

"B, listen to me," Cody pleaded. "Your mother's right. It's time to book."

Berry released herself mechanically into her friend's arms and together they stumbled into the living room and out the front door. Drew, whose cream-colored Volvo was parked in the driveway, emerged from his protective trance and began shuffling through the house in the direction of the girls. At the door he turned around to face us and, with the most impeccable manners, said: "Thank you, Mr. Ullman and Ms. Darling. I had a really good time. And the meal was excellent."

When Freeman offered to drive them all somewhere, Drew assured us that he was "all there" and pointed to his head. Then he joined the girls in the car, and they sped off. Freeman and I were left at the door with no words to say to each other and no idea of where to begin. If this wasn't being *under attack,* I don't know what is.

In the weeks that followed, Berry began humming a cold, discordant tune, one that spirited her away from us and onto the streets, far from the comforts of home. I found this unacceptable—she belonged *to* us and *with* us. Wasn't that obvious?

Freeman and I had always been unsettled by the waves of unwashed children squatting on the avenues. Only now we understood that these "disposable" children were our daughters and our sons, and not all of them have been slapped or abused—in spite of their parents' shortcomings, many have been loved to pieces. Alas, it's the pieces that haven't come together, and time is running out.

Berry soon discovered that the street gave her unlimited power, or so she believed. Again, I don't think there's anything that Freeman and I could have done differently. While, in the early years, we might have focused more exclusively on Berry or, God knows, been a tad less permissive, I believe that she came into the world ready to raise hell. I also believe that love was hers to uncover, again and again, whenever she went looking for it.

This isn't to say that Freeman didn't blame me—just a little. While he was a man with a formidable imagination, he just couldn't imagine that he'd had a hand in this; on the contrary, he made me out to be some sort of wacko who'd sent our daughter packing.

My entire life, I had never been much of a drinker, choosing not to truck with realities that were alternative to the island; but if ever there was a time to pick up a new habit, now looked good. A margarita or two each night seemed harmless in light of what had happened to my life. As a countermeasure, Freeman began to retreat, as was his habit, into a world of reverb and timbre, suggesting that my drinking was proof of my guilt. "My *life* is proof of my guilt!" I screamed over the phone one night when he was working late. After a long pause and the crunching of corn chips, he said: "Go write yourself a little story, Wends. One that ends well. No, let me rephrase that: one that *ends*."

You might think that talk like this was cruel, but I knew he was right.

The first time that Berry left us, she stayed away a week. The night of our outdoor dinner, Freeman and I spotted her on Telegraph Avenue, sitting cross-legged on the sidewalk with a group of young people in various states of decomposing denim; two of them cuddled large cats in their laps. We waved from our car and made all sorts of vague promises: "We'll be good! We'll be better! No more therapy!" But it was not to be and we went home empty-handed. Frantic, we began making morning, noon, and nighttime drive-bys, if only to ensure that our daughter was eating and taking her prescription medication. On each occasion, we called out to Berry, solicitations that too quickly turned shrill. Invariably we were met with the clinking of coins in metal cups that the kids shook in our faces. "Pay for your sins!" one severe boy cried. After five days of increasingly desperate entreaties to get our daughter back, I sent Mummy out on reconnaissance. While she was famously unstable herself, we thought her eccentricity might buy entrée into more extreme social circles. Like me, Mummy recognized the street urchins as urban cousins of the Lost Boys and accorded them a nobility that evaded most adults.

The first time Margaret Darling showed up on the Avenue, Berry shooed her away, insisting that she was "mega cool." When Mummy showed up a second time with a tray of cappuccinos, she was invited to hover with the gang in front of Moe's Books. In a matter of minutes, Mother was regarded by the group as something of an elder freak, a matriarch who demanded respect. She gave out chewable vitamin Cs and zinc tablets to anyone who held out his or her hand; lip glosses were awarded the young women who crowded around her. Emboldened, Mummy took the opportunity to read from *The Pan Pathology*, ingratiating herself with the females of the tribe. When she arrived at the Darling chestnut, "Males don't mature, they just get worn out," one of the older boys grabbed the book from her hands and began ripping out its pages. "We're gonna use this thing for tampons and snot rags," he proclaimed, proving at least part of her point.

When it came time for Mother to cart Berry home in her Ford Galaxie, Berry wouldn't budge. "Hell, no, I won't go!" Berry chanted. Mother explained how vulgar that sounded, that certain protests are practically holy. "What's *vulgar* is you making out like a teenager," Berry snorted, which sent chills up Mother's spine. Of course Berry was right: Mummy was no longer a member of this club, not since she'd left the Boys of The Neverland for those on the Mainland. "You stinker," was all Mother could say; she wasn't referring to Berry's hygiene but it was too late. Berry spit on the ground and told her grandmother to "please fuck off."

The next morning we asked the Berkeley Police Department to pick up our daughter, with instructions "not to humiliate." By 4 P.M., Berry was returned to us like a UPS package, a little bent and waterlogged, but with all the parts there. For the rest of the day she sequestered her thinning body in her bedroom, refusing to speak. But she didn't object to the take-out chicken salad and coleslaw we set at her door. Or to the video of *Alien*.

DURING Berry's age of homelessness—how I wish I could call it a phase—the voice that followed me around like a dog suddenly went silent. As a source of wisdom the voice had already failed me, for my feelings no longer seemed illusory in the least: I was panicked about losing my daughter and nothing could change that. The more gradual loss of my husband troubled me, too, but I'd grown accustomed to Freeman's relaxed sense of time and obligation, and had learned to chew quietly on my regret.

My indifference to his kisses didn't help—as I have noted, kisses had always worked in the past when Freeman couldn't find the words to make things right, or good. He wondered now if I was sick in an old-fashioned way (cancer, heart disease, consumption) or perhaps in a newfangled one (chronic fatigue, fibromyalgia, lupus). Despite being surrounded by head cases, he never had had a feel for the psychological, the mental. He was a sensate guy through and through.

At a loss for how to live in the world of problems, Freeman fell back on what had always worked for him. On a balmy Monday afternoon I found him parading around our redwood deck, shirtless, barefoot, bandana tied round his forehead, and sporting his lowest slung jeans. He was wailing away on his Stratocaster, his amp blasting the sound all the way to Marin County. I recognized the song as one of Hendrix's—"The Wind Cries Mary." The noise was deafening; I wish I could tell you it was beautiful.

With all the decibels shattering the air I couldn't concentrate on my writing; some new parable about a rabbit's swift decline had been circling in the sink of my mind for days. I tried listening to some of my own music with the volume turned up, but the Hendrix rocketed through the walls of the house. I tried wearing headphones. I tried eating foods that fortified me: Grape-Nuts doused with half-and-half, a whole wheel of smoked Gouda. But Freeman's guitar-playing had become all-powerful—it peeled the paint off the walls, it scraped the very bones of my head.

Wendy, hold on, I told myself. *You know you love his music.* But my love couldn't change the tyranny of the sound. Furious now about having to look after *two* children, I stomped into the walk-in closet we called the library, and scanned the shelves for some novel that would transport me. Oddly, it was a nonfiction book that called to me, a book of Mummy's. I pulled it from the shelf and held it up to the light like a rare gem.

The Pan Pathology, Margaret Darling's first effort and the book that had put her on the map, had also received the most ridicule. While lauded for dissecting "the problem of the *puer aeternus,*" the book had been criticized for failing to offer a solution. Yet the readers who flocked to it had recognized themselves writ large in its pages and felt confirmed, felt *seen.* It's a big deal being seen, and Mother had helped a whole generation of women cope with their growth-arrested partners. While, through the years, I'd heard her talk animatedly about this book, I had never read a single page. To do so seemed criminal. I would have to admit that men were problems, and I had never been ready for that. To my mind, men were beautiful enigmas, not something to be solved.

I carried the book to our breakfast table and with the chords of "Foxy Lady" underscoring each paragraph, I read from Mummy's most scandalous work. I had to admit she was a marvelous writer—each sentence packed a punch and was elegant to boot. Her outrage and her humor were one and the same, and I felt a kinship with the writing and the writer. Occasionally Mummy went too far: "Men may be lovable turds, but in the end they must be flushed." More often, though, she made fun of her own lack of subtlety. I found it interesting that Mummy was an absolutist whereas I was seduced by doubt, and wondered if Mummy's certainty had somehow drained my own confidence. And then I chanced upon a page that was empty, save for one sentence in boldface:

When all else fails with your Pan-Man, you must do the loving thing.

My eyes misted up until I could no longer see the line. *Had Mummy forgotten to do the loving thing with Daddy? Did she regret leaving him?*

The explosive chords of "Purple Haze" now blew away my

thoughts; Freeman was putting on a real concert outside. And then I heard a faint pounding in between the cracks of his vocalizing. "Open up! Open up!" a voice hollered.

I ran to the front door and there was Officer America Fuentes, her club out of its holster. "The Shiva Darling residence?" she said huskily.

I nodded, machinelike, and let her in. She shambled through the living room, momentarily stunned by the panorama of the bay. Recovering, she slid open the glass door and tramped out onto the deck in her heavy police boots. Freeman rushed up to her and sang his heart out, the cord to his amp wiggling behind him like a tail.

A poker-faced Fuentes held up her large hand. When Freeman didn't respond she walked over to the amp and nonchalantly pulled the plug. "Sorry to interrupt the creative flow," she said. "But we've got complaints."

"Shoot," Freeman said, lowering his head like a boy who knows he has misbehaved. Tiny rivers of sweat made his chest glisten.

"We've also got requests."

"Requests?" Freeman said.

"Yeah, from me. If you're gonna play Hendrix, you gotta keep it down. But you also gotta play 'Manic Depression' or I'll have to take you downtown." She grinned broadly—even her teeth were big.

"Okay, okay, okay," Freeman said. With his bandana, he mopped the perspiration off his neck. Then he ran into the house and returned with his hulking twelve-string guitar. Resting his hip on the picnic table, he played an exquisite acoustic version of the song: "Manic depression's captured my soul. . . ." As Officer Fuentes fixed her eyes on the horizon, silently grooving to the music, I saw the sadness in Freeman's eyes, the pain rushing in. Even diversions had their limits; they could only work their magic for so long. Freeman would have to deal with reality soon enough, and I hoped I could be there when it happened. I wanted to be a great partner, to do the loving thing.

XV

FTER Berry left home, and school, a third time, Freeman and I held a powwow at Brennan's, a working-class bar near the freeway. For a single night he joined me in my campaign to rely on alcohol to do the hard work of relationship. The truth is, I'd never made peace with my margaritas— why *induce* a feeling of displacement?—but I liked to buy time with a drink, and an hour of not caring appeared to be a real bargain.

It was at Brennan's where I got the Big Idea. On multiple TV sets suspended from the ceiling, a commercial for Disneyland caught my eye. I spotted the usual suspects—Mickey and Cinderella and Donald and Doc—but in the back row and on the side was dainty Tinker Bell, waving and blinking her light. The group of old friends sang and danced in unison as fireworks exploded above their giant heads. Psychedelia for the rest of us, I mused. Freeman just shrugged, and hovered low over his beer.

"Look, Man!" I shouted, gesturing with my drink towards the closest TV screen. Using Freeman's nickname in public always sounded so dumb, and we both took turns laughing. "Look," I said again. "It's Tink and she's all in pink! Do you think . . . ?" We broke out in a second round of giggles.

"Whaddya think?" he replied, taking a sip of beer.

"No, I mean, do you think we could go?" I set my goblet down, and with my forearm brushed my damp bangs off my forehead.

"You want to leave already?" Freeman said.

"No," I said. "*Go.* To Dizzyland!" I cupped my mouth with my hand, trying to muffle the volume.

"Aha," was all Freeman said before he rose from his chair and made his way around an obstacle course of tables to the men's room. When he returned I was hunched over my margarita, sucking my lower lip. "What's up?" he said indifferently.

"The commercial. It was so poignant." I blew my nose into a cocktail napkin.

"Mmm," Freeman said.

"I mean it, Man. It stirred up something in me—something huge."

"That's the margarita talking." He looked away; a baseball game had supplanted the Disneyland commercial on every set in the room.

"No." I elbowed him. "I think we should go. There's that ride, you know. I think it would brighten Berry's spirits."

"Does it comes with klieg lights?" Freeman said.

"Come on. It would help her make some important connections. Let's go as a threesome," I said, tugging on his shirtsleeve.

"I can't. Remember, I've got *Jumanji*. But you and Ber should give it a whirl. Yeah, that would be good." His pale-blue eyes remained drilled on the ball game.

"I will, you know. I'm going to do it," I said with a half-baked conviction, and clinked my goblet with the beer mug resting in his lap.

★　★

GETTING Berry to accompany me to Disneyland wasn't the contest I'd anticipated. All along, she'd been nurturing a fantasy of going on the rides under the influence of LSD, just not with a parent in tow. For two days Berry lobbied hard for Cody and Drew to join us, but I finally put my foot down: "For some strange reason, honey, I pictured a mother-daughter trip with all the girly frills— you know, deep talks about art, lots of hugging and winking?" She made a face. "I did *not* picture taking care of three teenagers wigging out." On this issue Berry caved when I promised that our diet would be really, really bad for us—cotton candy, gooey-sweet cinnamon buns, and fried everything.

Choosing not to cash in on the Braverman name, we flew anonymously on Southwest Airlines, and quickly settled into our room at the Cruella DeVille Motor Lodge in Anaheim. Berry wouldn't consider any motels named after Disney heroines, and I'd had to work fast to come up with alternatives. The sad thing was, our motel's name was the single witty thing about it; what was "cruella" was the absence of decor.

With a backdrop of perpetual traffic just outside the motel room walls, we peeled off our heavy, dark Bay Area garb and draped ourselves in thin cotton pastels—cropped pants and tank tops. We were ready to "go native." At the last minute Ber kicked off her flip-flops in favor of platform tennis shoes and bee-striped, thigh-high stockings; she pulled a plaid miniskirt over shell-pink Capris. To cap off the look, she shrugged on her army backpack studded with Black Sabbath buttons. "It's a *theme* park," was her endearing defense. I snickered when I checked out my own theme in the bathroom mirror: my attempt at "surfer girl" was a bust, the bright white skin a giveaway. As a coda, I swept a scarf featuring the bridges of Paris around my neck. The idea of it trailing behind me on the faster rides was irresistible.

In the delicatessen across the street—the Pinocchio Nosh—Berry and I plowed into a breakfast more fit for a lion king than a puppet. Disoriented by the plane trip, the constant stream of cars, and the prodigious sunlight, we consumed large amounts of refined sugar and fat. It was here, in the deli, I realized that we were dangerously close to being companionable. The richness of our meal seemed to have a positive effect: I didn't bring up any business about Berry living regularly on the street, nor did she accuse me of any number of wrongdoings. We were suspended in a rare moment of parent-offspring peace, made all the more memorable by the sight of a snow-blanketed Matterhorn out the window to our left.

We decided to make our way on foot, though everyone who offered directions insisted that we approach the park by car. We could see it just beyond two luxury hotels—the elegant sweep of the monorail, the blur of purling rocket ships. Disneyland was so close we could smell it.

By the time we arrived we were sweaty and eager to find shade under the roofs of Main Street. I bought us twin sixteen-ounce Cokes and giant suckers in the shape of Mickey's head. When Berry made a bee line for a Disney character tchotchke shop, I suggested that we move on. I was afraid she might chance upon some upsetting retail item: a Peter Pan sword, a stuffed version of her great-great-grandmother.

Disneyland, I reminded Berry, was originally divided into four distinct tracts—Frontierland, Adventureland, Tomorrowland, and Fantasyland. I thought it best that we traverse these in a logical order, working our way up to the Mother of All Rides. Which is how we spent a fortune before arriving in Fantasyland. Once she bought and slipped on a "Pirates of the Caribbean" tee-shirt—she admired its outlaw cachet—Berry decided that a collection of kitschy tees was in order. I confess that I could deny her nothing, for she seemed unusually present; as far as I could tell, only Coca-Cola coursed through her veins. We spent the afternoon boarding all manner of transport: raft, riverboat, submarine. We visited the animatronic President Lincoln, the see-through denizens of a haunted house; we took in a saloon show, a jungle cruise. While Berry made fun of every uncool thing, she found certain joys and real epiphanies in all the simulations. At one point she even squeezed my hand in a show of undiluted glee. Then she caught herself and sniffed: "What amazing bullshit!"

We arrived in Fantasyland after a light dinner of corn dogs, still well before nightfall. No matter that the sun had let up on our backs and necks; we stumbled around like drunks. All that pounding blonde light, sugar and salt, and so many rowdy images vying for our attention had the cumulative power of an acid trip. I drained my last cola of the day in one obnoxious gulp, and when I accused Berry of palming a pill, it turned out to be a Motrin. "I'm having a sunstroke," she explained as she reclined on a bench. Her child-sized tee showed off her curves, its picture of Maleficent stretched to the max.

"But the teacups," I reminded her. "We got to do the teacups or we'll regret it the rest of our days."

"Regret barfing? I seriously doubt it." She rotated her tiny frame on the sticky planks of the bench. As three young men passed by, they turned into oglers—something a mother never should see.

"And here I thought you teens are really into getting all, you know, *disoriented*. Well, your loss," I said before giving her right arm the heave-ho. She pulled back hard, and we commenced a tug-of-war, really a pantomime of parent-child relations. Finally I was able to cast her off the bench and onto the gravel. The good news was: she was still smiling. With the efficiency of the young, Berry brushed off her skirt-pants combination, and hoisted her backpack, now plump with purchases, onto her back. After making a big deal of pointing at her and then at the giant china vessels in the distance, I gamboled off in the direction of the Mad Tea Party ride.

"Mothership!" Berry hollered and raced to my side. "Not now," she cautioned. "It'll toss our cookies for sure."

"No, honey, this is it! Your one chance to exact revenge. You can spin me as hard as you like. Or not."

"You're on," she said, eyeing me suspiciously.

After a ten-minute wait in line, during which we maintained a fatigued silence, Berry and I positioned ourselves in a teacup the size of a VW Bug, and entrusted our lives to a buff college student. The student wasted no time: he commandeered the steering wheel and at once we were spinning, nearly unhinged, in our saucer. Berry brazenly seized the wheel from the student—perhaps her outfit scared him off—and began to inflict more damage on our equilibrium. Just when I'd had enough—the nausea I'd so skillfully suppressed was now rushing to the surface—the ride stopped and we staggered off in a cluster of like-minded people. I sat down on a convenient cement toadstool, and tried to focus on the ground.

"Had enough for one day?" Berry asked.

"I've had enough for a lifetime," I answered, and our eyes

locked. For months we'd avoided speaking about our stay at the hospital, and now seemed like a bad time. "Berry, there's just one more ride I've got to do before we call it a day. Can you indulge your mother one last time? I swear, this is it." This time she gave in without a fight, and we shuffled off on sore feet to one of the oldest rides in the park—the ride called Peter Pan's Flight.

The line of people waiting to get in wandered back and forth six times around a roped partition. "It's now or Neverland," I said nervously. Berry rolled her eyes, too tired to openly ridicule me. As we advanced glacially to the front of the line, I began to experience a dense, cloying claustrophobia; it felt more mental than physical, although the cramped quarters were enough to make anyone woozy. Each time we took a symbolic step forward, I gripped the rope to stabilize my legs. I tried my best not to alarm Berry as her full attention would be required for the ride. When we were no farther than five yards from the gated entrance where the little pirate ships sweep their passengers away, I began to wobble, then tilt. Ultimately, I gave in and sat down on the hard earth, sipping in air between the cracks of everyone's legs. From this position, I scanned the sky, now blue-gold and darkening, and drank in its coolness.

Berry tugged at my arm like a three-year-old, slightly embarrassed for me, but concerned too. "Mu-Mu," she whispered, "please." When a light breeze rippled overhead, I took a whiff and rose to my feet. By this point we were flush against the shingles of the English Tudor cottage that housed the ride. I brushed my hand against a flower box and steadied myself.

As the line inched, with increasing strain, towards the dark mouth of the ride, we were approached by a few attendants dressed in character—a pretty girl in a sailor-collar coat; a young man in tights and a tunic of felt leaves; an American Indian chief with a magnificent feathered headdress. One attendant in particular stood out: a tall, bony adult in a flashy pirate getup. His face was hidden by a comically large, three-cornered hat that was festooned with the kind of gold tassels that look best on theater drapes; his legs were encased in canary-yellow tights; and a mauve-velvet greatcoat hung open over his blouson shirt, a white muslin affair with an excess of ruffles. The shirt was laced up the front with a black satin cord.

"Jason?" I said, startled.

"Come again?" The employee scratched distractedly at the bulbous tip of his long, crooked nose.

"Oh come on, it's me."

"Sorry?" He looked out at me, as through a telescope.

"Wendy," I said, hands flailing.

"Doesn't ring any bells." He fluffed the ruffles at his neck.

"Wendy *Darling.*"

"Ha!" he spat out. "That's terribly novel. I'm afraid, dear, you're just another wannabe. You'd better stand in line 'cause this place is crawlin' with Wendys."

"I *am* in line, you idiot. Hook, I'd know you anywhere."

"Of course you would. I'm Captain James Hook. At least that's what the coat says." He pointed to a name embroidered in bloodred thread on his lapel.

"You *know,*" I said between clenched teeth, "I mean Jason. *Jason Hook.*"

"Sorry, kitten, but you really got to get with the program." He reached out with a lace-encircled wrist to pat me on the shoulder, which was when I felt the cold sting of a cheap aluminum claw.

"Don't you lay a hand on me." I stepped back as far as I could into the line of squirming children.

"Lay a hand? Now why would I want to do that?" he drawled. "That wouldn't be very Disney of me." He winked at Berry and she winked back, even blowing him a kiss. Surely he flirted with all the girls?

Miraculously we had arrived at the front of the line where the pirate galleons await their fares; each ship boasted a proud skull and crossbones on its lacquered black sail. As Berry and I climbed into our seats and drew back the safety bar, the "pirate" stuck his mug in my face and said, "See you in hell, darlin'!"

Before I could give his remarks due weight, we lurched forward into the ride's thrill-packed chamber. Berry let out a throaty bark, the sort the ride deserves, and I clasped my palms together prayer-fully. No sooner had she yelped than we were hoisted high in a child's nursery trimmed with purple-striped wallpaper and white lace curtains. *Great-Nana's bedroom!* In seconds we burst into a counterfeit sky above the ghostly, flickering lights of London, skim-ming through the clouds past Big Ben. An expanse of stars loomed overhead as I watched the heartbreaking movement of tiny cars with their blinking lights down below. Tears streamed down my cheeks. Thanks to the genius of the ride's engineers, our flight plan was a canny replication of Peter's, that most fabled itinerary that Sir James set down on paper so long ago. As if suspended in time, our crossing of the night-sky appeared to be in slow motion—ironic for a ride that delivers its kicks with speed—and I imagined myself young and giddy, as long as I didn't sneak a peek at Berry, whose cringing presence suggested a world of need. I clapped my hands together and let go with smart observations such as "Wow!" and "Oh, oh, oh!" Such was my rapture that I began to soar on the inside, too. But it couldn't last: with a brutal disregard for beauty, the ship sped ahead, dipping rudely to the right as if trying to pitch us overboard. Finally we entered a more spacious chamber, drop-ping low over a spectacular island. We were instantly in the thrall of lagoon, forest, and a bubbling volcano. *Volcano?*

I exhaled, perhaps for the first time, and felt Berry's hand relax. But the ride didn't want us to rest: each time we made sense of the tableau before us, it betrayed us with another. A confusion of dis-embodied voices assaulted our ears—heckling and mocking us—and the background music swelled to manic extremes. I half wondered if Freeman had had a hand in it. The blunt tick-tock of a clock unnerved me and I threw Berry a cautionary look. But her face was turned away from me. With one hand cupped over her mouth, she pressed the other on my knee. She didn't seem to be having a good time. After the ride veered sharply to the left, I couldn't believe my eyes.

"Something's wrong," I whispered to Berry. "I can see the walls! There's a bolt, Ber. A screw."

"It's okay, Mu-Mu." She patted my arm maternally. "You just see more now."

Could it be my perception was so fully ripened that I could make out the interior walls of an amusement park ride? The moment of clarity yielded to anarchy: we were thrust down another dark alley, our trusty ship swooping low, then banking sideways. I heard Berry wail but couldn't take my eyes off the silly cardboard faces that assailed us—caricatures of Hook and his sidekick Smee, and oh, dear me, was that a dewy Wendy Darling? Before any of this could register, we were spit out of the ride. "Thank you for flying with us," the sound system echoed. Our ship came to an unkind halt and sat dully in place, cruelly illuminated by the park's party lights. The lights also revealed my daughter, sitting as still as a statue. She was not visibly *un*happy.

The safety bar released us and I helped Berry from the ship, guiding her over to a bench that, I swore on my life, wouldn't move. She smiled at this, and then I knew the ride had gotten to her. If I was right, and here I could only make a wild assumption, she'd experienced something of history. Despite the ride's corny stylings, she'd flown to The Neverland like all the Darlings before her had. Of course, without Peter—without the Boys and the birds and the wind at our backs—it was just a three-minute whirl.

"Mommy, it was so beautiful," Berry said, warming her hands inside her tee-shirt. "I see what you mean."

"What, darling? What do you see?"

"You and Grandmummy and Triple—you shared something totally cool." She shifted her weight on the bench. "And what's more, it was *radical*."

"I'll say." I hugged her to my breast, if for only the briefest of pleasures, and then let her go. We sat there, stupefied in Fantasyland, until the park attendants asked us to "Please depart the park."

As we started back to the motel, the sky above us was nothing like the sky on the ride; between the smog and the haze of headlights, we could see very little at all.

XVI

s it not surprising, then, that Berry left us again, in spite of the flicker of happiness she had known? I daresay that happiness is not a reliable measure of one's well-being; there are other, more trustworthy criteria. Self-tolerance, for one, if not self-love—because who ever achieves *that*? For another, a brand of chemical makeup you can't find at the drugstore or in any fine shop. And, since I'm going out on a limb here, how about the faintest glimmer of structure? If I hadn't disciplined myself to write during the first two hours of my day, I wouldn't have lasted long, either.

And so she didn't last. Berry fell apart, every other month it seemed, sometimes theatrically in public, where the city of Berkeley would pick up the tab; other times at home, in the pristine rooms of her mind. Whereas Berry's initial breakdown had been pinned on a drug overdose, Dr. Song ultimately defined Berry's mood shifts, instability, intense anger, and self-damaging impulses as borderline personality disorder. This gave us something to say to her friends, but offered little help. As before, she still experienced moments of stabbing clarity, times when her stew of "bad" chemicals simmered on a low burner and she'd coast along for weeks. During these intervals she'd make us vow to keep her out of institutions, insisting that she'd die, even promising that she would.

Eight months after our trip to Disneyland, Berry and I began to make a little progress by using movies as a way to be together. We'd go off on Sunday mornings to see the most emotionally brutal films available—*Pulp Fiction* and *Interview with the Vampire* and,

God help us, *Natural Born Killers.* The bleak wordviews expressed in these films comforted Berry, and she even gave some thought to becoming a screenwriter. "Movies know how I feel," she said.

One morning in November after sleeping in her own bed, Berry dropped her guard at breakfast: with a languor I found chilling she spoke about a relationship with a guy named Mason or Jason or Chazz, an older man who frequented Telegraph Avenue and preyed on smart, potty-mouthed girls. With a sleepy smile, she described how she allowed him to dominate her for a few hours each week, an unsettling scenario whereby she'd pretend to be frail or in jeopardy. The older man enjoyed "saving" her again and again, and during each visit they'd concoct a new fantasy—Berry snared by a shark, Berry tied to the tracks, Berry forced to walk the plank. *The plank!* In each episode, Chazz or Jazz or Mazz would show up at the last possible second, swoop her into his arms, and carry her off to People's Park. They had their own spot there, a hedge of ivy, where he would press her into the dirt and they'd eventually make love. She maintained that it was worth it: he'd leave her with a few dollars and some great take-out, usually a goat cheese *pizzetta* with sweet potato fries. The only drawback, she said, was his smell—like moldy books or something that had died long ago—and she'd be in need of a shower, pronto.

Berry possessed a flair for making the kinds of statements that quarter your heart and then make you wonder how there could be any heart left to slice. I might have written a book on the regeneration of the heart organ, but I was under deadline to my publisher. Over a year before I'd promised them a trilogy of issue-oriented fables—*Bunny's Blue, Bunny's Bored,* and *Bunny's Got a New Stepmother*—and was trying my best to concentrate, lest my bunnies would end up homeless too.

By now my so-called healthy anger, the rage that had erupted at the hospital, had blessedly gone underground: I couldn't imagine how it could be of any use. Still, the gloom that had descended upon our house in the hills was no mere fog—it looked and smelled like smoke, for my daughter's mind was surely burning up. Freeman and I staggered through our rooms, like firemen looking for the source of the burn. We hardly recognized each other, and spoke slowly in order to prevent new and even more grievous errors. We became isolated and wary of outsiders. Wisely, our few friends stayed away. Mother couldn't handle the inertia and soon found herself in more exotic climes and more hopeful vistas. I would have handed her an Oscar for Crowning Achievement in Selfishness, if her strategy didn't appeal to me, too. Staying away was a *good* idea. If only we could do the same. At least Freeman could rely on work that was all-consuming, but I suspected that even he'd grown tired of his job's upbeat nature. Imagine having to work on a cartoon when your own child is going loony tunes. I didn't envy him.

I finished my children's book trilogy in spite of myself. I was certain that the deadness with which I approached it had worked its way into the prose, but for once I didn't have the strength to worry about quality. My editor stood by me: he felt the illustrations would carry the weight of the stories, going so far as to tell me that "no child paid much attention to the text anyhow." This was of little consolation as the drawings had been done by a gifted twelve-year-old boy living in New Zealand; his star was on the rise, my editor assured me. When it came time for the usual bookstore appearances, he suggested that I stay in the background and let the boy do his meteoric-rise thing. I spent one afternoon gnashing my teeth about this and then let it go. I didn't have the courage to read to strangers about depressed bunnies anyway. Berry was on the streets again, and the temperature at night was threatening to dip below forty degrees.

ONE morning in early February, when the world was fast asleep and dreaming avariciously of Spring, Daddy pounded like a madman on the front door. Already in town a week for an industry conference—"Revisiting the Golden Age of Air Travel"—he had yet to make time for our little injured family. Now panting and wild-eyed, he greeted me with a bear hug. My eyes, only partially open, made out a wiry man in a rumpled business suit. For the first time in recent memory, Daddy's eye patch covered his left orb.

"Snap to it, princess. Daddy's got a surprise for you. It's absolutely huge!"

"Daddy, it's five. In the A.M." I rubbed my eyes. "Besides everything's huge with you. You find clichés exciting." I tightened my robe, but the air bit right through it.

"Are you even listening?" he said. "I tell you, Wends, this is it!"

"All right, all right," I said, secretly happy to spend time with him. While our relationship was as sketchy as ever and our visits as infrequent as meteor showers, I happened to be in the mood for a surprise.

"Daddy, I'm sorry," I said, now stepping outside. "I can't stand this thing a minute longer." In a bold move, I stripped Daddy of his eye patch. It snapped against my wrist, then hung from my fingers like a limp bra. "I haven't been able to look you in the eye for forty years!"

"But princess," he protested, forgetting which eye to protect. "You don't expect me to look *plain*? Plain Jane Daddy?"

"Impossible. Couldn't happen." I smiled as widely as possible for the early hour.

For once, both of Daddy's pupils regarded me. Then, cocking his head like a spaniel, he gazed blankly at the house. "Can't see a bloody thing," he said.

"It's the *fog*, Daddy. We're socked in."

Recovering from the strangeness of his vision, he nodded. Then, ever the showman, Daddy steered me by the elbow to his car, what turned out to be a military-issue Humvee.

"Why are you putting me in the backseat?" I asked.

For a fleeting moment he actually reflected on something I'd said. "Don't know, really. I just thought it made everything more *special*." He regarded my thin flannel robe. Why don't you glam yourself up a bit, yes?"

I slipped back in the house and scribbled a note to Freeman, in case he noticed I'd gone missing. The loss of Berry had been too much finally and he'd taken to sleeping on a cot in his studio at the Ranch, returning only to wash clothes and rummage for music gear in the garage. We were treating each other respectfully, albeit with a vagueness that would have broken my heart if my heart wasn't busy breaking over Berry.

I threw on an ankle-length, gray-flannel skirt, a white fisherman's knit sweater, and some thick socks and boots, then coiled a muffler around my neck. In minutes I was out the door and ready for life to smack me in the face. I only hoped the occasion wasn't a formal one.

Daddy's Humvee cut across the summit of the foothills, negotiating the curves of Grizzly Peak with unexpected zip. We were heading south, in the direction of Oakland, taking the most treacherous switchbacks too swiftly for my taste. "The thing's not a Porsche!" I hollered into the wind.

"Jolly good!" Daddy called out. "I can really see better. So, ladybird, care to hear the company's new slogan?"

"Slogan?" I repeated.

"Straighten up and fly right!" he shouted over the noise of the road. "Brave Hearts Airlines does it in the air. Sheer genius," he said, clearly dazzled with himself.

I nodded sleepily; the rearview mirror confirmed the twinkle in his newly visible eye.

The vehicle now coasted downhill, making short work of the endless blocks of Broadway and speeding through the flatlands of Oakland, heading towards those square miles of concrete I recognized from serial childhood visits. In twenty minutes we were at Oakland International, the general aviation airport reserved for small planes.

"Let me guess," I teased him, "we're taking the train?"

Daddy's smile was a wonderful thing to behold: movie-star pearly-whites, but lots of exposed gum, too. A cross between Jack Nicholson's and Bruce Dern's, the grin looked hungry and sexy at the same time.

As the Humvee pulled up to the tarmac, a young man in a tan

jumpsuit ran up, threw open the doors while the vehicle was still moving, and took great pains to hustle us out. "All systems go?" Daddy asked once we were safely out of the vehicle.

"Four by four," the assistant answered, without fear of mixing metaphors.

"Roger," Daddy said, further confusing the issue. Then he turned to me and said, "Can Daddy give you a twirl?"

"What?" I said, at a genuine loss.

"It'll be just like old times."

I couldn't fathom the meaning of this but I recognized genius, too, when I heard it. "Sure," I said, "yeah."

And so I allowed him to scoop me, his grown daughter, into his arms. With the finesse of Fred Astaire, he spun us in circles on the runway, rotating our twinned bodies faster and faster. Though I was long out of practice, my childhood training kicked in—my arms spanned out in a vee and my legs followed suit, size-ten feet flexed for balance.

"Round we go, dear petal!" Daddy shouted into the wind.

I am not under attack, I whispered as the cosmos wheeled around me. My cheeks burned in the nippy air and happiness came to me like my natural inheritance. "Cowabunga!" I yelled.

This had to be the ultimate journey in my brief history as a bird. For in spite of the blur that enveloped me, one thing was clear: The Neverland should have been more like this, an experience that embraces flight while holding you tight. One without the other won't do.

About to crash us both into the pavement, Daddy returned me to the ground, coughing as he took in air.

"Daddy," I said, regaining my balance. "What brought *that* on?"

"Sssh," he ordered.

"Don't shush me. I'm not a child."

"Not now," he instructed. "Look!" He pointed to a vintage Sopwith Camel partially cloaked in vapor. It sat on the tarmac about fifty yards away.

Emerging from a corona of blue haze, a tall handsome woman with sandy, cropped hair, khaki slacks and knapsack, and a chocolate-brown bomber jacket sauntered towards us. Her resolve was frightening.

"Amelia?" I said, with a shudder. "Amelia Earhart!"

"No, princess," Daddy said. "Your grandmother."

"Nana?"

"No, *Jane*. Granny Jane."

The slender, boyish woman now stood before us; she gave Daddy a curt if solid hug, then bent over formally and extended an athletic arm to me. "Wendy," she said. "My dear, dear girl." She seized my right hand and shook it firmly. When I went to kiss her, she shifted her weight and rose to her full height. She must have been at least six foot one. "It's very good to see you," she said in the wake of my awe. "It's been an awfully long time. One could say, a lifetime."

"Yes," was all I could think to say.

"Come, let's sit down, shall we?"

Daddy nodded for me. He escorted the two of us to Johnny K's Cantina on the second floor of the terminal, where we could peer down at the planes as though we were minor deities. We were about to seat ourselves when Daddy waved his cell phone in our faces. "Sorry, girls," he said. "I've some desperately boring business to attend to. You'll have to get by without me."

"How will we ever manage?" I said, smiling.

I settled into a sparkly, emerald-green booth across from Jane, all the better to ogle her strangeness, her lithe, laddish beauty. Granny Jane—if indeed this was who sat before me—appeared preternaturally young. She must have been a good eighty years old in Earth years, yet she betrayed no signs of advanced age. While her face flaunted a few winsome character lines, she carried herself like a twenty-year-old, moving with grace and speed.

"Well," we both said, nearly in sync. "Well," Jane began again, "tell me everything. No, tell me something small, something I can digest."

Now where had I heard this voice before, a voice with such startling self-possession?

Shy and suddenly skeptical, I faced the window and watched the coastal fog recede. A ghostly landscape revealed itself, one I had memorized over the years like a favorite painting: dove-gray waves licking the deserted shoreline; rows of dew-slicked planes patiently waiting, waking up only in the presence of their pilots; blips of scrub on the tarmac, spindly weeds and stubborn grass. "I can't. I can't tell you what you want to know."

"Little Wendy," she said, affectionately fluffing my bangs. "Why on earth not?" Then she peeled off the heavy flight jacket, unknotted her wool scarf. She rolled up the sleeves of her blue Oxford shirt, and waited for an answer.

"I can't tell you about me because you—you don't seem real yet. You better start first, you better tell me about *you*."

"Oh. Well. Fair enough. Let's see." She instinctively reknotted her scarf. "I suppose you already know about your mother and me." I shook my head no. "Oh, dear. Now *that* would be a mouthful." I remained silent. "I won't start at the beginning, then, the whole bit about me as a fetus? Perhaps I'll begin a little later in the story?"

"Yes," I encouraged. "That would be better."

The waitress set two mugs of coffee before us, which Jane largely ignored. Out the window I observed a suspicious, Daddy-like figure climbing into a small plane; soon after I heard the roar of its engine, watched its silver wings glint in the first light of day. So Daddy was out of here.

Jane stretched her long, tanned arms over her head and yawned expansively. "Where was I? Oh yes, the nightmare called your mother." There was no doubt about it: she was one of us. "I suppose that she says terrible things about me, says I abandoned her?"

"Not really," I answered. "Actually, Mummy says nothing about you at all. Any details about you, we've had to make up ourselves."

At this, Jane threw her head back and laughed throatily. "Oh, that's rich," she said. "So, what myths and lore have you cooked up for me? Am I hero or villain? God or mortal?"

"Neither," I said quietly. Jane looked crushed, her equanimity fading. "You're what in books would be called a cipher. A blank."

Jane stood up woodenly in the dimly lit booth and cast shadows down on me. "And I suppose you're content to leave me that way?"

"No, please," I prodded. I rose to meet her eye. "Tell me your story. I deserve to hear it."

Jane slipped her hands in the deep pockets of her khakis, refusing to look at me.

"Grandmother, please."

"Grandmother?" She brightened visibly, then coaxed her long frame back in the booth. "God, that sounds ancient. Like a ruin. Do I *look* like a ruin?"

"No. That's what's so strange. You look, well, beautiful. Fountain-of-youth-ish."

Her mouth stretched open to reveal two rows of small, even teeth. I felt as though Mother were regarding me: the same violet eyes, the same soignée neck. But unlike Mummy, Jane was androgynous, possessed of a sporty, earthbound nature the other Darlings lacked. "Well, I suppose I could stay awhile longer. If we order real drinks." Pushing away her coffee, she flagged the waitress and demanded a pint of ale. I ordered a margarita, the slushy strawberry kind. This seemed to amuse Jane and suggest that I would not be able to keep up with her.

"So, Wendy, what sort of story do you *think* you deserve?" Her bluntness took me by surprise.

"The true kind. The kind that is true."

"Ah, the truth," she sighed, toasting me with her mug. "*Per aspira ad astra*. To put it loosely, 'Over thorns, to the stars.' And let's face it, there are more thorns on Earth than all the stars in the firmament."

At once a silence befell us, but one that was necessary, therapeutic. In the space of minutes I saw the collapse of her brave face, the face she'd no doubt presented over a lifetime of skirting thorns. The ale arrived and she took a few meaningful sips.

"Grandmother," I said again, so oddly pleasurable it was to say it. "Are you . . . okay?"

"Okay? I'm marvelous," she said, eyes clouding over. "You see, it was your mother who left *me*. My husband left us first, of course, but he went out like a champion! You should have seen your grandfather, Wendy. He was an inventor extraordinaire. He reinvented the world for Margaret and me—gadgets, bicycles, scooters. Unlike your father, he preferred the ground. Come to think of it, most of his inventions paid tribute to staying on the ground—but in the grandest style and at the greatest speeds." With both elbows on the table she leaned in towards me. "One evening when your mother was only eleven, he tested the most bizarre contraption: a motorcycle with canvas wings and shiny tail fins. 'Introducing the Janecycle!' he roared. He even christened the bike, smashing a bottle of Chateau Lafite Rothschild against the handlebars before he took off down the road. I remember waving to him thirty times, I was so proud. And then, you know, it happened. He, well, crashed. Suffice it to say, your grandfather crashed as magnificently as he'd lived: he hit an enormous hole, flew off the bike, and landed in a pond."

"But—" I broke in.

She put a dirt-stained finger to my lips. "He couldn't swim, Wendy. That's the thing. He couldn't swim and thus he drowned in only twelve feet of water. How appalling is *that*? Therefore, when it came time for your mother to go off with Pan, she was—despondent. I didn't get in Margaret's way. I thought a trip might be good for her. So, imagine my surprise when she didn't come back after the first Spring. When she didn't return the second Spring I was beside myself. I had to retrieve her. Well, that was the plan. But there was a hitch, of course: the flying bit. You see, I'd lost my touch. No matter how hard I tried, I couldn't generate those essential happy thoughts. There were reasons for this, not the least of which was—I was a zombie, utterly frozen with grief!"

"Oh, Grandmother," I cried, and moved to take her hand. Like Peter, she withdrew it reflexively.

"I spent the next year learning how to feel anything remotely pleasant. What came as a complete shock, then, were the Zen teachings of my neighbor Mr. Sudo. I wasn't prepared for his revolutionary ideas about suffering and acceptance, and here I floundered for many months. (You know, the Buddhists aren't even interested in lovely thoughts and yet they are full of them!) Then, one evening in Summer, while I was reading the love poems of the Sixth Dalai Lama out loud, I giggled for no reason. Without a shred of proof, I knew that everything and everyone—including Margaret—was all right. I felt certain of this. And, voilà, I found myself lifting up!" Jane stood up again in the booth, this time touching the ceiling with both hands. Then, noticing that a few regulars were staring, she folded her legs back under the table.

"My journey to The Neverland was not without drama. Several birds decided to make a target of me, and throughout the trip I felt humbled by my large size. But verily I made it all the way to the island, landing in a marsh so thick and fragrant I believe it coated me in maple syrup."

"I know the one!" I said.

"Well then, you know that I was not far from where the Boys dwell."

"What did Mummy say when she realized you'd come for her? Was she outraged? Was she grateful?"

"Oh, that." Jane inspected her glass, shook the last drips her way. "Maggie was all of twelve at the time, twelve going on twenty—a hormonal hurricane. She was furious at me, ashamed to be seen with her mother. She called me 'the old bat' and set about ruining my reputation on the island first thing, telling the Boys that I had beat and whipped her—that I was a monster who refused to let her sing or dance or play. Since I hardly looked like the Jane they'd known, I didn't have much credibility. And Maggie—well, you know how persuasive her beauty can be. When it became clear that she would not come back with me, I decided to remain on the island until she returned to her senses. With the help of a couple of Indians, I took up residence in a small cave and kept mostly to myself. Sometimes I would watch Margaret from afar, as she bumped and grinded against the Boys in a slinky dance she must have picked up from the Americans. I watched as she kissed the more developed boys, using moves I've never seen before or since. She was always laughing gaily but a little shrilly, and I suppose she was the picture of contentment, if young women are ever content. For me, the weeks crept by in slow motion and I seemed to lose heart. I know I lost my Zenlike calm, for I lay about the cave in a state of terrible gravity, waiting for my daughter to remember me.

"When my depression lifted a bit—when it felt more like a cotton jumper than a winter coat—I decided to visit Maggie. But, abracadabra, there was no sign of her. For all intents and purposes, she was gone. I was careful not to bother the Boys, for Margaret had told them to ignore me, and kept out of sight as much as possible. The good news was, if she *had* returned to London, it was just a matter of getting back to town myself. The bad news? My return ticket had been lost or, more precisely, was forgotten. The flying, I simply couldn't master it. And without the help of my neighbor Mr. Sudo, I could barely recall the tenets of Zen. I was half crazed, if you will, and wholly heartsick, convinced I was shipwrecked in a place that was supposed to bring happiness, but had brought only a depth of misery that I'd assumed wasn't possible. And hence, I spent the bulk of my adult years in a place that's not on any map. 'True places never are,' Melville said."

"Herman Melville told you that?" I gasped.

"Good God, Wendy, I'm not *that* old. Living alone, I did manage to keep fit, and learned how to make do in the wild. I ate quite well— the vegetables!—and took on a few friends, though no one directly connected to the Boys. No, my companions were strictly members of the tribal cultures and a couple of animals—dogs, if you must know. Stray dogs and the occasional horse. After hundreds of days, life wasn't so bad, though I hadn't a clue as to how many years I'd gone missing. Eventually I lost interest in returning to the Mainland, whether or not I could manage the feat. Life became more than just grin-and-bearable. I didn't feel so much alone on the island as quiet, composed. There's a happiness in that, too. And so I grew 'old' in a very young place, where nobody aged or became wise—they just appropriated the latest songs and gestures and jargon by sitting on other people's windowsills and *absorbing culture.* It's the way of all young people, I suppose."

"But Grandmother, how? How did you find your way back after all this time?" I shooed the waitress away when she came to freshen our drinks.

"The question is *why,* not how. Why did I return. Another Guinness!" she called to the waitress. "And the answer is Berry. Berry is the answer."

My arms pimpled with goose bumps and, like a fish, I opened my mouth to take in air. I reached for Jane's hand, expecting to be rebuffed; this time she took it and squeezed hard.

"When your daughter didn't make a successful . . . transit, the island was all abuzz. Even in my remote neck of the woods I got wind of the news. First it sickened me, rekindled the old, outsized anger I'd carried inside me for years. I hated this place anew, everyone and everything. Then, one afternoon when I was washing the very clothing I'd brought with me from London, the dungarees I arrived in and this button-down shirt—it was your grandfather's, you know—I decided that I'd had it with the cycle."

I shook my head. "You mean the ritual of sending off our daughters? Of bequeathing them to callow young men!" I was a little tipsy now, enough to express what I'd barely known I thought.

"No, we all survive that. I'm talking about the cycle of resentment, verging on contempt, of our mothers. It's a Darling trademark, or hadn't you noticed?"

"Yes," I whispered. "I have."

"It's our mothers who give us an unparalleled opportunity to spend the Spring abroad." She winked. "But all we make of it is, they want to boot us out of the house or they're pushing boys at us. Or we get so wounded by Pan that we make up our minds to never recover. But look, Berry didn't even make it to the island and her resentment is O.T.T. Over the top."

"Now where did you pick that up?" I asked, amused.

"From the Boys, naturally. I emerged from my hole, one could say literally, when I heard about Berry's fall from grace. I told myself, she's my great-granddaughter and she needs me! Not to mention, it was high time to meet you. And to see my own daughter and mother again."

So she had no idea that Great-Nana was gone.

"I worked like the devil to make it happen. With the help of the Indians I jumped off bridges, flung myself into rivers, pirouetted into ponds, anything to regain my sense of flight. All the while Pan was eavesdropping, it turns out, wondering what the dickens I was up to. When it was clear that I wasn't the fearsome ogre I was rumored to be, he approached me. He even bowed in my presence and made a sort of pathetic apology: 'Sorry, Jane, I rather forgot you were around.' 'That's old news,' I told him. Then I explained my mission, how I needed to help Berry whether or not Margaret would welcome me back. Pan saw me as a girl again, all fired up. So, before you could say Jack Robinson"—she snapped her fingers—"he delivered me to your father in London. I'd promised Pan I'd recommend him as the new mascot for Brave Hearts Airlines. And your father had me flown here. Of course now that I've landed, I'll suffer a *coup de vieux*."

"A what?" I'd finished the last of my margarita, and found myself gaping at her.

"A sudden and jarring jolt of age. I'll begin to age again. As I was saying, your father brought me here and the rest is history. Well, in time it *will* be. Since you've experienced this sort of thing yourself, I expect you to believe me."

"Oh yes," I said. "Daddy's really generous with his planes."

"No, you twit. The part about being escorted by Pan. I'm not quite sure you're listening."

Jane was right. In view of what she had said, I would have to know whether Peter had mentioned me. I would have to confirm, for all time, that he wasn't a forgetful creep. "Did Peter say anything?" I asked.

"He said lots of things," she answered crisply.

"About me?" I said, feeling all of thirteen again.

"Yes, dear. He asked about us. He finally gets it: we are an *us*."

"I'm not sure *I* get it. You mean he asked about each of us?"

"Not in so many words. He finally understands that the Darling women are a force of nature, that we are connected and that our well-being depends on the mothers and daughters *staying* connected. He loves us as though we were one girl, albeit over and over again."

"Well, that strikes a blow for individuality," I said.

"It's time," Jane said abruptly. "Let's make like a leaf and blow."

Now where had I heard *that* before? She stood up decisively in the booth and crossed over to the stairs. Starstruck, I left some cash for the waitress and headed for the exit. We both emerged from the terminal to find the runway marbled with sunlight, the sky a true blue. The fog had vanished and in its place was an unambiguous landscape, a most familiar world. Daddy's jumpsuited assistant approached in the Humvee and we hopped in with the engine running. On the drive home on the freeway, Jane was as entertained by the urban sprawl as I was dazzled by my company. Being tired was out of the question.

WITH no small delight I ushered Jane into our living room. I threw open the maroon-velvet drapes to let in some light and to introduce the view—that heart-stopping panorama of the bay crowned by the sheer dome of heaven. All visitors eventually succumb to the view, for it really is too vast, guaranteed to humble even the most haughty personality. I offered Jane an overstuffed chair, but she settled her frame in one of two rocking chairs that are fixtures here—one for me, the other for Freeman, should he decide to join me. I hurried off to prepare a room for my guest, hoping she would stay the night and perhaps several more. But sleep was not an option: when I returned to the living room, I found Jane flat up against the sliding-glass panels, clearly struck by something.

"Jane?" I asked.

"You have it all, Wendy. Do you know that?" I nodded vaguely. "All of life is right here in your picture window. And yet you are a sad girl. Clearly miserable."

"I'm a grown woman, Grandmother. No one seems to notice."

"Come." She took my elbow and led us to the rocking chairs. "I deserve to hear *your* story, do I not?"

"Which version?" I asked slyly.

"The true one, the one that is true."

AND so we spent the rest of the day and all of the night, me dishing out my life story in the most excruciating detail—the ascents and descents, the farce and melodrama—the warts and all-of-it. I had no idea there was so much to tell, but I must have been starving to tell it! Did I feel cleansed, purged, exorcised after the fact? Not really. But I did feel fond of much of the tale, for it is all mine. Peter got it wrong, though. It's living, not dying, that's the awfully big adventure. Living requires more imagination.

I told Jane that I wasn't really happy. That happiness didn't seem to be the point. It was up to me and Mummy and Freeman and Berry to create that for ourselves. If I could just remember that I love us. Would that be enough? *Should* that be enough? If I could see these people as characters in their own stories, perhaps I could give up some of my pain. My pain had been very important to me. I'm not so sure I *wanted* to give it up. And where would I stash it anyway?

All through the night we rocked in our chairs like the old mothers of the world. Around 4 A.M. Jane stifled a yawn, then rose to her full height and hovered over me. With her long, lithe fingers, she stroked my forehead. "Funny thing about forgiveness, dear. It has a stunning, one could say magical, effect of its own. Who would have thunk it?"

"Who said anything about forgiveness?" I asked her.

She bent down to look me in the eye, then came round and sat on the rug in front of me. Without blinking, she began to say the most exceptional things. "Wendy Darling. *You are not under attack.* Your imagination is not under attack. While telling your story, you've held up a looking glass to your life, you've begun to forgive it. Well, that's my theory." She smiled, faced the bay.

"What's your theory?" I asked, trembling.

"Finally, you see that what you *thought* was a curse—your unbelievable, unreliable childhood—has made you who you are today."

"A fraud?" I said in all sincerity.

"No, child. The moral of your own story. You see, those imaginative powers which *you swore* had permanently abandoned you are, in fact, your birthright. By telling your tale, I'll wager that you've reconnected with that so-called extinct imagination of yours. You've removed it from the shadows of time and sewn it back on, just as my own mother fastened Peter's shadow to his shoulder blades. At last you can recognize your depression for what it is—"

"True evil?"

"No, you silly sausage. As another kind of shadow—one that actually slips off. You may decide to try this shadow on, now and then, to see if it still fits, or store it in a bureau drawer for the rest of your days. It's your choice. For it belongs to you and no one else. You're right, of course. Who else would want the bloody thing!"

I threw my arms around Jane's reedy body and held tight, just as Great-Nana used to crush me to her bosom. "Oh, Grandma Jane," I cried. "I have no need to make up one more thing! I'm done with stories."

"Child, watch the merchandise," she said, brushing me off.

We spent the remainder of our time together rocking in our chairs, but exchanging no further words. After speaking for nineteen hours, my voice was a wisp and Jane's ears deserved a rest. The planets, tired of spinning, faded from view and we watched the colors of the day supplant the early-morning grays and blues. It was time to sleep; for once the thought of dreaming about nothing appealed to me. Like most aspects of my life, I wasn't certain of what had taken place here or if any of it would stick come the next day. In the thick stew of memory and history, a single idea made itself known: maybe there was a third reality I could live in, one sandwiched between California and the island. Maybe it had room, too, for an inspired husband, a wayward daughter—for a fantasy life as big as a barn. No one said I had to stop at two realities.

For all my fears, Freeman was still around; in fact, he'd never once threatened to leave. His desertion was all in my head, it seemed. And there was the question of Mother, of breaking the cycle of blame. I couldn't promise any miracles, but I could try to make a little room in my heart for the possibility. *Over thorns, to the stars,* I whispered.

LATE morning, there was a tap at the door. Roused from a shallow sleep, I rose from my rocking chair and shuffled in stockinged feet to the entrance hall. The front door stuck. After several false starts, I cracked it open an inch to find my daughter, hands tucked in her armpits, shivering with all the dignity she could muster. Greasy curls hung at her ears like weeds, and in the place of her wool scarf she'd wound a frayed bandana around her throat. "Hello Parental Unit," she said evenly.

"Hello Offspring," I answered. I looked past her twitching form to the road, searching for evidence of transportation. I couldn't believe she'd mounted our steep hill on foot.

"Thanks for the birthday card," I said at a loss.

"Yeah, well, I just came by to borrow something." Her sandaled feet shifted back and forth on the porch to keep warm.

"Yes?" I said.

"The, um, you know." She pointed inarticulately, indicating somewhere in the house.

"Berry. I really don't."

"You know," she repeated. "That book of yours." I pursed my lips. "The one about the rabbit. The rabbit in rehab."

"Oh, that," I said. "Sure, let me get it. Would you like to come in?"

No, she waved her hands, chewed the inside of her cheek. Peering around me to the living room, her dark brows knitted. "Who— who's that?" she asked.

"What?"

"The mysterious lady."

"Oh, her," I said, smiling helplessly. "I think you'll want to meet her."

"I'm busy," she demurred. But she was interested. "She looks kinda familiar," Berry said, craning her neck.

"And she has quite the story," I added.

"Doesn't everybody?" Berry smirked.

"Well, hers is long and tangled."

"They're, like, only the best kind," she said.

"Let me get that book," I said, wandering off.

From the hall I watched as Berry padded into the foyer, then tiptoed over to Jane. She studied Jane's breathing, noted its rhythm and depth, its low-pitched hum. I shouldn't have been surprised when the two began breathing in sync—Berry's gift for mimicking sound could have an eloquent beauty.

Now Berry stood over Jane, taking hold of her chair. I was astonished at how gently she rocked it while gazing out the great wall of glass, studying the bare trees, the city's distant towers. Then she lifted her chin, and her melancholy eyes took in a universe of unseen things. The sun, a bit late for its debut, winked and placed her inside a column of gold. Contrary to what Berry had always maintained, she didn't care much for the night, far preferring the company of light. I know because she seemed so at home there.

I proceeded down the hall to fetch *Bunny's Blue*. It occurred to me that, at the first opportunity, I would have to rework the ending.

A Final Word on Flying

REUD was wrong, you know. Flying is not about sex—it's sex that's about flying. Because flying is about the spirit leaving the body behind, escaping the harrowing world of flesh, the deficient world of bone. But it's not about abandoning pleasure—pleasure comes along for the ride!

As a young thing with precious little life experience, taking my maiden voyage was my first exercise in faith. An education in free will and New Physics, being air-bound literally upended my ideas. It taught me that I would never be merely a body: there was so much more to life than corporeality.

When I first flew out my bedroom window in a sincere attempt to follow in Peter's footsteps, I had logged barely a mile before I came to a shattering conclusion: *I am not a body at all. I am something entirely new.*

I decided then to dedicate my life to whatever invisible force had brought me here—aloft over the emerald hills, soaring above the Bay Bridge, over the glittering swells of seawater. I made a promise to myself to always remember this day, a day when I was the opposite of fear and the very picture of freedom. The moment when I became *pure energy.* And I vowed that this mysterious force would never be suppressed or consumed by a life down on Earth.

In a formal gesture, I raised my right hand, spread my shaking fingers, and executed the Darling pledge: a tender blow to the forehead with the flat of the hand. It was a done deal and there would be no turning back. I was married to metaphysics now and, like my great-grandmother, would be forever counted among the passing strange.

DEEPLY FELT THANKS

O MY EDITOR at Simon & Schuster, the radiant, passionate, and wise Marysue Rucci; to my Simon & Schuster family, especially to David Rosenthal, Carolyn Reidy, Melissa Possick, Victoria Meyer, Aileen Boyle, Emily Remes, Alexis Welby, Victor John Villanueva, Jonathon Brodman, Jason Warshof, and Ellen Sasahara for their inestimable contributions. To Tara Parsons, for daily sustenance and assistance.

To literary confidante and muse Judith Ehrlich. To those gifted readers who donated their time, ear, and brilliant ruminations on the ways of the world—Carolyn Cooke, Emma King, Nina Byornsson, and Joyce Engelson. To Donna Bulseco and John Kalpus, my daring, intrepid researchers. To those generous, talented, and exacting friends who reviewed early portions of this work—Joanna Pulcini, Laurie Chittenden, Randall Babtkis, Tim Farrington, Kathleen Caldwell, and Claire Farrington.

To Mary Ann Naples, who found me. To Lynn Goldberg and Megan Underwood for their invaluable support.

To Robert Levine, Jonathan Kirsch, and Liza Nelligan for their wisdom, counsel, and emotional support; Mark Chimsky for his gift of Pan; Melissa Rallis for her gift of stars; and to James Le Brecht of Sound Artists for his time and knowledge. To Karen and Darryl Darling of the Darling House in Santa Cruz for their hospitality.

And most especially: to Linda Chester, my luminous agent, treasured friend, and kindred spirit who makes the writing life possible and oh-so-real. To my cherished colleague Gary Jaffe for a million daily things (and that's a low estimate). To Harriet Frank, my tenderhearted, supportive mother, and to Larry, my wildly creative brother, who is ever an inspiration. And to my husband, D. Patrick Miller, who, in spite of being Peter Pan–illiterate, served this book and its author in boundless ways, and who every day offers me a world more fabulous and durable than The Neverland. Patrick, come fly with me!

ABOUT THE AUTHOR

AURIE FOX is the author of *Sexy Hieroglyphics* and *My Sister from the Black Lagoon*. A former bookseller and creative-writing teacher, she has worked in the publishing industry for seventeen years. Laurie lives with her husband, author/journalist D. Patrick Miller, and her cats, Lewis and Gracie, in Berkeley, California. For more information about Laurie's work, please refer to: lauriefox.com